FIRST DATE

"So, are you asking me out for New Year's Eve, Jack?"

He clears his throat. "I'd, um, rather ask you in person, Diane, and by then I ought to know where we can go. So, will you go with me or meet me somewhere for lunch tomorrow?"

I smile. "Sure. How about Bandini's on Market?"

"Could I pick you up in front of the library at twelve-thirty-five?"

"That would be great."

"Okay. I'll see you tomorrow."

"Great."

More silence, but it's the kind of silence you swim in and enjoy, waves of silence filled with tingling, sweaty fingers and warm hands.

"I'm glad you called, Diane."

"Good bye, Jack."

Click.

I . . . have . . . a . . . date!

I, a twenty-five year old suede sister with some junk in my trunk am going out to lunch with a six-foot, skinny, ashy, blond-haired, blue-eyed scarecrow.

Lord, we are going to clash so badly!

And, for some reason, I can't wait!

It's about time I had *some* kind of life.

Books by J. J. Murray

RENEE AND JAY

SOMETHING REAL

ORIGINAL LOVE

I'M YOUR GIRL

CAN'T GET ENOUGH OF YOUR LOVE

TOO MUCH OF A GOOD THING

THE REAL THING

Published by Kensington Publishing Corporation

I'm Your Girl

J. J. MURRAY

KENSINGTON PUBLISHING CORP.
http://www.kensingtonbooks.com

KENSINGTON BOOKS are published by

Kensington Publishing Corp.
119 West 40th Street
New York, NY 10018

All Kensington Titles, Imprints, and Distributed Lines are available at special quantity discounts for bulk purchases for sales promotions, premiums, fund-raising, and educational or institutional use.

Special book excerpts or customized printings can also be created to fit specific needs. For details, write or phone the office of the Kensington special sales manager: Kensington Publishing Corp., 119 West 40th Street, New York, NY 10018, attn: Special Sales Department, Phone: 1-800-221-2647.

Kensington and the K logo Reg. U.S. Pat. & TM Off.

ISBN-13: 978-7582-1396-9
ISBN-10: 0-7582-1396-4

First Trade Paperback Printing: November 2006
First Mass Market Printing: March 2010

10 9 8 7 6 5 4 3 2 1

Printed in the United States of America

For Amy

1

Diane Denise "Dee-Dee" "Nisi" Anderson

This game is rigged.

I know it's only solitaire, but these cards just don't want to fall for me tonight. For seven games in a row, the ace I've needed to win has been hiding in the last pile on the right, and twice it's been the bottom card.

It serves me right for playing solitaire on Christmas Eve.

Solitaire is a funny game. It takes a long time to win, and when you do, you keep playing—and losing—until you win again. It's just something to do with my hands, to keep them occupied. "Idle hands," my mama used to say to me, and I'd finish the phrase: "are the Devil's playground."

I'll bet even the Devil cheats at solitaire.

Solitaire is kind of like life, I guess. You fuss and scratch to get into college, take the right courses, get the degree that you hope will take you through the rest of your life, get that diploma . . . then lose your mind trying to find a job that matches that diploma. I have a degree in library science, and, yes, it *is* a science to run a library. I figured that this country, with thousands of libraries, would have openings wherever I looked, especially for a suede-skinned sister like myself.

I was wrong.

While I was doing some part-time work at libraries in my hometown of Indianapolis, Indiana—and living with my mama, but that's another story—I was sending résumés to libraries all over the country. Most never responded, and four wrote nice "no-thank-you" letters, leaving me with interviews in Chicago, Louisville, and Roanoke, Virginia.

I had to look up that last place on a map.

And, of course, Roanoke is where I ended up. My official title is Grade Four Clerk, because I actually have a library science degree. I'm a clerk. I'm not "Assistant Librarian," not a "Media Specialist"—just a Grade Four Clerk, as if I'm working in an elementary school somewhere. I shelve books, reshelve books, scan bar codes, compile overdue lists, conduct reference interviews until my voice gets hoarse, and occasionally help coordinate Saturday morning readings for the kids. Yeah, that's me behind the circulation or reference desk, eyeing every person wandering into the library, forcing a smile and making change for the copier.

And . . . that's . . . about . . . it.

"Give me a king, please!"

And I'm talking to a deck of cards on Christmas Eve.

It's better than talking to my mama, though. She had called earlier this evening to bug me about coming home for the holidays.

"Meet any interesting men today?" she had asked. That's all Mama cares to know, and that's how every conversation starts.

"No, Mama." Though there's this homeless man who winks at me all the time. He's a nice man, I'm sure, but he only comes into the library to bathe in the men's room sink and dry his wet socks with the hand dryers.

"Well, you remember what I've always told you, Dee-

Dee." That's what my mama calls me, and I hate it. "You can have any shade of a man as long as he's black."

She has a million sayings just like that one. I should write them all down and call the book *Things My Mama Says That Make Absolutely No Kind of Sense to Anyone But Her.* The title would barely fit on the cover, leaving only a little room for my full name: Diane Denise "Dee-Dee" "Nisi" Anderson.

And though I tell her that Roanoke is 30 percent black, she's convinced I'm living in Caucasian-land.

"I'm more open-minded than that, Mama," I had told her, though I'm not as open-minded as I want to be. Roanoke is, well, Southern, despite its location on the map just east of West Virginia. Folks frown on mixing salt and pepper people around here.

"As long as you have a black man up in there in that open mind, I don't care."

"That's not what having an open mind is all about, Mama."

"It isn't?"

"No."

"It is to me."

But you're wrong! I had wanted to shout. "Mama, that's not it at all."

"Well, you tell me what *you* think having an open mind is all about."

"Okay, you see, you have to be willing to accept anyone into your life, regardless of race. That was what Maya Angelou was all about. That was what Dr. King was saying when—"

"Don't you bring Dr. King into it!"

Mama has had some, well, *issues* about Dr. King ever since she found out he wasn't faithful to his wife. We can't talk about Bill Cosby, Magic Johnson, or Jesse Jackson anymore either. Oh, and Kobe Bryant, too, but I mentioned

Kobe once, and all Mama said was, "Those Asians took over baseball, and now they're taking over the NBA." My mama, who lives in basketball-hysterical Indiana, knows next to nothing about Hoosier Hysteria or the Pacers.

"Mama, you know what I look like."

"I look at your picture all the time, and it's like looking in a mirror."

Not. I've got Daddy's skinny face, which doesn't quite fit the rest of my . . . let's say *healthy,* twenty-five-year-old body, and though Mama's body only jumps out in front (Mama's got a bad case of "no ass at all"), my body jumps out only in back. I'm not flat in front. I'm just not "well-rounded."

"Mama, I'm plain." With a train. A caboose. And though I walk the stacks at least half of the time I work, I will never be able to uncouple that caboose.

"As soon as you have a husband and a baby, you'll get some titties to match your behind."

And Mama's a churchwoman. Forty-three years she's been a member of her church, and she's the only woman I know who says "titties" like it's any other word like "chair" or "kitchen." She even points out other women's chests sometimes, saying, "That woman over there has some tig ol' bitties"—as if anyone listening can't figure out what she really means.

Yeah, she embarrasses me sometimes.

"Mama, come on. I'm too plain for any decent-looking black man to notice me." Not that I've been trying, and not that any decent-looking black men ever come into the library just to meet me. "But I've got just enough . . . exotic-ness"—is that even a word?—"to attract any—"

"Don't you say 'white man,' because you *know* I won't have that. Not since that Bobby and you in the seventh grade."

Which was thirteen years ago. It was my first sock hop, an in-school dance, you know, all sweaty palms, red hair bows, not enough lotion on my elbows and knees, and Bobby, who was plain and quiet like me was the only one to ask me to dance, and I really wanted to dance, so . . . I danced with him. That was it. One dance to some old El Debarge song, something like "Love Me in a Special Way." Our hands kept slipping off each other because of the sweat, and neither of us looked the other in the eye. He had an ashy nose. Not that I remember much about it—

Okay, it was a turning point in my life. I can't deny it.

There I was, plain, flat as a board, just brown enough to be called black, the beginnings of my caboose slowing me down, and I was totally ignored by every black boy in the gym because I didn't have titties. Or a weave. Or make-up. Or fingernails. Or bicycle shorts. What was that all about anyway? Hey, everybody, look at the veins in my butt! And the only boy in the room who consciously made a decision to think I was good enough for him was a white boy named Bobby. I wonder where Bobby is now. I hope he's not a doctor with those sweaty hands of his.

"Mama, that was so long ago."

"I remember it as if it were yesterday," Mama had said. "The *shame* of it all. Getting told on Easter Sunday by Imogene Blakeney, of all people, that my youngest daughter was bumping and grinding with a white boy in plain view in public. It was a *shame*."

"We weren't bumpin' and grindin', Mama." I'm starting to drop all my *g*s whenever I talk, and I've only been in Roanoke for a year. I refuse, however, to use the phrases "might could" or "How you doin'?"

Mama had growled. "Like I said then, and I'll say it to you now. You should have danced by yourself before you danced with any white boy any time, any place."

And that's what I've been doing ever since. I've been dancing with myself. It isn't so bad. I'm on my own, have my own place, my own car, my own bills, and my own savings and checking accounts. The only time it isn't fun being independent is late at night, especially if there aren't any C batteries in the house.

And Mama will *never* know about any of *that.*

Her Baptist heart couldn't take it. The shame of *that.* She'd probably find out right before another Easter service or something, and Mrs. Imogene "Couldn't-Hit-a-Note-if-You-Hit-Her-with-a-Hammer" Blakeney would be screeching it all over the sanctuary. I know Mama has only gotten her "pleasuring," as she calls it, from Daddy, my uniquely handsome, skinny-faced, shovel-handed, wide-footed, gap-toothed Daddy. They make a cute couple, but I doubt Daddy would ever buy Mama C batteries for anything but a flashlight.

"Now your *sister* . . ."

As soon as Mama had mentioned Reesie, I had tuned her completely out. Reesie is my older, supposedly wiser, *African* sister, who has only made babies (three and counting) with *African* boys since she was fifteen. And Mama never had any shame about any of that. None at all. I danced vertically with a white boy once, and Mama was ashamed. Reesie has danced horizontally with three *different* black boys, and Mama's proud as she can be.

If that isn't dysfunctional and worthy of an entire segment of *Oprah*, I don't know what is.

And Reesie, who I have no respect left for, once told me, "They *found* you by the side of the road, Nisi." After Mama had straightened that lie out, Reesie told me, "They were gonna adopt a puppy, and they adopted *you* instead." I have too much of Daddy in my face to be adopted, but sometimes I wonder if they switched my mama at birth or something.

"Are you listening to me?"

"Yes, Mama." I had yawned. "I have to go."

"Go where?"

"Out, Mama." As in, out of the living room to the kitchen to get a slice of orange cake left over from the library Christmas party.

She had sighed. "I still don't know why you had to move so far away."

"Roanoke is where my job is, Mama." And Indianapolis is many blissful hours away. Luckily, Roanoke isn't connected nonstop by air to any city except Pittsburgh, Charlotte, and D.C.

"And why did you have to have your own place, and a whole house at that, and not even in a black neighborhood?"

"There are plenty of black people in my neighborhood. The family across the street and the neighbors to my right—"

"They aren't really black if they live where you live."

No, I had wanted to say, they're just middle class enough to live here and just happened to be able to scrape up enough money for a down payment so they don't have to live on top of other people in an apartment complex.

"Child, you could still be living in your own room right here in this house, you wouldn't have a mortgage, and that city library you said you liked working at the most is just around the corner."

That particular city library in Naptown was the first to turn me down for a full-time job after graduation, but I purposely screwed up the interview. I didn't want to be working a stone's throw from my mama! I might have picked up those stones and thrown them at her! It did, however, offer me part-time work at minimum wage; I accepted . . . and I endured three dreary years with Mama and Reesie's three little monsters I collectively called "the Qwans": J-Qwan, Ray-Qwan, and Qwanasia. If it weren't for Daddy, I would have gone out of my mind.

"Mama, they didn't want me for the position I deserved four years ago."

"Well, there are plenty of other libraries around here, and maybe they have some openings now—"

"Look," I had interrupted, "I'm blooming where God planted me, okay?" Mention "God" to Mama, and she at least takes a breath. "Staying and working the stacks in In-

dian-no-place at minimum wage was a waste of my time,
Mama, and—"

"Excuse me?" she had interrupted. "Living with me and
your daddy was a waste of time?"

"That's not what I said."

"It sounded like you said it to me."

My mama only hears what she wants to hear. "I said that
the *job* was a waste of my time. It was a waste of my degree
and all that money you and Daddy paid for me to go to college. Look, Mama, I'm tired. I'll talk to you later." Then I
had waited for her to get the final word.

And this time, Mama didn't speak right away. That gave
me time to walk down my hallway, clutching a cordless
phone I paid way too much for, wearing an outfit I bought
with my own money at regular price at a store Mama would
never shop in, into my library. Yes, I have a library. What else
do you do with a three-bedroom ranch (advertised as a
"handyman special") when you only need one bedroom? I
know it's redundant and stereotypical for a librarian to have
her own library. But I'd much rather buy books and shelves
than beds no one will ever sleep in. If Mama and Daddy
threaten to visit someday, I may have to buy a sleeper sofa or
something. I'll probably end up just sleeping on that sofa
since I'm leaving the other bedroom "fallow." It's my storage
room now.

But I don't want to think about that. Not the buying of the
sofa—the visit from Mama and all her criticisms. She'll
look at my house as *her* house and spend the entire visit "fixing" everything I've done wrong.

"You make sure to be in church on Sunday," Mama had
said eventually. "Maybe you'll meet somebody."

Just once, I'd like to go to church *only* to meet Jesus.
"Good night, Mama."

"And go to a black church this time, Dee-Dee, okay?"
Click.

Oops. I had hung up on my mama. I had only been thinking about hanging up on her, and my finger had hit the button before I could stop it. The phone had rung a second later. "Sorry about that, Mama. My finger slipped and I—"

"Are you coming up for a visit or not? At least come up for New Year's."

I had taken a deep breath and closed my eyes. "No, Mama. As I've told you before, I have—"

"Your own life now. I know, I know." Silence.

"And I only have one day of vacation left this year." More silence. "I promise to come home for Thanksgiving."

"Thanksgiving? That's in . . . *eleven months!*"

"Bye, Mama."

Click.

I had waited a few minutes, and the phone didn't ring. After that, I had started shuffling cards and . . . here I am.

I really shouldn't be playing solitaire at all. I should be making cookies for Santa, which only I would eat in the morning. I should be wrapping gifts (mainly for myself) or listening to carols or even looking out the window for the snow showers they're predicting. Roanoke might have a white Christmas for the first time in anyone's memory. But aren't all Christmases white anyway? You have a white Jesus, white shepherds, white angels, and white stars. It's a Caucasian Christmas. At the library, we've been listening to a country station that plays only Christmas music from Thanksgiving to New Year's Day. Our library isn't completely quiet, because Kim "Prim" Cambridge, the library director says, "We have to compete with the mall, and they're playing that music, too."

Kim is . . . odd.

So, I've been subjected to eight hours of "Jingle Bell Rock," "Silent Night," "White Christmas," and "I'll Be Home for Christmas." Oh, and "The Christmas Song" sung by some white guy with a twangy voice. Where are Nat King and Natalie Cole? Or just Nat? Mmm. I could get used to Nat's creamy-butter voice in my life. I doubt I'll hear him on that station, though I did hear a little Luther Vandross one day. It surprised me so much when he belted out "O Holy Night" that I did a little chair dance right there at the reference desk.

Francine, the other Grade Four Clerk, had then had the nerve to ask if I needed some lotion for my behind. "You look all itchy and twitchy," she had said.

White folks just don't know a good chair dance when they see one.

I was listening to that station earlier tonight, but I'm all Christmased out. Those reindeer keep hitting grandma—because grandma is *drunk*—and the little drummer boy (all seventeen different versions, three every half hour) is giving me a headache with all that rum-pum-pum-pumming. I'm no Scrooge, but when you start hating "The First Noel"—the first Christmas song I learned to sing when I was five years old—you don't have any Christmas spirit left.

I look at the gifts under my Charlie Brown Christmas tree, a remnant of a tree I actually bought at a Christmas tree lot. "Topped it off a real big one," the man had told me, and I had talked him down to three dollars.

You know you're *horrible* at celebrating Christmas when you talk a man down to three dollars for the top of a "real big one" and your tree fits in the front passenger seat of your Hyundai.

And, you know you're lonely when there are only four gifts under that tree. Two are from anonymous coworkers (one from a gift exchange with the circulation staff, one from a gift exchange with the reference staff), and both are books: *The Da Vinci Code* and *The Handmaid's Tale*. Neither book is my cup of tea, but they'll look nice in my library. The third gift is a sweater I bought for myself at Lane Bryant. I had tried on several sweaters ranging from sizes ten to eighteen, and though my heart had said, "Give yourself a size ten, girl," and my mind had said, "You'll look just *fine* in a fourteen," my *body* ordered me to wrap up the size eighteen. It actually fits me better, though I'm embarrassed *that* it fits me better. It will give me an excuse to get out after Christmas to exchange it . . . for a sixteen . . . or a fourteen, who knows? I may take a couple walks around the block tomorrow.

And the last gift really isn't a gift at all. They're books I get to review for the Mid-Atlantic Book Review, an on-line book club I've belonged to since I arrived in Roanoke. "We're MAB, and we're Mad about Books!" is our slogan. I didn't make the slogan, and, for the most part, I'm "Mad *at* Books." The trifling stuff they publish these days . . . At least these books will keep me busy for a week or so.

Until then, I'll just—

"Finally!"

Now if I can only find a red jack, I'll be . . .

Set.

Time to shuffle.

Again.

Merry Christmas, girl.

2

Jack Browning

I don't know why I'm putting up this tree. *Old habit, I guess.*

Yeah.

It's something to do.

There are so many ornaments. Baby's first, second, where's the—There it is. Baby's third. Stevie opened it last year . . . before tearing into his other presents.

Without a second thought.

He was a kid. He was excited. He opened this bear on a train in about five seconds. He loved his bears. I wanted to get him a plane, or an old car, or even a Harley-Davidson ornament, but Noël said to stay in sequence. "We're creating heirlooms for him to share with his own family one day."

One day.

Don't think about it.

I can't help it.

You and Noël were just keeping Hallmark in business, you know.

I was getting to like that tradition.

You can't miss putting together his toys.

They were fun.

You cursed the directions too much.

They weren't written in decent English half the time.

I look up at the goofy tree topper, a star I picked out at Wal-Mart. Half of the lights have the colors of the rainbow, and the other half are clear white. I don't know why they keep burning out.

That's what lightbulbs do.

But they only put in two replacement bulbs. How nice of them.

That's how they keep you coming back, year after year.

Noël always winced and shrugged when we had completed the tree, but she took the picture anyway with Stevie in front of the tree, all warm in his footy pajamas, his stuffed teddy bear named Mr. Bear in his arms, his eyes sparkling like all the tinsel—

He was a cute kid.

The cutest.

I'm sure Mr. Bear is still in Stevie's closet. I ought to donate it and all the Christmas gifts Noël bought for Stevie during the year to the Salvation Army. She was always thinking about Christmas, even in July.

You thought she was crazy.

Yeah.

I just can't open her closet door to get at them yet, mainly because I can't quite get myself to open the door to that room. My back aches from sleeping on the bottom bunk of Stevie's bunk bed, and I ought to wash those sheets . . . but that little boy smell is still in them.

Have I done everything correctly?

Something's missing.

The train! Why didn't I put that together before I hung the ornaments? I did the same thing last year. We put up the tree, wrapped it in lights, hung all the ornaments, and threw on lots of tinsel, so much so that it choked Tony the cat.

Tony deposited a very interesting, shiny fur ball in the kitchen the next day.

And then Noël said, "Don't forget the train" . . . and here I am forgetting the train again.

There are some outdoor decorations in the laundry room. Don't forget them.

It's too late. It's Christmas Eve.

It's never too late to celebrate Christmas.

It is this year.

I piece together the track around the base of the tree, getting tinsel in my hair and pinesap on my forehead. "You look silly, Daddy," Stevie would say. Then I place the train on the track, hooking all the cars together and hitting the switch on the locomotive. The batteries are still good.

Chug-a-chugga, chug-a-chugga.

But where's the smoke? Oh, yeah. I have to add cooking oil to the smokestack. Maybe later.

Tony the cat hated the train, and I keep expecting him to appear out of nowhere to swipe at the caboose. He left soon after . . . that day. He's better off anyway.

You forgot to feed him most of the time.

I forget to feed *myself* most of the time.

Yeah, your diet should consist of more than alcohol and pretzels.

I wonder if Noël bought *me* anything before . . .

You know she did.

But my presents would be in that closet, too. I'll bet she got me some clothes. Yeah. She was always trying to dress me better.

Anything would have been an improvement.

But I've lost a lot of weight. I'll bet there are ties in that closet. Noël wanted me to look professional on the job—

which would be over for a while anyway, at least until after New Year's, though I'm sure I'd have plenty of papers to grade. I'm on an extended *holiday break* from teaching. You can't call it "Christmas break" anymore.

That isn't politically correct.

And you really shouldn't say "holiday," because it comes from "holy day." So I guess you just say, "Have a good whatever."

Try putting that phrase on a button and see if you don't offend anyone.

The school, Monterey Elementary, called me in again to substitute last week. It's nice to know they're thinking of me, but I'm on permanent sabbatical, prematurely retired at the ripe old age of thirty-two. I should have gotten hazard pay to teach social studies to fifth-graders, and they want me to substitute? No way, I said, even though subs are now making eighty bucks a day. I'm okay for funds—for now. The life insurance . . .

I don't want to think about the reason I have so few debts now.

You will anyway.

I don't want to, but . . . they only gave me $5,000 for Stevie! That's all he was worth! Five thousand dollars for a priceless little life! I got more money from the settlement on the van! A child's life *has* to have more value than a van!

Stevie was priceless.

It was as if he were leased to me for a few years, and I could trade him in for . . . for this . . . for this.

Stevie was on loan from God, Jack. We're all only on loan to this world.

It's just not fair.

I get up and walk down the hallway to Noël's door. All the times I used to come up from grading or writing, turning this doorknob silently, easing the door open only to have the hinges squeak, but Noël slept through it, even though I bumped a dresser drawer with my knee almost every night.

Your bruises must have healed by now.

They have. I even have a few scars.

It was a sharp dresser. Get it?

Ha-ha.

I'd feel for the corner of the bed on my side, slide in beside her, kiss her cheek, maybe spoon with her a while before returning to the cold side of the bed. . . .

I can't turn the knob today. I just can't. Maybe tomorrow.

You've been saying that for the last six months.

I know. Maybe tomorrow.

I return to the tree, plugging in the lights. Then I take a picture of . . . no one with big eyes giggling into the camera.

Oh, God, this is so hard.

No one said it was going to be easy.

I down the rest of my eggnog, toasting the tree and carrying on a conversation with myself while the train chug-a-chugs in circles.

3

Diane

I like living alone, and I even like living in a house that continuously falls apart, all at once sometimes. I've met some interesting men that way, and they don't have to bathe or dry their socks in my bathroom.

It all started about three months after I moved in, not that my house in northeast Roanoke—which *is* mostly blue-collar and white—would ever be the first cover home of *Better Black Homes and Gardens*. At first, it was a series of little things. Nothing major, just minor problems to fuss at like drafts, creaks, funny smells, and peeling paint and siding.

After all these minor headaches, the small deck at the back of the house simply fell into the yard, taking a huge strip of siding with it, after some heavy rains during my only week off from the library last summer. Why do bad things always seem to happen on your vacation? I called around for estimates, didn't have the $2,000 (over my dead body!) necessary to rebuild it "to code" (whatever that means), and ended up taking a card off a wall at the entrance of Food

Lion for a handyman. I called and left a message, and the next day Robert Maxwell showed up.

I have only dropped my jaw past my ankles once or twice in my life, and when I saw Robert Maxwell, my jaw was dragging on the ground behind me, grass and little stones and dandelions all up in my teeth. Imagine a six-five black Fabio with good hair, muscles on top of muscles, a smile right out of *GQ*, and hands the size of tree stumps. I showed him the damage to the deck and the siding.

"It'll take me uh couple uh three days," he had said real slow. "It won't be no trouble 'tall."

Except for his constipated, country accent, I had enjoyed my handyman. I had watched that mountain of a man through the miniblinds in my bedroom. That man could dig him some holes and cut him some wood, and the way his sweat dripped down his massive back to his behind . . . I had even thought about smoking cigarettes afterward. I had felt like such a ho. When it rained on what was supposed to have been his last day and he hadn't shown up, I had been depressed all day and prayed all night for a sunny day.

On his last day, while he was laying and nailing the floorboards, I had brought him some sweet lemonade and sat on the finished section wearing my tightest shorts and an electric pink tank top.

"You do nice work," I had said in my hoochie voice.

"Thanks," he had said.

"You sure five hundred will be enough?" I had wanted to tip him real nice with my body. I had wanted to climb Mount Maxwell. I still do.

He had looked at me with those sleepy eyes of his. "My wife says I shoulda asked for more."

His *wife*. Of *course* he had a wife. She has to be the happiest woman in world history. She probably has an orgasm every time Robert opens the front door to their house.

"She say one of our boys needs him some braces, and my

oldest daughter needs her car fixed." That added up to at least four children. Robert Maxwell was a potent man.

I had felt terrible for taking advantage of him just to save me some money, so I had paid him $750 cash after taking an advance out on my MasterCard. I had reached up to shake his hand, and I had watched my hand disappear into his. "Take care," I had said, hoping to see my hand again.

"Call me anytime."

And I do. I call that man, a real man that only the Lord God in the highest heaven could make. I have Robert Maxwell's number on speed dial, and I call him every time something inside or outside the house breaks, just to see him in the flesh.

I even break stuff . . . just because.

Hmm.

I think I'll need him to redo my sidewalk. It's all pitted like the surface of the moon. Yes. He'd have to break it up with a jackhammer or sledgehammer. . . .

That makes me dizzy just thinking about it. And maybe I'll get some real cigarettes this time, you know, to support Virginia's economy.

But can I see the sidewalk from my bedroom window? Hmm. I may have to get comfortable in the living room. But can you pour concrete in December? I bet you can't.

What else can I break around here?

4
Jack

Merry Christmas, Daddy. . . .

"Stevie?"

I sit up too quickly and hit my head on the slats for the top bunk of Stevie's bed.

Again. When will you learn?

How did I get here?

You were drinking heavily.

I only had three—

Five.

Okay, five mugs of eggnog. At least I won't need breakfast. I've already had my dairy and eggs for the rest of the week.

I look up at the torn black lining under the top bunk. One little hole, and Stevie had found it, taking one tiny finger and rrrrrrrr-ip. And instead of fixing it properly, I had only duct taped the sides and put a few pushpins here and there.

It did the job.

But it looks tacky.

I'm a grown man sleeping in my boy's bed. Funny, I hardly had to do that when he was . . . when he was here. Noël did most of the soothing in this house, whispering him back to sleep whenever he had a bad dream. He would call out only to her in the night.

And here I am calling out to him in the morning.

Merry Christmas, Jack.

What am I going to do today? There's no need to check the mailbox since it's a holiday. That's one of my few daily errands. It takes forty-seven steps to get to the mailbox. The fact that I know this makes me sad.

It took you forty-three yesterday.

It was cold. I had to move fast.

I've been waiting for my first novel to come out, a romance of all things, as if romance will ever happen to me again. I had waited too long to find a wife, to start a family . . . and to buy a safer vehicle than that van.

Stop thinking about that van.

I go to the kitchen and turn on the coffeemaker before I realize I haven't put in any coffee. The water that drips into my cup is slightly brown and smells like coffee, but it tastes like . . . hot brown water. Instead of searching through the mess I've made of the kitchen pantry for the coffee, I take a tea bag I used yesterday and dunk it into the water. It should be good for at least two more cups.

You're going to need vice grips to squeeze out any flavor.

Probably.

I return to the living room and plug in the lights of the tree before curling up on the love seat with my "coffee water tea."

"It's a nice tree, honey."

It never was, but Noël was always looking for something positive to say. The four trees I bought for us before . . . the accident . . . leaned right or left, were too bushy or had bald spots, or were too short or too tall.

One even had a bird's nest.

Yet, after we decorated those trees, they always looked better—in Noël's eyes, anyway—than any tree in any window in the neighborhood. We used to walk through the neighborhood looking at other people's trees, and though there were many grander than ours, Noël always said, "It's a nice tree, honey."

"Thank you," I say now. "Thanks . . . honey."

Change the subject. You're already out of Kleenex.

I'll use napkins.

You're out of them, too.

Oh. Paper towels?

Just the part stuck to the roll.

I've killed a lot of trees.

You're the champion of the forestry industry. Think about the novel.

My novel has been sent out to reviewers, and my agent, Nina Frederick, is supposed to be sending their reviews to me the second she gets them. My editor, Trina Lozell, has told me to keep my fingers crossed, but I'm not superstitious. "It's a great summer read," Trina says.

Then why is it coming out in April?

Beats me.

My book will finally be on the shelves in bookstores after all those late nights away from Noël and Stevie. I had wanted to make it big as a writer to allow Noël to stay home with Stevie instead of working as a medical transcriber at Roanoke Memorial. And if the money was good enough, I could quit teaching and write full-time.

All those dreams . . . and only mine came true.

Until the insurance money runs out.

All those dreams!

Change the subject, Jack! What's left of the paper towels will feel like sandpaper on your nose!

And I'm all out of lotion.

There's bound to be some lotion on Noël's vanity.

I'm not going in there. I'm . . . I'm thinking about the book.

I'm not nervous about the reviewers as much as I was about the revisions Trina suggested I make. She had me add more profanity, sex, attitude, and drama to what was originally a simple love story. I'm a little embarrassed about it all. I even had to add stereotypical, one-dimensional characters who are more like caricatures than people. Noël would barely recognize the novel, mainly because it wasn't originally multicultural.

You mean, it wasn't originally interracial.

I prefer the word "multicultural." We are all, after all, from the human race.

True.

My simple, sweet little novel had two lonely white people meeting, getting together, and falling in love. Nina had agreed to represent my manuscript if I changed a few "colors" and added some more "colorful family and friends." I ended up padding the word count with gratuitous sex, adult humor, and cursing—all of which seems to be in vogue in today's literary world. "The book needs more dramatic, guilty pleasures," Nina had advised, and I had still wanted that dream even if I didn't have Noël and Stevie to share it with me, so . . . I did it. I even rationalized that since there is a glut of same-race romances out there, I would be breaking new ground. The world was changing, the literal face of the nation was and is darkening, so I supposed with a few touches here and there—

If Noël had been here to do the final edit, I know it would have come out better. She had helped me to write the original woman's part, and in many ways, she's like Noël: sensibly curious, honestly shy, spiritually worldly, and glamorously uncomplicated. My character and my wife were beautiful homebodies.

Like I've become.

Except for the beautiful part.

True. I can't remember the last time I've left the house.

You bought eggnog, Kleenex, and coffee two days ago at Food Lion, remember?

That was two days ago?

Yes.

Time flies when you're not having fun, too.

Get back to the book.

I had told Trina early on that I wasn't up to making appearances or traveling to promote the book because of what's happened, and she had understood. "That's okay, Jackie," she had said, in her Brooklyn accent, "we weren't planning on you making any appearances anyway. You'll be the non-gender-specific D. J. Browning on the advance review copy."

Non-gender-specific, a name that could apply to either a man or a woman.

You've been neutered.

So, here I am on Christmas Day, an anonymous, neutered man waiting on the next day's mail missing . . . Noël and Stevie.

God, I need to stay busy.

So, get busy.

But where to start . . . where to begin? Time to get up off this love seat and do something.

Right.

The toys.

The toys?

Yeah. Stevie's toys. Other kids need a nice Christmas, too, and though they'll be a few days late in getting to them, at least—

At least you'll be moving.

At least I'll be moving.

Start with the simplest things first, and then it will become easier.

I hope so.

5

Diane

When I'm not working at the library, I stay home nights and read.

A *lot*.

As in four to five books a week, up to three books on the weekends alone.

I used to read like this as a kid, but it took joining the Mid-Atlantic Book Review to kick-start my reading habit. At first, we'd all read the same book and post our reviews at the MAB.org Web site. When authors started using blurbs from our reviews for their book covers, we later branched out into posting reviews at Amazon.com and Barnes & Noble's Web site. Now, since we're one of Amazon.com's top one hundred reviewers, we get advance review copies from publishers and authors from all over the world.

And I don't have to pay a single dime for any of the books I read anymore. Just about every other book in my library is an advance review copy from some author or another.

If I like a book, I give it four or five stars and write extremely long, glowing reviews in the hopes that my name will travel around the world on the back of some best-seller. At least my name will get out of the house. That's only happened a couple of times, but it is still quite a rush to see my own name in "lights" whenever I go into a bookstore.

Now if I hate a book—and I've hated a *lot* more books than I've liked—I give it one star, though I often write something like, "If I could give this book no stars, I would." Then I write reviews so short or so overly critical that not even the most imaginative writer or publisher can squeeze a kind, ellipsis-filled comment to put on the back of a book.

It's funny, but of the hundreds of books I've reviewed, few have scored between one and four stars. I guess you could say it's all or nothing with me as a reader. "Grab me early and grab me often, Mr./Mrs./ Miss Author, and don't you let me go"—that's my reviewer's credo.

I like reading romances the most, not that romances aren't ridiculous at some level. Most of them are pretty out there, but occasionally I run into one that almost sounds realistic, like what happens to the woman in the story could really happen to me. I usually give those books higher marks, even if they aren't or will never be best-sellers or be made into movies.

I don't watch many movies, romantic or otherwise. They are so much more unreal than even the most far-fetched books I've reviewed. I mean, in real life, brand-new cars usually start 99 percent of the time and don't break down on lonely wilderness roads where beady-eyed strangers with maniacal thoughts happen to show up out of the Technicolor blue to help, despite the fact that the population of said wilderness is 0.5 people and 95 squirrels per square mile. In real life, drivers usually insert the correct key in the ignition the first time, and home owners find the front door key in milliseconds, not dropping the key ring while the masked man with the machete slinks closer at 0.2 miles per hour. In real life, most dead bolts hold and don't break the first time the cop or villain (or cop/villain) kicks in the door, and the doors don't splinter because most of them aren't made out of real wood anymore.

And the people in the movies aren't real, either. In real life, people have gas, runny noses, diarrhea, weak and/or small bladders, and constipation. Unless filmmakers want to do a teen comedy or get an R rating, their people have to be sniffle free and regular so no one will have to use the restroom for one hundred minutes.

In real life, children aren't always cute; don't have snappy, adult-sounding comebacks; usually have some piece of green snot or other bodily crud somewhere on their bodies; aren't always clean or dressed perfectly; and *occasionally* say the darnedest things. I ought to know. I work in a library that literally crawls with snotty kids every Saturday morning.

Movies also have unreal scenes and settings. In real life, meals don't always taste good—or all that bad either—even at Grandma's house, and families don't always sit down together so they can have some snappy dialogue and food hijinks involving what's *really* in the meat loaf. In real life, the average yard is . . . average, the grass more beige than green, the flowers not always alive or blooming, the trees and bushes not always coiffed like a new hairstyle, the leaves not always raked, the weeds not always pulled, the deck . . . not always attached to the house. And in real life, the house isn't that spacious or grand. I doubt I'd ever see my house in a movie. My windows are dirt spotted and grimy on the outside.

Robert Maxwell to the rescue? Hmm. Maybe this spring when I want to see what the outside looks like, but not now. Everything is so wintry and gray.

My carpet is worn and dirty, though I vacuum often, and my hardwood floors are so scuffed that I have throw rugs everywhere. My bathroom is clean, but it's anything but gleaming. Hard water will do that to your fixtures. My sink, however, is not full of dishes . . . because I use lots of Styrofoam. My refrigerator is often bare (except for condiments) by the end of the week, and I sometimes hear echoes from my cupboards and cabinets. No, my home will never be in a movie, unless they do a sequel to *Animal House*.

And please don't get me started about the so-called jobs people in the movies have. Yeah, I have lots of issues with the movies, and I've even thought about being a movie critic, too, but I doubt my reviews would ever go on any poster or DVD cover. In real life, jobs are tedious and frustrating at times, and there's rarely enough time to flirt, cheat, make conversation, or develop relationships. Folks generally *work* at work, and the only people hanging around the copy machines are the people *repairing* them.

Movie people just aren't real enough for me. In real life, folks spend a lot of time in line: at the Department of Motor Vehicles, in traffic, at the supermarket, or at the "big game." They do nothing but wait and think, "Here I am again in line, waiting to get into another line." In real life, people actually read newspapers, novels, magazines, and cell phone manuals silently to themselves in bed late at night until they fall asleep. And in real life, every phone call isn't life changing, life affirming, mind-blowing, or the least bit shocking—or all that interesting, for that matter.

If Hollywood followed the average person around for twenty-four hours, it would be real, but who would watch it? Who would watch a movie about, well, nothing?

Just look at the average romance or "chick flick." These movies do pretty well at the box office if there's chemistry between the two principles, but what real-life romance has chemistry, heat, and passion *all* the time? In real romance, so much *nothing* happens that eventually *something* has to happen—which is usually a burst of passion followed by *more* nothing. Nothing has the ability to happen for minutes, hours, days, weeks, months, and years at a time (don't I know it!), leaving the average person time for introspection, a few collected thoughts, a nap, trips to the bathroom, chores, vegging out in front of the TV, another nap, and/or a shower. Can Hollywood put all that in a romantic movie? Of course not! While it is logical and everyone can relate to it, it's ultimately boring. Something has to happen every nanosecond in romantic comedy, or the romance (and the movie) fizzles.

I know, I know, romance is about hope, about possibilities, about chance encounters, and Hollywood doesn't have time (or the budget) to be completely real. Hollywood wants to get to the juicy stuff, to get to the passion, to get 'em rolling and writhing in bed, so Hollywood can get to the sunset, to the limo, to the church, and to the credits scrolling during a song that just might win a Grammy.

Maybe I'm too cynical, but *reel life* can never be real. And though many of the books I review fall short, at least they *try* to be real.

I flop into my comfy chair, an overstuffed leather lounger, and open four packages, each addressed to "Nisi." That's right. I'm just like Madonna or Cher. I am the one-name MAB reviewer. Mama thinks I should use my "Christian" name, but Mama doesn't know how angry some of these authors can get. My pseudonym gives me a little security, and in a way, I have made a name for myself. If "Nisi" gives a book high marks, the book is *good*.

The first book is called *The Quiet Game*, by Anonymous. Hmm. Anonymous? Maybe it's a big-name author afraid to ruin sales of his or her other books. Either that, or this is a stinker, and the publisher doesn't want anyone to know who wrote it. No title graphic, just plain black text on a white cover. Most advance review copies I receive are dull like this to save money, I guess. I open and read the first page:

> *I've been playing the quiet game ever since I was a little boy.*
> *I'm good at it. No one has ever beaten me. No matter how much they tried to make me talk, I didn't talk.*

No matter how much they tried to make me laugh, I didn't laugh. No matter what they did, said, or threatened, I didn't make a sound.

And I still don't.

I am the champ.

If they only knew what was going through my mind. . . .

If they could only see what I see through my little lens. . . .

I'm not sure that I want to know or see, but at least this book isn't full of typos so far. I hate that. You wouldn't believe how sloppy some authors and editors have gotten in their rush to get a quote or two from a reviewer. It's almost as if I'm reading a first draft half the time. This reads smoothly, but I don't think this is going to be my cup of tea.

Virginia is as good a place to play the quiet game as any. It's already quiet. Except for a little strip of rat-racers in Northern Virginia (NoVa) and around D.C. and Richmond, even the people are quiet, silent almost. Not much has changed since the Civil War. I guess Virginians are just as dead as all those ghosts on the battlefields, the ones they charge admission to. I don't visit them, though.

There might be a ghost out there who can outquiet me, and I can't let that happen.

Besides, I have my own personal battlefields, and you don't even have to get a park permit or sit in traffic or stand in line to see them.

All you have to do is read the headlines. . . .

And if you're not careful, I'm going to put a bullet in your head.

I don't have to read this one. It has to be a rip-off of the sniper killings a few years back. When will authors get some innovative plots? There is definitely nothing new under the sun. I mean, where's the mystery in this? I enjoy reading mysteries, I really do, but after reading this first page—and knowing what it's based on—there's no point in reading this at all. And I'll bet the movie version of the whole sniper mess is either in the works or "in the can," as they say.

Overkill. That's all this is.

Yeah, it shocked me that a black man was the sniper, just like it shocked all those fool criminal profilers out there who thought he *had* to be white to be such a sophisticated criminal. The only thing that shocks me more is the book sitting in my hands. This is old news, and it gets published. Sometimes I don't think the publishers in New York have a single clue about what folks really want to read. "Hey, here's something that scared the crap out of Americans on the East Coast, Bob. Let's sell it." Yeah, and it kept us inside *reading*. Now that the sniper has been caught and convicted, we're outside again . . . and reading *less*.

I set *The Quiet Game* aside and wished Vanessa—the president of the Mid-Atlantic Book Review—would stop sending me every book that takes place in Virginia. I wasn't even living here during those sniper shootings, and I know there are at least ten other women in Virginia who post reviews for MAB. Why me? I pick up *The Quiet Game* and flip a few pages, the word "blood" jumping out at me several times on page six. Great. A black serial killer sniper is the narrator, he looks at life through his "little lens," and I live alone on part of his personal battlefield.

I'm going to pass on this one for now. I'll probably skim it later, and I know I'm not the only book reviewer who skims books on occasion. So many books come out every year in the United States, something like 100,000 titles, and it's difficult for reviewers to keep up. I officially reviewed 106 books last year in addition to "unofficially" reviewing 140 of my own choosing at Amazon.com, and I might have read half of the 106 all the way through.

The title of the second book, *Thicker Than Blood*, by J. Johnson, doesn't make me feel any safer, although when I open to the first chapter, I'm mildly intrigued:

> *"They say that you men think about sex every seven seconds," Jeanetta says, sipping her mega–Mai Tai during the happy hour at Bensons Bar and Grill after work.*

When's the last time I went to a happy hour? Or even a restaurant that serves mixed drinks, for that matter? It has to be years. I doubt I'm missing much. But men think about sex every seven seconds? Who determines this stuff? Do *I* think about sex that often? Who has the time?

> *I don't answer right away because I'm looking at the cute woman sipping on some ice water sitting next to Jeanetta. She's small with a cute face, zigzagged cornrows, little dimples, a shy smile, and very nice legs that are smooth and silky, with cut calves. She has small hands and the nicest brown eyes. And she's wearing some cut-off jeans, you know, with all the strings hanging down from where she cut them, and a tight, plain white T-shirt that almost gets to the shorts, a tattoo of some kind edged around her belly button. She's quite a package. I wish I were sitting where Jeanetta's sitting—*

"*Cute* woman"? Hmm. That girl is a hoochie. When will authors realize that most of their female readers are *nothing* like the women in the books they write? When will authors realize that we do not aspire to *be* them? If other female readers are like me, they have some baggage, and the only time they have smooth and silky legs is just before a trip to the gynecologist's. Cute Woman sounds like a trifling ho.

I know, I'm just jealous.

"Are you listening to me, Robert?"

Oops. "Call me 'Rob,' Jeanetta, and I know that can't be true."

Jeanetta, a fix-up date from Tony, a real estate buddy of mine, is bustin' out all over in a beige dress with buttons that go all the way from her breasts to her thighs. The girl is thicker than thick, but she's one of those sisters with an agenda, you know, like she has to save every man from himself or something. Too much make-up anyway, though I haven't exactly been looking at her face. She must have triple Ds up in there.

Mr. Johnson—at least I assume that a *man* wrote this—is obviously writing *with* his Johnson. Why is it the big women in men's books (and some women's books, too) have to have attitudes and agendas? Jeanetta sounds blessed, not cursed, and just to have some triple Ds for a couple hours might be nice to balance me out so I wouldn't have to lean forward so much when I walk.

"I bet it's true," Jeanetta says.

"Just add it up," I say, sipping my Coke. "That means men think about sex eight times a minute, right? That's almost five hundred times an hour, over ten thousand times a day, close to four million times a year." I was, after all, an accounting major before I went into real estate. "How would anything ever get done?"

"Like anything ever gets done anyway," Jeanetta says.

Amen to that! Maybe nothing gets done *because* men are thinking about sex so much. So, whenever Congress has trouble passing a bill . . . I don't want to think about that.

The woman beside Jeanetta is quiet. I like that. She's kind of like me, just taking life in, watching and thinking. Maybe she's waiting on someone. Lucky guy.

I'll bet Cute Woman is a ho, and a pro ho at that, and Rob is about to hook up with her.

> *"Okay," I say, "let's say a group of fellas are play-ing a pickup game of basketball. Don't tell me all they're thinking about is some booty while they're ballin'."*
>
> *Jeanetta blinks at me. "You just said 'ballin',' right?"*

Jeanetta is obviously not a proper lady of color. Such language!

> *The woman beside Jeanetta bites her lip and looks away. Cute. Definitely cute, and she's eavesdropping on us. I had better not sound like a complete fool then.*
>
> *"I meant," I say, "they don't have time to be think-ing about sex when they're shooting hoops." They'd better not be, especially if they're playing tight defense on me."*
>
> *"Yeah?" Jeanetta says. "Isn't the object in basket-ball to put it in the hoop more than the other guy?" She takes a longer sip of her Mai Tai. "Sounds like they're thinking about sex to me."*
>
> *"That's not what I'm saying—"*
>
> *"And what about football?" Jeanetta says. "You take a ball from between some sweaty fat man's legs, and if you hit the hole just right, you might score."*
>
> *Damn. I never thought of it that way before.*

Neither have I. Yuck. I will not be watching any of the bowl games this year, not that I make time to look at TV. About all I do is dust off my TV.

> *"And in baseball, you try to keep your balls in play so you can hit a home run and get to home plate."*

Jeanetta nudges the woman next to her with her elbow. "All the sports men play are all about sex, right?"

The woman turns to us. "Maybe," she says in a cute voice. Everything about her is cute. "Sports can't be all about sex."

What sport isn't sexual? What sport puts most folks to sleep on a Sunday afternoon? I got it. "Golf isn't that sexual," I say.

"Long skinny clubs, drivers, ball in the hole," Jeanetta says.

Hmm. Okay, what's more boring than golf? "Chess, then," I say.

Jeanetta smirks. "A bunch of men trying to gang up on the queen."

Damn. Jeanetta is sharp as a tack. Smart and thick. I know this will be our only date.

"Okay, enough with the sports analogies. I just know that I don't think about sex that much." I don't know why I'm admitting that to them. I have to talk fast. "It isn't because I don't enjoy it." Whenever there's a blue moon. When was the last time? Was Clinton or a Bush president? Damn.

I know this is false. Any man who's this hard up has to remember his last time in glorious, graphic detail.

All *two* minutes of it.

And as for me . . . hmm. I don't have a last time to remember, though that one time with Petie Whatshisname in the tenth grade . . . No. *We* didn't. *He* did, but I didn't. The boy didn't even get his pants off. I thought he was having a seizure!

And now I've depressed myself.

"Don't get me wrong. I just don't have the time because of my family."

"Amen to that," I say aloud this time. Yeah, I talk back to books. They don't argue back—much.

Jeanetta arches two perfectly shaped eyebrows. I bet she gets them waxed. "Tony told me that you weren't married."

"I'm not. I'm talking about my family *family, the family that raised me."*

"Oh." She sucks down more of her Mai Tai. The girl thinks and drinks too much. "Well, you know what they say: blood is thicker than water."

Blood is thick, but what is thicker than blood? Is it supposed to be love? That's not something I've ever thought about. Love is thicker than blood. Hmm. I guess it makes sense.

I know they—whoever the hell "they" are—say that. But "they" have never met my family.

"You got to stand by your family no matter what, through thick and thin," Jeanetta says. "Your family has to come first."

I finish my Coke. The woman beside Jeanetta looks bored. Shit. I better liven up the conversation. "But what if your family is completely out of its damn mind?" The other woman turns to me, her eyes focused on my face. We have this little moment, you know, like we recognize something in each other. Maybe her family's messed up, too.

Either that or Cute Woman is upset you said "damn." Or she's the hoochie I know she is. I'm beginning to like him, but the women? They're ridiculous.

"Are you saying that your family's dysfunctional?" Jeanetta asks.

"Dysfunctional?" I say. "That's a word for white folks and talk shows."

True. Though sometimes I think my mama . . . No, I'm not going to say she's dysfunctional. Blood *is* thicker than water. Mama's just . . . eccentric.

The other woman smiles. Nice. We're connecting. Cool.

"My family is crazy," I say. "My family is damaged. My family is . . . completely out its damn mind. Trust me. Your IQ will shoot up thirty points just being in the same state as them."

Jeanetta clears her throat and takes her purse from the bar. "No one's that crazy," Jeanetta says, turning to the woman beside her. "Come on, Chloe. Let's go."

Chloe? Geez, Cute Hoochie Woman is a perfume. Rob is getting played.

What the hell?

Jeanetta turns to me with a bland, no-this-hasn't-been-fun look on her face. "It was nice meeting you, Robert."

"It's Rob, and who—"

"Uh-huh." Jeanetta slides off the stool, but Chloe stays put. "Come on, girl. Happy hour's almost over. You don't have to chaperone me anymore." Jeanetta turns to me, dipping those triple Ds into my face. "No offense, Robert. I have to be careful. You understand."

"Uh, yeah." I smile at Chloe. "It was nice meeting you, too, Chloe." I think.

Chloe slides off her stool, letting just the tip of her tongue flick over her lower lip. "It was nice meeting you, too, Rob."

And she got my name right.

*"And I'd like to meet your family someday," Chloe
says directly to me.*

Cute and *daring? "What?"*

*Chloe hops up on Jeanetta's seat. "I'd like to meet
your family."*

*Daa-em. "Um, I'm going to see my grandpa Joe-
Joe and my daddy this evening. You . . . want to come?"*

Grandpa "Joe-Joe"? Where do authors get these funky
names? One author came to the library to do a reading last
fall, and he said he used a phone book for all of his names. "I
prefer the randomness of it all," he said. I doubt there's a listing for "Grandpa Joe-Joe" in the phone book.

"Sure."

Riiiiight. Just like that. Chance meeting, a "date" to see
Grandpa Joe-Joe, then lots of sex where Rob will analyze
Chloe's tattoo. Only in books. Or in Las Vegas.

Or so I've heard.

Yes! "Cool."

*Jeanetta sighs and shakes her head. "How are you
going to get home, Chloe?"*

Chloe smiles. "Rob can take me."

Rob. That's my name. I like this girl.

*"Whatever," Jeanetta says, and she walks out of
Bensons.*

*I don't watch Jeanetta leave, though every "man"
cell in my body wants me to, and I focus on Chloe's
hands. Short nails, no nail polish. I'll bet her hands
are soft. "Are you sure you want to meet my family?"*

Chloe nods.

*I leave a ten on the bar. "Well, okay." I look down at
her feet and see sandals. This could be a problem.
"Just watch your step when we get to Grandpa Joe-*

*Joe's house. You never know what might be hiding in
Grandpa Joe-Joe's jungle. . . ."*

Not bad. Not great. Adequate. It reminds me of some
book I read a few years ago, what was it? Some book about
a dysfunctional white family that made most of the top ten
best book lists. Maybe this is the darker version of that. Yet
another rip-off.

I toy with turning the page. I haven't quite been grabbed
yet, though I have a feeling these two—Chloe and Rob—
will be bumping uglies by page thirty. So predictable.

I need a challenge!

6

Jack

This isn't easy at all.
But it has to be done.
I know.

I'm sorting Stevie's toys into two big boxes: toys from kids' meals, which still smell like French fries, and toys fit to be taken to the Salvation Army. He took good care of his toys, not that we showered him with that many. The xylophone still rolls and plays a tune. Now where is the . . . hammer? What do you call it?

Call it the "banger."

Here it is. He used to bang all day on this thing, and some days he'd fixate on a single note and play that one note wherever he went.

Good ol' Stevie "One Note."

I hit a note several times.

Put it in the box, Jack.

I know, I know.

After half an hour, I realize something: fast-food restaurants give away a *lot* of toys. We ate out a lot, even though Noël could cook like a master chef, and we have all the Magic Chef accessories to prove it. But we liked going to places with indoor playgrounds so Stevie could work off his chicken nuggets and fries while we nursed sweet teas and . . . talked.

I miss that. I miss watching him sliding and climbing. I miss hearing him say, "Daddy, look!" I miss talking about nothing with Noël. So much of our "romance," if you could call it that, was a long series of nothing moments held together by a frolicking little boy.

You're almost done. Don't stop now.

The boxes almost filled, I hold Stevie's teddy bear, Mr. Bear, the one I bought at the hospital gift shop the day Stevie was born. While Stevie called him Mr. Bear, I used to call him "Chuck," because Stevie regularly threw him around his room.

Mr. Bear has seen better days.

The seams under each arm are ripped, one glass eyeball almost dangles, and his fur is fuzzed out in all the wrong places.

I'm keeping Mr. Bear.

No one's stopping you.

I set Mr. Bear on top of Stevie's dresser and take the French fry–smelling toys to the big garbage can outside. While every other garbage can on this street will be full of wrapping paper, bows, and boxes, mine will be full of fast-food toys. There's something . . . sad about that.

You need to start over.

Yeah, but it's still sad.

I look at the space in the driveway where Noël's Ford Mustang, her "baby," used to sit. It was too yellow for my taste, but it fit her and her sunny personality. She was always sunny, even on cold and overcast days like this. I hadn't touched the car except to put a blaze orange "FOR SALE" sign in the rear window. I hadn't expected anyone to notice, but a nice man, a World War II veteran who was wounded at

Anzio, like my Grandpa Jeff, had bought it and my memories of Noël in that car . . . three days ago?

Close. Four days ago.

Really?

And you haven't been to the bank to deposit his check yet. When are you going to do that?

If she had taken the Mustang instead of that tin can of a van, maybe she'd still be alive.

Don't think about it.

It's hard not to.

I return to the house to get the "good" box of toys, loading it into the Isuzu Rodeo I bought using some of the insurance settlement money. It sits parked on the street with only a minor dent in a door. Epoxy glue and duct tape hold one of the outdoor mirrors to the driver's side door, a victim of an errant garbage can a few weeks ago.

You weren't paying attention.

Yeah, I pushed the garbage can into the mirror. I should have called the insurance company about it, but I'm sure the people there are tired of hearing from me.

When I go back into the house, I hear the phone ringing, and at first, I'm not sure what I'm hearing. So few people have called these last few months.

Except for telemarketers hawking phone service, mortgages, and something about a fire safety house for kids. You donated to that one.

Anything for the kids.

The phone is still ringing.

I know it's not Noël's family—or mine. I've asked them to leave me alone for a while until I can . . . function, and they've respected my wishes for the most part, Noël's family especially. I'm sure deep down they still blame me for everything and wish that I had died instead of their only child and grandchild.

You're not thinking those thoughts again, are you?

No.

Good. I like talking to you.

You're the only one who does.

I check the Caller ID as it rings on. It's not long distance and can't be the school. Who else would be calling on Christmas Day?

"Hello?"

"Is this Jack Browning?" The man has a voice full of gravel.

"Yes."

"This is Bill Williams. Hope I'm not disturbing your Christmas."

It's too late for that. But who is—oh. It's the man who bought Noël's car. "You're not disturbing me, Mr. Williams. How's the car running?"

"I'm bringing it back."

"Why?"

"It's got a shimmy."

"A shimmy?"

"A shimmy. It was wobbling all over the place."

"When?"

"When I was taking it home."

"But that was . . . four days ago."

"Yep. Just haven't had the time to bring her back until today."

Oh, geez. He had to say "her."

Come on, Jack. He's a Marine. Anything that carries him somewhere is female.

I grip the phone tightly. "I don't understand, Mr. Williams. You said that you were taking the car to your own mechanic to get it checked out, and I told you I'd hold on to the check until you had done that. Has your mechanic checked it out yet?"

"Uh, no."

"He hasn't?"

"No, but I don't want to purchase the vehicle anymore because of that shimmy."

That car doesn't shimmy. That car is rock solid. "Well, look, Mr. Williams, it hadn't been driven in a long time. Perhaps one of the tires is lower on air pressure than the others. Did you check the tires?"

"I know a shimmy when I feel one, young man."

Think! "Well, you know those are after-market wheels on that vehicle, and my wife was always saying that they weren't as perfectly balanced as the original, so—"

"Will you be home today? It's the only day I can get another driver."

But I only want memories visiting me today! "Were you driving it, Mr. Williams?"

"No, my grandson was."

"Your grandson was?" During the test-drive, the grandson proved that he couldn't drive a five-speed.

He couldn't even find reverse.

"Perhaps your grandson was in the wrong gear going up or down a hill."

"He wasn't. I was sitting right there next to him telling him when to shift. Now will you be home today? I want to come get my check."

But of course! The check! It's all about the money.

It's not that I need the money. It's the principle of the thing. A man should keep his word. "I'll be . . . I'll be home all day, but please reconsider. My wife babied that car. You know how clean it is inside, and she had the oil changed religiously every three thousand miles."

"I'm concerned about the shimmy."

This man is fixated on the word "shimmy." Maybe it's a World War II thing.

"I understand your concern, I really do, but that car is *safe.* I wouldn't have sold it to you otherwise. And anyway, you said you were taking it to your—"

"I know what I said, and now I'm saying that I'm bringing it back today."

I can't have that car back here, all sunny and yellow and

full of Noël! Not today! "Look, it's been sitting in the driveway for two months, I haven't been driving it, so it's possible—"

"And the back windows leak."

And now it's about the windows! "I *told* you about the back windows, and you didn't seem concerned *then*. All you were concerned with was getting the car to your home because you knew you were getting a good deal."

"And now I'm bringing it back. Will you be there, say, around three?"

This can't be happening! "I know you want a safe car for your grandson. I understand that. What I don't understand is how you're not being a man of your word. I told you I would hold on to the check until your mechanic checked it out. *I'm* doing *my* part—"

"I got the law on my side, young man."

The law? What law? "The lemon law?"

"Uh-huh."

"Mr. Williams, that law doesn't apply to this situation at all. That's only for car dealerships."

"That's not what I've heard."

Geez! "Can you do me a favor, Mr. Williams? Can you take the car to your mechanic first and have him check it out like you *said* you would, and if your mechanic, whom you obviously trust, finds major problems, then we'll—"

"My grandson says he doesn't feel safe in it, and neither do I. We'll see you at three."

"Sir, you're taking the word of an eighteen-year-old driver who had difficulty finding the reverse gear during the test-drive."

"He was just nervous."

"I know he was nervous, but he was giving us all whiplash. And legally, you have the title, signed by both parties—"

"You know that isn't really a legal document, Mr. Browning. You had to forge your own wife's signature!"

I can't catch my breath. "Because she's . . . dead, that's why, and I told you why that day, and you said you understood."

"I don't want any trouble, Mr. Browning, and this car has trouble written all over it."

I sigh. Noël would have already said, "Cool, Mr. Williams, bring it back. We understand." And Noël wouldn't want me to sell her "baby" to anyone like Mr. Williams or his gear-stripping grandson. "Okay, Mr. Williams, bring the car back, and don't forget to bring the title. I'll be here waiting."

I turn off the phone, tossing it onto the sofa. "Unbelievable. I should have deposited that check the second I had it."

The Lord giveth, and the Lord taketh away—and on Christmas Day.

Maybe you'll need that car, and this is God's way of saying—

Don't bring God into this.

Oops. Sorry. I forgot. You and God aren't speaking.

I have never had any luck with any vehicle. I broke the grille of my mother's AMC Spirit, pushing it out of a snow-drift two months after getting my license. A few months later, I backed my father's Buick Regal into another car in a parking lot. The first car technically "mine" was an Oldsmobile something-or-other.

It was an Omega. They don't make those anymore.

That's why I blocked out the memory.

The Omega died outside Dayton, Ohio, on a sunny, below-zero day. Fixed, it lasted only a few months more, finally coughing up oil in Marietta, Ohio. My next car, a Toyota Corona, purchased from a mechanic in Charleston, West Virginia, was a bucket of rust, yet it served me well, despite losing the muffler on some train tracks in Indiana and having only an AM radio and a pretzel-shaped antenna that, for some reason, would only bring in stations that had nonstop farm reports.

"Wheat futures are looking good. . . ."

I still don't know what a wheat future is.

After selling that rust bucket to a man who planned to race it—

He was spooky. He actually thought he could get a 350 engine in there.

—I bought my first "brand-new" vehicle, a Nissan Sentra. It was a beautiful car until two fifth-grade boys decided to wrestle on it in the parking lot. There were a hundred other cars to choose from, and they chose mine. Two months later, I "won" a game of chicken with a pregnant deer outside of Elliott's Creek, Virginia, denting the brand-new hood.

She shouldn't have hesitated.

Two months after that during an ice storm in Boones Mill, Virginia, an ancient tree branch decided to fall on the roof of the Sentra—and the second hood—destroying forever its once aerodynamic design. I barely got a thousand for it on the trade-in for the van.

We're not thinking about the van today, remember?

Right.

A few minutes before three, Mr. Williams shows up with the Mustang, the grandson driving, Noël's Mustang bucking like, well, a mustang. I dig the "FOR SALE" sign from the kitchen trash can, smoothing out the strips of masking tape, then go outside.

And Mrs. Williams is with them again in . . . a Buick Regal? My luck.

Life has a way of making circles.

More like spinning wheels.

You're so negative.

I'm just full of positive negativity these days.

That made no sense.

I walk by Mr. Williams, who rests beside the Mustang and leans heavily on a metal cane, to Mrs. Williams in the Buick. I open my wallet and take out the check, handing it to her.

"Dry run," she says.

"Yeah. I guess so." I turn to Mr. Williams. "You have the title?"

Mr. Williams fishes in his pocket for the title, and then holds it out to me. I take the title, rolling it into a little scroll.

Now you'll have to go to the DMV to get that fixed.

I can't wait.

You'll have to get Noël's name taken off it.

I know. I'll have to find the death certificate.

If you sit in a DMV long enough, everyone you have ever known will eventually show up.

Yeah, the DMV is one of the only true melting pots left in this country.

I can't blame Mr. Williams for losing his nerve, but what did he think he was buying? It's a used car with close to 100,000 miles on it! I was practically giving it away!

If he really wanted a safe car for his grandson, he would have bought him a Volvo or something.

"I filled up the tank," Mr. Williams says.

Oh, that makes everything better.

I nod. "Are all the records in the car?"

"Yeah," the grandson says.

I don't look at the can't-drive-a-stick grandson. I open the back driver's side door and press the "FOR SALE" sign into the window, using my fingernails to smooth out the strips of tape.

You should trim them.

Yeah.

They look like claws.

They do, kind of.

And get a haircut. You look like a hippie.

Thanks for the compliment.

Mr. Williams takes out his wallet. "What can I give you for your trouble?"

Well, you gave me your word, and look what happened. "I don't want anything from you. This is a solid car, and I don't want you to think I was trying to put one over on you. The gas is enough."

Mr. Williams looks at his wallet. "I'm going to do some more investigating on this car. I might still buy it."

How can you investigate the car *without* the car? If I don't see you or your no-driving grandson again, I'll be a happy man.

Mrs. Williams can come, though. She seems apologetic.

I nod to Mrs. Williams, close the door, and take the key from the grandson. "Good-bye," I say, and I walk back into the house.

"Merry Christmas," Mr. Williams says.

I don't return the phrase.

Why not? It's Christmas Day!

It's a rotten thing to say.

On the day after Christmas while others are standing in line at the malls returning gifts, I'm giving slightly used toys to the Salvation Army, and I'm not the only one waiting in line at the loading dock. There are other dads and moms with boxes of "last year's" toys and clothes. I guess they're making room for the new load while I'm just . . . making room.

When it's my turn, I hand Stevie's toys to a stranger, a young guy in jeans and a red flannel shirt.

Let go of the box.

The man tugs a little on the box, saying, "You need a receipt?"

Let go.

I release the box, my hands shaking. "Uh, no." I look past him and see huge piles of clothes inside. "Um, do you need women's and children's clothes?"

"Sure do, especially boys' clothes."

You have some of those.

"I'll, uh, see you later today."

"Sure thing, chief."

I get into the truck, but I can't take my eyes off that box, still in— Oh! He's just thrown it down! There are *years* in that box! There's a little *boy* in that box!

Get a grip on yourself.

"I'm sorry, Stevie," I say, starting up the truck. "I'm so sorry."

Back at the house, I wander around upstairs for a few hours, avoiding Noël's door. The toys were hard enough. But her clothes?

You can't possibly wear them.

I know that.

Though you're certainly skinny enough now.

Very funny.

They'll make someone happy.

Not me!

This isn't about you. It's Christmas. It's about others. It's about giving gifts.

I go to the door to Noël's—*our*—room and extend my hand.

Just turn, pull toward you a little, and push. You've been doing it for years.

"Not today," I whisper.

Go in.

"I just . . . can't."

The furnace chooses this moment to whirr to life in the basement, and Noël's—*our*—door rattles. I had replaced the doorknob, and it had never worked right after that.

Open the door.

I grab the knob, turn it slowly, pull back, push gently, and then hear the familiar creak as it swings inside. The curtains are still pulled back, light filtering in through the miniblinds, to reveal dust on the TV, on the mirror on Noël's vanity, and on the candles resting on the headboard. I look up at the ceiling fan and see more dust.

You need to dust this room.

I know that.

On instinct, I tiptoe between the bed and the dresser, knocking a knee into a drawer that never would fully close.

When are you going to fix that drawer?

As soon as I dust; now be quiet.

I lift and push in the drawer, but it stays put. I never got around to fixing much in this house, and I never got around to building Noël that closet organizer she wanted. They make it look so easy on the box, proclaiming "simple, easy installation with only a few household tools." It's still in the box next to the washing machine. Maybe I'll—

One step at a time. Dust and fix the drawer first.

Right.

I open Noël's closet and see . . . *twenty* or more bags from various department stores, some with flattened white boxes.

Merry Christmas, Jack.

Most of them are for Stevie.

But some of them are for you.

I pull out all the bags, and arrange them on the bed, the receipts folded neatly in the bottom of each bag.

She always saved the receipts.

Stevie would have gotten a new wardrobe complete with four pairs of new shoes, a new church outfit, and . . . a belt. He used to take my belt and wrap it around him twice. He was such a good mimic of me. I remember one time—

Look in your bags, Jack.

I'm having a memory.

We are having a memory, but you have work to do.

I open the first bag and see some brightly colored "teacher shirts," collared knit short-and long-sleeved shirts, with matching pants.

So colorful.

Before I met Noël, I only wore gray, blue, and brown Oxford shirts and corduroys. She said my outfits made me look "dispassionate."

You did. You looked more like a funeral director than an elementary school teacher.

I wasn't in a fashion show.

But the kids noticed the change.

Yeah. They did. They didn't make as much fun of me.

Except for that Baxter kid. He could probably find something wrong with Jesus.

The second bag contains a new belt, two packages of underwear, and an economy pack of brown and black socks. The last bag contains . . . a watch.

She knows I don't wear a watch! This has to be a gag gift.

You're rarely on time.

I like being fashionably late, and now that I have new fashions . . .

But when I open the box and take out the watch, I flip it over to see an inscription: "Ecclesiastes 3: 1-8 I love you, Noël."

There is a time for everything.

A time to be born and a time to die.

Still so negative! Why not "a time to mourn and a time to dance"?

All this . . . *this* is a mourning dance.

Put it on.

I put on the watch. I don't fiddle with setting the time. There will be a time for that. Just not now.

I pull out a bright red and green shirt and put it on, wiping dust from the mirror.

Now you're in tune with the season.

I look like death warmed over.

With claws, Mr. Claus.

I need a haircut, a shave, and about thirty pounds added just to my face. How did I get so skeletal?

You're an anorexic Santa.

And wrinkled? Only my eyes are unlined, those hazel-blue eyes Noël liked so much. "Drink to me only with thine eyes," she used to say. She liked that old-fashioned poetry.

But would she like this old man in the mirror? Would any-one?

Get to work.

I'm getting, I'm getting.

And take off that wedding band.

Not yet.

You're not married anymore.

I spin the ring around my finger, a nervous gesture I have been performing ever since we got married. I had never worn any jewelry before, and I'm constantly losing things, so I check often to see if it's still there.

It's still there, and it shouldn't be there.

Lots of . . . widowers—what a crummy word—wear their wedding rings.

Lots of old widowers. You're not old.

I feel old. I slide the ring up to my knuckle and see a cal-loused circle. I wouldn't even take it off to do the dishes or work in the yard. Why would I take it off now?

You used to call it "the world's tiniest handcuff."

That was before I got married.

And you're not married now, so . . .

I slide the ring back down, spinning it. I still feel married, so as long as I *feel* married, I'm keeping it on.

At least you feel something.

Yeah. At least I can still feel.

I hoist Noël's clothes from the closet onto the bed, and for a moment, I feel guiltier than I've ever felt before. These are *her* clothes. These are clothes she spent hours shopping for, finding the best sale, getting the best deal, even waiting for the price to come down. Do I have the right to just . . . give them away? She would give them away in a heartbeat if she thought it would brighten someone else's day, but—

It has to be done.

It has to be done.

I rip open all her drawers, tossing her clothing behind me, trying not to think of her wearing any of it . . . and failing. The tears won't stop. Noël used to be inside these clothes, and I used to take these clothes off her, tossing them up into the ceiling fan, and they would shoot around the room while we—

She's in a better place.

And where am I?

You're here.

Yeah, I'm here crying over some clothes.

I leave the dresser, clutching a silk red robe Noël used to wear after a shower, and it still smells faintly of Dove soap and herbal shampoo. I look out the window at the backyard, clutching that robe. God, that swing set looks as if it's going to fall down. I was never mechanical.

The backyard isn't level.

Stevie didn't seem to notice. He didn't even mind sliding down the slowest slide ever built while Noël and I sat in the wooden swing and watched him . . . *grow* before our very eyes. One of his shoes would just . . . fly off, and it was next to impossible to get it back on again. His feet grew so fast!

He's in a better place, too.

I know, I know. But—

A single snowflake dances by the window. Snow? I wonder if it will stick. Even a thin blanket of snow would be nice. Stevie's snowsuit, which swamped him last year, would have fit just right this year. We would be running around in the snow, Noël would be in the kitchen making hot chocolate for us, and then we'd eat grilled cheese sandwiches with tomato soup. Stevie would say something like, "You know, Daddy, drinking hot chocolate is like drinking kisses."

Drinking kisses.

I rest my head on the windowsill.

I miss that boy. God, how I miss that boy.

You'll see him again.

I look out at the yard, as more snowflakes drift down.

That's the problem. I can't stop seeing him *now!* He's

right *there*, trying to get a snowflake to land on his tongue! And over there, he's chasing after a firefly! He's running through the sprinkler and pushing that plastic bubble-making lawn mower on the other side of the yard!

Then don't stop seeing him. See him as the happy, healthy boy he was, and get on with your life.

How? By boxing up my wife and son and giving their memories to someone else?

It's a start.

I don't want to forget them.

No one's asking you to forget them.

I don't want to . . . put them on the shelf somewhere to dust off and look at every once in a while. I want them back!

Then give them away.

I can't, and I won't.

They aren't yours to keep anymore. They belong to God.

They belong . . . to God?

They belong to God.

Yeah, God can be greedy that way. Only the good die young, right?

Nothing gold can stay.

Right. Nothing gold—or golden—can ever stay in this overcast world.

Except you.

I'm not golden.

You could be.

I'd rather be overcast.

God moves in mysterious ways.

Well, sometimes He doesn't move fast enough or at all.

The snow is starting to stick. The roads will be slick, but the truck ought to do fine. I wonder if I have enough boxes for all these clothes. I could use garbage bags. . . . No. That wouldn't be right. They deserve better than garbage bags.

I'll just have to make a couple trips and get my boxes back each time. Geez, the four-wheel-drive vehicle I bought to replace the van that cost me my family is going to be used to safely deliver their memories to the Salvation Army. What could be more ironic?

It can't be considered ironic if it's expected. You aren't the only one who has ever lost a spouse and child. This is all part of the process.

The process sucks.

Only for a little while. But when you're done with this part . . .

And when I'm done with this part . . .

Don't think too long, now. Do something fun.

And when I'm done, I'll . . .

Think sunny thoughts, now.

I'll make Stevie a snowman.

7

Diane

Instead of going into the library on the day after Christmas, when no patrons come to the library anyway because they're all out standing in lines at the mall, I use my last remaining sick day. And since it's snowing—okay, it's not *really* snowing like it used to in Naptown—I don't want to drive anywhere.

"Too much partying last night, huh, Diane?" Kim "Prim" says when I call in to tell her I've developed a nasty cold.

"Yeah, I guess," I say. Why spoil her stereotype of me? At least *she* thinks I have fun. *Somebody* should be thinking I have a fun life.

"See you bright and early tomorrow, okay?"

"Okay." I'll be early, but I doubt I'll be bright.

I hang up and blow my nose into an imaginary tissue. Then I pick up the next book, *P&Q*, by J. K. Growling. What kind of name is "Growling"? I can only hope for the best.

1: Venus Dione

Oh no she didn't!

I clutch the latest copy of Maxim *and see Psyche's flawless body glistening with sweat on the cover, one scrawny towel barely covering her unnaturally natural "yes-they're-real" breasts, one scrawnier towel lying along her caramel thighs, toned to perfection by daily aerobics, her stomach so tight lint would bounce off of it.*

So far, I hate Psyche. This is so fake. Venus has an interesting voice, though. But what's up with these names from Greek mythology?

I hate her beautiful ass, I hate her blonde highlights, I hate her perfect uncapped teeth, I hate her darker-than-Mississippi-mud brown eyes, and I hate that trademark orange and black monarch butterfly tattoo on her arm.

I still hate Psyche. She's too perfect. This might be lucky to get one star, though I like Venus's attitude. Maybe I'll give it two stars for Venus hating Psyche, too.

Psyche was only supposed to be quoted, and she was only supposed to be inside the magazine in a pictorial on all of Aphrodite Incorporated's models, including me. I barely get a black-and-white head shot on page 128 in a sidebar.

Here she is on the goddamn cover.

Bitch.

"Bitch," I say with a giggle. Oh, like Psyche really exists. But here I am, yet again, echoing a fictional character. I hate it when this happens. I start talking back to a book, and the book hooks me. I'm curious about Grandpa Joe-Joe's jungle, but . . . I'll keep reading this one for now.

Nearly two million men of all ages and races will be drooling and jerking off over Psyche, and where is my latest full-body shot? On page seventeen of the latest JC Penney fall catalog. Not many men check out hot black women in itchy-ass wool blazers and turtlenecks on page seventeen of the JC Penney fall catalog, and if they do, I don't want to have anything to do with them.

Neither do I! They'd have to be perverted to get their "pleasuring" that way. Even Mama would agree with me. But was the phrase "jerking off" absolutely necessary? Is the author a man or a woman? I can usually tell. If the women's voices sound authentic, it has to be a woman. I'll bet J. K. Growling is a woman.

This has to stop! I knew ten years ago that Psyche would be trouble when she was only Ginger Dane, skinny brown wench with high cheekbones and a perfect smile from Athens, Ohio, sister to Rosemary Dane, another skinny brown wench whom I let model for me because I felt sorry for her. I have tried to snap Ginger in two on many occasions, giving her shitty shoots near the equator, where I had hoped she would turn black as night or get yellow fever, but the bitch came through with flying colors—and fame. That damn Sports Illustrated *swimsuit issue catapulted her to glory. I never should have let her do that. And when I wanted her to get sleazy in a rap video to damage her holier-than-anyone image, she flipped the script on those rappers, dressing in a formal white gown instead of some coochie-cutter hip huggers—and sent that single platinum. And last year I thought I could ruin her for good by rumoring her into a tasteless affair with that fat, sloppy comedian, what was his name? Fat Daddy? Pudge Daddy? Whatever. No one believed the rumor at all, not even Jay Leno, who said Psyche was just too "pure to be with a porker" on* The Tonight Show. *Damn, the bitch is giving supermodels a bad name, being as pure and healthy as she is. She isn't high-strung, isn't anorexic, isn't popping pills, doesn't drink, and she somehow manages to stay out of most of the tabloids.*

Pure and beautiful.

But her purity and beauty will be the end of her.

A main character has to be flawed in some way, right? So far, Psyche is the all-American black girl with . . . with . . . a conscience? This is an interesting twist. Or is this book supposed to be a satire on the modeling industry? If that's the case, Psyche is going to get hers in the end, proving, I guess, that purity isn't *chic* in American society.

I am still Venus, I am still head of Aphrodite Inc., and I am still the world's delight. I am a classic beauty with bronze, luminous flesh. My beauty is intoxicating and suffocating. I still do four, five covers a year, and I'm nearly twice that wench's age. In other words, for a middle-aged sistuh, I am still da bomb. I am a weapon of mass destruction, atomic, neutron, and hydrogen bombs all rolled into one.

And since I sign Psyche's paychecks, Psyche is about to have a bomb go off in her trifling little life.

Yes. Psyche is about to realize that I am ugly to the bone.

And now I hate Venus. She sounds straight off some soap opera, like some Texas matriarch on *Dallas*. So one-dimensional. And jealous? Hasn't jealousy been overworked as a basic conflict in women's fiction?

> *And when I want things to get ugly, I call on my wayward son, Q. After I buzz him, I'll only have to wait a few seconds for him to come into my office. Men, as a rule, obey me, and my boy is punctual. I've had that boy on lockdown since the second he was born. He'll do anything for his mama.*
>
> *Mainly because I sign his paycheck, too.*

Hmm. What kind of a name is Q? If "P" stands for Psyche, "Q" has to be the main love interest. His name sounds wimpy, like some name from a James Bond movie, and we're not about to talk about those ridiculous movies.

> *2: Quentin "Q" Dione*
> *Mama's buzzing me again.*

Hmm. A new voice. This could be a challenge after all. Let's see if the author can give Quentin—and who on earth would give any child this name?—more than one dimension.

> *Must be time for a little mischief.*
> *I smile at the little mirror on the back of my office door and see my white daddy, a male model named Adonis from way back in the day, staring back at me. It's unmistakable. Adonis, who now raises show dog Alsatians, gave me good hair, gray eyes, a straight nose, and perpetually tanned skin. Yet Mama swears I'm Festus's boy. Not a chance. My "daddy" Festus is blacker than coal dipped in Hershey's syrup plastered with tar and covered with dirt, and I'm light skinned as a feather.*

More intrigue. Q is mixed. He's rare in literature, and I don't know why. This country has been the melting pot for a couple of centuries nearly everywhere except in novels.

Not that I'm angry, you understand. Being in between has its advantages, particularly with the ladies. Yeah, being mixed lets me mix with all shades of beauty, and no one grits on me when I have, say, an Asian doll on one arm, a fiery redhead on the other, and a dark chocolate bunny in front of me beckoning me with her silky brown finger. Because I am a rainbow, I can talk to and taste any flavor of the rainbow.

And the rainbow tastes good. *America: the melting pot that melts in your mouth.*

I don't like his "player" attitude at all. Why can't he be a normal man? I hope Psyche, even though I can't stand her yet, puts him in his place. If she does that, I might like her a little bit.

I fly by Grace, Mama's third replacement secretary this month, and open Mama's greenish blue seafoam door. Mama has this thing about seafoam that borders on the psychotic because some "certified fashion color consultant" once told her that she looked good in seafoam.

She doesn't, but no one tells her that.

I see Mama looking over Manhattan through her seafoam contacts past some roosting pigeons while sitting in her seafoam chair behind her seafoam desk, one finger curled around some seriously dark extensions tied up with a seafoam scarf. A few pigeons roost outside her window as if readying to fly her chair out over New York. Mama is still fine as hell, but I know her age is taking its toll on her. If it weren't for Botox,

*collagen treatments, and cosmetic surgery, she might
look like someone's hot, gray grandma.*

This is *sick!* "Mama is still fine as hell"? And what's up
with the seafoam? My own mama has a thing for dark blue
ducks, but . . . seafoam contacts? Grandpa Joe-Joe is sounding more *functional* the longer I read this.

    "Q?"
    "Yes, Mama."
    "I have a job for you."
    "Yes, Mama." Who are we firing today?
    *She tosses a magazine over her head, and it flutters
like a butterfly into my hands. "Check out who's on the
cover."*
    *Daa-em, Psyche is looking finer than fine, as usual.
And on* Maxim. *I always knew she'd be a crossover hit
with the white boys since that* Sports Illustrated *cover.
Psyche's been playing hard to get with me for ten
years and barely gives me the time of day, but when
that girl smiles at me . . . shit, she's the finest woman
on earth right now. Luckily, I have a subscription to*
Maxim *so I don't have to sneak this copy out of
Mama's office.*
    *"Not much left to the imagination," I say, trying to
remain noncommittal, my arms folded.*
    *I have learned never to compliment one of Mama's
models in her presence. I once said that a model was
"cute," and that's all I said, though she did have this
ass, ooh, that would make you smack your mama with
a stick. The "cute" model went from Cover Girl com-
mercials and a bit part in a James Bond flick to posing
with a "neck massager" on the back pages of some
smut magazine almost overnight. Mama ruined her
cute little ass big-time simply because I said she was*

*cute. I cringe at where she might have ended up if I
had said what I was really thinking about that ass.
She'd probably be in the maternity section of the next
Sears catalog, flaps down with a lost look on her face.*

That is *so* true! What woman in her right mind would
pose for those kinds of pictures? What is she thinking? Is
she thinking, *Well, I'm pregnant, so I'd guess I better go get
my picture taken with a flappy bra?*

> *Mama spins around in her chair, her fingers knitted
> together, her elbows on her desk. "I want you to fire
> her, Q."*
>
> *I try not to blink, but I can't help it. Psyche has
> been the flavor of the month for nearly ten years, ever
> since she was sixteen. She is the hottest hottie on the
> planet, billboards and ads everywhere, even a doll
> marketed by Mattel. Mama must be trippin'. I mean,
> Psyche is responsible for at least 30 percent of
> Aphrodite Inc.'s annual revenue.*
>
> *"Um, fire Psyche?" I manage to ask.*
>
> *"I don't stutter."*
>
> *This is serious. The board of directors, a bunch of
> wrinkled old men and women Mama uses to rubber-
> stamp her ideas, are going to freak out. "Um, the
> board of directors—"*
>
> *"Fuck 'em." She spins around. "She is to be fired
> by the end of the day today, a copy of her pink slip in
> my mailbox by six sharp."*

Too much profanity. Proper ladies of color should never use
the F word, especially foxy femme fatales who sleep around
and wear seafoam contacts. I know it's part of her character,
but . . . it's so unnecessary and a waste of ink. Now I know
black women *do* curse. I just don't want to "hear" them curse
in books. It's so . . . permanent in the reader's mind.

I could argue with her, but it won't do me any good. When Mama gets just a tiny bit mad, whole departments lose their jobs, and security puts them and their shit out on Madison Avenue for the entire world to see.

"Yes, Mama."

Mama flips a Rolodex card over her head, and I snatch it out of the air. "Those are her home and cell phone numbers, and when you're through with that card, burn it."

After I memorize those numbers, of course. "Yes, Mama."

I take one more look at that Maxim *cover. Damn, Psyche is fine, and I bet she'd put a hurtin' something fierce on me.*

And if I'm lucky, that's precisely what I'll get her to do. A hurtin' so good.

And then I'll fire her.

I have to. I'm a mama's boy.

Oooh! I hate him and his mama and Psyche and— I flip to the back and don't see a picture of J. K. Growling. I keep forgetting that most advance review copies don't have pictures like real books. Shoot. I wanted to sass her to her face. How can you write a romance where the reader despises every character in the book? I mean, it's funny at times, I'll grant that, but it's dysfunctional, trifling, and totally sensationalized. Venus is a model. Q sounds like a model. Psyche is a model. What, models represent 0.0001 percent of the population, and here they are hogging all the pages of a romance? How ridiculous! If I wanted to have this stuff fill my head, I'd watch *Entertainment Tonight* or read *The National Enquirer.* I'll give this book one more chapter, and if it doesn't improve, I'll have to write my famous "I couldn't even finish this book and I got my money back" review . . . even though I do get these books for free. Who's going to know? Get ready, Grandpa Joe-Joe. We may have a date in your jungle in a few minutes.

3: Ginger "Psyche" Dane

The phone is ringing, but I am not answering it.

Only a few people on earth have my unlisted number, and I don't want to talk to any of them. If it's Mama, she'll be asking about my love life. If it's Daddy, he'll be asking me why I don't talk to Mama— about my love life. If it's Rosemary, my hopeless sister who married for money instead of love, she'll be asking when she can get away from her ancient, dusty husband for a visit—so she can ask me about my love life.

The fact is, I don't have a love life, but they don't want to hear that. They all want to hear that their Ginger has found the man of her dreams and is going to move from the Upper West Side to a house on Long Island with a picket fence, a bidet, a three-car garage, 2.5 children, and a dog.

Hey now. I might like her a little bit after all. She doesn't seem to like being a model any more than *I* like her being a model. And her mama pestering her about her love life? I know all about that.

The phone rings on, so I bury myself in my down comforter.

I'll bet they saw the cover. No, Mama and Rosemary don't read Maxim. *It's probably Daddy. He'll tell me how I shouldn't flaunt what God gave me, that he can't show his face in church this Sunday, that he wished I had worn more clothes. But I know he's proud of what he helped create. He has to be. He didn't have any sons, but he did have two beautiful daughters, and I'm his baby. Rosemary did some modeling, too, but she quit looking good once she married and gave birth to the requisite male heir to the fortune two years ago. Her marriage is in trouble, but when I bring it up,*

Rosemary brushes me off with, "You're not married, Ginger, so you cannot possibly understand."

I may never get married. Oh, sure, I've been ru-mored into an affair or two on the pages of People *and* Us *simply because I'm seen walking with or talking to some movie star, pro athlete, or entertainer, but love has never found me. I haven't exactly had the time for love, what with shoots 300 days of the year on up to five continents. Maybe I should give love my unlisted cell phone number so I'll be easier to find.*

It's hard to feel sorry for her, but I do. I mean, I have a cell phone . . . that no one ever calls, not even Mama. Not that I've ever given out my number to anyone. I have only put five telephone numbers into the memory, and three of them are for the library. I sometimes call my own cell phone from inside my house just to make sure it still works. I even leave myself reminder messages sometimes.

I'm pretty pitiful sometimes.

The phone rings on.
Maybe it's an emergency, though emergencies, as a rule, aren't emergencies at all in my family. Rosemary will tell me that something's wrong with Shizzy, her Shih-Tzu: "Shizzy has intestinal distress, Ginger, so could you please come by to hold my hand at the vet?" Rosemary even fainted the last time when the vet re-moved a single tick from Shizzy's neck. If Shizzy isn't falling apart, then Rosemary will try to impress me with her husband's wealth: "Ginger, I'm going to send the driver to pick you up so we can go spend Fuller's money." As far as I can tell, money is the only thing she gets from her husband since he's pushing seventy. Daddy will tell me about his roses then plead with me to talk to Mama, and Mama, well, Mama will still ask me about my love life: "Ginger, girl, you aren't getting

*any younger, so you'd best find a man now who will
love you when your titties hit your knees and your behind drags on the floor."*

HAAAAAA! Another somebody's mama uses the word
"titties"! J.K., you're on a roll. Don't blow it.

> *I should have turned off the ringer before I took my
nap.*
> *I crawl out of my comforter to the nightstand and
turn over the base of the phone to slide the ringer button to "off," but as I do, the phone falls out of the cradle to the floor.*

Gee. What a coincidence. I know it happens, but it happens far too often in books. Why not just have her answer the
stupid phone?

> *Shoot. Now I have to answer it.*
> *"Hello?"*
> *"Psyche, hi, it's Q."*
> *Venus Dione's son, the anointed one,* People *maga-
zine's "Sexiest Man Alive" a few years ago, the dread
prince of the petticoats who loiters around Aphrodite
Inc. waiting to take over the company. Right now, he's
just Venus's errand boy, probably with a message from
Venus for my next shoot.*
> *I haven't talked directly to Venus in years, and
that's fine by me. She scared me the first time I met
her: "You ain't nothin' but a piece of meat, a piece of
eye candy, girl, nothin' but a Milk Dud," she had told
me. "So don't you go thinkin' you're a queen or
nothin' cuz I'm the queen." As sophisticated as she
acts in public, Venus Dione is as common as any chair
in a beauty salon, and rumor has it that a chair in a*

salon has more real hair on it than Venus has left on her head.

That wasn't nice! Funny and accurate, though. And I feel almost the same way about Venus. Hmm. I'm starting to identify with this Psyche woman, even though she is the exact opposite of me physically.

"Hi, Q." Isn't that a kid's game? I wonder what his real name is. I hope it's not Q-pid. "What's up?"

Ah, I get it. Cupid. Psyche and Cupid. I'll have to look up that story in my mythology book. I'll bet it explains the rest of the book. Ho-hum. Another author who steals a plot.

"That Maxim cover, ooh, girl, you got it going on."

Don't fall for it, Psyche. He's only after one thing, and then he's going to fire you. Be strong, my sister.
Sigh. I'm talking to her now. I'm almost hooked.

I draw the comforter around me even though I know Q can't see my nakedness. Something about the way he looks at me with those gray eyes of his makes me squirm. "Thanks. It was kind of unexpected."
"I'm sure it will set a sales record for them. Did you get my flowers?"
I haven't opened my condo door in two days. The Maxim shoot in the Bahamas took a lot out of me. That's not sprayed water on my body on that cover— it's my own sweat. Why we had to shoot a close-up on a hot beach in June in the Bahamas is beyond me. And even though it looks as if I'm naked under those towels, I still have everything important covered. I've been offered millions by Playboy, Penthouse, and Hus-

tler *to pose nude, but that's not for me. What God has blessed me with will be shared only with my future husband.*

I knew she had a conscience. Hmm. Up to two stars, J.K. I like the unexpected, and I *really* like a spiritual main character who actually *lives* a spiritual life.

And I hope my future husband doesn't send me flowers. At first, it was nice, you know, getting flowers from strangers for simply being beautiful. Now it's a chore. I'm sure Q's flowers are wilting gloriously just outside the door in the hallway. I get so many flowers and letters from admirers, and I can't have an e-mail account anymore, not that I have time to go on-line. I used to be propositioned about a hundred times a day on-line, and it seemed as if every male past puberty had me on his buddy list. The millisecond I'd get on-line, I'd get hit with a couple dozen instant messages. How they found out it was me, I don't know, and I changed my e-mail addresses almost daily. I even changed it once to whitegirl7845, and they still *found me. Then someone told me that my IP address—my laptop's address—can't be changed. So now, I turn off all instant messages and delete most of my mail before reading it.*

Same here. Not that I get bombarded by IMs. I've almost joined an on-line dating service. Almost. They all require a picture, and I don't want men scrolling past my face on their way to find a prettier woman.

"Yes, I got your flowers, Q, and they're beautiful." I'm sure they are—if they're outside my door and they're still alive. "Thank you. Um, where am I off to next?"

"I'd rather discuss it over dinner this time, if you don't mind."

Dinner? Q, the duke of drawers, the king of kinky, the prince of—no, I won't say that word—wants to meet me for dinner? In public? The paparazzi will have a field day, especially after that Maxim *cover. It is so hard to see your food with all those flashes going off. "Um, Q, do you think that would be a good idea?"*

"Oh, I didn't mean we'd go out, Ginger. We could order in."

He called me Ginger! I feel a flush come over my face, even though I don't want it to. Is he asking me out? That didn't make sense. We're ordering in, so how could he be asking me out? I've had a minor crush on him for ten years, but I haven't pursued him for fear his mama would put me out on the street. It seems that every woman Q has seen for more than two weeks has vanished from the planet, and I saw the last model he dated in a department store window as a living mannequin.

Harsh. But aren't all models living mannequins? Is this what J. K. Growling is trying to say about the modeling industry? I know, I shouldn't hate these women for their beauty. They were blessed. I just wish I could find a man who didn't "read" a woman with his eyes. I want a man who will "read" every chapter of me. . . . Whoo! Just the thought of any man turning all my pages is making me hot!

But my face is so hot! I haven't had this feeling in . . . I can't remember having this feeling. "Um, yeah, Q, that would be great." But where? I look at the random clumps of clothes on the floor of my bedroom. Definitely not here. "Your place, right?"

"I was hoping . . . yours."

My fingers tingle, and I get cottonmouth something

fierce. Lord Jesus, help me here. "Oh, I don't know. My place is a wreck. I haven't been home in weeks, so maybe not."

"I've already gotten us a pizza, and I'm calling from the sidewalk right under your window."

I wrap the comforter tightly around me, go to my bedroom window, and look down ten stories to the sidewalk. I see a man holding a pizza box and wearing a baseball cap. "Are you wearing a Yankees hat?"

"Yes. I'm incognito. No one has recognized me yet."

I look at the nothing I'm wearing. "Give me a few minutes, and I'll let security know it's okay for you to come up."

I can't be too careful. When I first started out and had Mama and Rosemary living with me, we had a few scary evenings with our backs pressed into the condo door because of several stalkers who got by the doorman.

"Don't make me wait too long. The doorman is looking at me funny. We wouldn't want him to call any photographers."

"He won't," *I say. But Dwight the concierge might. I'll bet Dwight makes more money tipping off gossip columnists than working here. I limped in one day last year after stumbling during an aerobics workout, and the* Star *had me as a victim of a mugging the very next day.* "The doorman looks at everybody that way, Q. See you in a few minutes."

I hang up, shut the drapes, and look at my messy bedroom. "He is not coming in here, no matter how much he wants to," *I say to the piles of clothes as I head to one of my bathrooms. I have three and a half bathrooms to go with three bedrooms, which was fine when Mama, Rosemary, and I shared the condo, but* *now . . . I live in a 2,165-foot, $15,000-a-month cav-ern with south views of the city, sunset views of the Hudson River, and breathtaking views of Central Park. I should really move out, but I haven't found the time.*

And now I hate Psyche again. Fifteen *grand* a *month?* I could pay off this little house in four months with a salary like that! Why in the world do we pay the beautiful people so much money? Oh, this world is getting too trifling to bear sometimes!

> *I stop in front of my bathroom mirror. "And he is not coming in here either, no matter how much I want him to," I whisper.*
> *Sorry, Lord. I can't help it if I'm horny. It's how You made me. And You made him . . . beautiful. Q's not too tall—those basketball players have always made me feel like a midget. Q's not too uppity—those rappers made me feel as if they were God's gift to women, and they weren't, with all those tattoos, piercings, and bee-otching. And Q's not too worldly.*

Yes he is, girl.

> *I bite my lip.*
> *Okay, he's worldly, Lord. Maybe I can, you know, bring him back into the fold, make an honest man out of him.*

Not a chance.

> *I bite my lip again.*
> *Then he wouldn't be Q. Hmm. This could be tricky.*
> *I feel my hands, and they're sweaty. See what he does to me, Lord? I hear he can be very persuasive,*

and I'm tired, and weak, and it's been so long since I was even kissed for real. Posed kisses in magazines do not count.

I throw cold water on my face. It's only a pizza, Ginger, and you don't even like pizza, because it goes straight to your thighs. And it's not like you can throw on a designer dress to eat pizza. I'll just throw on some sweats, not put on any make-up, and wear a Mets cap.

"He'll just have to take me as I really am."

Did I just say, "Take me"? Sorry, Lord. I meant that Q, in all his sexiness, will just have to see me as I am: sanctified sister Ginger Dane, from Athens, Ohio.

I shut the book. So far, I have a love-hate relationship with this novel. I like Psyche because she has a soul, even though she's far too pretty to be believable. Q has no soul, Venus sounds as if she's out to take Psyche's soul, and . . . and what else? Yes, it has my attention, but . . .

I pick up *Thicker Than Blood*. "Grandpa Joe-Joe, here I come."

8

Jack

After making three trips to the Salvation Army with Noël and Stevie's clothes, many of them tear-stained, I had made the world's worst-looking snowman in the backyard.

You've made worse.

The sticks I had used for arms were bigger than the snowman's body, the eyes were two mismatched wood chips, and the hat was an upside-down bird's nest.

At least it doesn't have crushed beer cans for ears like last year.

I had tried rolling the snow into balls, but it wouldn't stick together until I added some dead grass, old clover, and dirt. It sure was colorful.

I know Stevie is up there giggling about it.

And Noël is, too.

"It's a nice snowman, Jack. And thanks for skipping the beer ears this year," she's saying.

Beer ears this year. Yeah, that's something she would say. She was always better at rhyming than I was.

I had sat on the big swing for the longest time, gently gliding back and forth, as more snow floated down. It was . . . peaceful. It was as if Nature was covering up my world with a fresh, clean blanket.

Until the snowman had decided to fall. I had to prop him up with a couple of bricks.

So, now he's a snowman with red feet.

That point out behind him?

So, he's forever walking backward, like you.

I'm making progress.

You could be making more.

I'm inside the kitchen warming up and staring at a Russell Stover candy box sitting on the table. I'm afraid to open it, though it still has its plastic wrapper, because it has to be at least six or seven months old. It was a "just because" gift to Noël; I forget what for. Just one of those loony romantic things I used to do "just because" right before . . .

Don't think about it.

It was the last gift I ever gave her.

I'll bet they still taste good.

I'm not hungry.

A little chocolate never hurt anybody, and you need to gain some weight.

I won't eat the ones with the nuts. Noël loved the ones with nuts.

Because she said she married one.

I'm not that nutty.

Yes, you are.

If I keep talking to myself, maybe I will be.

No. It's good therapy.

While I eat only the nougats, I look around the kitchen. I should have carpeted the floor. It's so cold. Oh, and that border still looks so good! I thought it would come out crooked, but Noël was there to help me. I should remove all the latches on the cabinets that kept Stevie from messing around. But . . . maybe the next family will need them.

You can't stay here much longer.

I know.

I can't stay in a four-bedroom house alone. It's a waste of space. I haven't been downstairs except to throw dirty clothes into the laundry room, and some of the crumbs in this kitchen are starting to move. Most of the crumbs are at Stevie's place—

Don't go there.

I can't help it.

Get out of the kitchen, then.

I wander down to Stevie's—*my*—room and jiggle the top bunk. I'm sure it will come off the other one. Maybe I can set them up side by side and put Noël's king-sized mattress over top of them. That would save me a daily bump on the head anyway.

Good thinking.

Thank you.

Though your daily bump knocks some sense into you.

I grip one end of the top bunk and lift, and the entire bunk bed comes off the floor. Is that supposed to happen?

Evidently.

There must be some trick to this. Hmm. I should take off the mattresses first, maybe put the entire bunk bed on its side . . . What's this?

Sticking out from under the top bunk mattress is a picture book about planes, trains, and automobiles. As I slide it out, I see two more books wedged underneath, each of them a picture book about animals. How did Stevie get up here? And why did he hide them? And where and when did he get them?

I see a bar code on the back of the first book, "Roanoke Public Library" in bold letters underneath the dark lines and numbers. Noël used to take him nearly every Saturday morning to the library for story time. It gave me most of the morning to write since they would often go to a park or a museum afterward.

I guess I should return these.

Tomorrow.

Yeah, I guess tomorrow is as good a day as any. I have lots of nothing to do tomorrow, all day as a matter of fact.

Nothing to do and all day to do it.

Is "nothing" something to do?

Sure. And you're good at doing it.

The phone rings, and I answer without checking the Caller ID. "Hello?"

"Is Thomas Mann there?"

We used to get Mr. Mann's mail when we first moved in, and we—*I*—still get phone calls for him. "Thomas Mann hasn't lived here in six years. Please put me on your do-not-call list."

"Are you the new home owner?"

"Yes, but—"

"And is there still a VA loan on this property?"

"That's none of your business. Now please put me on your do-not-call list."

"Is your current loan at seven percent or higher?"

Pushy bastard.

"It's none of your business. Now please, put—"

"We here at the Financial Group can help home owners like yourself who have high-interest, VA loans and—"

I hang up. I doubt anyone can help me.

Don't be so sure.

Now what am I *really* supposed to be doing?

You're doing fine.

No, I'm forgetting something.

You're supposed to be writing another book, but don't rush it. Live a little first.

You call this living?

I had signed a two-book deal. I have no idea what to write about for the second book, and I've been avoiding even *thinking* about writing it.

You're good at that.

What?

Not thinking.

Thanks.

It's all a part of doing nothing.

My agent and editor are expecting something similar to the first one. It's supposed to be full of dramatic, guilty pleasures on every page. And I have a January 31 deadline for three chapters and an outline.

I'm screwed.

No, you're not. You'll think of something.

I can barely function in my own wearisome life, and I'm expected to create other, more exciting lives?

So, they'll be as dysfunctional as the characters in the first book.

What I should do is write the exact *opposite* of what they expect. I should give readers dramatic, *innocent* pleasures.

Like a picture book for children.

Yeah, like a— No. I write for adults.

It's not possible to write a book about innocent, adult *pleasures.*

Well, I'm going to try.

Your agent and editor won't like it.

What can they—or anyone for that matter—do to me that hasn't already been done to me?

Good point.

I am going to the library to return these books tomorrow, and while I am there, I will read up on some of my competition.

But you're supposed to be writing.

One step at a time, right?

You're the boss, chief.

9

Diane

I pick up the fourth and last book, *Wishful Thinking,* by D. J. Browning. Nice, colorful cover photograph of an average sister in a hard hat with a Mona Lisa smile. Different. Opening the book to the first page, I read:

1: Daniel "Dan" Pace

I know I am in trouble when Beth says she wants to eat at Hooters on a Monday night.

Asking a guy to Hooters has to be some kind of new test for men, and I'm failing miserably. I am trying not to look at all the reconstituted breasts and buttocks bouncing and all the pierced and tattooed belly buttons undulating around the restaurant. And all those tan legs! Pairs of them everywhere I look! How can a man not look at Darcy, his server, when the sun on her sunrise tattoo below her belly button has set somewhere lower? How can I not stare at the freckles practically staring back at me through Darcy's tight shorts? How can I not stare at Darcy's hooters at a place called Hooters?

You could respect your date and look into her eyes, Dan. Uh-duh. And is this guy white or what? He's staring at "tan legs." This must be one of those interracial books I've heard about. I read on:

> *"You remind me of my mother, Dan," Beth says, her eyes following Darcy instead of looking at me, a plate- ful of shiny clean chicken bones in front of her and five empty bottles of Sam Adams guarding her side of the table.*
>
> *Back to reality. "Hmm?"*
>
> *"I said, you remind me of my mother."*
>
> *I hope my one class in psychology will come in handy here. "I remind you of your mother?"*
>
> *Beth nods, sighing in Darcy's direction.*
>
> *"Um, is that a compliment?"*
>
> *Beth glances my way. "No, Dan. I hate my mother." Her eyes grab on to Darcy again, her tongue flicking over her lower lip. Damn, she's sexy when she does that. "I've hated my mother since the day I was born."*
>
> *Where's this coming from? "So what exactly did you mean by that?"*
>
> *She guzzles more beer. "You're pretty smart. You figure it out."*

Beth is gay, Dan. She and Darcy are going to hook up and leave you hanging at Hooters. So predictable.

> *"Figure out what?"*
>
> *Beth rolls her eyes and takes another sip, tossing her napkin on the table. "I'll be back."*
>
> *I watch Beth head for the bathroom and glance over at the semicircular booth across from us. Two*

black women sit on either side of a black man who either had to have played some football or had to have done a tour or two in the service. Lucky guy. He's got two women, one on either side of him, yet he's able to be hard staring at every implant in the restaurant. One of the black women, who has light brown eyes almost like a cat's eyes, catches me staring, so I quickly return to picking at the label of my Sam Adams.

Yep, this is an interracial book. I'm somewhat intrigued. "Cat's eyes," huh? They're probably contacts.

I have no idea why I'm here. I'm sitting alone at a table on my fifth date with Beth, and I'm still not sure why I'm with her at all. Nancy, a woman I teach with at Monterey Elementary, said we'd be "perfect" together. "She's so outdoorsy and spunky," Nancy had said. "And she is so into hiking like you are, Dan."

Hiking. Right. On two of our previous dinner dates, all she did was hike to the bathroom or talk our servers to death. On our other two dates, we sat in front of her TV watching college football on ESPN, the dramatic fall colors of the Blue Ridge Parkway screaming to be hiked through. And at the end of each evening, she rushed from my car or rushed me out the door of her condo without even saying good-bye. I have yet to find out if her tongue flicking feels as good as it looks.

"Because she's gay, Dan," I say. "Now hook up with the sister, and let's get on with this thing."

Beth returns. "You figure it out yet?"
I sigh. "Well, I know you don't like your mother."
"I hate my mother. There's a difference."
"Okay. Um, so if you hate your mother, and I re-

*mind you of her, you must hate me." I smile and wait
for Beth to contradict me.*

She doesn't.

"I, uh, I hope I'm wrong."

*"You're not." She gulps the rest of her sixth Sam
Adams.*

Huh? *"Let me get this straight. You're saying that
you hate me?"*

She nods. "With a passion."

*I sit back. "Then why have you been going out with
me?"*

"Just to see."

"To see what?"

*"To see if you interested me." She shrugs. "And you
don't. Sorry."*

This is messed up! *"Then why'd you agree to go out
with me tonight?"*

*"For the hot wings," she says, with a soft laugh.
"And the view." She raises her eyebrows. "Isn't that
why you come here, too?"*

Wait a minute. Something weird is happening here.
"This is the first time I've ever been here, Beth."

"Yeah, right."

*"No, it's true." I'd be too embarrassed to eat here
by myself, and Hooters is not the place to take a lady if
you want to keep her respect.*

Three cheers for Dan! Not. Wait a minute. This means,
then, that Dan doesn't think Beth is a lady . . . or something
like that. I'm getting to be as confused as Dan is.

Unless she likes good hot wings, I guess, or . . . she
really *likes the view.*

*Beth waves at yet another server. "I come here all
the time."*

"You come here . . . all the time." Oh . . . shit. I can
handle this. *"You're, um, you're bisexual?"* Please say
yes! This is every man's fantasy, and I am definitely a
man in need of a fantasy to come true at this time in
my—

"Hell no, Dan. I'm not even bi-curious."

Oh. I guess that's good. It would be so hard for me
to take if she were dumping me for a—

"I'm a lesbian, Dan. I thought Nancy told you."

Spunky. Outdoorsy. Into hiking. Beth, who looks
like an L.L.Bean model with her short, dark hair; high
New Hampshire cheekbones; jeans; Timberlands; and
blue and black flannel shirt, is a lesbian?

Gee. What a nice stereotype to see *again* in a novel. This
had better grab me in the next few pages, or I'm going to
slam this one.

*I run a checklist through my mind. Beth likes
sports. Check that—Beth* loves *sports. She can quote
stats, scores, and sports scandals better than any guy I
know. She plays on a softball team and everything,
and she even played field hockey in college. Lesbians
wielding sticks? Wait, they're curved sticks. Nothing
phallic there. And so what if she wears flannel shirts; I
mean, I know it's a stereotype and all, but I wear flannel shirts. And no one can drink more beer, belch
louder, or—*

*Geez, she's more of a guy than I am. About the only
thing she hasn't done is light some farts, though I did
see a lighter in her bathroom.*

Dan sounds like a fraternity boy. I hated the frat boys at
Purdue. All their secret this and that was just cover for their
insecurities.

And not a single one of them ever asked me out.

And she did ask if I had a cute sister. How'd that conver-
sation go? "You have a sister?" Beth had said. I had said,
"Yes." Beth had smiled and said, "Is she cute?" Hmm. I
should have connected the dots with those two questions.

"Uh-duh," I say.

"No, uh, Beth, Nancy didn't tell me that you were a,
an, um—"
"A dyke."
So glad she said it instead of me. Oh, sure, I was
thinking the word, but I would never say it. To a
woman, anyway. There were a few in the service with
me, but every one of them could have kicked my ass.
Come to think of it, even the nonlesbian women in the
Marines could have kicked my ass.

Dan's wimpy. Or at least he says he is. I bet he can handle
himself. Or, rather, I hope he can handle himself. The sister
on the cover looks rugged.

And as for Nancy, the bitch, we're going to have a
long talk. Nancy is still trying to get me back for that
one-night stand two years ago. I mean, other than
teaching fourth-graders in the same building together,
we have absolutely nothing in common. Except for
that bottle of vodka. And the whipped cream. Oh, and
the peanut butter. And the ice cream. Good thing I was
out of Hershey's syrup or the stains never would have
come out of the comforter while we made our "ba-
Nancy split." I still have a little peanut butter stain on
the wall. Something about peanut oil on latex paint
not coming out. Why did we—oh, yeah. Jewel had just
broken up with me, and I had no self-control that
night, and I was hungry, and I do have a sweet tooth,
but—

So far, Dan is clueless, unscrupulous, and loveless. And he's an elementary school teacher? Would any sister—or any *woman* for that matter—be interested in that combination? I don't think so. This writer flunked characterization—and logic—in a big way.

Beth pats my hand. "Don't worry, Dan. But, hey, you never know. Things might work out for you in the end."

"They, uh, might work out how?"

"One can always hope."

"Hope for what?"

Darcy chooses this moment to return with our check, and Darcy is doing that tongue-flicking thing. In Beth's direction. And it's sexy as hell. Either chapped lips must be catching or . . .

No . . . way. Was I just bait for a lesbian hookup? No wonder Beth said that she wanted to meet me here.

Darcy hands the check to me and slides a slip of paper to Beth. Beth peeks at the slip of paper and nods at Darcy.

"Have a nice evening, y'all," Darcy says.

"You know we will," Beth says, and Darcy walks away, occasionally looking back at Beth.

Beth gathers her coat. "Sorry, Dan."

"Wait a minute," I say. "Where are you going? What just happened?"

She stands. "I have a date."

"With whom?"

"With Darcy. Haven't you been paying attention?"

My dinner date has just picked up our server for a night of tongue flicking. "You and Darcy are going to . . ."

Beth nods.

"Just like that?" And I'm not invited?

She slips into her coat. "Hey, Dan, I tried to in-
clude you, but Darcy isn't into that."
　"Into what?"
　Beth squints. "I thought you were from California."
　"Yeah, but that was a long time ago, and just what
does being from California have to do with this?"
　Beth shakes her head. "I gotta go get ready."
　"And you're leaving me with the check?"
　She laughs. "Yes, but don't worry about the tip. I'll
tip Darcy later for us, okay?"

And this is the end of his version of the events, thankfully. I don't like him or find him believable for a second. I
turn the page and hope the sister is more likable.

2: Tynisha "Ty" Clarke

Tynisha? Hmm. Is Ty going to be ghetto? Is this another
one of those "opposites attract" interracial romances? You'd
think that just having two characters with different skin
color would be enough. Well, let's see if Tynisha is a believable sister:

I know I shouldn't be eavesdropping on someone
else's conversation in a restaurant, but when you've
been waiting as long as we have, you have to do some-
thing. That's so . . . twisted! Poor Dan!
　"Did you just hear what she said to him?"
　Mike sighs and pours out more salt onto the table,
flicking several grains toward Pat. "He should have
seen it coming, Ty. Look at her. She's wearing what he's
wearing and looks more comfortable in it than he does."
　Pat arranges the stack of Sweet'n Low for the fifth
time. "She is wearing a flannel shirt and work boots,
Tynisha."

"I wear work boots, Patricia. What are you trying to say?"

"If the boot fits," Pat says.

I am so glad to get out of those heavy, steel-toed Red Wings that I wear while I'm roaming Roanoke, Virginia, in my Verizon van—

Hold up. She said, "Roanoke, Virginia"? She works in my adopted hometown? So, the Hooters in the story must be the one out on Williamson Road, not that I've ever been there. I might just like this book a little. My new hometown is in a book. Imagine that.

—looking for some address in the middle of no-where, hopefully not having to gaff a pole or squeeze into a crawl space. Climbing poles for the phone com-pany is not glamorous at all, but the pay is better than good. I am one of the few sisters climbing poles for any company in the state of Virginia, but that doesn't mean I'm a dyke.

"That's right," I say. "It means you're a pioneer, girl."

"Forget you, Pat," I say. *"That's just wishful think-ing on your part. That's probably why you've been my friend since the seventh grade. Hoping you can get a piece of this action."*

"Come on now. You know I only pole climb, no pun intended. And unless you grow a dick, Ty, I don't want your . . ."

Oooh, Pat is nasty. I'm glad she and Dan aren't going to hook up. I shudder. But they might hook up anyway. Dan seems hard up enough. And did Pat really have to say, "Grow a dick"?

Mike elbows Pat and cuts his eyes to the left. "Finally."

And, naturally, it's the wench who has a date later with Beth. And Dan is still sitting there at his table peeling his beer bottle. Man has to be hard up, but why is he so calm? If I were Dan, I'd be breaking shit about now, and I wouldn't have been stuck with the check. And how clueless is he? I mean, he didn't know his girlfriend was a lesbian! The man should be wearing a stupid sign.

"Amen to that," I whisper. I like Ty.

"Hi, my name is Darcy."

She looks like that Darcy chick on Married with Children. *Wasn't she gay on that show, too? I know all Darcys aren't gay, but this is creepy.*

"I'll be your server tonight. What can I get y'all to drink?"

Y'all? Maybe she's from Hee Haw. *Do they do gay salutes on* Hee Haw? *Getting "down on the farm" has just taken on a totally new meaning.*

I giggle. If this book were written solely from Ty's point of view, I might be enjoying myself more. This should have been the first chapter anyway. A lady should always get to speak first . . . and last.

"I'll have a grande frozen strawberry margarita," says Pat, the alcoholic, *while I stare her down. "What?"*

"Who's driving?" I ask.

Pat latches onto one of Mike's muscular arms. "Mike is."

I roll my eyes. "So you two aren't trying to get any tonight? Just trying to get your drink on?"

"It's a Monday night, girl," Pat says. "Who goes macking on a Monday night?" She rests her head on Mike's shoulder.

Mike moves his shoulder away from Pat's head. "Go ahead, girl. You're blocking all the testosterone up in here."

Pat waves at the crowd of people at the bar, their eyes glued to Monday Night Football. *"How do you know if any of them are gay?"*

Mike only raises his eyebrows, and I shake my head at the two of them. Pat, who is the most heterosexual being I have ever met, goes on dates with Mike, the strong, silent gay guy. Yet if you ever saw either one of them on the street, you'd think Pat was a librarian with her granny glasses and old-fashioned clothes and Mike was a preacher all dressed up sharp in electric blue.

Oooh, that E. Lynn Harris! Every time you turn around there's another gay black man in a book. And what is Ty, who seems to be levelheaded, doing with a freak and a homosexual? I know they're friends, but come on! Is everything going to be "opposites attract" in this book or what? And that crack on librarians, oooh! I have never worn granny glasses in my life!

Though my mama has. Hmm. Two stereotypes so far. Maybe D. J. Browning is going for a record.

"Ahem," Darcy says.

Don't be a-hemming me, wench! You made us wait, so I'm going to make you wait. "Let's see now . . . I'll have . . . a strawberry daiquiri and . . . a glass of water, please."

"And I'll have a Sex on the Beach," Mike says. "And Darcy, I hope it won't take you fifteen minutes to

get our drinks to us since we've already been sitting here for fifteen minutes waiting to place our order."

Darcy fiddles with the gold cross on her necklace. Oh, right, Darcy's a Christian. Not. "Yeah, I'm sorry about that. Monday is one of our busiest nights."

And later, it's going to get busier, huh, Darcy? I look over at Dan. Still sitting there, still ripping labels off bottles. Pitiful.

Well, hook up already. Do *something.* I know they have to develop their relationship over—I flip to the back of the book—285 pages? This book is kind of light. I could read a book like this in a couple hours. Hmm.

"Would y'all like to order appetizers with your drinks?"

"We'll have an order of hot wings and an order of spinach dip, please," Mike says, and I blink at him. "What?"

"What if I wanted something different?" I say.

"Go ahead," Mike says.

I'm not really that hungry for anything but good conversation, but I can't stand anyone ordering for me. "Make it two orders of hot wings."

"Okay," Darcy says. "I'll be right back with your drinks and food."

Yeah, right. We'll be lucky to see Darcy before the second half of the game.

"Anyway, as I was saying," Pat says, "before I was rudely nudged with somebody's hard and crusty elbow—"

"My elbows aren't crusty," Mike interrupts.

"Dag, Mike, lube them things," Pat says. "So, Mike, we haven't seen your friend Paul around in a while. Are you two still kickin' it?"

Mike shrugs. "Yeah, we're still cool, but I think our relationship changed when I asked him to give me a little space. I'm just tired of partying all the time. I'm getting too old for that shit."

And this ends Ty's opening section. Not terrible, not wonderful. Adequate. I'm getting hints for what's to come, and it isn't as if it will take long for these two to get together. It's Dan's turn again:

3: Dan

I'm getting too old for this shit.

I've been peeling beer bottle labels ever since I had my first Michelob—or was it a Miller?—back in high school. I peeled quite a few bottles of Bud in the service, too. I know it means I'm horny. And I am. It's hard for me to admit that at thirty-two, yet it's true. I know I've just been dumped for another woman, and I know that this isn't the first time it's happened.

But at least the first time involved a woman dumping me for her mother.

Oooh, nasty! Why can't Dan just be a plain, ordinary man? Why does he have to have so much baggage?

Which isn't as twisted as it sounds. Okay, it does sound twisted, but there's a logical explanation. Given the choice between marrying me, the surfer boy Marine from California turned elementary school teacher from Virginia, and the traditions of her Thai, man-hating mother in Cleveland, Jewel chose . . . the Honda Prelude that her mother promised her if she broke off her engagement with me.

This is different. A white man with a Thai ex will be bumping uglies with a rugged sister—an interesting development. At least it means he's open to interracial relationships.

Either that or he'll mess with any woman, anytime, anywhere.

The freak.

Yeah, it's a little bit twisted. And it also involved her mother agreeing to pay for all of Jewel's med school bills, but I feel that I've been replaced by a two-door coupe that I hope rusts to dust up in Ohio, and I don't want to think about Jewel anymore. She's past history, end of story, archives, end of the road . . . yet she visits me whenever I have situations like this, as if she's sitting across from me right now in Beth's empty chair. The ex that keeps on giving me pain.

And I still have the ring I gave her that she threw back in my face.

Which means that Jewel will be back in Dan's life. That's how these books work. He's hard up and hurt from a past relationship, and as soon as he finds true love with Ty (though I still don't see *how*), Jewel will be back with a vengeance. Such a soap opera. I'm so glad real life isn't this way.

I look at the mess in front of me: seven beer bottles' worth of labels, two plates of chicken bones, and a pile of sticky napkins. Leftovers from a five-date relationship with . . . a lesbian who is going home to wait on my waitress, to serve my server, who is going to get the tip of Beth's tongue.

Damn. I hope the Sam Adams and all those hot wings give Beth some really bad gas. Or loose stools. Yeah, that would be perfect. Just an evening of Darcy and diarrhea. An evening of sucking down Pepto-Bismol instead of sucking face. An evening of starts and farts, fits and shits.

HAAAAA! That's a good one. Nasty, but good. Funny, but I don't mind it so much when a man of any race curses. That's how most men communicate when they can't think of anything intelligent to say, right? But educated sisters—no, they can't be cursing up a storm and get my approval.

I reach down to pick up a stray fleck of a label and turn my head just enough to see the delicious, sexy, toned brown legs of the black woman with cat's eyes in the booth across from me. Beautiful is the wrong word. Stunning. No, dazzling. Classy, definitely elegant. Cute toes, too. She must work out. So smooth, flexed just right, so well-proportioned, so—

So busted.

She saw me.

I raise my head too quickly, bump it hard on the bottom of the table, and see a few stars. When I finally am able to sit up, I steal a glance her way—and she's smiling at me. Perfect teeth gleaming like that gum commercial. Fabulous.

Or is she laughing? She has her hand over her mouth and—

Yeah, she's laughing. Private Sidney, a hot black woman from Alabama whom I hung out with in Saudi, used to laugh at me the same way whenever I tried to dance, covering her face with both hands. Yeah, I'm that bad of a dancer. I wasn't bad at dancing horizontally, though. Yeah, I wonder what Cyd's up to these days? We used to go at it—

Dan *is* a freak! Do I want him messing with Ty? What on earth could she *ever* see in him? Do all white men in their thirties behave this way? This is getting beyond ridiculous. A Californian former-Marine *freak* of an elementary school teacher is going to hook up with a trailblazing, cultured sister? Against my better judgment, I'm going to give it a few more pages, but it had better get moving, and it had better start getting real.

Geez, I need to get hold of myself. I'm too old to be reliving old relationships and flirting, yet that's what I'm doing, and who am I flirting with? A black woman sitting next to a guy twice my size just minutes after my lesbian girlfriend has left me to go play field hockey— or should I say tonsil hockey?—with one of Hooters's finest.

Yeah, life can suck in oh so many special ways.

I toss two twenties and a ten on top of the check. I know that will give Darcy more than a 20 percent tip, but who knows? Things have a way of working out. Maybe things won't work out between Beth and Darcy, and Darcy will see me in a new light because of my generosity, realize the errors of her ways, and give me a chance.

And then again, maybe Darcy will use her tip to buy Beth a new leopard-skin thong, and then they'll—

I down a full glass of lukewarm ice water, and as I set down the glass, I look once more at Cat Eyes. Such ripe, red lips, such devastating eyes.

And thighs. Don't forget the thighs. They are smokin'.

At least he's not a chest or booty man. Eyes and thighs. I have two pairs of those. They aren't "smokin'," but they can *smolder* when I want them to.

I nod once at her, and she nods back. I put on my coat and nod again. She nods again.

We've just had a nodding moment.

I don't have many of these moments. What do I do

next? If I had any guts, I'd go over and speak to her. But what would I say? "Hi, I'm the guy who's been scoping out your fine, sculpted legs like a drooling teenager, and I was wondering if I could have your phone number, maybe give you a call sometime?" But if the big guy is her boyfriend, I might be leaving with a busted nose to go with my bruised ego.

No, Dan, you might be leaving with *his* phone number.

Instead, I weave my way through the tables to the door, where I pause to look back at Cat Eyes and only see Darcy at her booth, serving their drinks. What's Cat Eyes drinking? A . . . strawberry daiquiri. Hmm. Kind of matches her lips. She takes a sip, those cat's eyes wide and painfully sexy.

I almost have an epiphany—something about cats' eyes, strawberries, and leopard-skin thongs—but the epiphany vanishes when stinging rain pelts my face outside the door. Rushing to my Subaru, parked away from the neon orange glow of the Hooters sign, I jump in, start the engine, and pop in my favorite cassette.

Eric B. and Rakim to the rescue once again.

At least he has okay taste in music. So, Dan's "old school." I just wish he wasn't such a freak. Now let's see Ty's reaction, and she'd better react. I wouldn't shrug off a man staring that hard at me for anything—not that it happens that often to me. Let's see, the last time a man really gritted on me was . . . I sigh. It was during my first year at Purdue. He was a fifth-year senior football player named . . . Kentrick? Kendrick? He had looked me up and down and up and even circled me once, like an African lion stalking his prey. I felt so . . . exposed. He never actually approached me. He just . . . looked.

And I graduated *before* he did, four years later.

4: Ty

A white guy nodded at me, and I nodded back. Twice. Either we just had us a moment—in his mind, anyway—or that boy has Tourette's. And what a perv! Checking me out like that, hard staring at my legs, like maybe he thinks he can get between them. That will be the day.

"Preach on, my sister!" I shout. But then I sigh. I bet they will be getting busy by page fifty, which is about all I'll probably want to read of this book. That's one of my rules. I'll give any book fifty pages, and if I'm not fully grabbed, embraced, and fondled by then, it's over for me.

Though I do have some fine legs. At least he has some taste. And he does have sandy blond hair and blue eyes. For whatever reason, I've always had a thing for blond hair and blue eyes on a guy, not that any of the brothers I've ever dated have gone that route.

So, *she* has never been in an interracial relationship. And Dan the vodka-drinking elementary school teacher/freak, who can't tell if a woman is a lesbian or a man is gay, is the one for her? What would Mike Tyson say about this? Oh, yeah. This is getting *ludicrous*.

But why did he tip Darcy? There isn't even forty dollars' worth of food on that table. He is obviously a generous fool when it comes to women.

With a "Stupid" sign around his neck.

I turn to watch Mike stirring his Sex on the Beach, still going on and on about Precious Paul. "Paul is somebody I can have fun with, but I don't see us to-gether five or ten years from now. He's just not settle-down material."

Pat slurps her daiquiri. Girl has absolutely no manners. "Speaking of settling down, Ty, are you and Mr. Tickler in it for the long haul, or are you going to get Charles to make an honest woman out of you?"

Oh . . . snap. Ty has a Mr. Tickler, too! I feel a rush of blood to my face. I know, I'm weird, but I'm feeling embarrassed by something that's happening to a woman in a novel. I wonder if Ty has the newest model. . . .

Before I can answer—and I really don't want to answer—Darcy returns with our appetizers, which gives me a wicked thought: good service means that the server is getting some later. Would Darcy be this busy with our order if she weren't getting busy after work?

"Here are your drinks, hot wings, and spinach dip. I also brought some extra plates for y'all. Are y'all ready to order your main courses?"

I shake my head. "I think this will be enough for me, thank you. Are you guys ordering anything?"

Mike pats his stomach. "No, I had a late lunch so I'm not that hungry. This will be plenty."

"This is fine," Pat says. "If I get hungry later, I'll attack some of the leftovers in the fridge."

Darcy winces. No big tip for you at this booth, wench. "Great, I'll bring your check in a few minutes. How should I divide it?"

Pat rolls her eyes. "Just bring one check, please. Whose turn is it to pay anyway?"

Mike pulls out his Visa and hands it to Darcy. "Mine."

After Darcy leaves, I see Pat staring at me. I know she wants me to answer her question, most likely because she wants yet another of my leftover boyfriends. The girl really likes her leftovers. I dump 'em, and she pumps 'em. She says they taste better the second time you cook with them.

And Pat's the librarian-looking one? Trifling, just trifling.

I decide to change the subject. "That wench didn't even ask if we wanted dessert. I guess she needs to hurry up and get ready for her date with home girl later."

"At least she has a date, and stop trying to change the subject," Pat says. "So what's up with you and your love life, Ty? You haven't been on a date with Charles in God knows how long. I know you've been dating that battery-powered Mr. Tickler, and if Mr. Tickler is that good, girl, I may have to invest in one."

I can't believe she's busting out with my business like that! Though I know Mike could care less, I'm embarrassed as hell.

And now I'm embarrassed all over again. In addition to giving librarian-looking people a bad name, Pat is just plain rude. What's the word? Uncouth. Yep, Pat is uncouth in the booth.

Though I plan to get some from Mr. Tickler tonight if Charles doesn't come through.

It sounds to me as if Ty has her priorities in order. I'll bet she has quite a collection of C batteries in her nightstand. She may even have rechargeable batteries warming up in one of those little rechargers right now. I should probably get a recharger, too.

It's good for the environment, you know.

"I'm just glad you got over Jason," Mike says. "He was a dawg with a capital D."

I'm so tired of where this conversation always seems to go. "Why is it we talk about the same damn thing every time we go out?" I ask. "I don't want to talk about the man I'm with or the men who dogged me out. I don't want to talk about Charles, and I sure as hell don't want to talk about Jason. I came out tonight to talk to two of my friends about normal shit, like working, or the last movie you saw, Pat, or the last book you read, Mike. This is depressing."

Neither Mike nor Pat speaks for a few moments.

"I, uh, I fixed that problem in accounting today," Pat says.

" 'Bout time, too," Mike says, and in no time, they sit and fuss about working for Wachovia, where Mike is a supervisor and Pat is a systems analyst. I don't understand a word they're saying most of the time, because they speak that computer-tech language, but at least they aren't grilling me anymore.

Darcy gives us exactly two minutes to start on our wings and spinach dip before bouncing up to the table and handing the credit card slip to Mike. "Here you are, sir. Thank you, and y'all have a good night." Then Darcy bounces away, and I know that isn't the ass she was born with. It doesn't fit her white body at all. I'll bet she got a real good deal on the sale of her single-wide at the trailer park and bought herself a booty. I'm sure her mama's real proud of her.

Ain't that the truth! All these no-ass-at-all white girls are trying to get cabooses. They could rid me of mine anytime!

But wait—how are Ty and Dan going to hook up when it's starting to sound as if Ty doesn't even like white people? There are far too many opposites in this book. Too much nonsense. This kind of thing would *never* happen, especially in Roanoke, Virginia.

Mike signs the slip. "She doesn't deserve a tip at all, but I'll give her fifteen instead of my normal twenty percent. Everybody has off nights. Are you all ready to go?"

When we get outside, the rain is coming down in heavy sheets. Mike and Pat share an umbrella to his Maxima, while I pop my umbrella and start for my baby, my brand-new BMW 525i, a car I may actually get to own outright in about ten years once the lease runs out. As I'm passing under the Hooters sign, I hear some thumping bass sounding like some old school rap from when I was little—and it's coming from the old Subaru parked next to me? How dare that little car sit next to mine! I park my car in the boondocks to keep hoopdies like that away from my baby. There will be no scratches, dents, or scars on my baby!

I look through the front windshield, you know, just to be nosy, and see . . . Dan? He hasn't left yet? What's up with him? Is he having car trouble? No, exhaust smoke fills the air just fine. Is he—I hope he isn't waiting for me. Just because I nodded to him does not mean—

He's waving. Do I wave back at the man who was feeling up my legs with his eyes? You're asking a lot, Mr. Dan. First nodding, and now waving. I know you've had a rough night, and though I don't know exactly how you feel—no man ever dumped me for another man—I feel you, Mr. Dan. I squeeze out a wincing smile but don't wave, get in my car, start it up, and pull out of the Hooters parking lot. I check the rearview mirror to see if he follows—you can never tell with white men these days—then head for home, humming along to that old school beat.

I close *Wishful Thinking*. The concept is different, but it's too far-fetched. Ty seems as if she has her life together—a strong sister with a job and a plan. Dan, though, has too much baggage and droolage. Is "droolage" a word? I know I'd probably trash this one, even though I usually give interracial romances the benefit of the doubt, since there are so few of them. I might pick this one up again one day when I'm bored out of my skull.

Good thing I stocked up on C batteries. The checkout girl at Wal-Mart didn't even blink as she scanned the Duracell megapack, the ones parents buy for all the electronic Christmas toys. Little did she know . . .

Or, what if she *did* know?

I've embarrassed myself again.

Three times in one night, two from a book, and one from a memory.

I must be crazy.

10
Jack

There's hardly anyone in the main downtown library today. No wonder I found a parking spot so close to the building.

It's the day after the day after Christmas. No one's reading today. The batteries are still good.

True.

I stop at the circulation desk, where a tan woman—check that—a light-skinned *black* woman is reading a trade paperback. I slide the books onto the counter, and she looks up briefly before scanning the bar codes on the books and looking at a computer screen.

"These books are very late, sir."

"I just found them today in my son's room." I look at her name tag: Diane. "He was, um, hiding them from me."

She squints at the screen. "The fine on these will be . . . sixteen-fifty."

"Ouch," I say, and I dig into my wallet for a twenty.

"For ten dollars more, you could buy all three," she says, reaching over and taking the twenty.

"I could? Here."

Diane finally looks at me, blinking her brown eyes once. "Oh, no. I meant you could buy these at a *store* for ten more than your fine." She gives me my change, her fingers lightly brushing my palm.

"Thank you," I say, as my palm tingles. "Um, where is your, um, African American section?"

She looks up, again briefly, before looking at the books on the counter. "The nonfiction section is—"

"I need fiction."

She blinks once, and was that a sigh?

It was a sigh.

"In the fiction section, sir," she says softly.

Oh, yeah. How stupid of me.

You said it.

"Right."

I walk away toward the fiction section, feeling foolish. Where will *my* book be?

In the fiction section.

I messed up. I hope I didn't hurt Diane's feelings.

I'm sure you did.

I'll bet she gets stupid questions like that a lot.

And she's just hung a "Stupid" sign on you.

She has to have a lot of patience to deal with stupid people like me all day.

I'm sure you made her day.

I look back. Her eyes are buried in that trade paperback again. Here I am, a writer of African American fiction, and I ask a stupid question like that.

Then I realize . . . that librarian . . . Diane . . . touched me. Her fingers grazed my palm, when she was giving back my change.

Don't read anything into it.

She's the first person to touch me since the funeral.

But she thinks you're stupid.

And she thinks I'm stupid.

11

Diane

What a fool!

The library isn't segregated, except when it comes to nonfiction, yet there he was assuming that we had a special African American fiction section. White folks think in little boxes sometimes.

Wait. The last bookstore I went into had African American fiction in its own section. Segregation *isn't* over. Maybe he doesn't come to the library that often. I mean, those books were six months overdue. And he's just finding them? What kind of parent is that? Either he's absentminded and unobservant or that child is good at hiding things. I look closely at the books I will have to reshelve later. They're picture books, meaning he has a child age four at the most. What four-year-old can hide books from his or her parents?

And why does a white man want to read African American fiction? He should be reading nonfiction so he'll know the real deal. I know that the fiction books I review aren't truly about the real black experience, and that they're just for entertainment, but I doubt anyone would want to read the real deal about being black in America.

Especially white men. Oh, excuse me, *Caucasian* men. He's a member of the world's youngest *named* race, "Caucasian" having been coined by some German named Blumenbach in 1807. And how do I know this nugget of information? Another white man came into the reference section to ask, that's how. And this Blumenbach was a piece of work, let me tell you. He is supposedly the father of physical anthropology, and he based his findings on studies of his own collection of sixty human heads. Sixty . . . human . . . heads . . . in his *personal* collection.

I will never understand white people.

And the man over there wandering in the fiction section is definitely white—and ashy. White people, as a rule, are the ashiest people on the planet, the reason Vaseline Intensive Care Lotion (for dry skin, of course) and Oil of Olay were invented, the reason SPF-48 exists, the reason alligators are not as self-conscious around vacationers and retirees in Florida. As George Bernard Shaw once said, "A really *white* man would be a horrible sight."

And that shaggy man is a horrible sight, indeed. If we had a children's reading today, they'd all run away from him. Skinny, unshaved, scraggly blond hair, light blue eyes, and more wrinkles on his clothes than straight lines.

Pitiful.

But what is he doing returning a few books on a Thursday morning? Maybe he's on his holiday break. I'll bet he gets the whole week off from his cushy job. Well, it can't be that cushy. He was wearing only a simple wedding band. I'll bet his no-ironing wife has quite a rock on her finger.

I pick up *Thicker Than Blood.* Grandpa Joe-Joe, please help me forget about that skinny, ashy, unobservant white man.

2: Grandpa Joe-Joe's Jungle

"I told you to be careful," I say. "Just find yourself a stick."

Chloe looks around in the tall grass in front of Grandpa Joe-Joe's two-story farmhouse for a stick to scrape off a wedge of shit from her sandal.

Nasty. From Mr. Shaggy White Man to crap on a sandal. I just can't win today.

"Does your grandfather have a dog?"
"No. The septic is probably backed up again."

Nastier.

Chloe finds a stick and begins scraping. "Yuck."
I shrug. "Grandpa Joe-Joe won't notice."
And it's true. He doesn't notice much of anything anymore. If it's raining, I have to tell him to come inside. If it's snowing, I have to tell him to put on a coat. If he's stank—and he's right stank most days—I have to tell him to take a bath.

Grandpa Joe-Joe might have some Caucasian in him. Mr. Shaggy White Man had some serious funk on him.

I look behind me. "Damn. He took down his mailbox again, and I'm not about to go looking for it today, as hot as it is."
Chloe tosses the stick away. "He takes down his mailbox?"
"Yeah. He thinks if he doesn't have a mailbox he won't have to pay any taxes."

If only *that* would work.

Chloe only blinks.

"Really. I pay his taxes anyway, ever since he got back from the VA hospital."

She steps up beside me. "Has he been sick?"

"He has post-traumatic stress disorder," I say, and I can't help but laugh.

"That's not funny." She swats at a swarm of gnats in front of her face. "That's a serious disorder."

"I know it is. It's just that Grandpa Joe-Joe was never in any war. He got in just after Korea and got out just before Vietnam."

"Oh."

"He's got everybody fooled, huh?" I continue through the grass. "Follow directly behind me if you want to."

She takes my hand, and it is soft. "Where's the sidewalk?"

"This is the sidewalk. Grandpa Joe-Joe doesn't believe in trimming anything. He likes everything a little wild." I part a thick shock of grass, and she steps through. Very nice calves. "See those bushes blocking all the first-floor windows?"

She shades her eyes and looks up at the farmhouse. "Yeah."

"They were planted by Great-Grandpa Bert in nineteen forty-eight."

What, no Great-Grandpa *Bert*-Bert? If you're going to be throwing funky names at your readers, at least be consistently funky.

"Really?"

"Yeah. I think they're holding up this side of the house now, and whenever Grandpa Joe-Joe locks himself out of the house, which is almost every other day, he just climbs the bush to the second floor."

*Chloe squeezes my hand, and I stop. "What's that?"
She points to the right at a hulking piece of rust.*

*"That's a DeSoto, Grandpa Joe-Joe's first car. I
spent many a summer evening racing that car as a
kid."*

"It . . . ran once?"

*I smile. "No. It wasn't running even then." I slide
my hand out of hers, put it around her shoulders, and
point to the back of the farmhouse. "If you look real
carefully at the kudzu over there in the backyard,
you'll see all of Grandpa Joe-Joe's cars and trucks
peeking out."*

"I don't see . . . oh. Oh."

*"Yeah, there are a lot of them, and when the
kudzu's down in the winter, all kinds of folks stop by to
ask Grandpa Joe-Joe for parts. He doesn't sell any of
the parts, though, but he lets them look, mainly so he
can mess with them."*

*She leans back into my arm, even slides her arm
around my waist. Where has this girl been all my life?
"How does he mess with them?"*

*"Oh, say a man asks, 'How much for that bumper
on the Ford?' Grandpa Joe-Joe will circle the man a
couple times, then say, 'How much you got?' The man
will ask, 'How much do you want for the bumper?' and
Grandpa Joe-Joe will ask again, 'How much you got?'
This will go on and on till the man says something
like, 'I got a hundred dollars.'" I stop and slide my
hand down to Chloe's little waist. Nice and soft. Nice
little shelf down there, too.*

Come on! Not all women readers have "shelves." Since
when has having a big behind translated into sex appeal? *I*
haven't felt it, and very few men have ever gotten close
enough to my "shelf" to feel it. The things men want in a
woman that women don't want *on* them.

And speaking of shelves, I don't see Mr. Shaggy White Man. I feel a chill. I mean, it's just Kim Prim and I here today until two, when Francine gets here, and Kim believes that every patron is harmless. "They're only here to be enlightened," she says.

Oh, there he is, and though I feel a little better just knowing where he is, I still feel a chill. I look at the front door and see it rocking back and forth. When is maintenance going to fix that thing? The tiniest bit of wind makes those doors move.

I look down at the page. Now, where was I? Oh, yeah.

> *"Then, um, Grandpa Joe-Joe will say something like, 'A hundred dollars? That all you got? Damn, you're poorer than me. How's that make you feel, boy?'" I turn Chloe to me, my chin nearly resting on the top of those zigzag cornrows. "He's always messing with folks, and he'll probably mess with you, too."*
>
> *She looks up at me. "How crazy is he?"*
>
> *"Pretty crazy." And Chloe is crazy pretty. I hope Grandpa Joe-Joe doesn't run her off like . . . No, I don't want to think about that day.*

"Oh, please do," I whisper. I look up slowly, darting my eyes side to side. No one heard me. I have to stop thinking out loud while I'm reading.

> *"Come on," I say, taking her hand, but Chloe doesn't move. "What's wrong?"*
>
> *She points at a long black gopher snake sliding through the grass in front of us.*
>
> *"Oh, that's just a gopher snake. Nothing to it. Only eats mice." I look all around us. "It's the coiled and brown ones you should really watch out for."*
>
> *She jumps up to me. "I don't like snakes."*

"Better not use Grandpa Joe-Joe's bathroom, then.
I had a gopher snake pop out between my legs once
while I was, um, doing my business."

Nasti*est*. That can't really happen, can it? If so, I am
never moving to the country. Never. I can barely make myself go in the staff bathroom upstairs.

"They can . . . do that?"
"Sure. They get into the plumbing all the time,
looking for mice, I guess. Lots of mice out here."
"Were you scared?"
"Hell yeah. It scared the shit out of me, all right.
No one can be constipated at Grandpa Joe-Joe's
house."

HAAAAA! But it's still nasty. Did I just laugh out loud? I
look around and only see Mr. Shaggy White Man pulling
books from the shelves. What's he got, five books already? I
sigh. He'll be back here in a few minutes, and then I'll have
to do some work.

I lead her to the porch, a small gap in the bushes
letting us hit the first step.
"Will the porch hold the both of us?"
"It ought to," I say, "but if it doesn't, you'll just tour
Grandpa Joe-Joe's root cellar first."
Chloe drops my hand and steps back through the
bush to the ground.
"I'm just kidding, Chloe. It'll hold us. Just don't—
" Damn. *"Just don't leave the sidewalk." I have to do*
something about that septic. "You still have that stick?"
Chloe retreats even farther, fussing and cussing,
looking for another stick.

"It's just fertilizer, Chloe. Why do you think the grass is so green and thick around here?" She isn't hearing me at all. Now both of her sandals have shit on them. *"It's the best land in Franklin County.*

Hey, there's a Franklin County just south of Roanoke. I wonder if . . . Nah.

If we could just find it under all this grass, that is. I've had so many offers to buy this land from other real estate developers, but Grandpa Joe-Joe won't have it. This is my home, he says, my . . . home. I know I could get at least $5,000 an acre for it, and that would give Grandpa Joe-Joe half a million to play with, but he won't even listen to me when I start talking numbers. 'This . . . is . . . my . . . home.'"

That's right, Grandpa Joe-Joe. You keep your family's land.

Chloe finds a stick and starts scraping, her face one big frown. Damn.
"Of course, we'd have to move Grandma and Great-Grandpa first, though."
Chloe freezes. "They're . . . buried out here?"
"Somewhere." I look around. "I used to know where they were, but with all this kudzu—"
She turns to leave. "I'm out of here."

I would have left at the first sign of human excrement. What took Chloe so long? Oh, that's right. Chloe is a hoochie-ho with zigzag cornrows and a nice "shelf."

"Where are you going, Chloe? We're only staying a few minutes. I just want to check up on him, see how

he's doing, and then we'll leave. Five minutes, I promise."

"I'll wait in the car," she calls out.

"It's too hot to wait in the car, Chloe. Come on. It'll be all right—"

Then I see a skinny, yellow, liver-spotted hand reaching through the grass for Chloe's ankle. Damn, Grandpa Joe-Joe, not today! I start to run to Chloe, but I'm too late. Her screams send a flock of sparrows up out of the grass into the sky.

What would I do if that happened to me? I'd probably scream, and then I'd stomp the living daylights out of that liver-spotted hand, crap on my sandals or not.

Chloe kicks Grandpa Joe-Joe's hand away and runs to me, which is a good sign. The last girl ran completely away, all the way to Atlanta, or so I hear. I wish Chloe's whole body wasn't shivering, though.

"Is that, is that—"

I put my arms around her. "Yeah. That's Grandpa Joe-Joe."

"Where . . . where—"

I don't see him, which means he isn't done messing with us. "He'll pop up eventually. He's like a big prairie dog."

"Why . . . why—"

"Like I said, he likes to mess with folks."

And then we see his hunched-over form moving through a patch of thinner grass before he disappears into a thick canopy of kudzu behind the house.

"He is crazy," Chloe says.

And this novel is as ludicrous as *Wishful Thinking*. Oh, I'm sure there are crazy folks in the Southern hills, but no woman—"cute" hoochie or not—is going to go running *to* the man who *brought* her to this place.

I look over to the fiction section. Where's Mr. Shaggy White Man? Ah, I see a neon-white hand pulling another book from a shelf. Oh, Lord, I hope he's not leaving books all over the place. That's what some folks do. They pull a book from the shelf, continue to look, find something better, and then they put the "not-as-good" book down wherever they please. I sometimes see folks do that at the grocery store, and I have to fight the urge to take somebody's unwanted peanut butter from the bread rack and return it to the condiment aisle.

Oh, he's coming this way. Dag, he's skinny. And tall, maybe six feet. Tall people should not be skinny. There's just so much more "skinny" to see. That red and green shirt he's wearing is nice and colorful, and the green matches the pants, but those wrinkles, and is that a price tag? Tacky!

He's stopped at another shelf, a thick stack of books under one arm. Only five of those books are leaving the building, Mr. Shaggy. I guess you didn't read the sign posted right in front of me on the counter.

He's moving away. He's still not done? I look back at my book.

> We hear Grandpa Joe-Joe laughing, more cackling than laughing really.
> "Hey, Grandpa!" I yell out. "It's me, Robbie!"
> More cackling. "Nice ankles!" he yells, and he cackles some more.
> I smile. "He likes your ankles."

I look at my ankles and see nothing special. J. Johnson has some strange fetishes.

> Chloe looks down at her ankles. "Oh."
> More cackling. "They smell like shit, though!"

Ouch. "I'll, uh, I'll clean up your sandals for you."

She looks down again. "They're ruined."

"I'll, uh, buy you some new ones, then."

More cackling, this time from somewhere over to our left. Grandpa Joe-Joe hasn't lost a step at all, and he's pushing sixty-five.

"What's her name?" *Grandpa Joe-Joe yells.*

"Chloe!" *I shout.*

More cackling. "Chloe? What the hell kinda name is that?"

It's a perfume.

I look at Chloe. "You want to answer him?"

"No." *Chloe looks pissed.* "What kind of name is Joe-Joe, anyway?"

No cackling this time. "Name my mama give me," *Grandpa Joe-Joe says, standing just three feet behind us, wearing his usual overalls, red flannel shirt, and shit-kicker boots. I wish he would shave and get a haircut or wear a hat. He's looking more like Moses every day.*

Chloe turns her head slowly. "Oh, I didn't mean anything by it."

"I did," *Grandpa Joe-Joe says, wiping his forehead with a blue bandanna.* "What kinda name is Chloe? Sounds like a name you'd give to a cow. Here, Chloe, Chloe, Chloe, here, girl, let's get you milked, now, Chloe."

For some strange reason, I like Grandpa Joe-Joe. He is, in his own odd way, calling Chloe a "heifer."

Chloe's little back stiffens. "My mama gave me that name." *Nice comeback.*

Grandpa Joe-Joe chews on his moustache. "What's ya mama's name?"

"Violet," Chloe says.

"Better name." He nods at me. "Robbie."

"Grandpa."

"Well, you seen me, now get on. I got things to do," he says.

I can't imagine what. "You need anything?" I reach into my back pocket for my wallet.

"Did I ask if I needed anything?" He spits out a hair. "Did you hear me say I needed somethin'?"

I take out two twenties and put them in his hand. He folds them twice and shoves them into his pocket. "Have you called anyone about the septic?"

Grandpa Joe-Joe grins. "Yeah."

This is a surprise. The last time he waited until the stream of filth backed up to the front porch. "Who do you have working on it this time? It can't be Roto-Rooter. They refuse to come back out here."

"Nah. Jes' me." He plucks a strand of crinkly gray hair from his chin and stares at it. "An' Jimmy."

Not Jimmy! Anyone but Uncle Jimmy! "He's out?"

"He *been* out."

"Oh."

Damn. Now I'm going to have to weed-whack Grandpa Joe-Joe's hundred acres looking for Jimmy's "medicinal" plants. The Franklin County sheriff found Jimmy's last crop growing in the bed of an old Ford Ranger pickup a couple years back, just under the kudzu. The plants weren't that big, but those fifteen marijuana plants got Jimmy fifteen months, and all Grandpa Joe-Joe cared about was getting his truck back after the trial.

"He's a good boy, Jimmy is. He visits an' stays."

Until he gets arrested. "Is, uh, is Jimmy here?" I look up at the house.

"He's around."

Which means he isn't here. "Where, uh, where are you pumping the septic to?"

Grandpa Joe-Joe winks at Chloe. "It's a secret."

As hot as it is, all I'd have to do is follow my nose . . . to more of Jimmy's plants. "Grandpa Joe-Joe, you know what happened last time."

He spits out another hair. "Won't happen this time, I guarantee it. We got us a good hidin' place this time." *He plucks a hair from his moustache and looks at it.* "Where'd you find Miss Chloe, Robbie? She's cute."

I watch Chloe blush, or at least I think she's blushing. "We met at Bensons."

He cackles. "Miss Chloe's an alcoholic, then?"

Here we go. "No. She was drinking ice water."

Grandpa Joe-Joe rolls his eyes. "Bet it was some corn liquor." *He wraps the bandanna around his head, looking every bit like an old gangbanger.* "Has to be corn liquor to hook up with you." *He steps next to Chloe.* "You a rabbit, girl?"

"What?" *Chloe asks.*

"I said, are you a rabbit?"

"No," *she says.* "Are you?"

Grandpa Joe-Joe smiles. "I ain't no rabbit, but you are. You're scared as a rabbit. You shoulda seen yourself jump out there."

"It's not every day a skinny old man grabs your ankle for no good reason," *Chloe says.*

"That's right, girl," I whisper. "You tell the old moustache-eating gangbanger a thing or two."

I look up again. I'll bet Mr. Shaggy White Man could eat his own moustache. He's *still* looking? He has only gotten to the *R*s. At least he's methodical, though it would have been easier for him to run a simple search on the computer to spit out some titles.

"Who said I didn't have a good reason?" He cackles once, then gives Chloe the evil eye. *"Now what you doin' with Robbie?"*

"I, uh—" Chloe starts to say.

"He ain't nothin' special. Just cuz he's college educated don't make him special. Just cuz he got a good job over in Roanoke sellin' houses to uppity colored folks don't make him special.

Two books *in a row?* What is so special about this place? As far as I can tell from working at this library, Roanoke is where literature went to die!

Just cuz he got himself a nice house and two bathrooms don't make him special. Just cuz he's thirty and don't have no wife and kid don't make him special. He ain't nothin' much to look at neither. Takes after his daddy, who was the ugliest man who ever lived, and I oughta know cuz I'm his daddy's daddy."

Chloe looks at me as if to say, "Is any of this true?"

It is, sort of. Daddy isn't a pretty man, but he isn't ugly. To me. And anyway, I think I take more after my mama than him.

"I tried to leave Robbie's daddy outside in the snow one day, but damn if he didn't keep on comin' back into the house. I even drove him down the road aways." He plucks hair from his chin and looks at it. *"He come back the very next day, can you believe it? Then I kept him in the house, made him stay in his room till he was . . . eighteen, I think. Didn't want him to scare the neighbors, don't you know."*

Chloe only blinks rapidly. What she must be thinking.

"Run, girl, run!" I whisper, a little too loudly. I look up and see Mr. Shaggy White Man juggling several more books between the *R* and *W* stacks near the window. He won't be long now, and just when this book was pulling me in. As ludicrous as this novel is, it's growing on me . . . like kudzu!

"How is your ugly-ass daddy anyway, Robbie?"

"Daddy's fine," I say.

"He still got that fool worm farm?"

"Yes."

Grandpa Joe-Joe cackles and gets right up in Chloe's face. "Robbie's ugly daddy has a worm farm, and everybody thinks that I'm *the crazy one. He got a couple million of 'em copulatin' and fornicatin' down near the lake. You wanna meet crazy and ugly, you go on down there."*

Chloe is looking very much like a scared rabbit now. Time to rescue her. "Uh, yeah, Grandpa Joe-Joe, we'd better be going." I turn Chloe toward the car. "It was good seeing you again, Grandpa Joe-Joe."

"No the hell it wasn't," he says, and he cackles. "You got nice ankles, Chloe. Get yourself a new name, and you'll be all right."

Chloe turns and stops. "What name should I get?"

Grandpa Joe-Joe blinks. He's not used to someone talking back. "Bess. Bess is a good name, a good solid name for a woman. Change your name to Bess, and you'll be all right."

Then Chloe cackles, and it's almost a perfect mimic of Grandpa Joe-Joe. "Now that's a name you'd give to a cow."

Oh . . . no! Bess was my grandma, Grandpa Joe-Joe's wife! "Uh, Chloe, um, please don't—"

"Here, Bess Bess Bess, here Bess Bess Bess, come get yourself milked, Bess Bess Bess," Chloe says, still mimicking Grandpa Joe-Joe.

Grandpa Joe-Joe's face drops, and he shoves his hands into his pockets. "Bess was my wife's name."

Chloe sucks a sigh through her teeth. "Oh, I'm so sorry."

"She weren't no cow."

Chloe leaves me and takes a few small steps toward Grandpa Joe-Joe. "I'm really, really sorry. I shouldn't have said that."

Grandpa Joe-Joe turns away. "She was as big as one, yeah, kinda spotted like one, had these big brown eyes, even had herself a cute tail, but . . ."

"I'm so sor—"

Grandpa Joe-Joe's cackle cuts her off. "Robbie, I like this one. She got spunk. I like her a lot. She ain't no rabbit. You can bring her around here anytime." He points at the ground at my feet. "And what you doin' standin' on my daddy?"

I look down. The ground at my feet doesn't look any different, but I step back anyway. "I thought he and Grandma were buried under the oak tree out back."

"I moved 'em," he says, with a scowl. "If you came around more often, you'd know that."

Chloe steps quickly back to me. "Let's go," she whispers.

"Why'd you move them, Grandpa Joe-Joe?"

He folds his arms to his chest. "So the shit wouldn't get to them is why. Damn. That'd be a fine howdy-do, wouldn't it? You're pushin' up daisies and then you're pushin' up shit. That ain't no way to spend eternity."

"Please, Rob," Chloe whispers.

"Uh, see you later, Grandpa Joe-Joe."

We turn toward the car and walk quickly through the heavy grass. "Shouldn't he be in a home?" Chloe asks.

"He is in his home."

"No, I mean—"

I squeeze her hand. "I know what you meant, and

*don't think we haven't tried. He lasted six hours in a
home I had all lined up for him, and I still had to pay
for the whole month."*

"What happened?"

*We get into the car, and I crank up the air-
conditioning. "At first, he seemed okay, you know, flirting with all the ladies, shaking hands with all the men.
I took him to his room, got him settled in, and gave
him a hug. A few hours later, I get this call. 'Come get
your grandfather,' they said. 'He's hanging outside his
window on a sheet.'" I turn to her and pull away from
Grandpa Joe-Joe's. "He tried to escape by knotting
sheets into a rope, but he didn't have enough sheets to
reach the ground."*

"They kicked him out for that?"

*"Well, he did, um, leave a mess on his mattress." I
stare at her, so she knows what kind of mess I mean
without me saying it.*

*"Oh." She slips off her sandals and puts them on
the floor in the back.*

"I'll buy you some news ones, I promise," I say.

*"Don't worry about it." I check out her feet and her
short toes, each one the same length as the other.
"Don't stare," she says. "I know they're deformed."*

"They're not. They're . . . unique."

Let's evaluate our author, J. Johnson. We know the author
is fixated on titties, "shelves," ankles, and feet. This is definitely TMI—too much information.

*"Uh-huh." She rolls down the window, letting the
wind ruffle some stray hairs above her cornrows.
"Doesn't he get lonely out there all by himself?"*

*I can't say that he has Jimmy now. Jimmy will only
show up to tend to his plants, wherever they are.
"Grandpa Joe-Joe's where he wants to be, I guess. He*

never complains about being lonely. And I visit as often as I can, just about every weekend."

"You ought to visit him more often, even help him keep his place up."

"I just don't have the time."

"Make the time."

"Why are you so concerned about my crazy grandpa anyway?"

She laughs. "That man isn't crazy."

"You said he was."

"Well, I was wrong. He's not crazy at all, Rob. I know crazy, and he isn't crazy."

I glance at Chloe. The only people I know who truly know crazy are either psychologists or crazy themselves. Is the crazy pretty girl sitting next to me a crazy crazy pretty girl?

"I was a psychology major at Tech," she says.

Whew. "Yeah?"

"Yeah. And your grandfather is smart."

"Even if he thinks you have cute ankles?"

She slaps my thigh. "I do have cute ankles. Anyway, he was just testing me, and I know I passed the test."

"What test?"

She rolls her eyes. "Where are we going?"

"Huh?"

"Where are you taking me?"

I haven't been paying attention. I've just been driving and thinking about Chloe's toes and cute ankles and Grandpa Joe-Joe being smart under all that crazy.

"Uh, I don't know. I don't even know where you live."

"I live in Roanoke, near Roanoke Memorial. I'm a nurse there."

Roanoke again. I pick up *The Quiet Game* and rush through the pages until I see . . . Roanoke mentioned *again. Three* out of four books I have to review take place in "The Star City of the South"? But I've only been here a year! I'm no expert on this place. But, I suppose I'm the best MAB member for the job.

I hear books fall and look up sharply. Mr. Shaggy White Man is trying to carry too many books, and the more he tries to catch them, the more they slip through his fingers. He's hunched down and collecting them into a huge stack. Oh, shoot! He's coming this way, and I just *have* to finish this chapter.

> *She turns to me. "The hospital is where I sometimes work with really crazy people, so I know your grandpa's not crazy at all. Eccentric maybe, a little rude, a little coarse, but not crazy." She sighs. "Your daddy probably isn't crazy either."*
> *"Wanna bet?"*

Who's she kidding? His daddy has a worm farm. He *has* to be crazy—

"I'd like to check these out."

Shoot. I close my book and look up at Mr. Shaggy White Man. "We have a policy about how many books a patron can check out at one time, sir." I count fifteen books! Geez, at around 100,000 words each, he'd have to read 1.5 *million* words in three weeks! He's out of his mind.

I'll bet he has a worm farm.

"Oh. Uh, what's my limit?" He hands me his library card.

I try not to stare at any part of Mr. Shaggy . . . whose real name is Jack Browning. I look up from his library card. "Five is the limit."

"Okay. I guess I'll have to weed a few of these out."

And I get the privilege of waiting for you to "weed them out." Wonderful. It's one of my many perks.

I watch him flip over and examine the backs of several books, and it's not a bad collection. He has Margaret Hodge-Walker, bell hooks, James Baldwin, Richard Wright, Tannarive Due, Alice Walker, Margaret Walker, Toni Morrison, Terry McMillan, Omar Tyree, Eric Jerome Dickey, and Yolanda Joe. He has made decent choices all around. He places *Paradise,* by Toni Morrison, on the counter, and I scan it. Terry McMillan's *Disappearing Acts* follows. Decent novel, but the movie was average. He turns Alice Walker's *The Color Purple* over several times before placing it on the counter. Great read, great movie, a good choice. Now he's debating between James Baldwin's *Go Tell It on the Mountain* and Richard Wright's *Native Son.*

"I want to read this one"—he holds up Ralph Ellison's *Invisible Man*—"but which one of these two should I get?"

Is he expecting me to make a recommendation? I look closer at this man named Jack. He has tiny lips; freckles (or are they moles?); a severe, sharp nose casting a shadow over a ratty, uneven blond moustache and beard; and more worry lines than my grandma. And he has a little boy? I'll bet he robbed the cradle. That's what these "don't-have-to-work-during-the-holidays" white men do.

"Um," he says, "which one would *you* recommend?"

And, of course, he said "you" louder, as if I, a black woman, would know exactly which black book to recommend. I slide his stack around until I find Ernest Gaines's *A Gathering of Old Men.* Instead of saying anything, I scan it. I really ought to hit him with June Jordan's *Technical Difficulties*, but it's not in his stack.

"*A Gathering of Old Men.* I've heard of that one."

Uh-huh. Right.

He collects his books. "Thanks."

"They're due back in three weeks," I say.

He smiles, and finally I have something nice to say about him. He has a nice smile full of straight teeth, a smile that makes his worry lines disappear. "I'll have them back well before then."

Uh-huh. Right.

"Are you open on New Year's Eve?"

I want to get smart with him and say something like, "Me or the library?" but I don't, partially because he's not the least bit attractive, but mainly because I do have to work on New Year's Eve. I have no life. I'll have to put up a sign behind me that reads "Dateless on New Year's Eve—Pity Me." I force a smile. "Yes, we're open until nine on New Year's Eve."

"Okay, I'll see you then."

He nods once, and he leaves.

He just assumed I'd be here. He's right, of course, but he *assumed* I would have nothing better to do than work in a library on New Year's Eve. And he's going to read, what, half a million words in two days? His no-ironing, teenaged wife must mind the child so he can do his thing.

I feel a colder draft and look toward the door. He's coming back in? I gave him his library card, didn't I?

He steps up to the counter and collects the books he didn't take out. "I should have put these back."

I would love for this man to put these books back so I can continue reading, but I want to make sure they'll be put back in the right places. "I'll put those back for you."

"It's okay," he says. "I have plenty of time."

I stand. "Don't worry about it. You can just leave them on the counter."

"Are you sure? I don't mind."

Don't you have to be getting on home to your teenaged wife and sneaky brat? "It's okay. I need to stretch my legs."

"Oh. Okay." He smiles. "Bye."

I don't say "bye" to him because he has left me with fifteen minutes' worth of work.

12
Jack

Well, at least I had tried to make her day a little easier. It was the least I could do for all her help. I'll have to ask Diane to recommend even more books, because *A Gathering of Old Men* is a crackling good story.

I spend the next two days reading and taking notes mainly on dialect and dialogue from these masters of the written word, and they teach me that love is love, hate is hate, and prejudice is prejudice no matter who writes it. I know I'll never even come close to their power, but they've inspired me.

And then I sketch out an outline, reminding myself to KISS—Keep It Simple Stupid. My setting will have to be good old Roanoke, the same as my first book, and my main characters will have to be an African American woman and a white man because that's what my editor expects. As for point of view, well, even though her voice was so much stronger than his in the first book, I'm going to try third-person omniscient and see what happens. I'm going to need the simplest of plots, something much less involved, contrived, and coincidental than the first book. It has to be deeper and more serious. It has to mean something to me. It has to speak from my heart.

In other words, it has to be everything the first book was not. I wish my first draft had stood up to the editor's scrutiny. That story had heart, soul, and emotion.

Heart, Soul, and Emotion—not a bad working title. A little vague, though. Hmm. How about . . . *Greetings from the Melting Pot.* Too long. *The Melting Pot Blues?* Why not? My editor will change it anyway. At least I like it. I might as well get started:

1: Interrogating the Sponge

Why "the Sponge"?

It's what Noël called me when we first met. I didn't have anything to say to her at first—

You rarely did—or do.

True. She said she liked a quiet man, and that I was just a sponge soaking up life.

And now you wring life out when you're writing.

Something like that. Now hush so I can get going.

"It looks like blood on the floor next to your computer!"

"It's not blood. It's—"

"And what about the stains on the walls?"

"I can explain that, you see—"

"And those muddy footprints all over the kitchen leading into the living room. What about those?"

"Oh, that. You see—"

"What happened today, *Mister* Jefferson? Can you tell me?"

And while you're at it, tell me. This is supposed to be a romance?

It will be. Give it time.

Arthur Davis Jefferson, with his ashy, calloused, scarred fingers nervously drumming on the table, a cold can of Diet Coke just inches from his grasp, didn't look at his interrogator.

"I want answers!"

So do I!
Be patient.

Where to begin, wondered Arthur. *Where exactly to begin*. He looked up and tried to smile, but it came out more as a wince. "It was an . . . interesting day, to say the least."

"Uh-huh. And?"

Arthur glanced at the door, willing it to open. His son could explain this better than he could. His son would clear all this up. He'd fill in all the blanks, and because of his age, he'd get mercy, something his interrogator was obviously denying him. Mercy. That's what Arthur needed. Just a small amount. Sympathy was out, and empathy was a pipe dream. A little mercy.

He reached for the can of Diet Coke, but his interrogator's dark brown eyes said, "I wouldn't be doing that just now." He withdrew his hand, folding it into his other hand prayerfully, hopefully.

"Well, you know, it, uh, it was raining earlier today, and—"

"I know that."

Why am I talking about the weather at a time like this? he thought. "And, uh, Stevie was outside playing, and—"

"In the rain? You let him play outside in that thunderstorm?"

Arthur sighed. "No, it was only raining then, not very hard, kind of a mist really, just enough to cool him off. It was so hot, and he had been swinging on the swing set, and—"

"What were you doing during all that lightning?"

Arthur sighed again, dragging his hands to his lap, where they wrestled with each other. "Writing." He looked up at the dark brown eyes. "Downstairs."

"Writing, huh?"

"Yes."

"You didn't even know it was raining, did you?"

Arthur scrunched up his lips. He could deny it, but it would do no good. *Who doesn't know when a thunderstorm is raging outside his window?* he thought. *Besides me, I mean.* He shook his head. "Once I heard the thunder, though—"

His interrogator's hands sliced through the air. "Are you that . . . unaware, *Mister* Jefferson?"

Is that a rhetorical question? he thought. *If I say, "Yes, I am that unaware sometimes," I'll be doomed. If I say, "No, I knew there was a thunderstorm churning through the backyard," I'll be lying. Mercy. That's all I want.*

He sat up straighter, still feeling the dull ache in the base of his neck from hours hunched over his laptop. "I was on a roll, a real breakthrough. I was, um, really cranking it out."

My fingers were flying, and I couldn't catch up to them! he thought happily. *Please understand! Please recognize that inspiration doesn't always come, that it's sometimes like a game of baseball where so much nothing happens for innings at a time and then—bam! Someone hits a home run, a grand slam, a grand salami, a towering shot over the bleacher creatures onto Waveland Avenue. That was me today, and I had to let it fly, set it free immediately with no hindrances, no attention to misting rain falling on a healthy, happy, albeit muddy boy on a summer's day.*

"So, you're downstairs 'cranking it out,' as you say, while your child runs around in the lightning."

There was lightning downstairs, too! he wanted to say, but he only thought it. Inspiration sometimes has a price. "I called him in the second I heard the thunder."

Which is not to say that Arthur had heard the first rumbles of thunder. He had only heard the loudest thunder, that rolling peal that had broken the inspiration, caught that towering fly ball and turned it into a can of corn bloop to center field, sent it wherever inspiration goes, perhaps to Cleveland? *Why Cleveland?* he wondered. *I haven't been there since the Steelers used to win games. Wasn't I with Dad then? It was raining then, too, at the old stadium. Yes! And we were in the front row—*

"Stevie came in right away?"

"Huh?"

"Did your *son* come inside right away?"

He winced. "Not exactly. He, uh, frolicked a little, um, in the mud." In the circle of mud where a pool used to be, where Arthur had attempted to plant grass, only to have the grass seed eaten by every robin and sparrow in Virginia. "On his way inside."

"And it didn't occur to you to make him take off his shoes before coming into my kitchen?"

I'm so glad I didn't marry a lawyer, Arthur thought, *though I suppose every woman has the lawyer gene.* "I'll clean it all up, I promise."

His wife's dark brown eyes met his. "Artie, we go through this every single day."

"I know." He brightened. "It's only gum on the carpet, cinnamon, I think. If I take an ice cube—"

She snatched his Diet Coke and took a long drink, shaking her head. She did that a lot, that head shaking, usually once in the morning and a whole lot more at

night. He couldn't blame her. It wasn't easy living with a
would-be author.

To be more specific, it wasn't easy living with him, a
man, raised in the melting pot, whose mind was three
parts stew and one part broth, a literal bouillabaisse of
lives and memories congealed within the goo of his
brain, spewed forth in staccato, home run–like bursts on
a laptop whenever inspiration returned from Cleveland.

"I'll, uh, be more attentive tomorrow. I just—" Her
eyes told him not to speak, so he stopped.

"Don't say you'll be more attentive because you just
can't be attentive." She backed up to the closet next to
the refrigerator and took out the mop.

He rose from his chair, but her dark eyes put him back
in his seat. "I'll do it," he said, feebly and without con-
viction.

She rolled her eyes. "Go back to your . . . typing."

Mercy? he thought. *Mercy from a woman holding a
mop? And on a rainy day in a muddy kitchen?* "Are you
sure?"

She blinked once, and that answered his question.

"Uh, I'll, uh, . . . well."

I am so well-spoken, he thought. *At least my characters can speak clearly when I want them to.*

He stood. "Thanks." He stepped to her as she turned
away from him, plopped the mop into the sink, and
turned on the faucet. He moved as closely as he dared,
his body millimeters from hers. "I'm sorry."

She used the sprayer to rinse some Frosted Cheerios
off the mop. "I'm used to it." She smirked. "For a man
who is such a sponge for details, the whole house could
burn down around you, and you'd still be down there
typing away."

He kissed her brown neck, marveling at its softness.
"Maybe," he said, slipping his hands to her hips.

"Maybe nothing. I know you."

It was true. She did. She knew him. It was why he had married her ten years ago.

He kissed the sensitive spot just under the hairline of the softest part of her neck, the tropical scent of protein styling gel tickling his nose. Her hair had texture, but it wasn't coarse. He had found out the hard way when he had brought the perm back from Food Lion. "I'm regular, not coarse," she had said. "Regular tampons, regular perm, regular . . ."

A real regular girl I married, he thought. *A regular girl for a regular guy. Two regular people in an irregular marriage. There is something . . . symmetrical about it all.*

"I'm glad you do."

She wrung out the mop with her hands. "Glad I do what?"

"I'm glad you know me."

She rolled her eyes, frowned, but gave him a kiss on the cheek anyway. "Am I in your next book?"

"You always are," he said. "You always are."

So, what do you think? It's not too . . . domestic, is it?

I like it. It's sweet. It's a nice memory. Noël was so angry that day, and yet she mopped up the mess and even sang while doing it.

But there aren't any guilty pleasures.

Have him put his hands on her ass or something.

In the kitchen?

Why not?

But it's muddy.

You never know. It might turn her on.

I roll my eyes, save the work, and sit back from the laptop, looking at the mess that is my cramped office. It really isn't an office, though it has all the prerequisites. My laptop rests on a pressboard desk covered with coffee cup–sized circles that Stevie connected together with twelve of the sixty-four colors of the Crayola rainbow. It is as if Spirograph has bloomed on every surface. The laptop itself has seen better days, the floppy disk drive occasionally functional, the CD-ROM drive held forever in place and inert by two pieces of masking tape. The blue industrial swivel chair I sit on swivels only ninety degrees each way before complaining to a stop, its movement impeded by several gobs of spent gum and two gummy worms.

The two-drawer dented metal filing cabinet under the desk holds all of my old rejections, and there's quite a healthy stack in there. My favorite rejection from New York proclaims: "I do not have room for additional commercial novelist on my list, and while I'm happy top have an abundance of great writers on my list, I lament that I cannot take on writers who seem to resonate with readers."

What a load of gobbledygook! Who would want to work for an editor who thinks "novelist" is both singular and plural, cannot spell "to" correctly, and uses the word *lament* in a rejection, as if this editor truly laments anything other than his or her inability to edit a letter?

I look at my printer and refrain from hitting it. It has been one constant, electric paper jam since the day I bought it. A trio of expended ink cartridges—ones I had planned to refill by hand—teeter on the top of the printer. I knock them over, and they jump to the floor to join a string of paper clips and torn envelopes. An overflowing waste can a sneeze from the empty paper shredder, which Stevie nicknamed "the 'fetti maker," sits under the first set of shelves holding miles of reference books. These books, collected or given as gifts or simply saved from oblivion by me at yard sales, make the shelves sag only in the middle. Yeah, my bookcases are smiling at me.

You shouldn't have used pine boards. They're soft wood.
But they're cheap.
My library has no organization whatsoever. *The Real*

Mother Goose is sandwiched between a current Roanoke phone directory and *Masterpieces of African-American Literature.* The 2000 JC Penney fall catalog balances on top of *In Search of Color Everywhere: A Collection of African-American Poetry,* Time-Life's *WWII,* a Bible (King James version), *American Indian Archery,* and *A History of African-American Artists.* My 1950 edition of *The Oxford Universal Dictionary* sits in the middle of the first "smile," surrounded by *The Autobiography of An Ex–Coloured Man* and the *1998 Guide to Literary Agents. Siddharta* follows *The Awakening,* which creeps up on *Emily Post on Entertaining,* which catches up with *Things Fall Apart.* I used to have one "smile" devoted to African American writings, and the left half contains titles by Toni Morrison, Brian Egeston, and Octavia Butler, but the rest of the shelf includes *The Bonfire of the Vanities* and *ABC's of the Human Body. A Tree Grows in Brooklyn* blooms next to *Native Stranger, Cultural Literacy, Parting the Waters,* and *Journey to Ixtlan* on the top smile. What's that? Oh, yeah. It's a wooden carving of an African elephant sitting on top of *To Love & To Cherish: Meditations for Couples, The Joyful Heart,* and the *Shakespeare Birthday Book,* a gift from my mother. Yeah, I guess my collection is eclectic and peripatetic.

And ultimately pathetic.

At least *I* read.

The only things that give this room any kind of order are Post-it notes. Affixed to every flat surface are more fluttering Post-it per square inch than any office has ever seen, each a piece of the puzzle I grandiosely call my "works in progress." So many scribbles and hieroglyphics. I guess it's my way of keeping my ideas a secret, even from me. These cryptic notes blot out most of the pictures on the shelves behind them, photographs of Stevie, Noël, my family, Grandma Ella, Noël's family, Stevie again, a few cousins, my nieces and nephews, Noël again in one of those Glamour Shots, my parents, Stevie again . . . and again.

Visible atop a speaker attached to no visible stereo is my

first baby cup, the silver now a dark black, and inside that cup is a two-dollar bill, given to me by my maternal grandfather after a particularly good day at the dog races in Juarez, Mexico. Next to this less-than-sparkling cup is a baseball autographed by Ted Williams, the Splendid Splinter, who, sadly, has passed away recently.

I would have more room if this office weren't also the guest room (complete with full-sized bed overflowing with files, newspapers, magazines, and books, each with numerous page corners turned down) and the catchall room. An old Tandy computer, its pride wounded from neglect, serves to keep the closet door closed, and a gargantuan monochrome monitor sporting a TV antenna for a hat stares blankly from atop a TV stand where once sat a thirteen-inch TV with no remote control.

I haven't opened the closet since 1999, when Noël had heard a rustling sound in the walls. I had located the rustling inside the closet where empty computer boxes and warranty cards (and other things manufacturers told me not to *ever* throw away) lived in harmony, evidently, with mice. I had played the mighty hunter that day, pinning one of the mice to the baseboard with my shoe. I thought, of course, that I had solved the "noises-in-the-walls" issue, but, of course, I hadn't. That one mouse dragged itself around in the closet using its front paws, struggling to chew through another warranty card or the corner of another computer box, just wanting to make its way in the world that is the closet.

I don't plan to open that closet anytime soon.

Other than the laptop on top of the desk, there are several coffee cups, each with brown residue at the bottom and at the top edges, each crying out to be rescued with a semiannual visit to the kitchen sink. In the "97.1 WQMG Smooth R&B . . . Classic Soul" cup, with the residue covered with fluffs of dust, are several red pens, their tops chewed to the quick or missing. And under my most recent cup, a broad yellow smiley cup in the very best seventies tradition—a Fa-

ther's Day gift from Noël—is a stack of paper ripped from a
steno pad.

I hardly remember writing this . . . rambling set of para-
graphs, notes, and squiggles, in no certain order, that formed
the basis for the remarks I had planned to make at Grandma
Ella's funeral over a year ago. I had written some of them
while stuck in traffic outside Philadelphia on I-76 the night
of the funeral service. The rest I composed in the pew at the
church.

I never read my remarks. I was too choked up, too intim-
idated by other family members making remarks, and simply too scared to speak in front of 500 people. But for some
reason, I saved these notes.

Intro: Start with last lines from Robinson's
"Lucinda Matlock": "Degenerate sons and daughters . . . It takes life to love life."

I smile. I had scratched out "Degenerate sons and daughters." That wouldn't have gone over too well with my father,
aunts, or uncles.

The ideal Ella was a fisherwoman, a fish cleaner, an
outdoorswoman in flannel shirts and funny hats, a
pianist, composer, and writer.

Grandma Ella was a true Renaissance woman. Noël said
that Grandma Ella was really my muse.
She sure could cook.
Yeah.

She survived polio, open-heart surgery, a late baby, a
Catholic president whom she thought was the anti-
Christ, knee replacement surgery, and cancer. I lived
most of my life scared of this woman, This saint

who once washed out my mouth with a bar of Camay for saying "dang," which she said was a derivative of "damn."

I doubt I would have read all of that. Saying "damn" in a church would have doomed me from attending any future Browning reunions.

I remember so many things:

   . . . The way she drove her Oldsmobile station wagon with one foot flat on the gas, the other foot bumping the brake, as if she were late for heaven or something and everybody had better not stop her from being first in line to see Jesus

   . . . The birthday cards she sent me, 40 in all, each with $2, the last card mailed from what would be her deathbed

   . . . I remember Red Rose tea and the ginger-snaps, pretzels, and saltines in the big tins up at the lake in Canada that she swore would "never rot or spoil" since they were made in Pennsylvania

   . . . Her telling me, "can't is spelled w-o-n-apostrophe t."

Grandma Ella, who had called me from her deathbed and asked if I had gotten any of my books published; Grandma Ella, who had asked me to write her story one day . . . The stories she told of her father, George T. the evangelist, who once patched a canvas boat using Teaberry gum and despite a raging thunderstorm stopped to pick up a fallen branch of colorful leaves for his wife Dessie, the best definition of love I've found so far . . .

Maybe I can work some of Grandma Ella's personality into one of my characters, maybe my main character's mother? She'd definitely be unforgettable.

The rest are notes I wrote at the funeral while listening to other speakers. I had thought that I knew everything about Grandma Ella, but I was wrong.

Grandma Ella:

*Put envelopes in the freezer so she could remove any uncancelled stamps later

*Cleaned and reused aluminum foil

*Put out half napkins on the table

*Had a list for just about everything; said Post-its were invented just for her

*Believed that a messy desk was the sign of a <u>working</u> mind

*Couldn't eat chocolate or ice cream because of allergies most of her life; in the end, the allergies went away, and at 89, she ate her first ice-cream sundae and loved every bite—"it's <u>so</u> delicious!"

*Of the three Stephens girls, Helen was the prettiest, Charlotte the smartest, and Ella—"Well," Uncle Bill said, "Jack got his money's worth."

*Had the ability to get folks to do things simply by asserting: "You will do the electrical work" or "you will make this shawl" or "you will sing a solo"

*Got a high school play cancelled in the 60s—play had rape scene—and received angry phone calls and death threats

*Gave "Are You Saved?" tracts to door-to-door salesmen

*Favorite line to her 5 children: "Do you really <u>need</u> it? Or do you just <u>want</u> it?"

*Dad's story: "Coach said to eat steak before the game." Mom asked, "Are you on the first team?" I said, "No." Mom said, "Then you'll get hamburger until you're starting on the first team."

*Planned own funeral; said: "It will be next Friday" (and it is!)

*On deathbed in last moments: "What time is it? I'm still here. This isn't heaven. Why am I still here?"

*She's having a reunion with her son, her parents, her husband—"But I'll see Jesus first"

*Once ran away from home (I didn't know this!); Left North Carolina for Philadelphia to play piano in a speakeasy during Prohibition; changed her name to Helen Brown; called the "best pianist in Philadelphia"; found by father and taken back to NC . . . later ended up founding a church with Grandpa Jack in Philadelphia . . .

Grandma Ella was quite a woman, but when I asked my agent if her biography had a chance to be published, Nina said no. "She isn't famous enough," Nina said.

I should still do something with this.

Yes, you should.

I return to my "five hundred–millimeter stare"—the distance from my eyes to the laptop screen—and reread my novel so far. I want to intrigue readers into thinking there is something seriously and fundamentally wrong with the scene, yet in the end, everything is seriously and fundamentally *normal.*

Normal is good.   .

Not when you're supposed to provide dramatic, guilty pleasures on every page!

No writer can do that!

The narrative begins harmlessly enough, though the average reader might be thinking, "I may have picked up the wrong book."

That's what I thought.

The novel opens with an interrogation, the interrogator trying to piece together the mystery of the "blood on the floor," the "stains on the walls," and "the muddy footprints all over the kitchen." Noël was never an interrogator like that, but I want my heroine to be like that. It's more dramatic, more . . . tense if she has an accusatory voice.

It isn't until the word "ashy" that the reader has a clue to Arthur's identity, and I'm sure Arthur's "calloused" and "scarred" hands will get me in trouble with the critics. A white man's hands being calloused, as in actually having to work so hard as to cause calluses to form on his hands? Not on our lives! Callous, maybe. "Scarred" is an equally puzzling description of a white man's hands. Unless, they will say, he is a farmer, an NFL lineman or a quarterback (two of a few positions white men are currently able to play in the twenty-first century), a lightweight Irish boxer, or an assembly-line worker, he can have no physical scars.

Now you're thinking too much!

So, what does the reader know about Arthur? The reader knows he is possibly an NFL lineman/Irish lightweight who works the land by day and the assembly line by night, the typical hardworking American white man. The reader knows that he is in trouble, but that doesn't worry the reader at all. The reader knows that though he may face a hail of bullets, a nuclear bomb or two, and the evil that naturally plagues white men wherever they go, our white man hero will be triumphant in the end. This is, after all, only the opening page.

My critics are going to skewer me! Maybe the interrogator will take the heat away from Arthur. No, they'll find fault with her, too. She's too angry and rude, and—

You think far too much. Let it flow. You haven't even had reviews of your first book yet. They might be wonderful reviews.

Of a book I don't recognize anymore?

I reread the chapter again. Geez, it's almost as if I've created a serial killer.

Yeah, I was sort of wondering about that . . .

The evidence against him is heavy, his responses weak and unresponsive, his choice of "interesting" to describe a day of "blood," "stains," and "mud" completely creepy. The reader will begin to lose sympathy/empathy for Arthur until he asks for mercy and folds his hands "prayerfully" and "hopefully."

He's not such a bad sort, a few bricks shy of a load in the verbalization department, but an okay Joe (though you've named him Arthur) who knows when to pray for deliverance.

But is he a good father? The critics will say, "No, he isn't because he let his boy play in a lightning storm." The critics *won't* say that Arthur is a good father because he remembers what it was like to be a boy and knows that a little thunder, a little lightning, and a little mud made us all.

You're thinking too much again.

I know. I can't help it. I have all this time to think.

When Arthur's wife—whom I haven't even named yet? Geez, I'm slipping. I'll call her Di for now.

Why "Di"?

I have my reasons.

Ah, Diane the librarian. You're going to name a character after her because she touched you?

Shh.

When Di asks, "Are you that . . . unaware, *Mister* Jefferson?" I'll bet the readers start nodding.

I was nodding.

Shh.

They'll think that he is completely unaware. He does not hear the thunder, he does not know it's raining, and he most likely doesn't know where his son is. But are these traits of the average father? Can the reader really fault Arthur for being clueless? Or for being a writer? My main character doesn't work, *per se*, though writing is, of course, a job *someone* has to do.

But so is doing the dishes or taking out the garbage or trimming fingernails and toenails.

Yeah, you're right. The reader will lose respect for my "would-be author" almost immediately.

I've created a puzzle, a conundrum inside a poser folded into an enigma, a man whose mind is "three parts stew and one part broth," the results of his living in the "melting pot."

It's not so bad. It has your *attention, right?*

Oh, it does all right. It has me criticizing my own novel before I've gotten ten pages into it! Who does that to his or her first draft? No one!

I'll bet all writers do this.

I'm . . . I'm not a writer. Gaines, Morrison, Ellison—they're writers. I'm just a . . . storyteller.

Then tell a story. Let it flow.

But they don't want a story! They want drama! They want guilty pleasures! They want . . . they want everything I know *nothing* about!

Tell a story anyway.

I sigh deeply, take a sip of lukewarm tea, and shake my head. "This will not do."

I toy with deleting my first chapter, such as it is, with a single touch of a button.

Keep it. You might need it.

When will I need it?

It might make a nice last *chapter.*

You know . . . you might be right. But what author writes the last chapter of a book before he or she writes the first?

They said they wanted three chapters and an outline. They didn't specify which *three chapters, did they?*

No. No they didn't.

I smile because I may have written the last chapter of my second novel.

13

Diane

I check the clock on Saturday afternoon. Four o'clock already? Where has the time gone? I haven't been that busy today, just the usual walking of the stacks and scanning of the books, and no shaggy white men have come looking for the African American fiction section. That gives me just enough time for one more chapter of *Thicker Than Blood*, and then I have to get to work reshelving a few books.

3: Daddy's Worm Farm

I make a U-turn and head to Pine Lake, taking a dozen country roads to Daddy's one-bedroom shack a few feet from a little backwater cove. I honk at all the ducks in Daddy's dirt driveway, and they part like white water, there are so many of them.

"What's with all the ducks?" Chloe asks.

"Worm farm . . . ducks. They go hand in hand."

I park under some towering pine trees next to the largest bin of worms. I call it a bin because I don't know what else to call it. It's like a huge sandbox raised three feet off the ground with several sheets of black tarp over it.

"Watch your step here, too."

She slips on her sandals, wincing. "I will."

She put those nasty sandals back *on?* Well, I guess it's better than going barefoot.

I look around her to the dock but don't see Daddy's boat. "He must be out delivering worms."

"He delivers them?"

"Yeah, and by boat. He traded in a brand-new Ford truck for this boat. You'll just have to see it to believe it."

"Where does he deliver them to?"

"He bought fifty old Coke vending machines at a thousand a pop, and he placed them all around the lake, mostly at marinas. All he did was use some gray duct tape to put the letters W, O, R, and M over the C-O-K-E on the machines. I told him that he forgot the S, and he said, 'No, I didn't.'" Which is one of the longest sentences he's ever spoken to me. "But that's about all anyone would get, alive anyway, if it gets too hot."

"They're not plugged in?"

"Yeah, they are, but not all of them are in the shade."

"That's . . . absurd."

"But it's not crazy?"

"Misguided maybe, but, no, not crazy."

She opens her door carefully, a flock of ducks staring right up at her. "Do they bite?"

"Yeah."

"You're kidding, right?"

I pull up my pants legs, and point at several red marks. "From my last visit. I was wearing shorts."

She shuts the door. "You go first."

You got that right, Chloe. Rob needs to shoo all those ducks out of the way.

"Watch this." I lean on the horn, and the air fills with ducks and feathers, and a huge greenish white splat of goo plops on the windshield. "We can get out now."

This author is definitely visual, I'll give him that.

We check out the biggest bin first. I pull back the edge of one of the tarps, and we see . . . dirt. Not much excitement at a worm farm. "Underneath all this dirt are about a million worms, and all they do is make more worms. They double every twenty-two days."

Chloe whistles. "That's . . . a lot of worms. Does he make any money?"

"Well, he's in debt because of the vending machines and all the bins he has to build every three weeks, and this land wasn't cheap, though I got him a pretty good deal. He sells two dozen worms for two dollars, which is a pretty fair price, and he says that each machine makes him about a hundred a week in quarters, so—"

"He makes five thousand dollars a week?"

"Yeah. In quarters. But only from late March to early November."

"That's . . . seven months, about thirty weeks times five thousand . . . He makes a hundred fifty thousand dollars a year from worms?"

I am definitely in the wrong profession. They didn't have this major at Purdue.

"Give or take."

"That's . . . that's amazing."

I shrug as I watch several gangs of ducks closing in. "He ought to be raising ducks. That's where the

money's at." I take Chloe's elbow and guide her to-
ward the dock. "But he's got some major problems this
year, and it's all because of these ducks."

We walk out onto the dock, and Chloe flops down,
taking off her sandals, and dangling her feet over the
edge.

"I wouldn't put your feet in there," I say.

"Why not?"

"Just look."

She looks down. "I'm looking."

"You used to be able to see the bottom. It's only
three feet deep here."

"Eww." She pulls her feet under her. "What hap-
pened?"

I sit next to her. "The ducks happened. The worms
attracted them, they hang out, they shit everywhere,
and this cove just . . . died. That water is duck-shit
soup.

And I was going to have some clam chowder for dinner
tonight! Not anymore.

Daddy's neighbors all recently signed a petition to
have the worm farm removed so the ducks will go
away and they can go swimming again. A news crew
even came down here a couple weeks ago, so now folks
think all of Smith Mountain Lake is duck-shit soup."

"I think I saw that story."

"Yeah. Didn't do much for business down here. All
that publicity cut down on fishing on the lake, and that
cuts down on Daddy's sales. . . ."

She sniffs the air. "It does smell . . . metallic."

"Today's not so bad because it rained yesterday.
But go a few days without rain, and this cove smells
like, well, Grandpa Joe-Joe's yard. But that's not the
main problem. You see, Daddy doesn't sell the worms

*fast enough. He might sell two million worms a sea-
son, but whatever's left at the end of the season just . . .
copulates all winter. Eventually, he'll run out of land
for all his bins, even if he starts stacking them on top
of each other, and when that happens . . . well, I don't
want to be anywhere near here when that happens.
Can you imagine a couple million worms spilling into
that cove?"*

*Chloe looks down at the water. "Dag, the sunset
doesn't even reflect on the water."*

*I hear a boat approaching and look out into the
main channel. "Here comes my daddy."*

*We watch his busted-up Chris-Craft, a wooden boat
in the age of fiberglass, churn through the green water
to the dock. That thing takes so much water he has to
bail as he goes. I catch the front end and tie it up while
Daddy ties up the back. Then he starts stacking sacks
full of coins onto the dock in front of Chloe.*

"Hi," Chloe says.

" 'Lo," Daddy says.

"I'm Chloe."

*Daddy nods, and he keeps on stacking. She's get-
ting more out of him than I usually do.*

"Need any help?"

*"Nah," Daddy says after a pause. He glances at
me, but he keeps on stacking.*

*It's always been like this, ever since I was a little
boy. He hardly ever made eye contact with me when I
was growing up, hardly even spoke to me, like he was
either ashamed of me or ashamed of himself. He isn't
an ugly man, just . . . big featured. His eyes are too
wide and too round, his forehead is at least a foot
across, his nose is flattened all over his face, and one
ear's bigger than the other. He isn't exactly slow,
though it takes him a couple seconds to answer any*

*question, and I know he's not dumb. He's just . . . my
daddy.*

I'm beginning to like Rob. He has pride in his family,
warts and all. That's rare these days.

*And since Mama died two years ago, all he's been
doing is this worm farm. He could have invested
Mama's life insurance money raising any other animal, maybe even cows or pigs or even horses over at
Grandpa Joe-Joe's. I guess he chose worms because
they're blind, they don't make any noise, and they
breed like, well, rabbits. I don't know what he thinks
about all the ducks, or even the raccoons that try to
raid the worms every night, or even the petition his
neighbors have signed against him and his farm. I just
don't know my daddy all that well, even after thirty
years.*

"So, Daddy, how's it going?"

*He looks up, the last sack of change on the dock.
"It's goin'." He steps out of the boat and collects four
bags at once, each easily weighing fifty pounds. I grab
two, Chloe struggles with the last one, and we follow
Daddy up to the shack. He opens the only door and
goes in, extending one of his massive arms behind him
to take our bags.*

"Aren't we going in?" Chloe whispers.

"No. He won't let anybody inside."

"Why not?"

*I don't answer her, because I really don't know. I
tried to go inside once, but he blocked the way, not
saying a single thing, barely making a sound.*

*Daddy comes back out with a huge plastic bag
filled with Styrofoam cups and lids and heads past us
to the largest bin.*

"Are you going out again, Daddy?"

Daddy nods, pulling back one of the tarps. The second he does, the ducks flock over and surround him. They never nip at his legs. Never. Daddy lays out a line of cups in front of him, and then he starts digging into the dirt, coming up with fistfuls of worms. I've never seen him count them, but I've never heard of anyone complaining that they were shortchanged. Every third fistful, he flings several worms into the air, and the ducks go crazy, squawking and fussing with each other. I almost see a smile on his lips whenever he does this, and it seems to be the only time my daddy is ever happy.

Chloe wades through the ducks to stand beside him. "Need any help?"

Daddy blinks at her, then at me. "Nah," he says.

Chloe digs into the dirt with both hands. "I don't mind." She grimaces as she pulls up a handful of worms. "Two dozen in each, right?"

Daddy glances over at her hand. "You got twenty."

"Huh?" Chloe says.

"Need four more."

Chloe looks at me, and I shrug. I don't know how he knows. He just does. Chloe counts out the worms wriggling in her hands as she puts them in a cup. "Twenty," she says eventually.

"Need four more," Daddy says again.

Chloe nods. "How'd you know?"

Daddy touches his temple. "Just do."

Chloe puts four more worms in her container and snaps on a lid. "Come on, Rob. This is fun."

I've never done this. I've never wanted to do this, yet here I am, walking toward my crazy daddy's biggest worm bin, rolling up my sleeves while ducks nip at my pants legs. Daddy nods at me, and I dig in.

This is beyond gross, yet . . . it's kind of relaxing. The worms massage my hands when they aren't snotting on me,

Oh, that's sick! I may never eat clam chowder again.

and the ducks don't nip at me as much once I start feeding them. I find that I have "twenty-eight hands," so Chloe and I work together to fill our cups. She digs her twenty, I dig my twenty-eight, and then she takes four from me. In less than an hour, we have several hundred cups finished and ready to go. We help Daddy get them into the boat, he nods at each of us, and off he goes into the last of the sunset.

Chloe holds up her hands. "Where do you wash your hands around here?"

"Good question."

We end up wiping them off on an old towel in my trunk, but no amount of wiping will get all the dirt from under our nails.

"That was interesting," I say as we return to the dock.

"It was fun," Chloe says.

"Yeah?" I slide closer to her. "You aren't kidding, are you?"

"No."

I put my hand on top of hers. "What do you think of my daddy?"

"You mean, do I think he's crazy?"

"Yeah."

"What he does might seem crazy to the rest of the world, but the way he does it is completely sane. And he makes money, a whole lot more money than I do."

"But it's all he does. It's all he's been doing since my mama died two years ago."

"So he's just working it out. Nothing wrong with that." She smiles. "I think he may even be an idiot savant."

"A what?"

"An idiot savant, you know, someone who seems kinda slow but who has amazing mathematical abilities. I bet he could count all the pine cones in that tree over there in less than a second. . . ."

I look at the stack of books that need to be reshelved and count thirty. No sweat. At any rate, I'll be glad when I get back to the reference desk. The circulation desk gets so mind numbing sometimes.

And as I walk, I can't help but look for duck shit on the carpet.

I read *way* too much for my own good.

14

Jack

"A normal man—we'll call him Arthur—and a normal woman named Di meet at a . . ."

I'm telling a story in Stevie's—*my* (I keep forgetting)—room to Mr. Bear. Mr. Bear isn't blinking an eye, but I can sense his disapproval. Something about the way that eye just . . . dangles there.

"Well, anyway, they meet somewhere, uh, *normal,* and at first, they don't really like each other—which is *normal*—because they don't know each other very well. We human beings are paranoid that way. We don't like what or whom we don't know."

And this human being is a little drunk. That's why I'm not talking to myself tonight. I don't want any competition when I'm drunk. And besides, Mr. Bear isn't nearly as judgmental as I am. I mean, as judgmental as the voice in my head is. Or something like that.

And even if I were sober, I couldn't possibly make that last bit make any sense.

I had gone to Food Lion to buy some fingernail clippers and some more Kleenex, and it had a whole refrigerator section dedicated to Kris Kringle Eggnog, twelve-proof and half off, limit of four, be sure to use your MVP card.

I took four, and three are already . . . somewhere.

"So these exceptionally *normal* people are wary of each other at first, you know, checking each other out, maybe occasionally catching the other's eyes." I take a swig. Too sweet! "Or, in your case, Mr. Bear, catching each other's *eye*. You really ought to see a bear optometrist."

Mr. Bear seems to grin. I blink. Wait a minute. He always seems to grin. He's frozen that way. It's why I don't trust him. He smiles too much.

"Oh, ha-ha, Mr. Bear. I didn't mean you ought to see a bear *naked* optometrist. I meant that you needed to see—"

A phone rings somewhere in the house. I wonder where I put it. Probably next to the Kris Kringle Eggnog bottles.

The phone stops ringing by the time I get to the kitchen. Figures. I turn to go back to Mr. Bear, and it rings again.

I snap up the phone, but I don't speak. Sometimes you can catch people off guard that way.

"Hello?" It's a woman's voice, one unfamiliar to me. I keep silent. "Is anyone there?" she asks.

I can't resist. "I'll check."

"Excuse me?"

"Did you burp?"

"I must have the wrong number. I was calling about a Mustang."

The damn car. "You have the right number, and no, I haven't sold the car yet, and yes, it has a lot of mileage on it, and no, it's never been in a wreck, and yes, the back windows leak."

"Uh, okay."

It's one of those long "okay"s, like o-kaaaaaaay. It's a cute "o-kaaaaaaay," though. It's even kind of sassy.

"Is there a place where I can drive by and see it?"

A unique choice of words. "You want to do a drive-by?"

"Um, yes."

"Then come by twenty-eight Frances Avenue anytime. It's sitting in the driveway, and it's yellow. You can't miss it."

"Okay."

Another long "o-kaaaaaaay," even cuter and sassier than before.

"When is it convenient for you?"

I blink. "When is *what* convenient for me?"

"For, uh, for me to come by to see the car?"

For a minute there, I thought she meant something else, something full of dramatic, guilty pleasures. "Oh, anytime is convenient. Just not now." I'm in the middle of a long story with Mr. Bear, my story critic, and we can't be interrupted.

"Oh, I couldn't possibly come by this evening. How about tomorrow, say, around ten?"

Tomorrow is . . . Sunday. I should be going to church. I've been saying, "I should be going to church," for the last six months. I wonder if they miss me at First Baptist . . . or if they even know I'm not there. Oh, I'm sure they do. We were members, and Stevie was in the children's choir—

"Hello?"

"Okay." I say it short like "okay" is supposed to be said.

"And if I like what I see, can I take a test-drive?"

"Sure." Now go away.

"See you tomorrow. Bye."

Click.

I return to Mr. Bear and stare him down.

He wins. Note to self: never have a staring match with a stuffed animal.

"Now where was I? Oh yeah. Let's say that Arthur is a man like me."

Mr. Bear doesn't look too sure. He's such a skeptic sometimes.

"I'm normal. Most of the time. I think. But what really is normal anyway?"

Mr. Bear looks bored.

"Okay, okay, no philosophy tonight, I promise." I go to the window and see what's left of the snowman. The sun, that yellow sun, is so cruel sometimes. My snowman has become a watery gray amoeba with brick feet. "Mr. Bear, you're being very tight-lipped tonight. You need to learn to communicate better. So, tell me, how are we going to get these two together? How are they going to meet?"

He could be selling her a car.

I squint at Mr. Bear. How'd he do that without his lips moving? Or do bears even have lips? They have jowls, don't they?

"Okay, he could be selling her a car." I pause to collect what few thoughts I can catch. They're running away so fast tonight. "But it's not just any car, oh no. It's his dead wife's car, and . . . he tells her that right up front. He says, 'Before you go any further there, Di, there's something you should know. This is my dead wife's car.'"

Mr. Bear seems to look away. I can't blame him. This is all so painful for him.

"'That's right,' I'll tell her, 'this is my dead wife's car, and as you can see, it's a car to die for, Di.'"

You don't want to sell that car.

"No, I don't, Mr. Bear, but I have to. It's far too yellow for this neighborhood."

I flop onto the bed, my head clearing some. Sadness will do that, you know. "Okay, uh, seriously now, we're going to take a sad, divorced man . . . Yes, a sad *divorced* man who really didn't want to be divorced at all, a man who still loves his wife and son dearly, and they're still alive, and . . . and we'll hook him up with an equally sad and lonely woman named Di at . . . a church?"

Mr. Bear seems to shrug.

"No, that's been done before. How about a restaurant?"

Mr. Bear seems to roll his one good eye.

"You're right. That's been done before, too." I turn to Mr. Bear. "Well, you've been far too quiet all this time. I want to know what you think. Where can we have them meet?"

Mr. Bear only looks out the window.

"Outside? You want them to meet outside? In this weather?" I laugh. "You bears are all alike. Humans are fur challenged—I keep telling you that!"

Mr. Bear still stares out the window.

"I didn't mean to hurt your feelings." I follow his line of sight out the window and see two trees. "You want them to meet in some trees? Like Tarzan and Jane?"

Mr. Bear doesn't laugh. He has no sense of humor. It's probably why they had him stuffed.

"Okay, you're being stubborn, but I can see by your eye that you're on to something. Okay, trees, trees, trees . . . are used to make paper." I turn to Mr. Bear. "A-ha! You want them to meet at a newspaper stand!"

Mr. Bear doesn't bat his eye.

"She might not have the correct change—those stands don't give any change, you know—and he might have an extra quarter and a dime. . . ."

Did Mr. Bear just blink?

"I'm warmer, though. I can feel it from the softening of your eye. Let's see . . ." I pace the room. "Paper, paper, paper . . . is used to make . . . toilet paper. You want them to meet in the bathroom?"

Mr. Bear doesn't seem amused.

"My editor would find *that* dramatic. She'd say it was kinky-cool-*chic* or some other screwy New York phrase." I lie back on a pillow. "She'd probably even like this conversation we're having. A drunk man having a conversation with a stuffed animal. It would be *très chic*." I open my eyes, and the room spins to the left. "Just think of all the cameras they'd need to film this little scene, all those angles. You'd get all the close-ups, Mr. Bear."

The phone rings, and it's ringing somewhere close by. Did I bring it in here? I see it behind Mr. Bear on the dresser. I reach for it, but it doesn't fly through the air to me. It always works in those *Star Wars* movies. I get up, stumble once, and take the phone.

"Jack's Party Mart, Jack speaking."

"Mr. Jack . . . Browner?"

Close enough. This man has a strange accent. Is he even American? "Yes."

"Mees-ter Browner, I eem call-ing from Ci-ti-corp in Sout *Da*-ko-tuh. How are you today?"

I look at the Caller ID. It's an 866 number. Is this how they talk in South Dakota?

"Mees-ter Browner?"

"Yes?"

"We would like to offer you a spee-ci-ul plan in case you are ever dis-*ah*-bulled and cannot pay your bill."

Dis-*ah*-bulled? "Are you really calling from South Dakota?"

"No, I eem call-ing from Sout *Da*-ko-tuh."

"It's Sou*th* Da-*ko*-ta."

"That's what I said."

I roll my eyes at Mr. Bear. He understands. "No, you said Sou*t Da*-ko-tuh."

A slight pause. "Dis plan gives you peace of mind should you ever become dis-*ah*-bulled, and it only costs twenty-nine ninety-nine a mont."

"A mont!" I repeat, with a giggle. He got the money amount just fine. "I eem not inter-*est*-ed. I eem already dis-*ah*-bulled, and I don't have a balance on my Visa anyway." I don't even know where my Visa is. Probably hiding out with the fingernail clippers I couldn't find earlier today.

I hear a few pages turning. I know he's reading from a script.

"Dis plan—"

"I know, I know, it gives me peace of mind. Like I said, I eem not inter-*est*-ed, so please don't call me again. Good-bye."

I turn off the phone and the ringer.

"Now, where were we?" I stand in front of Mr. Bear. "We're going to have Arthur and Di meet . . . in . . . a . . . bookstore and that's final."

Mr. Bear's eye seems to brighten.

I sit on the edge of the bunk bed. "Yes. They . . . both like to read, so they meet in a bookstore, but not one of those new megabookstores with a billion books, because their workers don't know where any of their books are! No, it has to be a small bookstore, a dusty bookstore, an intimate bookstore where the owners give recommendations of books they've actually read and know where every single book is."

Mr. Bear is unmoved.

"You're right, you're right. If Arthur gets the recommendation from the bookstore owner, Di can't— Wait a minute. Di either owns or works at the bookstore." I jump up and shake Mr. Bear's paw. "You're brilliant!" I pace the room again. "Okay, so Arthur asks Di to recommend a book, just like Diane did today, and Arthur follows her to the right shelf. He can comment on her beauty here, of course, you know, watching her walk, filling his head with all sorts of nasty thoughts, the perfect place for a guilty pleasure or two. You know, 'nice ass,' or something like that. And when she hands him that special book, their eyes will meet, and she won't be able to let go of the book right away, which Arthur will take as a sign that she's interested in him, only it's really because he has a green booger dangling from his left nos-tril." I smile at Mr. Bear. "But, of course, Arthur doesn't know what to do because he hasn't dated anyone but his wife in what seems like forever, and he still loves his wife, and it's awkward for both of them, and—"

Is Mr. Bear asleep? Maybe he's just holding his breath. He's good at that.

I shake my head. "You're right, you're right. It's too much like that movie with Tom Hanks and Meg Ryan." I sit again. "The bookstore is out." I look at the bottom of the top bunk. "But . . . maybe . . . the library . . . is in."

Where's my steno pad? I run to the kitchen, can't find a steno pad, and end up writing on the back of today's Food Lion receipt:

D. works in library; A. goes to library to return over-due books; likes what he sees; decides to research her for his next novel; tells her he's researching

Researching what? Black history? No. Too obvious. His own history? A white *Roots*? Too . . . bizarre. Maybe he's just researching a book on local history for now. Maybe Di is a longtime resident who knows everything about Roanoke.

Tells her he's researching local history. D. a long-time resident who . . .

Who what? She has to be black, and I know so few black women. I am so out of touch with black women. Should I interview Diane? No, that would be pushy. I can just observe her, see what she does, talk to her every now and then, maybe use some of the conversations we have in the novel. But, is there anything romantic about a library? So many walls of books, so many dark corners, so many places where no one ever looks at books. But, it can be quiet with lots of lights, yet . . . it's also an anal place with too much organization. And if Arthur is flaky like me, she has to have a button-down mind. But they both have to be normal, average people—no "beautiful people" this time—who are simple, down-to-earth, pragmatic, honest, and sincere.

But who would believe that scenario?

I look down at my notes and lamely finish with:

. . . who helps him

It's a start anyway.
Where have you been?
Your buzz wore off.
Oh.
And it is a good start.
Maybe that's all I need.
True, but what does Di help Arthur do?
Start over.
And find love again.
Yeah. That would be nice.

15

Diane

After making myself a strong cup of coffee, I relax on the sofa and pick up *Wishful Thinking*. Maybe it will get better, most likely it won't, but at least I'll have what's left of my Saturday evening to give it and all the others fifty pages of my time.

3: Dan

Why did I wave? What possible reason could I have had to wave at a complete stranger? I never quite know what to do with my hands. Private Sidney didn't seem to mind, but that was over ten years ago when I was in my sexual prime. Cat Eyes didn't wave back, and I can't blame her. It must have been hard for her to wave and hold onto her umbrella at the same time, and besides, she doesn't know me from Adam. I hope she doesn't think I'm stalking her.

And she drives a Beamer? That girl must be paid. Classy, paid, and smoking hot.

And out of my league completely.

You got that right. If *you* can't see the two of you getting together and *I* can't see the two of you getting together, *no one* can.

But at least she smiled. I think. More of a squinty smirk than a smile. Maybe she doesn't like Eric B. and Rakim. Maybe she has issues with Subarus. Maybe— Maybe she thinks I'm stalking her.

She thinks you're stalking her, Dan. First off, you're white. That's an obvious clue. Second, you're being rude and are gritting on her.

I ought to be going. I guess it's off to my favorite restaurant, the Williamson Road Pancake House, a retro diner complete with Formica counter and taped-up stools that still spin. I need to drown my sorrows in a slice of apple pie covered with cheddar cheese. I can always get the "Norm" treatment there. Gladys will greet me at the door by name, seat me in my favorite booth looking out on the taillights and headlights of Williamson Road, and bring me hot tea with lemon. Gladys will ask, "Where's your girl, Danny?" I'll say something like, "You're my girl, Gladys." She'll say, "Oh, go on," then I'll finish with, "I wish you were sixty years younger, Gladys." Then I'll pretend to read the menu, pretend to agonize over my decision, eat my pie, flirt with Gladys, and leave a two-dollar tip for a two-dollar check.

So, Dan has a nice streak with old ladies. I like that. As long as it doesn't progress into something kinky with Gladys.

*On second thought, I don't want to hit on an octo-
genarian tonight. It doesn't seem fitting somehow.*

And I don't have four dollars to my name.

*So, I go home to my gray squat apartment building
(also known as "the Cube"), right across the street
from the pancake house, and park next to the big,
green Dumpster. Tonight it's filled to overflowing, and
because of Election Day tomorrow, the city won't get
to it until Wednesday. That will give Cat Stevens, my
cat, more time to eat garbage.*

*Cat Stevens really isn't my cat. She's just a huge
black and white tabby with Groucho Marx eyebrows
who just happens to live in the alley outside my windows. When I first moved in, I threw some frozen leftovers into the alley and heard a nasty cat snarl. That's
how Cat Stevens and I met. All it took was a frozen
chunk of potato salad. I still don't know why I put the
potato salad in the freezer. I found my car keys in an
ice cube tray once, even found my driver's license in
the crisper. Yeah, that Kelvinator is a vacuum, a black
hole for all the things I can't find.*

Okay, you're overdoing the clueless part, D. J. Browning.
Let's speed this up.

*But getting back to Cat Stevens. The best thing
about her is that she's not picky. She loves my cooking.*

I have, however, stopped freezing the leftovers.

*I leave the Subaru and head up the sidewalk to the
lower entrance of the Cube as the rain subsides. I used
to hang out on the porch in front of the entrance with
the old super, Mr. Reardon. The man drank whiskey,
smoked unfiltered Camels all day long, and still kept
his wits about him as he sat on an overturned milk
crate. He never said anything worth remembering, but*

it was always nice to have someone to speak to at the end of a long day taming nine- and ten-year-olds. A shame he died, and it wasn't even lung or liver cancer. A city bus hit him while he was on his way to get some smokes. His milk crate now holds some of my old records, my little TV on top—my shrine to Mr. Reardon.

The neighborhood around the Cube has a long and storied past but not much of a future. Davis Pizza used to crank out strange pizzas, even using peanut butter as a topping, but not many people ever went in there, because the weekly hotel next door became, well, a whorehouse. Young (and I use that term as loosely as they behave) ladies hang out behind the sliding glass doors of the hotel. Kind of reminds me of what I saw in the red-light district in Amsterdam, though those Dutch women were much hotter. I don't know how many times I've whistled "How Much Is That Doggie in the Window" as I've passed by that hotel on the way to Ralph's One-Stop to pay too much for beer.

I'm beginning to recognize these places. That nice-looking hotel on Williamson Road is a whorehouse? Here in Roanoke, Virginia, where the Bible Belt is always tightened to the very last hole? I'm finding this hard to believe, too.

The tattoo parlor that used to be next to Davis Pizza was once a booming business, as was America's Cash Express, a check-cashing place. I'll bet they were in business together. So many teenaged girls went first to the check-cashing place then on to the tattoo parlor to get pierced somewhere new: eyebrows, belly buttons, noses, and I'm sure even other more tender places. I've never understood that. Paying someone to give you pain.

You wouldn't understand because you're a man, and not much of one at that.

Wait a minute. I just paid for Beth's meal. I've been pierced, too.

And no woman gets to see my tattoo until at least the sixth date. Actually, it's more of a brand than a tattoo, forever preserved on my ass, courtesy of the delightful Private Sidney and her Golden Hot curling iron. "Turn around," Sidney had said. Being naïve and dumb, I had turned around. And that shit had hurt. Twice she got me before I could wrestle that curling iron away. It's faded some, but it still looks like an X on my left cheek. I'm a white boy with an X on my ass.

Charming. I'll bet your doctor tells everyone about your behind.

I tiptoe down the linoleum-floored hallway, open the door to apartment #2, and enter as quietly as possible. As soon as I close the door with the tiniest little click, the door of the apartment across the hall slams opens, and I hear a knock. Stella must sit by that peephole all day. She needs to get cable or something.

"Mister?" Knock-knock. "Mister, have you seen my husband?"

"No," I say through the door. I don't look through my peephole at Stella's face anymore. Very large pores and acne scars. Bags under her eyes. And she's barely twenty. At least she didn't bring her colicky baby, Tito Jr., this time.

"You sure?"

"Yes."

"Okay."

I look down at the two-by-fours I've had to pound into my door on the inside, praying that they'll hold

*when her equally young husband, Tito, comes home
from his drunk and tries to kick in the wrong door,
looking for his Stella. It is one strange relationship.
She looks for him all day, but when he comes home,
she won't open the door. And since Tito has no sense of
direction and obviously can't discern a number two
from a number three when he's tanked, he kicks in my
door, shouting, "I loves ya, baby! Ya know I loves ya,
baby!"*

My neighbors across the hall: the happy couple.

And the author is going to bring Ty into this madhouse?
I don't think so!

*I haven't seen the man in #1 since he moved in, but
I know he likes to order pizza. I trip over empty boxes
that he just throws out into the hallway instead of carrying them to the Dumpster. Once I figured out that he
never left his apartment—or ran much water for that
matter, which is kind of gross—I took it upon myself to
take out his trash.*

My other neighbor: the unbathed garbage giver.

*I look at the ceiling and hear my upstairs neighbors
sloshing around in the tub again. Very thin walls and
floors in the Cube. They can't have much body hair
left, the amount of time they spend squeaking around
up there, and I'll bet they never have to scrub the tub.
One day I came home and found that a rectangle from
my suspended ceiling had fallen to the floor, narrowly
missing my La-Z-Boy, and a large puddle of water on
my shiny gray carpet. I had then looked up through the
ceiling into the eyes of one of the swimmers, who in-
troduced himself as "Rob."*

"You okay down there?" Rob had asked.

*"Uh, yeah," I had said, as if being able to look
through your own ceiling into the eyes of a man who*

*humped his woman in a tub above your living room
was a normal occurrence.*

You have *got* to be kidding. This kind of thing doesn't
happen! This is getting to be like a TV sitcom.

> *"I'll have this thing fixed and caulked in no time,"
> he had said.*
> *You or your woman? I had thought at the time.*
> *My upstairs neighbors: tub humpers.*

This is so tasteless. Why would anyone buy this nonsense?

> *When I first moved in, I decorated as cheaply as
> possible, focusing first on my books. I used cinder blocks
> and two-by-fours for shelving, and over the past few
> years, I've added quite a few more levels. One day
> soon they'll touch the ceiling. I don't know how many
> books I own, but it has to number in the thousands.
> And unlike some people, I've read them all, some more
> than once. I don't have them organized or anything
> anal like that. I just put them where they fit, and from
> the looks of things, I'll need to get more cinder blocks
> in time for the holidays. For whatever reason, my fam-
> ily thinks that as a teacher I need more books to read.
> And because they're all on the West Coast, and because
> they're cheaper than me, they mail me books—book rate,
> of course.*

Finally, Dan has something I can identify with. He reads
and collects books, but being organized doesn't make a person anal. *My* books are where they're supposed to be.

> *Other than the La-Z-Boy, the books, a stereo with a
> turntable, a collection of records from when rap was*

young and contained no "bee-otches," and a dusty thirteen-inch TV complete with rabbit ears antenna, there's only an oak coatrack and a futon in the main room. No reason to be in here tonight. I have no one to squint at the TV with me, no one to help me warm up the futon.

Don't try to make me like you, Dan Pace. So, you're lonely. Big deal. Get over yourself.

I turn off the light to the main room and enter my kitchen/office. Instead of a kitchen table, I eat all my meals on an old cherry secretary, an antique with a drop-down desk. Not many women have had the privilege of eating on an authentic, century-old cherry secretary. It barely has room for a plate and a glass, and I have to eat the runny foods like Jell-O, mixed veggies, or anything with gravy first or the juices will run off the plate.

I've been planning to level it, but not tonight. Nothing is on the level tonight.

I may have to write a special letter to the publisher for even putting this crap—and it *is* crap—out there. No one on earth could live like this!

The sink holds one spoon, one knife, one fork, and one chipped china plate—as it should. Okay, it only holds those because they're all I own. No sense in investing in more than I need, and I save a mint on dish liquid. I have one pot, one pan, and one dish towel, too. I am an army of one in the kitchen.

I have but one plant, a Ma Plub tree, which sits in the corner in a rattan basket next to the garbage can. It was a gift from Jewel over two years ago, and she told me that the Ma Plub tree has medicinal proper-

ties. "My mother's people"—the Thai—"use it to treat diarrhea and stop bleeding." How nice. I've been hoping that the tree would die a slow, horrible death. I don't water it, haven't replanted it, and haven't done anything but curse at it. I even keep the kitchen window blind down at all times, yet there it is, flourishing, dropping leaves and small white flowers occasionally, sprouting fruit that I hurl at the alley wall. I'd offer it to Cat Stevens, but I don't think she's a vegetarian. I just don't want to get rid of it in case Jewel should come back. That would be the first thing she'd notice. I know she's not coming back, but if she did, I'd take her back in a second, even regive her the ring she threw at me.

After I cussed her out for giving it back in the first place, of course.

The Kelvinator rattles on as I turn off the kitchen light and enter my bedroom, tossing my coat onto the king-sized bed. I don't have mirrors on the headboard. I have more class than that. But because the room is so small, I have to edge around the bed to get to the walk-in closet and bathroom. And it isn't as if I've been very busy on that bed. Yet, whenever a woman sees it for the first time, she automatically assumes that I'm some sort of a Rico Suave Don Juan out for a piece.

If a woman can stand, first, going to the Cube; second, walking down that nasty hallway; third, seeing your broken-down front door; fourth, marveling at your crummy book collection on cinder blocks; fifth, *not* laughing at your bachelor's kitchen—if she can stand all that, she deserves you, Dan Pace.

"So I'm an active sleeper," I tell them, but they don't buy it.

And neither do I, and after my review, neither (I hope) will a lot of people.

I tried to sleep in a single bed when I first moved in, but I kept falling out. Living in a tent in Saudi messed me up that way. I need space when I sleep.

After peeling down to my underwear and sliding into bed, I pick up my well-thumbed copy of the collected works of William Shakespeare, hold it out in front of me, and drop it into my lap. It opens to Act I, scene five of Twelfth Night. *A romantic comedy. How fitting. I've been using Willie's writing as a kind of horoscope ever since I read* A Tree Grows in Brooklyn *when I was a kid. I close my eyes and play "eeny-meeny-miney-mo" with the pages, ending on the right. I scan down the page looking for anything remotely relevant to my day.*

And I get an eyeful.

In this scene, Olivia, a countess, is unveiling her face to Viola, a young lady posing as a young man. Willie's on tonight. A countess and a she-boy. Shakespeare and his cross-dressers. Anyway, Viola the she-boy describes Olivia's face as "beauty truly blent" yet says the countess is "the cruell'st she alive."

The cruelest "she" alive, her beauty truly blended. Here's Jewel Mekla Manowong once again, that ungodly mixture of Thai and black, that marriage of Southeast Asian and African that made her the most exquisite, most exotic woman I've ever known. Her mother named her Mekla after a Thai goddess who used a crystal ball to blind Ramasura, her almost lover. I guess that makes me Ramasura the Second. Mekla soon became "Jewel" once she and her mother moved to Cleveland without her father, a young American soldier who left Thailand in the early seventies without even knowing he had a daughter.

I keep reading and see the countess listing her fea-
tures: "two lips, indifferent red . . . two grey eyes . . ."

Jewel's eyes weren't gray. They were so dark a blue
they were almost purple. Maybe Willie is referring to
Cat Eyes. Her eyes were light, but were they gray? I
should have stared longer.

The word "rudeness" jumps out at me from Viola's
lips: "The rudeness that hath appeared in me have I
learned from my entertainment. What I am, and what I
would, are as secret as maidenhead; to your ears, di-
vinity, to any other's, profanation."

Yeah, I was kind of rude, staring at Cat Eyes' legs
like that. She didn't seem to mind; I mean, she nodded
in my general direction, right?

No. You are mistaken. Though I kind of like an intelligent, well-read man, this man is too freaky and too flaky for
me. Using Shakespearean plays as a horoscope? Give me a
break!

I reread the page and realize that Willie's nailed me
again. Here's Jewel, Beth the she-boy, and Cat Eyes
staring up at me from a 400-year-old play. William
Shakespeare was a clairvoyant.

I shut the book and turn out the light, juggling three
women in my mind, none of whom I have an ice-cream
sandwich's chance in hell of ever getting with. Jewel's
gone, end of story. When a woman says, "Don't call or
write to me or try to contact me ever," and throws an
engagement ring at you, she means it. Beth's gone,
too, but she was gone long before I met her. When a
woman wears flannel shirts and boots and hangs out
at Hooters, she means business, and it doesn't involve
men. And Cat Eyes—I guess she's long gone as well.
As if she'd ever think of even speaking to me after I

stared so long and hard at her legs, nodded at her, and waved at her.

   I hear Cat Stevens howling away beside my bedroom window.

   "I know what you mean, girl," I whisper. "I know what you mean."

   And a few seconds later, I hear the sounds of wood splintering in my living room, a Hispanic voice shouting, "Stella, ya know I loves ya, baby!"

   The next howl I hear is my own.

Instead of reading Ty's next installment, I go to my library and get out my thesaurus. I look up "ridiculous" and find "ludicrous, preposterous, absurd, silly, nonsensical, farcical, foolish, daft, strange, illogical, meaningless, bizarre, incongruous, outrageous, outlandish, unreasonable, unbelievable, laughable." I circle the words with the most negative connotations: "preposterous," "foolish," "illogical," "meaningless," and "laughable."

I think I've found all the words for my first sentence of this travesty of a novel.

I also write down "travesty."

Time to give Ty her last chance to save this novel.

4: Ty
Ooh, shoot, these contacts are driving me crazy.

I knew it! Ty is fake, too. D. J. Browning, you're making this too easy to hate!

   I can't wait to get home and take them out. I just can't believe I left my rewetting drops at home, knowing good and well that I'm going to a bar where the cigarette smoke clouds are heavier than the ones outside dropping rain by the bucketsful. The clouds out-

side are not the only things dropping rain. My right eye is so irritated it's raining buckets of tears, thus the heavy foot on the gas pedal. I normally try to be extra careful driving in the rain, but right now, I'm having an eye crisis.

With my right eye closed and tearing, I make a sharp left onto Summit Hills Lane. I drive about another hundred feet and make a right into my driveway, hop out of the Beamer, hit the alarm, and race up to the front door of my town home, being careful to keep my mouth closed so I don't drop or swallow the contact lens that I rubbed out of my eye on the way home.

After slamming the front door closed, tossing my purse on the sofa, and kicking off my shoes, I hit the light switch on the wall and run upstairs to the bathroom. I squirt some solution into the contact lens case and put the lens from my mouth into the solution first. After removing the left lens from my eye and placing it into the solution, I throw myself on my queen-sized bed, close my eyes, and cover them with a cool, damp washcloth from the bathroom. It's ironic that I paid four grand to have Lasik eye surgery to get perfect vision and to get rid of the hassle of contacts, yet I still wear them. No, it's not that the surgery was a bust. I just want to have a different eye color to match my mood and sometimes my outfits. I wonder how I would look with blue eyes. Probably like a damn fool.

But that guy at Hooters wears them well. Dan has some of the bluest eyes I have ever seen. They are a Pacific blue, just beautiful. They had to have been contacts. So at least he has good taste in eye color, but that outfit he was wearing wasn't hitting on anything. I mean, the flannel shirt he had on, I wouldn't let my scarecrow wear that out for Halloween. It was red, which clashed with his beautiful blues, and the stripes, *checks, or whatever you want to call them, were black, white, and yellow. The black corduroys he wore were a little too faded and badly worn. I could see the wallet outline in his back pocket, and from the looks of his knees, he must spend a lot of time on them, hopefully begging and praying that the fashion police will come and put him out of his misery. And, of course, everything he wore was in dire need of an iron. I chuckle a little, thinking about what a mess he was.*

Then I frown because I can't believe I'm at home thinking about this man.

I can't believe it either. Dan is a mistake in so many ways, and anyone reading this book is making a mistake. I know I'm supposed to suspend my disbelief, but there are limits. This book is an insult to anyone's intelligence.

I add "insult to intelligence" to my list of synonyms for "ridiculous."

Speaking of man, I notice the light on my Caller ID unit is flashing, which probably means that Charles has called. I check the box and notice that both he and Kevin have called. I also see that there is a message waiting. I hit the speaker button on the phone base and say, "Check messages," and the phone dials my voice-mail service.

"Welcome to Verizon's voice-messaging service. Please enter your pass—"

I interrupt by putting in my pass code.

"Two new messages—"

I interrupt again by pressing one to listen to my messages. "First new message, today, eight-fifteen P.M. . . . Hi, Aunt Ty, it's me, Kendra, and I made the AB honor roll at school. I even got an A in Mr. Pace's class! When are you gonna come take me shopping

again? I love you. Bye." My niece and her Mr. Pace.
The only thing she says about school is Mr. Pace this
or Mr. Pace that.

No . . . way. Dan Pace? This is how they're going to
meet? As if this would *ever* happen in real life! The author
needs a reality check. I mean, it's almost like having two
people meet in a library to start some romance!

It *never* happens!

Wait. Didn't Uri and Lara meet by chance in a library in
Dr. Zhivago? Oh, and didn't Streisand and Redford meet in
a library in *The Way We Were*? Hmm. I mean, I guess it
works for white folks. The only black librarian I've ever
seen in a movie was in that *Men of Honor* flick I saw a few
years ago. And she was only part-time, helping Cuba
Gooding pass his tests. Only in the movies. That kind of
stuff would never happen for me.

And speaking of movies, why is it that librarians are
stereotyped so damn much on the big screen? We're all supposed to be elderly with our hair in a bun and our glasses on
tight, mean, intelligent, single, quiet, neurotic keepers of the
holy Dewey Decimal System with a "hush" ready to fly out
of our mouths at a moment's notice. And we're all supposed
to be lonely, too. I am *not* lonely, because I am *not* looking
for a man.

Just look at *It's a Wonderful Life*. Jimmy Stewart gets the
gift of never existing, and what happens to his sweetheart,
Mary? She turns into a shy spinster with a bun who works at
a library! And don't get me started on Marian the Librarian
from *Music Man*! Who stamps books and sings while she
does it? And not all librarians are intelligent at all. Take
Sleeping with the Enemy and that Julia Roberts, as if anyone
like her would ever work in the stacks. She intelligently
fakes her own death except for that ring in the toilet, but
when she takes on her new identity, she goes back to work-

ing in a library, making it easy for her psychopathic husband to find her!

And what's up with these movies that have scenes in libraries with no library staff visible? The main characters find the information they need the very *first* time without any help! Amazing! I wish every kid were like Harry Potter. He never needs *any* help when he's in a library.

And why am I stressing over this so much? I know, it does no good to fuss over what *Hollyweird* puts out. I know that I'm not a prim and introverted librarian, and that's all that matters. And I'm not all "anticensorship," like some of those movie librarians. I believe some things are meant for anyone to read. That's why I review books before they get out to offend and muddy the minds of the reading public.

Which is why I've just about had it with *Wishful Thinking*. It was "wishful thinking" on D. J. Browning's part to think anyone would buy this book. Hmm. That sounds like either the first or last sentence of my review. I had better read some more, you know, to get more fuel for the flames I'll be writing later:

> *"To repeat . . ." I press three to erase the message. "Next message, today, nine-thirty P.M. . . . Hey, baby, give me a call when you get in." Click. It's just like him. "Give me a call," he says. Put this all on me. After pressing three, I grab the cordless phone and dial Kevin's phone number. Charles can wait.*
>
> *"Hey Kevin, it's Ty," I say, as I walk downstairs to set the dead bolt and place the chain on the door.*
>
> *"Hey little sister, what's up? I was just about to call you."*
>
> *"Kendra called me asking when I can take her shopping. Do you all have plans this weekend?"*
>
> *"No, as a matter of fact, we don't. Her mother called to say she won't be able to get her this weekend."*

Figures. "Is Kim all right?"

"Yeah, she just has a business meeting out of town this weekend."

As usual. She's probably spending the weekend shacked up with some guy. "Okay, I'll pick her up around nine on Saturday."

"That's cool. I'll let her know. I also need you to do me a favor. I have a conference scheduled for tomorrow at six-fifteen with Kendra's teacher. I was just told today that I have a mandatory sales meeting tomorrow when I get off and . . ."

"So you need me to go to the conference for you tomorrow."

Uh-huh. What a coincidence.

"If you would."

"Okay, I'll do that, but you owe me one. Bye, Kevin."

Ah, man, I really don't feel like talking to Charles tonight. I'm tired, and I just want to go to bed. I have to work tomorrow. But I know if I don't call, he'll give me nothing but attitude when we finally do speak. Shit, shit, shit. Hey, I know—I'll just leave him a T-mail, so I dial my voice-mail number and skip through the prompts.

"Hi, Charles, it's me." *And he'd better know who* "me" *is.* "I just want to let you know I got your message"—*even though it was short and a tad rude—* "and I'll talk to you tomorrow. I don't want to disturb your sleep. Bye." *Whew. That's done. After snatching my Crips do-rag from the dresser, I start the water running in the tub, adding some Bath & Body cucumber-melon-scented bubble bath. After lighting the honeydew melon candles, I turn the radio to WQMG's Quiet Storm.*

I smile. I do the same thing sometimes. And here I was all fired up to torch this book. Okay, just a little more:

> *I tie my hair up and slide underneath the bubbles, closing my eyes to shut out everything and everybody. But, unfortunately, the next day's events slowly creep into my mind. After relaxing for half an hour, I get out, put on my black satin and chiffon baby doll, and head to the bedroom. On the way, I stop to check my contacts, making sure they are taking back their original shape, and they are, thank goodness. Colored contacts are not cheap. I gently yank the corner of the plum comforter back, sending the three accent pillows flying through the air. I tug slightly on the crisp lilac sheets and fall into the bed. I close my eyes and imagine how I would look with blue eyes.*
>
> *I fall asleep with the image of Dan's beautiful blues imprinted on my brain.*

Riiiiiight. This is all so wrong! Why would she be thinking about Dan at all? She has Charles. She said she had a thing for blue eyes, but is a "thing" enough to keep her dreaming at night about Dan?

Trifling.

I throw a look at *The Quiet Game, P&Q,* and *Thicker Than Blood*, but I shake my head. Three stinkers and a maybe. *Thicker Than Blood* has kept my interest best, but it's still trifling at times. When am I going to get to write another five-star review and have my name travel the world? I might as well keep going with *Wishful Thinking*. I have nothing better to do.

I flip through about twenty pages until I see:

> *I have just enough time to vote at Breckinridge Middle School, so I roll into the parking lot, park next to a Verizon van, pop my umbrella, walk past a black*

*man in a hard hat carrying a roll of phone wire, and
enter the gym.*

*It's not very crowded, and after showing ID, I stand
in the voting booth wondering which cookie-cutter
politician to vote for. Decisions, decisions. Warner?
Who are the other two? Okay, Warner. And this guy's
running unopposed? Why put him on the ballot, then?
Just give him the job. On to the bond issues . . . Blah
blah blah court system. Okay, I'll vote yes. Anything to
clean up that mess. Blah-ditty-blah blah parks. Cool.
Blah blah education blah-ditty-blah $900 million! I
wish I could vote yes twice! Blah blah blah-ditty-blah
blah— Is this written in English? What is this bond
issue asking me? I vote "no" just because it's poorly
written. Now what have I just done? Gee, I've put Virginia into even greater debt. After flushing my votes, I
get my "I Voted" sticker and rush out the gym doors,
nearly colliding with the Verizon technician who is
carrying even more phone wire.*

"Sorry," I say, and I check out his face.

Only it's not a him. It's a her.

Hello, Cat Eyes.

They literally *bump* into each other?
They *literally* bump into each other.
I shake my head. What kind of foolishness is this?

*"Uh, let me get that door for you," I say, and I leap
toward the door, pulling it back with force.*

*"Thanks," she says, walking by me sideways, her
back to me. I catch a whiff of some perfume or another
and wonder how all her hair fit up under that helmet.*

*She's inside now. Say something before she gets
away, Dan! "Uh, you here to put in new phone lines?"*

That was so lame.

Yes, it was. Sic him, Ty, sic him.

8: Ty

Oh, he's as smooth as those wrinkled clothes he's wearing. Here to put in new phone lines? No, I always wear a tool belt and walk around carrying twenty pounds of phone wire. Here's your "Stupid" sign. What do you think I'm carrying all this line in for?

"No. Actually, I'm just redoing the lines in the office today."

"Oh," he says. "All by yourself?"

What, you think a woman can't do this shit?

"Wow."

Wow? I do not respond to white men saying "wow," especially if they don't have the decency to iron their clothes.

"Uh, makes sense, being kind of a day off for teachers and everything, huh?"

I don't normally respond to "huh" either, but he did hold the door for me. "Not for me."

He looks at the line wrapped around my shoulder. "Oh, yeah, right. I, uh, had heard they were changing the lines in the schools. I'm over at Monterey."

Monterey Elementary? As what? I'll bet he's a gym teacher for the slow kids on the short bus. "You teach there?"

He smiles. What's wrong with that tooth? Looks almost vampire-like. Get that fang capped!

"Yeah, I teach fourth-grade social studies."

Not a gym teacher? He has sense and a real degree? "You know Kendra Clarke?"

He blinks. "Yes. I teach her."

I blink. So this is the amazing Mr. Pace I've heard so much about. Dan Pace. I thought he was black the way Kendra carried on about him, but I have a lot to teach that child. You can't have a crush on a man who wears corduroys! "Oh" *is all I can think to say.*

"Are you coming for a conference today, Mrs. Clarke?"

He thinks I'm Kendra's mama. Which, I guess, I kind of am, since Kendra's mama is no good, but for him to assume that I'm anybody's mama is wrong. But maybe he's being tricky, trying to get my name by being wrong. I'll keep him wondering. "I hadn't planned on it, Mr. Pace." *Just establishing my distance, Mr. Dan.* "But it depends on if I can finish this job in time or not." *Hint. Get to pacing, Mr. Pace. I've got work to do.*

"Oh, yeah, right." *He nods again. I'm not nodding back.* "Well, I hope to see you there."

"I'll try," *is all I say, knowing good and well I will be there. I have to see what Kendra is so hyped up about. I mean every time I ask her about school, it's Mr. Pace said this or Mr. Pace did that. I can definitely see why she has a crush on him. He is nice to look at. But I also want to make sure he isn't some kind of perv, leading little girls on.*

He *is a perv, Ty! Open your damn cat's eyes!*

After completing the job at the school, I take a short lunch break to go vote and have a quick sandwich. I finish up my workday with two jobs in northeast Roanoke. At four-thirty, I am in my Beamer and on my way home to get ready for the conference.

Do I want to turn the page and find out about this conference? Would anyone? I check my African monkey clock on the wall. It's almost midnight, and my eyes are tired. I flip a few more pages past some more nonsense to:

Before Nancy can curse me again, I see a slender, brown hand knocking on my door. A moment later, Mrs. "Cat Eyes" Clarke walks into the room as a lady should, her front preceding her back—which goes on and on and on. And she is dressed so sharp I'm afraid I'll be cut. She shows off that ass of hers with some form-fitting black slacks, and her breasts are popping out at me from behind a low-cut, V-neck, charcoal gray sweater. Most women seem to wear sweaters to hide something, but she definitely wants me to see her flat stomach. My hands start to sweat.

"Am I interrupting something?" she says.

10: Ty

That is the ugliest white woman I've ever seen. What the hell is that on her neck? Thing looks like an overgrown booger. And Dan is still wearing corduroys for a formal parent-teacher conference?

I may have to back up a bit. It's not every day you get to read about ugly white women with "overgrown boogers" on their necks in books. Maybe later.

"Hello, Mrs. Clarke," Dan says, motioning to a chair in front of his exceptionally clean desk. He has the ability to be neat? I'm almost impressed. "Won't you be seated?"

I will as soon as that chicken head leaves, and chicken head stomps out of the room. I check the seat for chicken feathers before I sit down.

"You must be very proud of your daughter, Mrs. Clarke. I think Kendra will one day be a lawyer."

Really? "What makes you say that, Mr. Pace?"

"Um, she has a sharp mind, and she's great with facts."

Don't give me that shit! If she were good with facts, she'd be acing all her classes. "Why is it that she's making As only in your class?"

He blinks. "I thought she was doing well in all of her classes."

"She's doing okay, but she's making As only in your class. Do you have an explanation for that?"

"Uh, no. Maybe she likes social studies. That's why I said she'd be a good lawyer. Most lawyers are history majors before going on to law school. Um, what was your major?"

Oh no he didn't just try to reverse the conversation. If I let him get started, he might be asking me for my sign or something. "I majored in business administration, but this isn't about me. I'm here for Kendra."

"As you should be." He opens a grade book and runs a finger across the page. "Kendra has turned in all her work on time, and her lowest grade is a B on any assignment." He looks up. "She's the most consistent student whom I have in any class." He smiles. "Does she take after you or your husband?"

"She takes after me."

"I can see that."

Is he flirting with me? His blue eyes haven't left mine. He's flirting. Time to burst his bubble. "So, Mr. Pace, tell me about this crush Kendra has on you."

He turns red. "What crush?"

"You haven't noticed?"

He sits back in his chair. "No. Has she said something to you?"

"No, but all I hear about is Mr. Pace. I was a schoolgirl once. I had a few crushes when I was her age, so I know all the signs." *And this man hasn't noticed any of them.* "I'm just letting you know."

"I'll, uh, try to be more attentive." He frowns. "So

you think that she's getting such high marks because she has a crush on me?"

"No, I know Kendra's intelligent. I just wanted you to be aware of this."

"Thank you for telling me."

Now what? "I can't say that I blame her for the crush." I lick my lips. "But you're one of the few male teachers she's ever had."

What the— She's actually going to say— And then she's going to— She *licks* her *lips?* I . . . have . . . just . . . about . . . *had it* with this book!

Did he just shake his head? And why did he just pull his hands off his desk? "Um, I was expecting Mr. Clarke this evening since he, uh, since he filled out the form."

"Well, he had to work late, and he asked if I would come instead."

He nods his head. "Um, do you or Mr. Clarke have any concerns about anything?"

"I don't, but I'm sure if he does, he'll contact you." I stand. "Thank you for your time, Mr. Pace."

He stands and extends his hand. What the hell am I supposed to do with that? I shake it, and, ooh, it's sweaty. What's he nervous about?

"It was a pleasure to meet you, Mrs. Clarke."

It was all right. "You, too, Mr. Pace."

He walks me to the door—such a gentleman—then stands in the doorway as I twist and sashay down the hall. I look back when I get to the end of the hallway. Yeah, he's still staring, and he isn't trying to hide it either. I like a bold man. I smile at him and give one more shake before I turn the corner, then head for home.

You little hoochie! And I had such respect for you earlier! I turn the page, though my fingers don't really want to.

11: Dan

Oh . . . damn.

I hope no other parents show up. My hands are dripping, my heart is pounding, and all it took was a long look at some serious ass shaking in the hallway.

So, Kendra has a crush on me. Right. I don't believe that for a second. It's Mrs. Clarke *who has the crush. Otherwise, why would she walk down the hall that way knowing I was hard staring? And she smiled at me before she left.*

I check the clock. If I didn't have to stay another two hours, I'd be running out to her car right now to see if she'd be willing to share that perfect smile of hers with me tonight all night. . . .

Pitiful, just pitiful. And this is supposed to pass for literature? I scan ahead because I am obviously a glutton for punishment and see that a storm knocks out Dan's power and phone service, and it just so happens that *Ty* is the one who comes to fix everything before they . . . yep, they're bumping uglies on the king-sized bed right here on page one hundred. Do I dare skip to the last page?

"I'll bet you never expected this," Dan says, snuggling closer.

"Not in a million years," I say. "Not in a million-trillion years."

I shut the book. What a waste of paper and ink! The publishing company should be ashamed of itself! And I'm ashamed of *myself* for giving this book so much of my attention!

But when I wake up tomorrow morning, I'm going to make D. J. Browning ashamed he or she ever even thought of writing this book.

After I attend church, of course.

I might, after all, *bump into* a man there.

16

Jack

I woke up with a splitting headache and found four empty bottles of Kris Kringle Eggnog on the floor of Stevie's room.

Your room.

Right.

Mr. Bear couldn't even look at me, but I don't blame him. I'll bet he doesn't talk to me all day.

I go to the office; boot up the laptop; and, using my mother's copious genealogical records, I delve into the abyss—Arthur Stephens Jefferson's ancestry. I know I can't start my novel with this, but I have to write something I know something about. If I want Arthur to be like me, he must come from somewhere familiar to me. I type in a chapter title:

The Genealogy of the Sponge

Why am I calling him the Sponge? I guess it kind of goes with the whole melting-pot idea.

You could use a few.

What?
Sponges.
What for?
Your bathroom, for one. The kitchen. The downstairs bathroom.
Later. I'm writing now.
Sure. Go ahead.

No history of the average white man could be complete without some humorous anecdote about crazy Uncle Phil or the insane Auntie Phyllis. But first, let's look at some general, random information gleaned from the endless genealogical findings of Arthur's mother.

Arthur Stephens Jefferson was named for seven consecutive generations of Arthurs on his father's side, none of whom used their full first names. They were "Art," "Arturo," or "Artie," and one even went by "King." But our Arthur is simply "Arthur" (though his wife calls him "Artie" when she's angry), not that he or his friends have no imaginations.

There is only so much you can do with "Arthur."

"Stephens" was a family name, some thirteen generations old, a name frequently used by its owner for "Steve" or "Stevie" or "Stephen/Steven." And "Jefferson" was an old, renowned American name, one associated with greatness— but it was only an association. His genealogically minded mother had pronounced Thomas Jefferson as Arthur's "fourth cousin twice removed."

To where? we might wonder, but we won't.

This sucks. Who gives a history lesson on his main character? Who would even care?

You care, or you wouldn't have written it.

I only wrote it to write *something*.

So, keep writing. Maybe it will smooth itself out. Go with the flow.

I'm going, I'm going.

As a child, Arthur had scoured his mother's genealogical records looking for his place in the Caucasian pantheon. By most accounts, he was Nordic (his blond hair and love for snow and those little water-filled paperweights with the snow inside), Scotch (his freckles and love for red, red roses), Irish (his temper softened by nostalgia, warm beer, and sad songs badly sung in bars run by anyone with an O or an Mc in front of his or her name), with a touch of German (his inability to laugh out loud unless ordered to). Yet, he was also descended from the French and English, two entities that had stretched the Hundred Years' War to 116 because, obviously, neither side could count anything but dead bodies and taxes.

Such a divided man is Arthur Stephens Jefferson. He could never be a hyphenated American. His true hyphenation would never fit on the census form.

Somewhat of a mutt, this Arthur.

Now you're cooking.

I am? I just called my main character a mutt!

He's A Mutt in the Melting Pot. That may end up being your title. Keep going.

Stop interrupting, then!

Is there going to be a sex scene soon? Your editor expects one every twenty pages or so.

Later.

Don't keep her waiting too long.

Who's writing this, you or me?

We both are, remember?

I'm not so sure.

Maybe an old-fashioned erotic dream out by the shed?

Hush.

Okay. How about a fantasy, then? A quick ten-second fantasy.

In the middle of my character's family history?

How do you think we get families, Jack? First a fantasy, then the stalking, then the taking . . . It's about time you did some taking, Jack.

I don't know.

You're getting better, Jack.

I am?

Yeah. You're almost yourself again.

Almost.

Now if you bathe, trim your nails, shave, and get a haircut—

Don't push your luck.

Well, at least get cleaned up before you take the books back to the library.

Why?

You might see Diane again. Maybe you'll have a fantasy or two.

I don't know.

Just one?

Okay. Just one.

17

Diane

The anonymously written *The Quiet Game* is a rip-off of headlinesmade a few years ago by the DC sniper, and it completely misses the target as a novel of suspense and intrigue. The narrator, while sufficiently creepy, isn't compelling enough to carry the plodding, predictable plot to anything but an obvious ending and a twenty-page prison diatribe borrowed liberally from *Native Son*—perhaps the reason the publisher decided to keep the author's name from the public eye. The publisher should have also kept this novel from the public eye.

☺ out of ☺☺☺☺☺
—Nisi, *Mid-Atlantic Book Review*

I'm worried the publisher will use ellipses to say, "*The Quiet Game* . . . is a novel of suspense and intrigue," but I'm not too worried. I skimmed the novel and found that the last twenty pages is a diary the older sniper wrote while in prison, and the more I read from that diary, the more I was convinced the author stole bits and pieces of it from Richard Wright. I checked, and sure enough, the author summarized many of Bigger Thomas's thoughts from jail in *Native Son*. And luckily, I was the first to post my review at Amazon.com, so *The Quiet Game* will be officially a one-star book in a few days, since it takes up to five days for my reviews to post on the Internet.

Except for Psyche, the remarkably drawn heroine of *P&Q*, by J. K. Growling, this novel fails as both a romance and satire of the modeling industry. The plot, taken from the mythological story of Psyche and Cupid, breaks no new literary ground, and of the four narrators (Venus, Q, Psyche, and Rosemary), only Psyche's voice rings true as she stays true to herself and her spiritual upbringing while surviving the evil, soap-operatic machinations of Q and his mother, Venus. Aside from Psyche, the other characters are nothing but living mannequins spouting melodramatic, meaningless lines. Growling should have told the entire story through Psyche's eyes and not through the *glands* of the other characters.

☺☺ out of ☺☺☺☺☺
—Nisi, *Mid-Atlantic Book Review*

I'm the fourth person to review *P&Q*, and except for the first one giving the book five stars—probably put up there "anonymously" by J. K. Growling or his or her publisher— the other two give three and two stars, respectively. The book wasn't terrible, but any editor worth his or her salt should have known that Psyche's narrative carried the book. In fact, I only read her parts and followed the story line just fine.

Because I actually read every word of *Thicker Than Blood*, I plan to give it high praise. Yeah, it is ridiculous and at times unbelievable (it will only get four out of five stars because of that), but it doesn't take itself seriously and leaves the reader with comfortable, homespun warmth. Every character, and I mean *every* character, is as dysfunctional as Grandpa Joe-Joe by the end of the novel, and though Rob and Chloe hook up—often, and in the strangest places, including Grandpa Joe-Joe's root cellar—they don't connect, going their separate ways in the end. Except for the Drug Enforcement Agency's raid on Grandpa Joe-Joe's farm (where the DEA finds nothing but a field of human feces), the worm spill that makes the ducks too obese to fly south for the winter, and a wild dream Rob has involving Chloe's toes, it is a bittersweet and memorable read.

But because I'm more bitter than sweet this afternoon—no man bumped into me at church, though I did kind of throw that request into a prayer I made during the service—I have to write my review for *Wishful Thinking* right now while my bitterness is fresh.

Okay, it's not bitterness. It's disappointment. The interracial genre has enough trouble being published in this monoracial, black *or* white (and not both) literary world, but to publish *Wishful Thinking* as a "shining" representative of multicultural fiction is a disgrace.

I punch in "Wishful Thinking" on Amazon.com's search box, and in a moment, I see Ty's rugged face on the cover staring back at me.

"Hi, Ty," I say.

"Be the first to review this book!" cries out to me from under the synopsis of the book.

And I *will* be first.

"Sorry, D.J.," I say.

It's weird apologizing to a nameless, faceless author five days before he or she will be wounded, but, hey, it makes me feel a little better.

I read my notes only once and begin . . .

18

Jack

*W*hy haven't you shaved?
   I had no reason to.
   Sixth months of blondish-browning hair—
   And a few grays.
   They're blond.
   If you say so . . .
   Okay, and a few grays. Was my father gray at thirty-two?
I don't think so. Anyway, 180 days of beard and moustache
and sideburns—
   I liked the sideburns.
   No, you didn't.
   They made you look like Elvis.
   A blond Elvis?
   Yeah. That's about as bad as a redheaded Sinatra.
   Junior or Senior?
   Both.
   Are you going to let me finish shaving?
   Knock yourself out. Be careful around your—

Ow. My chin.

Good thing you have plenty of toilet paper. And use lotion when you're done.

I'm echoing Noël in my head now. "Use lotion," she insisted, and I would always forget. I find a bottle of Vaseline Intensive Care Lotion on her vanity. "I never much used it when you were here, and now look at me." I lotion my face and look into the mirror. Who am I looking like?

Kind of a cross between Tom Petty and Andy Warhol.

Scary. I need a haircut so I can look like an unknown, anonymous author, widower by day, author by night.

Sounds like a really bad TV show idea.

I'm full of bad ideas.

After trimming my "claws," I pull out another outfit from the Christmas bags. Baby blue stripes on a navy shirt with navy pants. Pretty subdued.

Take off the price tags this time, though.

Yeah.

I look at the iron, the cord wrapped neatly around it.

You don't know how to iron.

I watched Noël do it often enough, just about every night, for that matter. I should be an expert.

They look fine as they are.

True, but . . . I think I can make them look finer.

But once I fill up the reservoir with tap water and turn the switch to "hot," I realize that I don't know what I'm doing. I spray some starch on the pants, expecting a white sheen. There's no white sheen. Have I used enough? I spray some more. It must be soaking in. Is it supposed to be soaking in? Hmm. I spray it one more time. Then, I iron, the inside of a leg followed by the outside (with three helpings of starch), followed by both sides of the other leg, burning my fingers with the steam whenever I try to make a crease just right.

They're a bit stiff.

At least they're not wrinkled.

You could prop up a house with them.

They're not *that* stiff.

You walk funny anyway, so maybe people won't notice.

I pick up the shirt and check the label. "Cool iron if needed," it says. I look at the iron. It looks pretty cool, all aquamarine and white. Kind of stylish, really.

Turn the heat down.

I know what a cool iron is.

Maybe you should have done the shirt first.

I'm learning.

A few minutes later, I think the iron has cooled enough, and I start with the sleeves. Five minutes of trying to get a single wrinkle out of one sleeve convinces me that I hate ironing sleeves. And no matter how I iron the collar, it still flops around.

So, I starch it.

It still flops around.

Maybe it's supposed to flop around.

Or maybe my neck will hold it up.

And maybe it won't.

I flip over the shirt and iron the front. It looks pretty good, but when I hold it up, I see wrinkles on the back that weren't there a few minutes ago. Now what?

Don't press so hard.

Maybe if I lift up the front, I can put the ironing board in between and . . . Hey, it works? It works!

Don't think you've done anything special. Noël did this for you for years.

Yes, she did.

Five days a week, ten months of the year, times five years . . . over 1,000 times.

And she did it with a smile, too.

Now, what shoes should I wear with baby blue and navy? I look under my side of the bed and come up with some black-and-white high-top Nikes I haven't worn in years.

No.

I pull out a pair of brown suede hiking boots.

No.

I end up putting on some black Rockport walkers with some new black socks. I use Noël's full-length mirror on the back of her door and give myself a once-over. Skinny, long-haired, dressed nicely. This outfit says, "Modern."

It says, "Get a haircut."

Time to get my ears lowered.

As I'm leaving the house, carrying only the library books and a steno pad, I look at Noël's car and remember that someone is coming to look at it.

And maybe take a test-drive.

Do I stay? Do I go? Do I wait? Should I call her back?

She said she was doing a drive-by.

I shrug; though I feel strange shrugging at myself in broad daylight; get in the truck; and drive out of the neighborhood. When I turn onto Shenandoah Avenue, I remember . . .

A phone call . . . "Your wife's been in an accident" . . . "Oh, God! What about my son?" . . . dead space . . . "Your son was with her?" . . . "Oh, God!" . . . sirens . . . "Where are they?" . . . "Off of Shenandoah . . . in the creek" . . .

Heavy rain that day. The creek was over the bridge. She couldn't have known how deep it was.

That van had no ground clearance. This truck would have made it. The Mustang would have made it. They would have plowed right on through.

I get to the bridge and slow down, looking at the spot where the van had been . . . underwater . . . rescue divers trying to get inside . . . they can't find my son . . . "He has to be in there!" . . . Noël laid out on the muddy banks . . . shocking her, a bag being pumped over her beautiful face . . . so pale, so pale . . . they've found him . . . he looks like he's sleeping—

The creek is barely a gurgle today, hardly flowing at all, even though almost all the snow has melted. They would have survived today. They would have walked away with rosy cheeks and exciting stories and we would have had grilled cheese and tomato soup—

It was an accident, Jack.

It was a *mistake. They* weren't ready. *I* wasn't ready.

You're holding up traffic. It's thirty-five through here. You're doing twenty.

I accelerate up to thirty, turn in to the parking lot of the barbershop, and park in one of several empty spaces.

Mr. Underwood isn't too busy today.

Maybe I should put up a memorial for them. I've seen them on the side of the road, sometimes with flowers, or stones, a cross, even names and dates on a sign.

You have other errands to run, remember? Get in there.

No, I don't want a memorial to their pain and suffering.

It's for remembrance, not pain.

I'd just be advertising my guilt. It would be swept away in the next flash flood anyway. They were going to the grocery store, just a few items, care to tag along? I could have gone. I was too busy reading that day. She could have left Stevie with me. I could have gone *for* them.

You might be dead.

What's the difference? And anyway, better me than them.

Maybe you should visit them.

Once was enough.

Just to see if they're keeping things up nice.

I don't want to go to a cemetery to see where they *aren't.* I see them in every room of the house already. I have to find a realtor.

Selling your first house? All that saving, paying down debt, doing without—all the sacrifices you two made to get into that house?

It's not a home anymore. There's no one to hug. There's no one to greet on the stairs at the end of a long day. There's no one to watch grow. There's no one to lie next to. There's no one—

In the barbershop but the barber. Go get your haircut.

When I enter, I walk past mounds of fishing magazines in the waiting area and see Mr. Underwood sitting in the only barber's chair reading a newspaper, a little bell ringing behind me.

He folds the paper and squints. Then he smiles and stands. "How ya doin', Jack?"

A loaded question.

Full of wrong answers.

Mr. Underwood, tall and gangly with dark hair and gray eyebrows, swats the chair with a hand towel. "How long's it been?"

I sit, Mr. Underwood's fingers wrapping the gown around my neck. "About six months."

"I'd given you up for dead."

It feels that way. I don't respond.

He jacks up the chair. "Were you on vacation?"

"Something like that."

"You still teaching?"

"Yeah." It's easier to lie than to explain.

"How much you want off?"

I look in the mirror. "Leave me an inch or so."

He spins the chair around and goes to work. Directly across from me is a sign that reads "Gone Fishin'—Be Back at Dark-Thirty."

He's going to tell you a fishing story.

And I'm going to let him.

I clear my throat. "Have you done any fishing lately?"

As he cuts, Mr. Underwood tells me of the fishing trip to Ontario he took in September, when "all the leaves—you wouldn't believe how pretty they looked—were like the Blue Ridge Parkway only everywhere you looked." He mentions sizes and weights of smallmouth bass and walleyes, pike and lake trout. "They may not all be big fish, but they love a good fight."

I look at the blond and gray hair floating down to the gown.

I told you there were some grays.

Yes, you did.

"I was using peepers, you know, little spotted frogs, and I was just settin' up near this island, you know, casting toward shore as I drifted in." A pause. Snip-snip. "Don't like using an anchor too much, scares the fish, you know."

Just drifting in.

Floating.

Snippety-snip. "Anyways, as soon as that peeper hit the water, *bam!* Swirled right up and took it, and that fish pulled my boat clear into shore." A pause. Snippety-snip-snip. "Jumped out of the water and just spit that hook out. So, as the boat bumped some rocks in the shallow water, I fixed my line, put another peeper on, cast out . . . *bam!* But this time, I got him in the boat." Snip-snip-snippety-snip. "Four and a half pounds, biggest one I caught all summer." Another pause. Snip-snip-snippety. "But don't you know, when I was taking out the hook, I looked inside the bass's mouth and saw a little green-and-yellow flipper. I used my disgorger, and what should pop out onto my hand but another peeper with a hook hole in its little snout. I had caught the fish that I had just lost!"

Say something. Let him know you're awake.

"Really?"

"I couldn't believe it, and since peepers are going for eight dollars a dozen up there in Ontario, I put that peeper on my hook, cast out . . ."

He's going to say, "bam!"

Shh.

"And *bam!* I caught me a little two-pounder. Two fish with the same peeper." A pause. Rrrr-rrr around my ears. "And the darndest thing was, that first peeper was still alive, so I let him go. He swam right over to that little island." He spins me around. "How's that?"

The man staring back at me looks almost like Dan Pace..

You need an earring and a curling iron burn on your butt.

Did Dan wear an earring?

He did in the first draft.

Oh, yeah.

And Noël's curling irons might make an X.

Shut up.

"It looks fine," I say.

Mr. Underwood removes the gown, carefully corralling my hair and shaking it out onto the floor. He whisks away some hairs from my forehead, ears, and neck.

"How much?" I ask.

The sign says ten dollars, Jack.

He had to cut off a lot of hair. Maybe it's extra.

"No charge," Mr. Underwood says.

"Huh?"

He looks down. "It took me a little while to remember, but as soon as I got to cutting, I remembered why you haven't been around."

It was just down the street.

It would have been a hot topic in this barbershop.

I pull out a twenty, but Mr. Underwood holds up his hands. "No, that's all right, Jack. Next time."

"Take it," I say. "Use it to keep your magazine subscriptions going."

He still won't take it, instead turning and sitting in the chair. "Next time, Jack."

I shove the bill into my pocket. "Thanks."

Mr. Underwood returns to his newspaper. "See you in a few weeks."

"Right."

That was nice of him.

I didn't need his pity.

Maybe it was sympathy. Mr. Underwood doesn't wear a wedding ring, and he's old, so . . . maybe he's a widower, too. He never talks about his wife.

It's a barbershop. Men don't talk about that stuff in a barbershop.

Maybe they should.

Parking is scarce around the library today, and I find a space at All-Rite Parking across the street, which costs "$3 first hour, $1 every hour after." I stand at the kiosk with all the slots to prepay, and I only have a twenty.

You're only going to be here for a few minutes, right? Get change inside the library.

I fold and slide the twenty into the slot, tapping it until it falls completely in.

What'd you do that for?

Maybe I'll walk home. I'm good for eighteen hours, right?

You're strange.

You know it.

I take my books to the circulation desk, and a different woman greets me, her name tag proclaiming that she is "Francine." She smiles. "How are you today?"

Does she really want to know?

She's just being friendly.

I want to ask Francine where Diane is so I can thank her for her suggestions, but I don't. "Fine."

Maybe it's her day off.

Yeah.

And then I just . . . stand there. I don't know why.

"Do you need any help?" Francine asks.

"No." I look up the stairs to the periodicals section. I smile at Francine. "Thanks."

I take the stairs one at a time to the top and walk past several men of varying ages and races reading newspapers.

What are you doing here?

I see a stand of magazines, and one magazine stands out.

You're going to read that one again?

It helped the last time.

I suppose it did.

19
Diane

Just once, I'd love to walk into the public women's restroom and *not* see the hot water running in the sink. What do these folks think we're running here, a laundry? And look at all these fools saving fifty cents reading the newspaper—

And there's a white man reading *Essence*. What is this world coming to?

By the time I get upstairs to the reference desk, I already have a patron waiting. I put on my fake smile and ask the woman waving a Harrison Ford video in my face, "How may I help you today?"

"I brought this in late, and they said I had to pay, and I'm not about to cuz I couldn't get out in the snow, you know?"

That wasn't snow, I want to tell her. That was just some white fluffy dust that stopped Roanoke dead in its can't-drive-in-snow tracks. I could tell her about the time last year when Kim made me drive through real snow—almost six inches—to make sure the CLOSED sign was up in the window. "Um, Kim," I had said, "who's going to go out in this snow to the library?" She had replied, "It's our policy, Diane."

"So, can you help me?"

I smile more broadly. "You'll want to talk to Kim Cambridge. She's the director." This, too, is policy.

"You're not the director?"

I should be, but . . . "No, ma'am. I can page her for you."

"They told me down there that she was up here."

It's a big library. "I'll page her."

I dial Kim's pager and put in the number 2, a code for Kim to report to the reference desk. We're all supposed to wear our pagers, but I don't. I'm where I'm supposed to be (most of the time), and the buttons are bad enough. Up in Indianapolis, we wore buttons that said, "YOU DON'T SCARE ME—I WORK IN CIRCULATION." I kind of liked those. The ones here, though? Forget it. They say, "GET IT AT THE LIBRARY." Now I know from something I read that the library is in the top ten for "best public places to have sex," but the buttons are going too far. We had a pregnant, part-time volunteer get so much grief from patrons—

Ah, here's Kim, and now it's time to watch her bend over backward for this woman who can't get enough of Harrison Ford's dimpled chin.

"Yes, ma'am," Kim says. "How may I help you?"

The woman, who smells oddly of onions and bananas, explains her case, Kim nodding and putting on her "I'm-so-concerned-for-my-patrons" look.

"I completely understand, ma'am," Kim says. She takes the video. "I'll personally take care of this."

As the woman walks away, Kim turns to me. "Where's your button, Diane?"

Shoot. "I forgot it."

Kim smiles. "I have extras. I'll bring another to you."

"Kim, don't bother," I say. I pull out an "extra" button from the drawer. "I found it."

"Great." Kim walks away.

I clip the button to the hem of my skirt. I'll wear it, but nobody is going to see it.

I open up *The Da Vinci Code* and read a few pages before a snot-nosed child bounces up to the desk. "Yes?"

"Why are you reading?" the child asks.

"Because I *can*," I say.

The child runs away. They seem to do that a lot when I work the reference desk, for some reason.

I get one more paragraph read when a horny-looking man—I can tell, something about his eyes—approaches the desk. "Yes, sir?"

"Um, I'm looking for a book called *Satanic Nurses*."

A few other folks line up behind him. It's going to be one of *those* days. "Are you sure you don't mean *Satanic Verses*?"

He blinks. "No, it's *Satanic Nurses*."

It sounds like a triple-X movie to me. "Are you sure it's a book and not a video?"

He blinks. "It's already in video?"

"I'm sure we don't carry it if it is," I say. "Why don't you try one of the video stores on Williamson Road?"

He blinks. "I did. They're all rented out."

And you thought the library would have X-rated movies to check out? "Well, we don't carry those types of videos, sir."

He frowns. "Well, could you maybe see if the book is here?"

I point to the stairs. "Try circulation, sir. They can help you."

"Okay."

The next man asks, "I need to know all the Revolutionary War battles that were fought on national park sites."

What battles weren't? "Sir, most if not all of those battle-fields have become national parks."

"They have?"

"I'm sure of it. Try running a simple search for national parks, and I'm sure you'll find all of them."

"Okay."

What? No "Thank you"? I'm used to it.

The *Essence*-reading white man cruises by, still carrying the magazine, and is that a steno pad?

"Excuse me," a teenaged girl says.

"Yes?"

"I need a color photo of Moses for school."

I don't laugh. I want to, I really, really do. "I don't think we have any photographs of Moses, but I can direct you to some paintings of him. Will that help?"

Shrugs. "I guess." She cracks her gum. "Where is it?"

I'm not leaving my stool, missy. "Run a search, typing in 'Moses' and 'art.' I'm sure you'll have several reference books to choose from."

She cracks her gum and rolls her eyes. "Okay." She slinks away.

I want to yell, "Next!" but this is a library.

A young black boy steps up, looking so cute in a black down jacket that cost more than my entire wardrobe. "Um, can you help me find this book for me?"

"Which book?"

"Um, I was reading it yesterday, and, um, it was big and green and orange, and I found it on the top shelf."

That narrows it down. I want to help him, but there are others waiting in line. "What was it about?"

"Amphibians."

Ah, a future biologist. I wink. "I'll find it." I run a quick search and come up with a list of books, and print them out. I tear off the list and hand it to him. "I'll bet it's one of those." After directing him where to look downstairs, I smile. "I know you'll find it."

He walks away, looking back and saying, "Thank you."

That boy had some home training. It makes me want to hug his mama.

Not all the kids who come in here are like him, no, sir. The kids today lead such pampered little lives. So did I, for that matter. My parents' and grandparents' generations, though, they had it tough. And I'm not talking about their trips up the hill *both* ways in *four* feet of snow on their way to milking the family cow or goat *without* Gore-Tex gloves or mittens or Vaseline Intensive Care Lotion before putting bituminous coal in the one-room schoolhouse's only Franklin stove while wearing paper-thin PF Flyers and a sweater knitted by the nearly blind but lovable Aunt Edwina, all the while being truly *thankful* that they had unboiled, frothy brown well water to wash down their dirt sandwiches, brown bananas, and melted Moon Pies.

That's not what I'm talking about. Sure, I heard my share of back-then-it-was-so-tough stories, and sometimes I got tired of hearing them. But as I've grown older, I've respected my parents and grandparents so much more.

I respect them for surviving their childhoods. They were all denied the *privilege* of attending day care. They actually had to stay home and learn how to bake or sew or whittle or clean or wash dishes or hang their own laundry outside on the line to dry gloriously in the wind. They rode in cars *without* seat belts or air bags and often rode in the backs of pickup trucks with the family dog, Max, the flea-infested, flea-collarless pet whom they often let lick them in the face. They ate Hostess Cupcakes and Twinkies that had more calories per square millimeter than any other foodstuff known to humanity, wonder-*less* bread with one hundred percent *real* butter, and drank soda laced with *lethal* doses of pure sugar, yet they were rarely obese because they were outside playing—which the kids today must think is too dangerous or something. They even *shared* sodas with their friends—from *one* bottle or *one* straw—and no one actually died. They would spend hours building rolling contraptions out of scraps of wood ripped from Flexible Flyer sleds, construction sites, and real red wagons only to roll down the hill to realize they had concocted no way to stop until they hit bushes, curbs, or someone's cement block front porch. They fell out of trees and skinned knees and lost teeth and got into fights and soaped windows and threw eggs and got bitten by the neighbor's arthritic Chihuahua Felix because they were baiting Felix with a stick, and—get this—there were *no* lawsuits. They actually took responsibility for their actions. Imagine! They even ate worms and ants and grasshoppers and honeysuckle and dandelions and buttercups and watermelon seeds and pennies and anything *anyone* dared them to eat—and they got sick, but they somehow survived.

And they were so much more active than the kids I see come in here to sit all day at a computer or play on a Game Boy. They often left home in the morning to play all day long, and as long as they were inside the house before the streetlights came on, they wouldn't get grounded. Not a single one of them had a cell phone or a pager, a vial of pepper spray or a Taser. And instead of spending all day and night on the phone or on the Internet, they actually went over to friends' houses and knocked on the door or rang the bell or just walked in and talked to them. Imagine! Walking over, knocking on a door, and talking to someone in person! That little boy, as well mannered as he was, wouldn't know what I was talking about.

And my parents and grandparents were never as bored as easily as these kids seem to get. They often had to sit through the movie at the movie theater, and none of them had Play-Stations, Nintendo, Xboxes, Game Boys, Walkmen, Palm Pilots, cell phones, personal computers, chat rooms, MTV, e-mail, Dolby Surround Sound, DVDs, microwaves, microwave popcorn, satellite TV, or the mall. All they had were four channels that required something called rabbit ears to tune in, their friends, their little transistor radios, and their unconventional imaginations. They actually made up games

that often involved no more than a ratty old tennis ball borrowed from Felix the Chihuahua, a broomstick, half a block
of street, and manhole covers or their own shoes for bases.
When they played dodgeball (also known as "murder ball"),
the ball actually *hurt,* because no one had a working bicycle
pump and needle and no one had invented Nerf balls yet.
They were even *cut* from Little League or other sports teams
if they weren't good enough. Just imagine the incredible
blows to their collective self-esteem! My goodness, they'd
actually have to suck it up and try harder the next time!

Yeah, I'm from a wimpy generation, all right, and it all
started with my schooling. My parents and grandparents actually went to school during snowstorms, floods, wars, and
police actions, and that taught them perseverance, pride,
courage, patriotism, and fortitude. They actually had to take
tests that weren't curved and sit in un-air-conditioned classes
where their grades weren't weighted. And if they didn't make
the grade, they actually got held back and had to repeat the
same grade. I wonder where the lawyers were when that was
happening. They didn't even have calculators to add, sub-
tract, multiply, and divide. They actually had to learn how to
do math longhand using nonmechanical pencils that they had
to sharpen with their own hands! And when they had a book
report to do, they actually had to read the book! They couldn't
rent the movie, they couldn't read *CliffsNotes,* and they
couldn't even find the book on tape. Imagine the horror of
actually having to turn the pages! Oh, the humanity! Oh, the
paper cuts! Some of the kids who come in here simply refuse
to crack a book unless they can "flip through it" on the computer.

The kids these days . . . I don't know what to do with
them. They'd much rather watch movies like *Jackass* or
shows like *American Idol* or pierce something new or tattoo
themselves green or get their nails done or hang out until all
hours doing absolutely nothing or play eye-hand coordina-

tion games in their rooms or blame others for their failures and problems.

I look up at a man holding a little girl's hand. "May I help you?"

"Does your globe have Australia on it?" I have to actually show the man that, indeed, Australia does appear on our globe. "And do you have a map of Australia to scale?" he asks. I try to explain what "to scale" means, but he's not hearing me. "I need the biggest map you have." I leave him with the biggest atlas we have.

Maybe kids are messed up today because of their parents!

And after "Australia Man," my day travels quickly downhill.

"I need an A-to-Z encyclopedia" is next. I ask, "You mean a dictionary, right?" I get a nod. And this was from a grown woman! Stupid parents equal stupid kids!

"Can you help me find information on genital arthritis?" After stifling a howl of laughter, I convince this kind, gentle old man that he means "congenital arthritis." Though as he walks away, I wonder . . .

"Do you have a copy of *Romeo and Juliet* in English?" I could direct this child to the circulation department or a computer, but I don't. I take the child to the very edition I used when trying to decipher Shakespeare. I show him the left side, and his eyes bug out. "That's English?" Then I show him the right side of the book, and his eyes relax. "This is what I need! Thanks!"

Two "thanks" in one morning. A record.

But when an older black woman asks me where we "hide" *Waiting to Expire*, I feel like expiring right then and there. And I'm only halfway through my shift. I direct her to the fiction section without correcting her, see no one in line, and put up my "I'll Be Back in a Minute" sign.

It's time for my lunch.

I slide off my stool and walk around the counter, nearly colliding with a patron.

"Sorry," he says.

It's the white man, and he's *still* reading *Essence*? It must be the year-end issue. Either that, or he's a slow reader.

I smile and keep on. I'm hungry.

20
Jack

You need to be more careful.
At least she saw me.
She didn't recognize you.
No, she didn't.
Must be your new do.
I sit in the reference section about three tables from where Diane sits, well, *was* sitting when I first saw her again.
She'll probably recognize you if you sit here.
She might not.
Is that a good thing?
I don't know.
I look back at the magazine. I'm only to page forty-five, and I've taken so many notes. I have several lists going, mostly for hair products:

Megahertz Hi-Frequency Styling, Optimum
Multi-Mineral Relaxer System, HiRez High
Resolution Haircolor, Feria Multi-Faceted

Shimmering Haircolour, Mizani Beyond
Conditioning Crème Haircolor, Aveda Scalp
Benefits Balancing Shampoo, Luster's Earth Secrets
Organic Eucalyptus & Ginseng Root Scalp & Hair
Treatment, Motions Shine Enhancing Pomade, Doo
Gro Medicated Hair Vitalizer (Mega-Thick, Triple
Strength, Anti-Itch Formula, Extra Light Original
Formula, Crème Complex)

And what does this tell us?

Di's hair is going to be important to her.

She can't possibly use all those products at once, can she?

I don't know. Maybe. But how do I know what the texture of her hair is like? I thought hair was hair.

It obviously isn't.

I mean, if her hair is coarse, what products would she use?

Is it that important?

It will be to her. Her hair has to shine, right? Does coarse hair shine on its own, or do you have to add something to it?

Diane's hair was shiny. Did you see how she looked at you?

Yeah. She smiled, didn't she?

Actually, it was more of a grimace. You nearly ran her down.

She was smiling. I like the color of her lipstick.

She wasn't wearing lipstick.

Then I like her lips.

Oh, put that in a novel and see how many people call you a racist.

They're . . . pretty. Kind of pouty and well defined. An off-brown.

You'll need to get out Stevie's crayons. "Off-brown" sounds redundant.

They make her teeth seem whiter.

Gee, um, maybe she just has white teeth.

No, no, it's the contrast that makes them seem whiter. I like her nose, too.

What about her eyebrows?

Yeah, how does she get them to be perfect half circles like that? Almost as if she . . . shaved them?

Ouch.

Yeah.

You saw the button, right?

What button?

You—we—saw it. You were looking at her legs.

I was not!

Yeah, you were. You're always looking down. She has some nice legs, all smooth and silky.

You're determined to get me to write a sex scene.

I'm just saying . . .

She wore sensible shoes. Some kind of walking sneakers.

I knew you were looking.

She must walk a couple miles a day, kind of like I used to. No wonder her legs are so . . . toned.

Now you're talking. What about the rest of her?

Pretty hands, pretty smile, pretty calves, pretty lips. She's pretty.

What about her eyes?

I haven't made eye contact yet.

You saw her eyebrows!

But they were close to her forehead. It's how I know about her hair.

Make eye contact then. How can you write a romance without a visual in your mind of her eyes?

Or her ears.

To nibble on.

Or . . . her, um . . .

Go on.

What do I call it without sounding nasty?

Her booty, her back, her backside, her ass, her bumpers, her boom-boom—

Stop. I like her form, the way she stands up straight, the way she holds her shoulders, the set of her jaw, the—

Way her booty talks when she walks.

Now wait a minute, I didn't stare—

Yes, you did. Right after you tried to tackle her, you took a long look, and it's given you some ideas.

Right. It has. For my book.

Uh-huh. Noël didn't have anything like that back there.

Don't bring her . . . *that* into this.

Why not?

Because I miss her . . . *that*.

It was so small.

It fit her. Just like Diane's . . . *that* . . . fits her.

Call it a booty, Jack.

I can't call it—

You know you want to. Diane's got a nice, round booty. Say it.

That's something Dan would say, not me.

There's a little Dan in you, Jack. And if you're smart, you'll let him come out to stretch his legs.

My editor made me give him *three* legs. I'm not like that.

You used to be. Back before Noël.

That was so long ago. I don't even know how—

Yes, you do. It's just like riding a bike.

I'm not talking about . . . *that*. I'm talking about not knowing even how to approach her.

Well, sitting thirty feet away from her reading Essence *is an excellent first step. She'll be all over you.*

Shut up.

Not until you say, "Diane's got a nice booty."

Diane's . . . got a nice . . .

Whoa. There she is.

And when I see her return to her stool, I feel my lips forming the words, "Diane's got a nice booty."

I feel so . . .

Horny?

No. I feel . . . honest.

Honest?

Diane *does* have a nice booty.

Now get ready to check out her eyes.

21

Diane

To whom is he talking? Or does he have to move his lips to read? And why is he staring so hard at me? Do I have a patch of mustard on my lips?

I pull out a Kleenex and dab my lower lip. Nothing. I swivel away from his gaze anyway. How rude!

He had pretty eyes, though. Hmm. I look at him sideways, and he's back into his magazine. Figures. He has the attention span of a gnat.

Hairy-knuckled hands rap the counter, and I look up into the face of the oldest black man currently breathing on planet Earth. And he wears a nice dark suit and tie that fits him nicely.

"Where's your gynecology department?" he asks.

This is the tenth time this has happened since I've worked here. "You mean, the genealogy—"

The old man winks. "I know the correct name there, lady. I was just teasing." He leans an elbow on the counter. "So, how have you been?"

Nuh-uh. No way this old man is stepping to me. "Uh, fine."

"Care to help an old man find his kin?" he asks.

"Um, sir, there are—"

"Charlie," he says. "Call me Charlie Brown."

Oh . . . my. "Um, Charlie, there are some folks up in the genealogy department who can help you better than I can. They're experts at it, and I—"

Charlie scowls. "Oh, they're just a couple white women who don't know how to find black folks."

Which may be true, but . . . "Listen, Charlie," I say more softly, as I lean across the counter, "you wouldn't just be hitting on me, would you?"

Charlie's eyebrows rise and fall, his lips twitching. "Maybe."

I touch the back of his hand. "You're sweet, but you're also old enough to be my great-grandfather."

He steps back and adjusts his lapels. "Not interested, huh?"

"No."

Charlie winks. "Then I guess I'll go hit on those two white biddies upstairs again. Do I look all right?"

"You look charming, Charlie."

"Do I look . . . virile?"

I nod.

He smiles. "I'm not, but they don't know that. Want to know a secret?"

"Sure."

"I already know who all my kin are."

"You don't say."

He winks once more and leaves the desk, whistling something bluesy.

And as soon as he's gone, I'm instantly depressed. The *only* man in a suit to hit on me in twelve months is a man named Charlie Brown who dresses up to impress two ancient white women in the genealogy department.

22

Jack

That's how it's done. That's how you approach her.

She turned him down.

He was old!

And black.

So maybe . . . you know . . . she likes white men.

Or she has a boyfriend.

No rings.

I still have mine.

And hopefully she hasn't seen it yet. Put it in your pocket.

No.

Still determined to be happily widowed, huh?

Shh. Here comes somebody.

I watch an older woman carrying an ancient text of some kind approach Diane's counter. "Do you work here?" she asks.

"Yes," Diane says.

What a stupid question!

Shh.

"Can you appraise this book's value for me?"

You've got to be kidding!

Shh!

"I need to know its value. I want to sell it."

Diane looks at the book but doesn't touch it. "I don't do that sort of thing."

The woman looks around her. "Does anyone here do appraisals?"

"You might try a used-book store over on the Market. I've heard they sometimes appraise books."

She's so helpful.

I like her voice.

You mean, you hear voices.

I'm just listening to myself; now be quiet so I can hear Diane.

The old woman turns toward me then turns back, slamming the book back on Diane's counter and upsetting a cup of pencils. "Oh, pardon me, I didn't mean to—"

"It's all right," Diane says, collecting the pencils. "Is there something else you need?"

"Well, while I'm here, my grandson needs a book on raising chickens and fish."

At the same time?

Shh.

"Let me check." Diane does a rapid series of keystrokes. "Ma'am, I have two books, one on raising fish, one on raising chickens."

"Oh, they aren't all in one volume?"

She's loony.

Shh.

"No ma'am." Diane writes out what I assume are the call letters and numbers, and the old woman leaves, forgetting her book. "Ma'am? Your book."

The woman smiles. "Could you watch that for me, dear? I'll only be a second."

That was rude.

Did you see how Diane bristled when she called her "dear"?

I watch Diane slide the book to the side as a short, pudgy man approaches. "Does your *Wall Street Journal* have a business section?"

I turn away to laugh.

They heard you!

That was a *stupid* question!

I know, but . . . we didn't get to hear what she said.

I'm sure she said, "Yes, sir." And if I wrote down everything I've overheard today in a novel, no one would believe it.

Two young girls no older than twelve approach Diane. "Do you have a book about a famous person written by a famous author?"

No way!

I need to go back to teaching.

"We have plenty of those," Diane says. "Do you have a famous person in mind?"

"Well," the shorter one says, "I kinda want to know more about Elvis."

"Yeah," the taller one says, "we've been looking, and we can't find him anywhere."

Because he's dead.

Shh.

After Diane sends the girls to search for Elvis, I see her eyes traveling to the ceiling. Yeah, I'd be talking to God, too, if I had this job.

But you don't talk to God anymore.

Right.

A girl, maybe seventeen or eighteen, rushes by me, fluttering my magazine. "Hi, I, um . . ." She leans closer to Diane, and all I can catch is one phrase: "vaginal spermicide."

No way!

Unbelievable. I watch as Diane walks the young girl, who

looks younger the more I look at her jean jacket all covered in patches, her hair done up with little pink bows, away from us to the stairs. Diane seems to be giving directions.

To the hospital?

I don't know. Maybe the free clinic.

Diane returns to her stool—

You're looking at her booty again.

I am not. I'm still trying to see her eyes.

Right.

A little boy . . . about Stevie's age . . . goes up to the counter. "You got cramps?" he asks.

I watch Diane's eyes dance, and I feel . . . sad that I know what the boy is asking for. Crayons. He wants crayons. Stevie used to say it the same way.

"What?" Diane says.

"You got cramps?" the boy asks again.

Diane's mouth opens and shuts several times. "I'm not sure what you mean."

"You know, cramps. You color with them."

Diane smiles, and it beams out onto the boy. "Oh, crayons."

"That's what I said. Cramps."

Diane reaches under her counter and pulls out a box of crayons. "You be sure to bring these back when you're done."

The boy takes the crayons. "Okay."

That's your cue.

My cue?

Your cue to talk to her.

No, it isn't.

A little boy saying "cramps" just like Stevie?

Lots of little boys and girls say cramps when they mean "crayons."

But just now . . . here . . . while you're staring hard at Diane's booty when you say you are trying to see her eyes?

It's . . . it's just a coincidence. That's all it is.

Go on.

Go on and do what?

Ask her a reference question. It's her job, isn't it?

I don't know what to ask.

Sure you do. But before you do, take off your ring.

To ask a question?

Just for a little while. A few minutes at most. It won't kill you.

I spin the ring once and slide it into my pocket.

Now, what do I ask?

23

Diane

"Cramps"! I never would have guessed, though the kid was right about something. My back is *killing* me, and that usually means my time of the month is a few days away.

What a strange day! I mean, I usually get a couple strange questions, but nothing like this. I have barely had enough time to catch my—

The white man with the nice eyes is coming this way with his magazine and steno pad.

"Hi," he says.

"Hello," I say. I am a professional librarian. I do not say, "Hi" to anyone.

"I was wondering . . ."

That voice. I've heard that voice before. I look at his hand. No ring. No, it couldn't be . . . I glance up at his face. Same face. I think. He had a beard then, but . . . those eyes. They're . . . he's . . . and I didn't—

It's Mr. Shaggy White Man without the Shaggy.

What, has he been stalking me? And where's his wedding ring? What was his name . . . ? Think! I'm so stupid. He reads all those African American authors, and then he walks around with *Essence* likes it's his security blanket or something, and now . . . What is he saying?

"I'm sorry," I say. "I must be tired. Could you repeat your question?"

"Oh," he says, with a breathless little laugh, "I didn't ask a question. I was just saying that I was wondering if every day was like this for you. I couldn't help overhearing some of the questions people were asking you."

Is every day . . . like this, with another person asking me "normal" questions? "I guess." He has such an old face for such young, blue eyes. "Um, it's actually been pretty normal."

"This was a normal day?" He shakes his head. "I don't know how you keep a straight face." He drops his eyes. "I'm sure you heard me laughing at the guy who wanted to know if the *Wall Street Journal* had a business section."

"I did." Dag, is this a shy man or what? But he *is* talking to me. That's not a shy thing to do. And where's his wedding ring?

He touches the counter with his fingers, his nails neatly trimmed. "Anyway, I, uh, I admire your patience. You would make a great teacher."

Where is this going? Is this a come-on? "I would?"

He nods. "Yeah. I teach . . . well, I used to teach fifth-graders."

"Used to teach" sounds . . . bad. "You no longer teach?"

"I'm on kind of a permanent sabbatical."

He was fired.

"By my own choosing," he adds.

He quit.

"They keep calling me in, but . . ."

Wait a minute. They . . . want him back? He only retired? How old *is* he? Young eyes plus old face equals . . . stress.

Fifth-graders must take their toll on a teacher. He can't be a day over thirty-five.

He pulls his hand back from the counter. "I'm sure you have work to do. I didn't mean to bother you." He turns to go.

"What are you writing?" I ask before I can stop myself.

He turns. "Hmm?"

"You were taking notes."

He steps closer but not as close as before. "Just . . . researching."

I look at the magazine. "Using *Essence*?"

"Well, sort of, I mean, yeah."

I know he's hiding something, so I wait for him to explain.

He doesn't explain.

"Well, I guess I'd better be—"

"What are you researching?"

Why can't I let this man just . . . leave? Maybe it's because I've been answering so many questions today that I have to interrogate someone, I don't know. Or maybe it's because he's hiding something. And he *has* been stalking me. Who stalks librarians? Or maybe it's the fact that he says "he'd better be" going, which I wouldn't let him say for some reason, only he doesn't move. When most people say, "I'm out," they *go*. Not this guy.

He smiles that nice smile of his. "You'll probably think it's crazy."

I blink. "I work here, remember? I listen to crazy all day."

"Oh, yeah." He steps close enough for me to notice how stiff his pants are. His teenaged wife must have discovered starch and couldn't find the "off" button. "I'm researching a character for my next novel."

Next novel? I'm in the presence of a novelist. He doesn't look like a novelist. But what's a novelist *supposed* to look like? I mean, Stephen King looks perfectly ghastly as a horror writer, but some of the others—

"And . . . um," he looks into my eyes, "you're it."

"Excuse me?"

"I'm researching a character, and you're it."

I have trouble catching my breath after that one. "I'm . . . it?" As in, "tag, you're it"? What kind of thing to say is that? And who gave you permission to use me in your book?

He looks at his hands. "I told you it was crazy."

At least he's honest. Rude, but honest. "I don't know. It's not *that* crazy." It's actually kind of flattering, except . . . the man's been stalking me. And where exactly is his freaking ring? "What's your next book about?"

He shoves both hands into his pockets and sighs. "Well, I've only written three chapters of it so far, so I'm . . . I'm not really sure. I can tell you that it's a romance, though."

This might be a scam. This might be some sneaky way white men lure women to . . . to what? I decide to play along. "And I'm a character in this . . . romance?"

He nods. "You have a lot to offer."

What did he say? I have a lot to offer? What am I offering? And to whom? One day he's shaggy, the next day clean as a whistle. I can't help but widen the heck out of my eyes. I hope he didn't see—

"I meant, you have a lot to offer as a *character* in any book."

He saw my eyes. "Oh."

"I mean, for one, you have a job everyone can relate to. Who hasn't made contact with a librarian?"

Contact? My hands are starting to sweat. "True."

"And, two, you're, um, African American." He holds up the magazine. "The reason, um, I've been reading this."

I nod, though every fiber in my being wants to ask him one simple question: "Why are you writing about African American women, especially since you thought there was an African American fiction section in the library?" Okay, two simple questions: "Why are you reading *Essence* when you could be talking directly to me?" I know I'm not representative of an entire race, but I'm more of an average African American than any sister in that magazine.

"And, um, three, well, you're, I don't know how to say this, but, um, you're very attrac—"

"Is your other novel here in the library?" I interrupt. Lord, why did I do that? I had no right to interrupt a compliment; I mean, I get so few. It's just that . . . I'm afraid where the rest of number three might be leading. I felt a compliment coming on, and I don't do compliments from strange white men who are shaggy and wearing a wedding ring one day and clean shaven, shorthaired, and ringless the next.

"Oh, it's not due out until April."

I grab a pad of Post-its. "What is your novel's title?"

He squints.

"Oh," I say, "I just want to know the title so the library can preorder it. You're a local author, aren't you?"

"Yes."

I poise the pencil over the Post-it. "So, what's the title?"

"It's called *Wishful Thinking*."

No . . . way.

This kind of thing doesn't happen.

I break the tip of the pencil and get another. I must have heard wrong. "What's it called again?"

"*Wishful Thinking*."

No. This *is* happening. This is D. J. Browning. This is the writer I trashed the other day. This isn't someone else. My hand shakes as I write down the title. "And, oh, I've forgotten your name."

"Jack Browning."

I don't look up. Whew. Wrong name. Blue Eyes here didn't look like a "D.J." He looks like a "Jack," which makes no sense, I know. So, his book is titled the same as the other one, which is kind of strange, and they're both bound to come out at about the same time, but there aren't trademarks on titles—

"The publisher is using only my initials."

Is Jack Browning D. J. Browning? I have to know more. "Is, um, do you have a middle name?"

He squints. "Actually, Jack is my middle name. My first name is David. Why do you want to know?"

David Jack Browning. D. J. Browning. Oh, they really went all out disguising him. "Oh, just curious." Talk fast. "Why'd they want you to use your initials?"

He shrugs. "I guess they were afraid or something. I mean, it's not every day a white man writes, um, multicultural fiction."

No, it isn't. Jesus, help me!

"I originally wrote *Mr. Pace and Ms. Clarke*—that was my working title—and it was about two dysfunctional white people."

That explains a *lot*.

"My agent and editor, though, they thought it could be . . . transformed—that was the word they used—transformed into a multicultural romantic comedy."

They transformed it into something, all right.

"Anyway, they want me to write another, and, well, I'd like to model my main character after you."

That's so sweet, but—

"You were so helpful that day I came in looking so . . . bushy." He laughs. "I normally look this way." He looks down. "Not like Grizzly Adams."

Oh, God, I wish he were a jerk or something. He's nice! And I've written so many reviews, but I've never come face-to-face with any author I've criticized, and here he is—in all his skinny white flesh—and I have a review trashing his book—

Which won't post for another three days.

Maybe I can stop it. Maybe I can get Amazon.com not to post it. That's what I'll try to do. And then I'll read the entire book, cover to cover. Maybe I was a little too judgmental in my assessment—

But then again . . . the book wasn't that good, the parts I

read of it anyway. And now that I know it was meant to have two white people getting together . . . No, I can't let on in my review that I know that. Oh, geez, he's still talking, and I haven't been listening.

". . . six months without a haircut. I won't let that happen again."

This is crazy! Calm down, girl, calm down. Everything will be okay. And anyway, here's a man who is hiding his wedding ring. He's a dog. He's no good, even if he does have some fine blue eyes. I look up. "I'll bet your wife is proud of you."

His eyes fall.

Aha! Gotcha!

"She was."

Past tense. Was. She *was.* Separated? Divorced? What?

"She isn't proud now?" I can't believe I'm prying.

He turns away. "I don't know. She's . . . I have to be going." He takes a few steps away. "Um, it was nice meeting you, Diane."

"It was nice meeting you, too, Jack." Or should I say "D.J."? No. I can't let him know I know what he doesn't know. Did that make sense? No! This is all so confusing! "Uh, Jack, could you give me your phone number?"

"My what?"

I'm asking for this possibly divorced/separated okay/so-so novelist's phone number. What am I thinking? "Um, your phone number. So that . . . the library can contact you, say, for a reading or even a book signing."

He looks at his feet. Nice shoes. They look comfortable. "I don't think I'll be doing any readings or signings. I'm, um, supposed to be anonymous."

"Oh, yeah." Think! "Well, then, why not just . . ." What am I doing? I'm about to ask him for his phone number. But why? "Why not just give me your number?"

He doesn't move.

"I mean, um . . ." I can't think! "So I can call you . . ."

He moves closer. "So you can call me?"

"Uh, yeah, you know, so you can give me . . ." What? Give me what? Whew. Thank God I'm a librarian. "So you can give me the ISBN number and the Library of Congress control number for the book. It makes it so much easier for us to preorder your book."

He moves to the counter. "You could get the ISBN number from Amazon.com."

I should have thought of that. "But not the LOC number." And now I'm speaking in abbreviations.

"Okay."

He gives me his number, I write it down, and this time my hand doesn't shake. It vibrates. It literally hums. "Thank you, Mr. Browning."

"You're welcome, and please call me Jack."

"Okay, Jack." And I don't know Jack, do I?

"Bye." He walks away.

Say something! "Um, say hello to your little boy for me."

Jack's shoulders slump as he nods and continues toward the stairs.

That was strange. Maybe his wife has the kid and he won't see him for a while. That's so sad! I should have kept my big mouth shut.

As soon as Jack's bobbing blond head disappears down the stairs, I put up my sign and leave the counter. I have to find an open computer in the Internet Room—

Damn. Sorry, Lord! They're all taken! These . . . people without computers in their homes should be shot, and I mean it.

Okay, I don't really mean it, but, well, today—now, this *second*—I do. I have to undo my review until I've read the entire book, Lord. I wasn't fair in my review. And I know that I still might hate it even if I read the entire thing, but . . .

Somebody finish! Click-clickety-click your way out of here! These computer hoggers are just as bad as those cheap people who come into the library to make copies from cookbooks. They're just as bad as people who return books with toilet tissue or used Band-Aids or condom wrappers for bookmarks. They're just as bad as those snot-nosed children in the big chairs downstairs coughing up phlegm on every book their grimy, disease-infested hands touch. They're just as bad as anyone who comes into the library only to take a dump!

"Excuse me!"

I see a computer hogger waving his stank hand at me. I'm not on duty here! No one is on duty in here since we don't have enough funding! I walk over anyway. "Yes?"

"I'm having trouble getting on Yahoo!."

I look at the address line. He has typed "Youwho.com." I smile. Fool. "There must be something wrong with this computer, sir." I switch it off without properly shutting it down. Kim would have a cow. "We've been having lots of trouble with this computer, for some reason."

"Oh," he says. "It was running real slow, too."

Yes, now run along like a good dog.

"But all the other computers are taken."

Then go buy one, you cheapskate! They're on sale at Best Buy!

"I need to check my e-mail."

In my best teacher's voice, I say, "You'll have to wait your turn."

He stands and grabs his coat from the back of his chair. "I'm out of here."

"Do come back tomorrow, sir. I'm sure this one will be fixed."

"Whatever."

I had to do some damage control. "We don't want any patron leaving in a huff," Kim is forever saying. Though Jack left in one, didn't he? I'll have to call him, you know, just to get that LOC number . . . tonight . . . and to find out if I'm still a character in his book after being so nosy.

And as soon as the computer hogger's greasy, dark-haired

head bobs down the stairs, I boot up the computer, and, like he said, it *is* slow. Someone needs to clean out the cache file. I would do it, but I'm in a rush.

Once I'm finally on Amazon.com, I type in "Wishful Thinking" in the search box. Ten seconds later, the page finally loads. "Hi, Ty," I say to the screen. "You miss me?"

And then . . . I see *Wishful Thinking* by D. J. Browning.

"Do you work here?"

I look behind me at a well-dressed white man with silver hair carrying a briefcase, an overcoat, and an umbrella. "Yes, sir."

"There's a problem with the copy machine."

Do I look like I care about the damn (sorry, Lord) copy machine? "What seems to be the trouble?"

"It won't copy."

"Did you put in exact change? Sometimes it runs out of change."

He blinks. "You mean I have to pay?"

No, well-dressed white man. Only *you* have to pay. "Yes, sir. Fifteen cents a copy."

"You're kidding."

I shake my head.

"But this is a *public* library!"

We have to pay for toner and a service contract just like anybody else. "I'm sorry, sir. If you need to make change, go to—"

He waves his hand at me. "Never mind."

Normally, I'd be mad at someone like this man, who has been waiting all day to be rude to someone, and I just happened to be the lucky woman.

But today I'm too confused.

24

Jack

I'm sitting in space #38 in the All-Rite Parking lot having yet another conversation with myself.

I have no life.

Why did you leave?

You heard what she was saying about Noël and Stevie. It was too much for me.

She was just starting to get interested, and you just . . . left. What kind of a man are you?

Look, I know you're the part of me who wants to start a new life—

And you're the part of us who wants to live in the past. You're taking this "divided man" idea too far. She asked for your phone number, Jack! Diane, a woman you just met, asked you for your phone number.

So she could get the ISBN and LOC numbers to make it easier—

You don't believe that, do you? You saw her hand shaking. You know she was excited.

Only because I told her I was basing a character on her.

Come on, Jack. She kept trying to keep the conversation going, and most of it wasn't about the book. She wouldn't let you go.

Maybe she wanted some intelligent, adult conversation.

She was trying to get to know you, Jack. Why didn't you just spill it all?

I didn't want to depress her.

No, you didn't want to depress yourself. Get over it. It's been six months. Life shouldn't end because two lives ended. They wouldn't want that.

They were part of me. They made me . . . *me!*

I don't know what to do with you, Jack.

I don't know what to do with me either.

My mind is quiet for a while, which is strange. Of course, it's strange to see a man sitting in a car arguing with himself, too.

Her eyes light up, don't they?

Yeah.

And you know she's going to call you, maybe even tonight.

I doubt it.

You won't know if you don't get home.

I have to get some groceries.

And more Kleenex, right?

Not this time.

Really? You're thinking with your stomach for a change?

I want my clothes to fit right.

To give Diane something to hold on to.

I don't answer myself right away.

Maybe.

I don't normally shop at this Kroger, but I know I have a Kroger-Plus card on my key chain. Noël collected those things. I even have one for Harris-Teeter, though I don't even know where one is in Roanoke. All I know is that I'm going to save money.

You paid twenty dollars to park for five hours.

Time well spent.

I pick up a basket inside Kroger, then cruise the aisle shopping a la carte without a cart.

You should have been a poet.

No money in that. Yet, people respect poets more, because they're better able to distill life into a few words and phrases.

As I pass the Lunchables—Stevie's favorite lunch—an old poem creeps into my head, something about my best work is under the snow. Something like that. Robert Lowell? I think so. Yeah, Stevie was my best poem, my best work.

The signs read "3 for $7," so I take three ham and cheese Lunchables with Spiderman on the front. He would have liked these. He went as Spiderman at Halloween last year. He didn't scare anyone, but at every house—

"Ah, he's so cute," they said.

Yeah.

You didn't give out candy this year.

I will next year.

I walk a few more aisles until I decide to make Noël's famous Crock-Pot chicken.

You don't even know the recipe.

Ah, but I know what's in it. I buy a pound and a half of skinless chicken breasts, the largest Vidalia onion in the bin, a package of dry onion soup mix, and a can of mushroom soup. Is that all?

What are you going to put it on?

Oh yeah. Rice. I know we have a few boxes in the pantry.

Don't forget the spices.

The pantry is full of those.

Oh yeah. Noël was always experimenting with different spices. Remember the time she asked you for the paprika, and you handed her the cayenne pepper instead?

It was the same color.

What a disaster that would have been.

So, her egg salad would have had a little more kick.

You liked her egg salad.

She made it look so easy.

A woman pushing a small boy in a cart catches my eye in the frozen-food section. She has dusty blonde hair—

Another brunette having an affair with bleach.

Shh.

I sidle closer to her and the boy, acting as if I'm looking at . . . frozen turnips?

They freeze everything these days.

And then, I listen. . . . He wants to ride in the cart. She says, "Not now." He wants to ride on the side, hanging on like a fireman. She says, "No." He wants to push the cart. She says, "Sit still."

He wishes he were older.

Yeah. He wants to help. He wants to be a big boy.

Just like Stevie.

Noël and I indulged Stevie's every wish on our infrequent shopping trips together. We made him an active part of our shopping experience.

Saying "yes" more than saying "no."

As it should be.

If it had Spiderman on it, it went into the cart.

Yeah.

She's looking this way. Check out the rock on her finger.

I look back at the turnips, listening to the boy. They roll by behind me, and I look again.

Right into her eyes.

You're not very sneaky.

She smiles, her eyes soften, and she moves on, looking back once or twice.

Flirting with a married woman in the frozen-food section of Kroger?

I wasn't flirting. I was looking.

Looking at a ready-made family.

No, I was just being the sponge that I am.

Too skinny anyway.

And too mean to her child.

Instead of having a cashier overanalyze my purchases—at least I've heard they do that to customers—I try out the U-Scan for the first time.

"Welcome to Kroger. Press the touch screen to begin."

I press the "start" button.

"Do you have a Kroger-Plus card?"

I press "yes."

"Scan your Kroger-Plus card now."

Why does she have to be so loud?

I don't know. I scan my card and hear a beep.

"Welcome, Kroger-Plus-card member. Scan your first item, and place it in the bag."

I scan one of the Lunchables, hear a beep, and put it in the bag. It comes up as $3.29.

I thought it was three for seven bucks.

So did I. Maybe it will recalculate at the end.

I scan the other two Lunchables and the rest of my purchases. But when I get to the onion, I'm stumped.

You can't scan an onion.

I know.

I press the "produce" button.

"Key in the number on your produce item."

There's no number.

Why couldn't I just type in "onion"?

The world is number driven.

Don't I know it.

I look up at a plastic roller filled with numbers for asparagus, carrots, green peppers, lettuce, onions . . . but "sweet Vidalia" isn't listed.

"Key in the number on your produce item."

I look at the attendant, a sweet-faced teenaged girl. "I'm having trouble finding Vidalia on here."

She steps over, picks up my onion, puts it down, then goes to her computer. In a few moments, I hear, "Place your item in the bag."

You filled only one bag.

Hey, that's three lunches and at least three dinners right there.

What about breakfast?

There's cereal in the pantry.

There's some really old cereal in the pantry.

Cereal never decays.

I press "finish" and hear, "Do you have any coupons?"

"No."

Press the button, Jack.

I press "no."

So now you're talking to computers.

She . . . it . . . whatever asked me a question.

A new screen with payment buttons appears. "Select your method of payment."

Geez, there are eight different ways to pay.

What, no "give blood" button? Your total seems high.

Yeah, it does.

I press "debit."

"Do you want any cash back?"

I press "no."

"Insert your card into the card reader, and follow the instructions."

I slide my debit through, punch in my password, and wait for the total to change.

It doesn't.

"Take your receipt, collect your bags, and thank you for shopping at Kroger."

I pick up my bag and analyze the receipt. The "3 for $7" didn't take effect for some reason. I approach the attendant. "Something's not right here."

I hand her the receipt.

"The sign back there says three for seven dollars," I say, "and I don't see it reflected on the receipt."

She smiles. "There's nothing I can do here. You'll have to go to customer service." She points to a counter at the front of the store.

I take my receipt. "Thanks."

I walk to the counter, only there's no one behind the counter. After a four-minute wait, a woman with short hair and a tattoo on her neck shows up. I hand her the receipt and explain what happened.

She grabs a phone, hits a few numbers, and says, "I need a price check on ham and cheese Lunchables." She hangs up. "It will only take a moment."

Several moments pass. Then several more moments pass.

Moments shouldn't take this long.

Shh. I'm about to save three dollars.

Finally, the oldest living Kroger worker, a woman wearing a plastic cap on her head, sidles up to me at barely a stumble. "Those aren't on sale," she heaves. "Those are full price."

"But every sign back there under every Lunchable says three for seven."

She shakes her head. "Not under those."

"But I saw the sign."

"Did you read the numbers under the sign?" she asks.

"No, ma'am. I just assumed that what was above the sign meant that the Lunchables above the sign were three for seven dollars."

She leans on the counter. "Every other one is three for seven, just not the ham and cheese."

You know how to pick them.

Shh. I'm getting my Irish on.

"Then there shouldn't be a sign under the ham and cheese proclaiming that they are three for seven when they aren't three for seven. It's deceptive."

"They weren't under the ham and cheese."

She's calling you a liar.

"But they were!"

"No, they weren't." She looks at the customer service woman. "Long day, huh?" She looks back at me. "Want me to go back and show you?"

She may even be calling you a blind liar.

"So, you're saying that the customer is wrong."

The customer service woman steps closer. "We can give you a refund, sir."

"I don't want a refund," I say. "I'm hungry. Perhaps you can fix your signs so you don't have to tell another Kroger-Plus-card member he or she is wrong."

The old woman rolls her eyes. "The signs aren't wrong. You are. Those signs are clearly marked."

"So clearly marked that they confused a valued customer?"

"You must not have been reading closely enough," she says, with a smile.

I hate it when they smile.

Especially when they don't mean it.

"You want your money back?" the customer service woman asks.

I look from the old woman in the smashing plastic cap to the bored customer service woman. "No." I put my Kroger-Plus card on the counter. "I won't be needing this anymore."

"But, sir—"

I stare hard at the old woman. "I paid the wrong price."

"Oh," she says, "listen to him."

I stare harder at the old woman. "You know I paid the wrong price. I'll bet you didn't even check the prices."

Ask her if she went to school with the original Mr. Kroger.

This isn't about age. This is about justice.

She's old enough.

Shh.

"I checked the price." She flutters a withered hand in my face. "You just can't read."

I step around her, saying loudly, "I know, I know, the customer is always wrong. Thank you for shopping at Kroger." I stop and turn. "I paid the wrong price."

And as I leave Kroger, I realize that I've been paying the wrong price for a long time.

25

Diane

I had no luck retrieving my review on my own, so I wrote e-mails to Amazon's customer service and technical support for help before clocking out and going home. I should know within twenty-four hours how to fix everything, but I wish—

I wish I hadn't been so hasty to judge that book. And the things I said about D. J. Browning—who is really David Jack Browning, blue-eyed, somewhat handsome blond man—were harsh! I did everything but call him a racist, and now that I know him a little better, I know in my heart that he isn't a racist. He's a little misguided, maybe. I mean, he's using *Essence* as his handbook for the modern black woman. Though *Essence* tries, it cannot possibly cover every aspect of the modern black woman.

And he wants to put *me* in the book! *Me*, of all people! I'm not in *Essence*. My body type is not in *Essence*. The clothes I wear are not featured in *Essence*. The hair products I use . . . Okay, they're in *Essence*, but that's not the point.

Jack needs a real, live, actual sister to be his technical advisor, not some made-up, done-up, skinny models with their curves in all the right places. He needs someone like me to help him write a decent book.

He needs me.

A man needs me. This is . . . odd. But does he know he needs me? I mean, does he know that he needs my help? Maybe my original review will prove to him that he does. Maybe I don't need to take back what I wrote. Maybe my review is the kick in the pants that he needs to write a real book.

And maybe it will shatter his ego. I've heard of authors pitching a fit over Amazon reviews they thought were unfair, and I've heard of some reviews simply disappearing because an author—

That's an idea. I'll convince Jack that "Nisi's" review was unfair. Then, he can get it removed, and I don't have to do a thing. Yes, that's the way to do it. I'm sure his publisher will do something to protect him.

No, no. It was my mistake, and I'll have to fix it.

But what if the review can't be taken back, and Jack finds out that I wrote it? That's silly. How would he ever find out . . . unless I told him? I can never tell him that I wrote it. Never. It would break his heart.

And mine, too.

I have to call him. Our conversation didn't end as I wanted it to end. Actually, I didn't want it to end. He was so easy to talk to, despite all his "ums" and "uhs." Wait. I was "uming" and "uhing," too. I probably sounded so desperate.

But, what if his wife answers? If she's even there. And why wouldn't she be proud anymore? If she's white—and she has to be to dress Jack that way—maybe she's not proud of him writing about Ty. Maybe she thinks he's writing about his fantasies with a black woman. I'll bet that's it. She's jealous of Ty, and maybe his original white woman was based on his wife, and she's not happy about the changes. I know it would piss me off if my man wrote about someone like Ty. "Where'd you meet her?" I would ask. "How do you know so much about her?"

Jealousy may be overworked in fiction for a very good reason: it's *everywhere* in real life.

Yeah, that would be hard to explain. I mean, he could say, "Honey, they're only fantasies. They're not real. This is fiction. I made her up out of my head."

Hmm. I wouldn't buy it for a second.

I look at the phone. I should call him anyway, at least to get the LOC number, like I said I would. But . . . it's late. Strange black women calling late at night could confirm his wife's fears. But how would she know I was black? I speak clear, "white" English as well as if not better than most white people in Roanoke. Oh, but then she'd ask, "Who was that, honey?"

I know *I* would.

Shoot. Whom can I talk to about any of this? Mama? Not a chance. As soon as I say "blue eyes," she'll be clutching her chest. Reesie? No way. She'd say something like, "I *knew* you were adopted." Daddy? Hmm. Daddy might understand. I'm his "baby." He always listens to me . . . and reports *everything* I say directly to Mama.

I look at the ceiling. God? I know You don't share my business with the world, and I'm kind of confused right now. I don't know what to do. I don't know if I should get my review back or not. I don't know if I should call Jack or not. I don't know if I should even care so much for a man I just met who might be married!

Help a sister out.

Amen.

26
Jack

I'm cutting fat off the chicken breasts while the Crock-Pot warms up, and though it's a mindless task, I can't stop thinking.

You really told her off.

No, I didn't.

I was impressed. The old Jack wouldn't have even gone to the customer service counter. He would have folded up his receipt, stuffed it in his pocket, and gone home.

I still don't like conflict.

But didn't it make you feel good to speak your mind?

Yeah. A little.

You asserted yourself with plastic bag head, just as you asserted yourself with Diane.

We only talked a little bit.

It was the most you've talked to anyone except me in months!

I was babbling, wasn't I?

No. Not really. You might have given her too much information about the book. You're not the book, Jack.

I know that.

You should have told Diane about Noël and Stevie.

Diane was—and is—still a stranger to me. I can't dump all that on her.

You left her with too many questions about you.

So, I'm a man of mystery.

You should have asked her out.

Huh?

You should have said something like, "I know this is kind of sudden, but would you like to have lunch with me sometime?"

I couldn't say that.

You make your characters say things like that all the time. Just . . . write yourself something to say.

Not a bad idea. I always think better on paper. But why lunch?

So she'll know it's not serious. Lunch is friendly. Dinner, though, that means serious.

Why?

Because . . . because it's dark outside usually, and darkness was made for love.

Quit quoting from *Wishful Thinking*. I'm trying to put that book behind me.

It was a good line.

It could be considered a racist line, too.

You think too much.

But obviously not enough. I should have asked her out, right?

You still can. Go back to the library tomorrow and ask her.

Tomorrow?

You have any plans?

No.

And, if she accepts—

If?

Okay, when *she accepts, that could lead to a New Year's Eve date.*

She's working on New Year's Eve.

Right. Until nine. The celebrations don't start until midnight . . . when it's dark . . . and darkness was made for love.

Geez, I nearly just cut my finger off. I have to stop thinking about Diane. She's not like any of the women in *Essence,* and yet she's . . . more.

Now you're thinking.

She did ask for my phone number.

She sure did.

Noël didn't do that. I had to ask.

Maybe it's a black woman thing.

Or simply a "Diane thing."

Maybe.

You need to think outside the racial box.

While I slice up the onion—and tear like crazy!—I think of Diane. It feels so strange. For five years only Noël has been in my head, and now . . . Diane. She has a clear, distinct voice. It's not a lilting, melodious, or "cute" voice. It's a voice I can listen to. And her eyes aren't, well, "pools of starlight" or some other such nonsense I wrote to describe Ty's eyes. They're . . . soft and open, though they roll around a good bit. And her smile? It doesn't set the world on fire or stop traffic or sparkle. It just . . . moves me. And her body wasn't anywhere in *Essence.* She isn't "bootylicious" or "fly" or "da bomb." She's plainly . . . attractive. That's it. She's attractive. From the tone of her calves to the curve of her . . . *form,* from the light from her face to the kindness in her eyes, Diane is . . . genuinely attractive to me.

I like her.

I wipe tears from my eyes, some of them caused by the onion, the others caused by a single thought: I like her.

Noël would like her.

How can you say that?

They might even have been friends.

Yeah. They might have been.

The phone rings.

It's Diane!

No, it isn't. It's dinnertime, so it's probably some telemarketer.

I pick up the phone, and it nearly slides out of my hand.

Your hands are sweaty.

Shh. "Hello?"

"Hi, this is Jenny Dwyer."

Who?

"I called about the car yesterday."

"Oh, yeah." The drive-by lady.

"I must have missed you today. The car looks real nice. How does it drive?"

"Uh, I don't normally drive it. It's my wife's car."

"Oh, is she there? I'd like to talk to her about it."

I sigh. "Um, she's not here at the moment."

Why didn't you tell her the truth?

I'm not ready.

Yes, you are.

"When will she be back?"

I clear my throat. "She won't be back, uh, Jenny, because she died six months ago."

"Oh, I'm so sorry."

Not as sorry as I am.

"Well, um, hmm. Uh, when can I drive it?"

I feel a little weight come off my shoulders. "Anytime."

"How about tonight?"

She is so eager! You're a magnet for eager women, Jack!

No, I'm not. One wants information on a book, and the other wants a car. Neither wants me.

You never know . . .

"How about tomorrow . . . morning, around nine?"

"Sounds good. I'll see you tomorrow morning. Bye."

"Bye."

I hang up.

See how easy that was? And Jenny is a perfect stranger.

I didn't have to face her or see her reaction. That made it easier.

Easier is good.

Yeah.

So when Diane calls . . .

Shh.

After mixing the onions with the soup and the soup mix and pouring the goop over the chicken, I turn the Crock-Pot on low and head for my office. As soon as I sit and get a fresh screen, I start typing:

Where do rainbows go when they're done . . . rainbowing?

"Rainbowing" isn't a word.

Shh. I think I'm on to something.

English is too limiting sometimes. "Rainbowing" should be a word. I mean, what else do rainbows do? They rainbow.

"Rainbow" isn't a verb, either.

It is now.

Roy G. Biv. Hmm. He sounds foreign. He probably isn't from around here, which is somewhere lost in the South, where everyone has the same old, dull Southern names and accents. Good ol' Roy G. flies in during a storm as if to mock the thunder, sneer at the rain, raise a colorful eyebrow at the lightning, shrugging clouds off his back. That's my kind of man, and if he *is* foreign, he can marry me to become an American citizen. I can give Roy G. Biv his green card.

So much potential color for my life . . .

What makes a rainbow anyway? Maybe the clouds do, pressing them out like linguini or sweating them out like Play-Doh. And what makes them go away? Do breezes blow them around? How do they stay locked in place during a storm? And who would ever chase them?

Besides me?

I'll bet there's a rainbow with every storm, and I just haven't always looked with my soul hard enough to see it.

I'm not after the pot of gold at the end of the rainbow. Just a man.

A man like Roy G. Biv.

That was poetic.

It's a bit too flowery.

At least it sounds like a woman might say it.

It wasn't a woman saying it. It was me.

You want . . . a man like Roy G. Biv?

No, but I wouldn't mind having a woman who thought like she did.

You're getting heavily into your feminine side, aren't you, Jack?

Maybe.

I reread the screen. There's something . . . wrong with it.

It's soft.

It's crap, and I should delete it.

Noël would have liked it.

Yeah, she would have. I'll keep it.

Good.

27

Diane

The phone is staring at me. It's been staring at me all night. Occasionally it even shouts, "Call him!" As a result, I've read the same freaking page of *The Da Vinci Code* at least fifteen times!

I've picked up the phone at least ten times, but I can't force myself to punch in the number. I've never called up a man *first* in my life . . . which might be one reason I'm twenty-five and still an unmarried virgin. Hmm.

But the man is *supposed* to call the woman. It's in all the romances I read. I mean, there she is, by the phone or window or up on a lighthouse, waiting for her man to call/visit/come home from the sea.

He doesn't have your number, Diane.

Oh yes he does! He could always call the library!

You're not at the library, Diane.

Oh yeah.

I need more courage.

There's pound cake in the fridge. That will give me enough courage. Sugar can do that.

No. I shouldn't eat sweets after nine. I need to just pick up the phone and call him.

I pick up the phone.

What if he's not there? What if his wife answers? What if no one's there?

I set the phone back down.

If no one's there, do I leave a message for him to call me back? I could do that, but . . . then I'll fall asleep with the phone in my hand, and since I'm an active sleeper, I'll most likely make a long distance phone call to Fiji by accident. If his wife's there and he isn't, I could . . . play it off as a . . . fund-raiser for the library. It might work. And if no one answers, I'll . . . just hang up.

But he'll see my name on his Caller ID! And so will she! Unless he doesn't have Caller ID, but who doesn't have Caller ID these days? He has to have Caller ID, and when he checks for a message, there won't be one from me. I hate when that happens to me. Someone calls for whatever reason and doesn't have the decency to leave a message. That's just plain rude.

Yet, I always call the person back anyway. Why is that? Am I a "rude person" magnet or what?

I dial Jack's number, and after five rings with no answer, I become rude and hang up.

That was dumb. He might have been in the bathroom or the shower or out walking his dog. He seems like a dog person, and I don't know why I think that. It must be his former shagginess. He might have even been giving his son a bath or reading his son a bedtime story or taking out the trash or . . . messing around with his wife!

Eww.

Or he might have been asleep! He looked so tired.

It is kind of late. Oh, Lord, I probably woke him up, he couldn't find the phone, and now he's seeing my name on his

Caller ID, his wife is seeing my name on the Caller ID, and—

Time to play it off. I dial Jack's number again.

He answers on the first ring. "Hello?"

He doesn't sound groggy. "Hi, Jack." Good grief! I just said, "Hi, Jack"! I'll bet he hates that joke!

"Hello, Diane Anderson. Did you just call a minute or so ago?"

He has Caller ID all right, but at least he has my number somewhere in his house. Or apartment? No, he seems like a man with a house. And a dog. "Oh, yeah. I didn't think you were home."

"I was downstairs writing."

Of course he was, Diane! He's a writer. What else would he be doing? "Well, I don't want to disturb you."

"It's okay. Do you want the LOC number?"

Oh, yeah. That. And that number is the reason *he* thinks I called. "Of course. That's why I called."

I write down the numbers as he reads them, and I read them back to him. "Thanks. I'll be sure to get our preorder in tomorrow."

"Great."

And then there's silence. We've just taken care of the "reason" I called, and now there's static-filled silence. I hate silence, unless Mama's on the other end.

"So, uh, how's your writing going?" Whew. Hopefully this will start a conversation.

"Better."

Better? Just . . . better? How vague is that? I want to ask him if he's been writing about me, but I just can't. "Well, that's good."

"I've been writing about you."

And now my face is on fire. How do you respond when a man says *this,* especially if he's writing "better" and about you? "You have?"

"Yes."

"Um, great." Why can't I put together a decent sentence? And why didn't I eat some of that pound cake? I don't have enough sugar going to my brain! "That's, um, that's great, Jack."

I hear him sigh. "Listen, Diane, I have something to tell you that I should have already told you."

I brace for the worst. "Okay." Time to hear about the wife and kid . . . or kiddies? Maybe there are other rugrats or there's one on the way. . . .

He sighs again. "When I brought those books back that day, um . . . this is hard for me."

Books? Oh, yeah. Strange way to start, but . . . okay. He's going about this from the very beginning.

"I found those books in my son's room . . . where I've been sleeping for the last six months."

Teenaged no-ironing wife kicked him out of their bedroom? Is this where he tells me he's leaving his wife?

"And I've been sleeping in his bed because . . . my son, Stevie, and my wife, Noël . . . died in an accident last July."

Died. They . . . died. He's a widower. Oh, that's so sad! And now I'm sad! I was pestering him about his wife and son, and he was standing there . . . dying inside. I can't even imagine the heartbreak he's feeling! But why was he still wearing the ring when he was shaggy?

"And anyway, I don't know if you even remember, but when you gave me my change for the fine, you touched my hand. I hadn't let anyone, I mean, no one had touched me for the longest time, and, um, you did."

I hear him sobbing, and I start to tear up. I've given change to countless patrons, and to think that this one time . . . just a *touch*. And the next time I saw him, I didn't even *see* him because he had changed so *much*.

And now I'm rhyming while I'm thinking.

Why didn't I see him? Was it because he was a cookie-cutter white man? Or was it because I really wasn't looking?

But he saw me. Jack saw me. A man saw me as more than just a name on a badge behind a counter in a public library. Lord, I need to work on my blind spots.

"I'm sorry," he says, finally. "I shouldn't be dumping all this on you."

"It's okay." I walk into the kitchen to get a napkin and dab it at my eyes. "It's okay, Jack." And it is. It's okay. I'm okay with this.

"I've been meaning to thank you for . . . touching me, even though you didn't know you did it. This must sound so strange."

"It's not so strange." The slightest touch *can* change a life. "Remember, I work at a public library."

"Right," he says, his voice less weepy. "But if I put any of this in a book, no one would believe it."

A few minutes ago, I wouldn't have believed it either. Right. A touch exchanged with change. Sure. But now . . . "I believe it, Jack, because I know it can happen. It just did, right?"

Silence.

"I'm, um, sorry I didn't recognize you right away today, Jack."

He laughs, at least I think it's a laugh. Kind of . . . throaty, but nice. "Today is how I used to look. I mean, well, you know what I mean."

"I understand."

More silence.

"I've lost so much weight."

I smile. "You did kind of look like a scarecrow." Now why did I say that? I mean, other than the fact that he *does* look like a straw-filled stickman in his clothes. He's a blond Ichabod Crane . . . who saw his own headless horseman this past summer. Oh, what a shame!

"Yeah. I forget to eat sometimes." He coughs. "Speaking of eating, would you like to have lunch with me sometime?"

Whoa. I just called the man a scarecrow, and he asks me

to lunch. I would trash this whole scene if I had read it in a book, but here it is happening to me!

"Uh, I mean, you know, Diane, to discuss your character, the one in my book. I could maybe . . . interview you."

He's trying to play it off as a "professional" arrangement. Should I let him?

No.

"You mean you'd be taking notes during our date?" Oh my Lord! I just used the D-word. He was just asking me to lunch, and I think I've just made it into a date.

"Oh, um, yeah, that would be tacky. I won't take notes."

It *would* be tacky.

"I'll, uh, just take you in."

Blink-blink.

"I mean, I'll . . . I'll just talk to you, Diane."

I don't know, getting taken in sounds kind of fun. But he hasn't questioned the D-word yet. Maybe he didn't hear me say it. "So, we'll just talk during our lunch date."

"I'd like that."

Is "lunch date" the same as "date"? Hmm. I have to be sure. "Are you asking me out on a date, Jack?"

A slight pause. "If I were asking you out on a real date, I'd ask you out to dinner on New Year's Eve." Another pause. "But I know you have to work, so it would have to be a late dinner."

I smile. He has actually thought this through. But has he thought it *all* the way through? "It would probably be hard getting a dinner reservation this late. I mean, it's just two days until New Year's."

"I can call around. I have plenty of time."

He still hasn't asked me officially. "So, are you asking me out for New Year's Eve, Jack?"

He clears his throat. "I'd, um, rather ask you in person, Diane, and by then I ought to know where we can go. So, will you go with me or meet me somewhere for lunch tomorrow?"

I smile. "Sure. Where?"

"I was hoping you'd tell me. I don't normally eat downtown, so I don't know what's good and what isn't."

I don't eat out downtown much, either. Hmm. But, I've always wanted to go to this one place. . . . "How about Bandini's on the Market?"

"Great. What time suits you?"

"My lunch hour starts at twelve-thirty, so . . . twelve-forty? It's only a ten-minute walk for me." Hint-hint: Pick me up, Jack. It's supposed to be cold.

"Could I pick you up in front of the library at twelve-thirty-five?"

He's quick! "That would be great."

"Okay. I'll see you tomorrow in front of the library at twelve-thirty-five."

"Great."

More silence, but it's the kind of silence you swim in and enjoy, waves of silence filled with tingling, sweaty fingers and warm hands.

"I'm glad you called, Diane."

I'm glad I did, too, but I can't just . . . jump for this man. "And I was only calling about the LOC number."

"Oh, yeah. Well, I'm glad you listened . . . and accepted."

I'm glad about that, too, but I'm still not jumping. "I'll see you tomorrow, Jack."

"Okay. Bye, Diane."

"Good-bye, Jack."

Click.

I . . . have . . . a . . . date!

I, a twenty-five year-old suede sister with some junk in my trunk am going out to lunch with a six-foot, skinny, ashy, blond-haired, blue-eyed scarecrow.

Lord, we are going to clash so badly!

And, for some reason, I can't wait!

It's about time I had *some* kind of life.

28
Jack

You are so smooth when you want to be.
   I wasn't trying to be smooth. I was scared to death!
   Fear works for you. You can put the phone down now.
   Oh, yeah.
   I put the phone in its cradle and wiped my hands on my pants. I had to switch hands several times during the conversation, they were sweating so much. I felt like such a kid.
   Was I babbling? I was babbling, wasn't I?
   It takes a while for you to get going, but once you do, you flow out loud, too.
   Geez, Bandini's. I hear it's good.
   Just don't wear white to an Italian restaurant.
   Yeah. What *do* I wear?
   The same thing you've been wearing. Be casual.
   But I'd be wearing the clothes Noël picked out for me on a date with another woman.
   So?

There's something . . . wrong with that.

Look, unless you do some laundry, the only clothes you have that are clean are—

Okay, okay.

Just don't iron them this time.

I don't even know if I have any clean underwear.

Go "cowboy," then.

No way!

You're changing, Jack. You're getting better. Live a little.

Without underwear?

How will she know?

That's not the point. *I'll* know. It'll be cold tomorrow, and I know I'll feel a draft.

So, do a load of whites.

I'll do a load of whites.

Ten minutes later, I realize something: I have a lot of "off-whites" to wash. Why is it that whites don't want to stay white? Maybe the entire universe works toward color or something.

Nothing white can stay, either.

You said it.

I am shin deep in six months of unwashed clothing in the laundry room, none of it Stevie's or Noël's, thankfully. She must have done the laundry that day. . . .

You've let them pile up for far too long, Jack.

I know, but . . . how can someone live this way?

You weren't really living, Jack. You were just getting up in the morning for lack of anything better to do, wandering around the house, and drinking yourself to sleep. But now, you have a purpose.

And that is?

To start over. You have a woman coming over tomorrow morning to drive the car. She sounded pretty on the phone.

How . . . Just because her voice sounded pretty doesn't mean—

"Pretty choices made by pretty voices."

Will you quit quoting that . . . novel I don't want to think about anymore?

I'll bet she's hot. Mustangs are babe magnets.

Noël drove the Mustang.

And she was a babe.

You're talking about my wife and Stevie's mother, now. "Babe" isn't used to describe—

It should *be, especially by her husband. You still thought she was a babe, especially when she pulled up in that Mustang the first time you went down to Smith Mountain Lake.*

Yeah. She was a babe that day. The Mustang *is* a babe magnet.

Right. It's a muscle car.

I have no muscles, but that's not the point. I can't pick up Diane in that beat-up old truck! I'll have to take the Mustang.

You're going to pick up Diane in your dead wife's *car in the clothes your* dead wife *picked out for you? Gee, Jack, you're pushing the envelope now.*

I can't sell that car, and not because I think Diane will like it better. It's . . . it's a link to my past.

And now you'll use it to link to your future.

Something like that.

The best of both worlds.

Or the worst.

I dump as many whites (and plenty of grays) as can fit in the washing machine, dump in a full scoop of Tide, and pour in at least a quart of bleach. I turn the right knob to the longest wash setting—

Use hot water, Jack.

I turn the center knob to "hot," set the left knob to "oversized load," and pull out the right knob. Water streams into the tub, splashing up on me.

After six months collecting dust, it still works!

Yeah.

And so do you, Jack. So do you.

29
Diane

So . . . I have a date.

I keep saying it over and over again in my head. I even say it to the cake, to my glass of iced tea, to my reflection in the mirror, to my toothbrush—

I'm so glad I live alone.

I've been kind of floating through the rest of the evening. I'm even actually watching TV while ironing. It's some reality show or other I've never seen before where the kids try to get their dad a new wife. It's kind of . . . charming, though I doubt all those women's breasts or faces are real. What some people will do for love.

Like calling up strange white men, I guess.

I finger through my wardrobe and pick out a burgundy pantsuit. I'll wear a plain crème blouse underneath and a push-up bra I haven't had the nerve to wear. The first time I put it on, my breasts . . . moved. They just . . . smiled up at me.

The phone rings. Mama? It's not a holiday yet. "Hello?"

"Dee-Dee, it's Mama."

"Hi, Mama."

"Your father is taking me out on New Year's, so I won't be able to call tomorrow."

That saves me from asking why she called. "Big date, huh?"

"Oh, nothing special. Dinner and some dancing probably. You know your father."

Knowing Daddy, I am sure it will be more dancing than dinner. My daddy can dance. I used to stand on his feet in the kitchen, and he'd let me feel his "moves." I wonder if Jack and I will dance. . . .

"How about you? What are your plans?"

I finally have some news Mama will be happy to hear. "I, too, have a date."

"You . . . do?"

"Don't sound so surprised, Mama."

"I'm not. It's just . . . it's wonderful!"

Ah, now she's happy. "And I actually have two dates."

"With *two* men?"

She's probably clutching her chest. "No, two dates with the same man."

"You've already been on one and you didn't tell me?"

Yes, this is a bit confusing. "No. I have a lunch date with him tomorrow and a dinner date with him on New Year's."

"Oh. What's his name?"

"His name is David Jack Browning."

"Does he go by David?"

"No, he goes by Jack."

"What does he do?"

Mama defines men by what they do, not by who they are. "He is an author of multicultural women's fiction."

"What kind of fiction?"

I'll have to keep this simple. "He writes books for black folks, Mama." And please don't ask how skinny and ashy he is.

"A writer, huh? What does he look like?"

Hmm. "Well, he's tall, about six-feet—"

"As tall as your daddy," she interrupts. "That's good. I'm glad I married a tall man, especially now when I can't reach as high as I used to. The arthritis in my shoulders is acting up something fierce. It must be the weather. I'm taking . . ."

As Mama lists her "therapy," I wonder how she can turn my big news into her arthritis. It's magic. Anyway, it saves me the trouble of describing Jack more.

"Is he a Christian?"

From arthritis to a man's religion. Mama needs to work on her transitions.

"Yes." Though I really don't know, but I can't tell Mama that. I'll bet Jack is . . . a Lutheran. Yeah, there are lots of blond Lutherans.

"Is he single?"

"Yes, Mama," I say, trying not to strangle the phone. "Of course he's single."

"Just checking. Never been married?"

Hmm. "He's a widower, Mama. His wife and son died in a car accident last July."

"Oh, how terrible!"

Yet, in the grand scheme of things, that tragedy has brought us together.

"Was he driving?"

I never asked. Why didn't I ask? "I don't think so."

"You don't know?"

"Mama, we've only just met. I'm still getting to know him."

Silence. "And he writes books for black folks."

"Yes."

"Which ones?"

"Oh, only one so far, and it comes out in April, but he's working on a second book."

"What's the first one called?"

"*Wishful Thinking*. It's a romance." Sort of. "But it's kind of an adult romance, Mama, not like the ones you read."

"Adult? So, it has sex in it?"

Oh, yeah. "Yes."

"And he's a Christian?"

"Yes, Mama."

"Hmm."

I don't fill the silence or even attempt to argue with her.

"It isn't smut, is it?"

"No, Mama. Look, I'll send you an autographed copy as soon as it comes out."

"Okay." She doesn't sound too happy. "Is this serious, Dee-Dee?"

It might be, but I can't tell her that. "Mama, it's only our first two dates, and I've only known Jack for about a week. I'll let you know, okay?"

"Do you want it to be serious?"

It's none of your business! "I said I'd let you know. So far we're just friends."

"Is he serious?"

Serious enough to ask me out! "Mama, you'll have to ask him about that."

"Okay, give me his number."

She has to be playing, though she *would* call if I gave her Jack's number. "No, Mama."

"I'm just teasing, Dee-Dee. Is he nice?"

Very. "Yes."

"Handsome?"

Well . . . in a way. "Yes."

"And he's a Christian who writes smut?"

She just can't let it go! "Mama, he writes modern romance, and yes, there's sex in modern romance."

"Christians shouldn't be writing that sort of thing."

I'm not going to argue with her there. "Well, it's what he's publishing, so accept it."

"I don't know if I can." She sighs. "Well, tell me how you met. Was it at your church?"

"No, we met at the library. He just . . . came up to me, we started to talk—"

"Then how do you know he's a Christian?"

She thinks she has me. "He *told* me, Mama."

"He just up and . . . told you in the middle of a conversation."

Hmm. "I *asked* him, Mama, okay? You raised me right, remember?"

"Well, you make sure he's a Christian, okay? A man can say just about anything to get what he wants."

I don't respond. Mama considers herself an expert on all men because she's been married to one man for thirty-five years.

"So, where are you going on your dates?"

"Tomorrow we're going to an Italian restaurant for lunch."

"Italian? He likes Italian food?"

Who doesn't like Italian food? "It was *my* choice, Mama, and it's one of the nicest restaurants in all of Roanoke."

"Oh."

"And as for New Year's, Jack says it's a surprise."

"A surprise, huh? You make sure you take your own car or have plenty of taxi money."

"Mama, hush."

"Especially if he's driving. He doesn't drink, does he?"

Another thing I don't know for sure. "I've never smelled alcohol on his breath." Not that he's gotten that close to me.

"You've been smelling his breath?"

Geez! "I won't let him drink around me, okay?"

Silence. "Well, it's obvious that you like him."

"I do."

"Well, what do you like about him?"

"His eyes," I say, before I can stop myself. Shoot! Now I'll have to go into more details.

"Nice dark brown ones, huh, like your daddy?"

Can brown be light enough to appear blue? No. "His eyes are lighter than Daddy's." And that's the truth.

"Has he . . . kissed you yet?"

"No." Though the thought of kissing Jack starts my hands sweating again.

"You want him to, don't you?"

Of course I do! "Mama, that's none of your business."

"That answered the question. You want him to."

"Mama, I said it's none of your business."

I hate it when she's right.

"He's not too dark, is he?"

I try not to laugh or bite off my tongue. "No."

"That's good. The darker the berry, the darker the children."

Another one of Mama's sayings. "But what does that matter?"

"I'm just asking questions, that's all."

Of all the things that matter to Mama, the "skin issue" takes precedence. Daddy and Mama's skin tones are almost exactly alike, and she even told me she looked for boys with skin tone similar to hers in high school. Yeah, I have suede parents with dark suede lips so they could have suede children.

"It's getting late, Mama, and I have some ironing to do."

"You'll call me after your first date, won't you?"

"It's only lunch, Mama."

"You can tell a lot about a man by watching him eat. Now your father . . ."

I have heard this story too often to listen, so I continue ironing. Daddy's daddy, my grandfather, was career military, and Gran Anderson, my grandmother, thought Emily Post was the solution to every racial problem that existed. "If we all learn to eat *properly*"—meaning "like white folks"—"we'll be fit for anyone's table," she used to say. Naturally, Daddy eats like a perfect gentleman, but only when Mama is at the table. As soon as she gets up, he's a slurping, talking-with-his-mouth-full man.

"Mama, I have to go."

"Well, you take care of yourself. Say hello to Jack for me."

That was nice of her to say. "I will. Bye."

I hang up and stare at myself in the mirror. Was I being deceitful? No, not really. Mama just wasn't asking the right questions. What would I have said if she had asked, "Is he white?" I would have said . . .

I have no idea what I would have said.

And that makes me a little sad.

30

Jack

I wake up at a reasonable hour, shave, shower, and put on fresh clothes.

For a change.

And I start calling restaurants at 8 A.M. I choose the ones in the phone book that have the biggest ads, some even with full menus, assuming that these are the most expensive. By 8:30, I realize something: there's no one at these restaurants this early in the morning.

Because they're all open at night, Jack.

I'll have to call later.

What will you tell Diane?

What I've already told her: it's a surprise.

To both of you.

And that doesn't bother me in the least. Surprise, at least recently, can be a good thing.

A little before nine, the phone rings. "Hello?"

You're not even checking the Caller ID.

Just inviting more surprises.

"Hi, it's Jenny."

I smile. "Good morning, Jenny."

And you suddenly have phone manners?

"I'm here for my test-drive. I hope I'm not too early."

I walk into the living room and part the drapes near the Christmas tree. I see an old Crown Victoria parked behind the Rodeo on the street. "You're already here?"

Jenny gets out of the car, still talking on the phone. "Yeah. I hope I didn't wake you."

She's hot.

"No, Jenny. I've been up for a while."

Long, flowing blond hair surrounds a classic pale Nordic face of high cheekbones and red lips. She smiles up at the window. "So, what do you think of my mom's car?"

"I can see why you want the Mustang."

She walks behind the Crown Victoria, and she seems to . . . dance. No, that's not right. She . . . bounces.

That girl is toned to the bone.

She wears a light blue sweat suit that leaves little to the imagination.

She's a babe.

"I'll be right out," I say.

"Okay."

I get the keys for the Mustang, throw on a Windbreaker, and go outside.

"It's good to finally meet you," she says, extending a hand.

I shake her hand, though I feel awkward doing so. She has such small hands, and they aren't smooth at all. "I'm Jack."

She must work out.

"And now I have a face to go with a voice," I say.

Smooth.

I hand her the keys. "Thank you," she says.

She opens the door and gets in, then immediately adjusts the front seat and all the mirrors.

Why are you just standing here? Get in!

"Aren't you getting in?" she asks.

Green eyes. A few freckles on her nose. So young!

"I trust you," I say. "There's plenty of gas. And you can take it out on the interstate if you want to."

"You don't want to come along?"

You'd be crazy not to, Jack!

"How'd you hear about the car? I didn't advertise it." For that matter, how did she get my phone number in the first place?

"Oh, a friend of mine up the street saw it, knew I'd love it, and took down the information from your sign."

"Oh." I blink. "But there's no phone number on it."

"She knew your name, and I looked it up in the phone book."

"Oh."

Quit thinking so much!

She pats the passenger seat with one of those small hands. "Get in."

Yeah, Jack, get in!

I get in the Mustang, and for the next thirty minutes, I learn everything there is to know about Jenny Dwyer. She's fresh out of college with a psychology degree, hasn't found a job to match her degree, so she works as a fitness instructor at Gold's Gym. Her family has lived in Roanoke for "ages," she's thinking of pursuing a master's degree in child psychology, she loves working with children, she used to be a lifeguard, and she just loves the car "to death."

She's . . . perfect.

She's young. She couldn't be a day over twenty-two.

"Your sign didn't mention the price," she says once we finally pull into the driveway. "That kind of scares me, you know. I want this car, but I'm worried it will be out of my price range."

How do you put a value on your wife's "baby"?

"I looked it up on the Internet, at the Blue Book site, and I have a feeling you'll want at least four thousand."

Is she pouting?

She's pouting.

She's trying to manipulate me with her fresh face, body, and pout.

Is it working?

Not quite.

"I'm asking forty-five hundred."

Jenny's head drops, her chin pressed to her chest. "I was afraid of that." She turns to me. "I don't have that kind of money right now, and I doubt any bank will give me a loan since I owe so much for college."

Worked her way through college, needy, hot, cute as a button. A babe. Cut her a break.

Let her talk.

Yeah, she has the cutest voice, too.

"But . . . I can put some money down and maybe pay you monthly?"

You'll get to see her again and again.

Unless she mails it.

So, make her deliver it to you in person. Imagine how she'll look this summer in tight shorts and a tank top.

"I don't know, uh, Jenny. I was hoping to be paid up front. It makes reassigning the title easier." Which reminds me that I still have to get that title fixed.

Ask how much she can put down.

Why? It's obvious she doesn't have enough.

Just ask her. She looks so sad.

It's part of her manipulation. She is, after all, a psychology major.

"How much were you thinking of putting down, Jenny?"

"Two thousand."

Whoa! That's a lot of lunches and dinners with Diane . . . or Jenny, here.

Shh.

Maybe she can put some muscles on you. She could be your personal fitness instructor for a few months.

"And then how much could you pay comfortably per month?" I ask.

She crunches up her lips, and they touch her nose. It's a . . . cute gesture. "My insurance is kind of high. I got a few speeding tickets going to and from school, so I was hoping . . . a hundred fifty?"

I do some math in my head. Jenny would be paying me for almost seventeen months.

Sounds like the beginning of a beautiful friendship.

"Hmm," is all I can think to say. I get out of the Mustang, and she slides out of her side, shutting the door.

"I love this car," she says, putting her small hands on the car, smoothing out all the yellow on the hood. "I can see myself in this car."

She is definitely the right girl for this car. She's . . . sunny. Jenny is a sunny soul, just like Noël. The car deserves her, too.

"Well, Jenny, I'd like to think about it, at least for a day, okay?"

What are you doing?

If I agree to her terms, she'll want the car today. I have a date with Diane in a few hours, and I plan to drive this car. And the DMV will be packed today. It's December 30!

She hands me the keys. "Okay."

"Um, I have your number," I say, "so I'll give you a call tomorrow."

That's more like it.

"I can give you my cell number," Jenny says.

Yes! Take it!

"You could call me anytime."

All the better! Take the number!

Jenny pulls out and hands me a Gold's Gym business

card, of all things, and listed along with the Gold's Gym numbers are her home and cell phone numbers.

And her e-mail address, too? You are set!

"Thank you."

She steps closer, looking up at me with a . . . wistful look? "Please call me soon, okay?"

"I will."

And often!

Shh.

And that was no wistful look, Jack. That was the look of a woman who wants you.

I doubt that.

I watch her walk back to her mother's car, get in, and drive away in a car, which swallows her up completely. She looked good in the Mustang and drove it as if she already owned it. Noël would want her to have the car. Noël would say she's a perfect match for that car.

She sizzles, doesn't she?

Yeah, Noël could sizzle.

I was talking about Jenny.

Like I said, she's too young. When I graduated from high school, she was in the first grade, and she was only in the fifth grade when I started teaching.

She has a crush on you.

No, she doesn't. She just wants the car.

But think of the benefits! Picture this: it's ninety degrees in August, humidity at 50 percent, and Jenny comes over to pay you wearing the tightest shorts, maybe only her sports bra, and she's dripping with sweat, and I'll bet she has a tattoo somewhere sexy and a pierced belly button and—

I should be calling you "Dan Pace."

Dan Pace has it goin' on, yo!

I'm not like that. I've never been like that.

You could be.

I'm too old to play around like that.

No, you're not.

What would I look like with a child like that in my life?

Happy? Imagine the sex, Jack.

I'm not going there.

You're no fun. Dan would have lowered the price on the Mustang provided she could get him a discount at Gold's Gym and some one-on-one, sweaty instruction both at the gym . . . and in the house.

No, Dan would have said the wrong thing at the wrong time and gotten slapped in the face.

True. But, he wouldn't have washed his face for a week.

At noon, I leave the house just as the mail carrier arrives. Other than the usual mail trying to interest me in equity loans and credit cards, there is one piece from my agent, Nina Frederick.

The reviews have arrived!

I get in the Mustang, and adjust the seat back several inches.

Jenny was short.

Shh. I'm reading.

The seat's still warm.

Shh.

As usual, there's no cover letter from Nina, just two blocks of type on one page. The first review is from Kirkus: "*Wishful Thinking,* by D. J. Browning, is a promising debut novel," I read. Promising. Hmm. Not really an endorsement there. "Quirky . . . blah blah blah . . . innovative . . . entertaining; a solid first novel."

Not a single negative—or true—word.

I read the other review from Booklist. "Blah blah blah surprising social commentary . . . blah blah blah . . . colorful characters and warm humor . . . a sizzling summer read."

Not bad.

Not correct.

Don't be so hard on yourself. It's a first novel. You're al-lowed to make mistakes.

The whole novel was a mistake.

I toss the reviews onto the passenger seat and drive down-town, find a spot in front of the library, and wait, watching the digital clock change from 12:15 to 12:16 to 12:17. . . .

You're nervous.

A little.

It's only lunch.

It's my first date in seven years. I have a right to be ner-vous.

At 12:35 exactly, Diane walks out the front entrance, car-rying an umbrella and wearing a tan overcoat.

Curvy.

Shh.

I get out of the Mustang, and she smiles.

Nice smile.

Yeah.

I walk around, open her door, and watch as she has trou-ble getting settled into the bucket seat. She hands the mail up to me.

"Oh, sorry about that," I say.

"It's okay."

I close my door, return to my side, and get in, tossing the mail in the back. "You look nice."

She looks straight ahead. "But you can't see what I'm wearing."

Hmm. "What are you wearing?"

"You'll see when we get there."

I look in the side mirror and see a jam of cars coming our way. Instead of punching it and racing out ahead of them, I let them pass.

"How long were you waiting?" she asks.

"About fifteen minutes."

Why'd you tell her that?

It's the truth.

But that makes you sound desperate!

It makes me sound punctual.

The traffic doesn't want to end. "Is it always like this downtown?" I ask.

"It's the lunch rush. I usually walk."

I turn to her. "Would you rather walk today?"

"It's supposed to rain."

"Oh."

I see a gap in front of a Suburban and hit the gas pedal, and the Mustang leaps out ahead. I glance to my right and see Diane's hands pressed into the dashboard.

"Sorry."

"It's okay."

You're driving too fast.

I slow down. "Um, where should I park when we get there?"

"There's a parking garage across the street."

"Okay."

I take a ticket on the first level and circle higher and higher until I find a space on the top level in the cold, open air. Diane gets out before I can get my door open.

What's her hurry?

She only has an hour for lunch, remember?

I catch her looking back at her seat and frowning as she shuts the door.

That bucket seat must not have been kind to her booty.

Shh.

"Is this your wife's car?" she asks.

"Uh, yeah."

She blinks once.

"I'm, uh, trying to sell it."

Diane only nods.

"I may have found a buyer this morning."

We walk to the elevator as the first drops come down. I should have brought my umbrella, and it isn't proper form for a man to share a woman's umbrella, is it?

You'll be closer to her.

True.

The elevator doors open, and Diane steps inside. We're not the only ones on the elevator; another couple stands in the corner. I stand behind Diane as the elevator descends.

Get closer!

We're being watched.

So? At least make small talk.

But I can think of nothing to say!

31

Diane

He's nervous.

Me? I'm just glad to get out of that car. It was creepy being in his dead wife's car. They were in a car accident, right? But there was nothing wrong with that car except for the seat. That seat wasn't made for my booty. His wife must have had no-ass-at-all. So, maybe they wrecked in a different car. And from the way Jack was driving, *he* might have been driving. I can only imagine that kind of guilt.

And why are those two in this elevator gritting on us? We could just be coworkers out for lunch, or two perfect strangers who just happened to get on the elevator at the same time.

Perfect strangers. I guess that's how all relationships start out. We're all just perfect strangers . . . who can't think of a single thing to say to each other!

The elevator opens, and we walk out through the bottom level to the street, and like the weatherman said, it's raining "cold and hard." I open my umbrella and hand it to Jack. "You're taller than me."

Now anyone seeing Jack and me will know we're together, but I don't care. I spent far too long this morning getting my hair just right to have it sopping wet and ruined, and I don't want to be sitting next to or across from a soaking wet Jack.

Bandini's is already pretty crowded by the time we get there, so we have to wait a few minutes behind several other groups. When it's our turn, the hostess asks, "Two?"

"Yes," Jack says.

I was wondering if he could speak. He hadn't spoken since we got on the elevator.

And why is this place so crowded? I don't mean the number of people. I mean, why are the tables so densely packed together? I have to walk sideways to a little table off in the corner, and I know my booty brushed quite a few backs.

The hostess places two menus on the table. "Enjoy."

Jack pulls my chair out—how nice—but I need to take off my coat first. He gets the hint and takes my coat from me and drapes it over the back of my chair. I pose in all my burgundy glory for Jack, he smiles and nods (as he should), I sit, and he scoots the chair in as far as it can go. I pick up the menu and actually feel the heat from the back of the man sitting directly behind me.

I feel like a suede sardine!

Jack removes his jacket and sits. "Is it always this crowded?" he asks.

"This is my first time."

In oh, so many ways!

"Mine, too."

I look at the menu and check out the lunch specials. Prices and selection are decent, and "15-minute service on lunch entrees or your meal is free" makes me feel less rushed. I look side to side, you know, to see who's here (as if

I'd know anyone) and to see who else might be gritting on us.

No one is.

They're all grubbing—as they should be.

"What are you going to have?" I ask.

"The lasagna," he says, putting down his menu. "What about you?"

I'm torn between the fettuccine Alfredo and an antipasto salad. "I haven't decided." I look up at him. "If your lasagna is good, will you share it with me?"

He smiles. "Sure."

"Do you like fettuccine?"

He nods.

"Good. I'm having fettuccine."

We don't have to wait long to place our drink orders—we both get sweetened iced teas—and then . . . we stare at the table.

Awkwardly.

"Um, I got my first reviews today," he says, after three solid minutes of silence.

I look up. "From whom?"

"Booklist and Kirkus," he says.

I breathe a sigh of relief. "Were they . . . favorable?"

He looks up at the ceiling. What's up there? I don't look, though. "They were okay."

"Just . . . okay?"

He looks directly at me. "They didn't tell the truth."

"They were bad?"

He shakes his head. "They were great. They say my book is 'quirky,' 'innovative,' and 'entertaining.' But they're all lies. I'll bet my publisher paid for them."

"Why do you say that?"

He sighs. "It's really not that good of a book, Diane, and I'm sure once real readers get hold of it, they'll be trashing me on-line."

I need to change the subject, but before I can, a huge

hairy man wearing an apron comes over to us. "Hello," he says, in a sexy Italian accent. "I am Paolo Bandini. Is this your first time?"

We both nod.

"Then let me welcome you to my restaurant." He looks around. "We are a little shorthanded today, so I will personally take your order."

Italian men are *hot!* Hairy, but hot. We give him our orders, he does this little nod thing, and we watch him go back to the kitchen.

"The owner himself," Jack says.

Did Jack plan this? "Do you know him?"

"No, but I know his girlfriend."

Say what?

"I mean, I know *of* her. He's dating Marissa Thomas."

Is this supposed to mean something to me?

"You know, Marissa Thomas, the black woman running for mayor."

Oh, *her.* Pushy thing, and a truly *black* black woman. Not bad-looking for a woman pushing forty. And she dates an Italian man? Hmm. Maybe Jack and I aren't being trendsetters at all. But how does Jack know . . . "How do you know Marissa Thomas?"

"She spoke to the kids at Monterey last year on career day. She's a dynamic speaker, let me tell you, but what do you expect from a lawyer? She had those kids in the palms of her hands."

I need to change *this* subject, too. "Jack, how old are you?"

He smiles. "How old do you think I am?"

"I don't know. Thirty-five?"

He blinks. "I'm thirty-two."

"Sorry." Oops. Tragedy ages people. "I'm twenty-five, in case you want to know."

More opposites. When Jack graduated from high school, I was in the fifth grade. When he graduated from college, I was just starting to get my caboose. He's been married. I've never married. He's as white as a ghost. I'm suede. He's had a son. I've never even had sex, and—

I've never even had sex.

I had a few close calls, but nothing so close that I couldn't escape. I traded hands in high school with boys who, um, burst before I knew what was happening. My prom date only gave me a good-night kiss, which was fine with me. He had an overbite.

And I had two consecutive men in college (forever nameless to me now) who broke up with me because "I got needs, and you ain't givin' me what I need." Oh, the second man was more eloquent than the first. "I am a man," he had said. "I have the needs of a man, and you aren't making me feel like a man."

He was an English major.

Then . . . nothing. It's not that I don't have the desire—I do. I have wicked desire and a battery bill. It's not that I'm afraid of the act itself. I know what I want to do. It's the after part, the part that either becomes "happily ever after" or "see you after a while."

I look up to see Jack staring at me.

"Are you okay?" he asks.

"Yes."

"You seemed lost in thought."

"Sorry." Just reliving my sex life. What did that take? Sixty seconds? I need a life!

"Here we are!" It's the owner again with our order to save me from explaining. "Enjoy!"

And then . . . we enjoy. The table is small enough that we can put the plates side by side and eat easily off both. I'm afraid I'm eating too much at times, but it is delicious! And other than sharing food on our first date—I'm sure Gran Anderson and Emily Post are turning over in their graves—we don't act as if we're on our first date. We smile, laugh, and . . . hardly talk at all. Hmm.

Yeah, we're on our first date, and the food is taking the place of conversation.

"Where are we going for our New Year's date?" I ask once we've polished off all our food and a basketful of breadsticks.

"It's going to be a surprise," Jack says, wiping his lips with a napkin. "I will pick you up in front of the library at nine."

And leave my car downtown? "What about my car?"

"Oh, yeah, um, I guess I could pick you up at your apartment."

Do I look like an apartment dweller? "I own my own home, Jack."

He blinks. "Yeah?"

"Yeah. Over in Northeast behind Breckinridge Middle School."

He smiles. "I know where that is. Noël and I looked over there when we were house hunting."

He said her name. It's a pretty name, but it's . . . distressing for me to hear it, for some reason.

"We were going to get a ranch on . . . some street back there, I think, but I'm no handyman. It had a great big backyard, though."

"I'm over on Fleming," I say. I write the address on a napkin. "And you can pick me up around nine-thirty." Wait a minute. He said nine. He must have a reason. "Unless you've made reservations for earlier?"

He smiles. "Nine-thirty will be fine."

Hmm. A later dinner date. This could be interesting.

Mr. Bandini brings the check. "How was everything?"

"Marvelous," I say.

"Delicious," Jack says.

Mr. Bandini leans down. "Since this is your first time and your order took so long to get to you," he whispers, "I would like to offer this meal on the house, provided you return for dinner sometime soon."

I blink at Jack, and Jack blinks at me. We have a blinking moment.

"Is that okay?" Mr. Bandini asks.

"Uh, thank you," Jack says.

Mr. Bandini straightens. "It is good to see you two here. You must come back often."

Then he leaves.

"That was weird," I say.

"Maybe he, uh, likes the fact that we're . . . you know?"

That almost made sense, but I know what he's saying without saying it. "You think he gave us a freebie because you're white and I'm black?"

"Don't you?"

I decide to be cynical, though I kind of agree. "He just wants us to come back at night when we'll have to pay higher prices and drink lots of wine."

Jack smiles. "Is that so bad?"

"No."

"I like this place," he says. "Maybe we could come back here on New Year's."

What? "I thought you already made reservations."

He shakes his head. "I haven't been able to, Diane. Nothing was open when I called around this morning."

Then you *should* have called last night! I don't want to come into this . . . claustrophobic place on New Year's Eve! It will be wall-to-wall people. We'd be packed in here . . . tightly.

Wait a sec. That might work out.

"I guess it would be all right," I say. "But what if it's crowded?"

Jack shrugs. "Then we'll just . . . go for a walk or something."

"Okay."

Either way, I'm going to be with Jack. Either I'll be pressed up against his body with a wineglass in my hand, or I'll be out walking with him hopefully with his hand in mine.

I check my watch. "I have to be getting back."

It's a different kind of ride back to the library. Not only does Jack seem more relaxed, but the seat also seems more comfortable, for some reason. And he drives more slowly, more smoothly than before.

I just had a nice date with a nice man. And it took less than an hour.

The rain has stopped by the time we park. Jack gets out, comes to my door, opens it, takes my hand, and helps me out of the car. He just . . . takes my hand as if it is the most natural thing in the world.

"Thank you," I say.

"May I walk you to the door?"

I giggle. This is all so old-fashioned! "Sure." It's so . . . high school.

But it's wonderful.

We don't walk fast, we don't walk slowly—we just . . . meander to the door, not speaking, not humming, barely making any sounds. He holds the door to the foyer, and I walk in.

"May I call you later this evening?" he asks.

Music to my ears. "Sure."

He steps a little closer. "Um, Diane?"

Here? Just inside the foyer? People can see us! "Yes, Jack?" I don't look up into his eyes. I don't want him to see my fear.

"May I . . . give you a hug?"

Whew. At least it's not a kiss. And if anyone says anything, I can play it off as a friendly hug, nothing serious about it at all. "I could use one, Jack."

He steps closer and puts his hands around me, drawing me gently to him, my cheek brushing his neck. He's bony, all right, but it's a nice hug, not too long, not too short. He steps back. "Thank you. I needed that."

Whoo! So did I. But I can't tell him that yet. I even want to say something wild like, "Come in for change anytime,

Mr. Browning, and I'll touch your palm a certain way," but I can't. I'm sure I could eventually say something like that at the rate we're going. Instead, I say, "See you tomorrow at nine-thirty, Jack."

"I can't wait, Diane," he says.

I watch him go. "I can't wait either, Jack Browning," I whisper.

32

Jack

Ah, you got a hug.

Yeah.

Why didn't you kiss her cheek? It was right there waiting to be kissed.

I was too busy smelling her hair.

Researching your book during a hug?

No. Just . . . smelling her hair.

You were so stiff.

I wasn't trying to be.

You put your hands flat on her back. You could have gone lower.

I still might. Tomorrow night.

Now you're talking.

The skin on her cheek . . . so soft.

The firmness of her flesh . . . so curvy.

I feel . . . happy.

It's about time.

Now, what do I do for the rest of the day?

More nothing?

I think . . . I'll clean the house.

And that's exactly what I do. I spend two solid hours in the kitchen and go through seven Brillo pads getting the sink and the counters to shine again. I even sweep and mop the floor and remove all the unknown food products from the refrigerator that have been shoved into every nook and cranny.

You should call some high school kid to use this stuff for a science project.

Yeah, on "Biological Agents Found in Refrigerators."

Was that a former taco?

I think it was a Danish.

Eww. You had better not open the microwave, then. Something died in there.

Right.

Um, what about the minibar you've accumulated?

I look at six bottles of Kris Kringle Eggnog, fifteen cans of Miller Lite, and several bottles of Boone's Farm wine, the only alcohol Noël liked to drink.

I might need them.

And then again, you might not.

True. I'll keep them, just in case.

Right. What about the tree?

I'll leave it up for a while. We didn't usually take it down until New Year's Day.

You might want to water it.

Oh yeah.

There isn't much to straighten in Stevie's room—

You mean your room.

No, I mean Stevie's room. I'm going to sleep in the master bedroom from now on. I am, after all, the master of this house.

What about her things?

There's room in the laundry room for her vanity.

Taking big steps today.

Just hitting my stride, that's all.

After taking Noël's vanity and all its contents to an empty corner of the laundry room, I fold clothes for the next hour or so and put them into Noël's empty dresser. Then I eat two Lunchables for dinner. I want to have more flesh for Diane to feel.

You dog, you!

I just mean I need to start eating right and more often.

Then I sit in front of my laptop, going on-line to Amazon.com, just to see if—

I have a one-star book.

We have a one-star book. Why do we have a one-star book?

A Mid-Atlantic Book Reviewer named "Nisi"—

What kind of name is that?

Short for Denise? I don't know. Anyway, she has given *Wishful Thinking* one whole star.

The review pulls no punches . . . and even inflicts quite a few:

Wishful Thinking is an insult to anyone with intelligence. It is a travesty that the publisher found this book fit to print. The two main characters, Dan, a white man who thinks with his glands, and Ty, a black woman who doesn't use her intelligence, are preposterous. The plot, which belongs in a funeral plot, is a series of laughable, illogical, and ultimately meaningless coincidences. This novel is a farce, a lame attempt by a writer who obviously does not know the first thing about African American women. It is demeaning, belittling, and cruel to *any* woman, regardless of race. It was *Wishful Thinking* indeed for the publisher to think that anyone with half a brain would ever call this book literature.

She must have used a thesaurus.

Yeah.

She's just one reviewer, Jack.

And the only honest one so far.

She sounds shrill.

And angry.

Well, don't dwell on it.

It's hard not to. My book has insulted somebody.

Why not think about your next one?

About Arthur and Di?

Does she have to be "Di"?

How about Delilah?

Too biblical.

Della?

Too musical. And why does her name have to begin with D?

I have Diane on the brain, I guess.

Why not call her . . . Nisi?

Definitely ethnic.

And you could get some payback that way. . . .

But Nisi, whoever she is, was right! She nailed a book ripe for nailing. I have more respect for her than for anyone at Booklist or Kirkus. She was fair. Perhaps a little harsh on a first novel, but she was still fair.

Okay, how about . . . Deborah?

That's biblical, too. I need a normal name for a normal person.

And "Di" is a normal name?

Diana, then.

Fine. Go.

Arthur and Diana meet at the library. Exactly *how* do they meet at the library?

At the reference desk, just as you met Diane.

Okay. What is he researching?

His family tree.

She'd have to work in the genealogy department.

Maybe she floats from department to department.

I'll have to ask Diane if that happens. So, she helps him research his family tree, and he finds . . .

A black person in his ancestry?

I'm not writing a white *Roots*.

It could happen.

But how will that bring Diana and Arthur closer to each other?

They'll find out they're related.

How V. C. Andrews of you to think that. No, there has to be another way.

Okay. It's closing time, and Arthur walks up to Diana and says, "What are you doing after work?"

She'd dial 9-1-1 and spray Arthur with mace.

Our Diane/Diana?

Yeah, that might be a little ridiculous. I don't know what to do. This is going nowhere.

Okay, why not write about what's really happened between you and Diane, all the way from that first touch until now?

That's so . . . autobiographical.

It has really happened, and no one named "Nisi" could call it "preposterous."

I'll bet she could, because there are still quite a few coincidences.

So? Love stories are full of them. Your relationship with Noël began with a happy coincidence, didn't it?

She lived in the apartment upstairs in the Cube.

But you helped her move in that day.

I was being nice, and I had nothing better to do. It was so hot that day, and there was no way she was getting that dresser up there by herself.

What if it weren't your summer break from teaching? Would you have been there? And that apartment-warming gift of that Ma Plub plant didn't hurt, did it?

I was just being neighborly.

Are you saying that being nice and being neighborly are coincidental events?

No.

You made a choice *to be nice, though helping Noël in all her "babe-ness" wasn't that hard of a choice.*

Her T-shirt was so tight.

And the shorts.

Yeah.

You made a choice to help her, Jack. Choices can't be co-incidences. You chose to help Noël, and she responded. Was that a coincidence?

No. She made a choice to respond to me.

All I'm saying is this: once you have created two people in a book, they have to make choices, right?

Right.

Coincidences might help them meet, but the choices they make bring them closer together. That "Nisi" person focused only on the coincidences, not the choices. Maybe "Nisi" doesn't know what can happen in a love story or in real life, for that matter.

Wishful Thinking was more of a "lust" story, though.

True. But there have to be coincidences in any story. That's what makes life—and novels—interesting.

But I had them bump into each other, and fifty pages later, they were in bed!

Diane's fingers brushed your hand, and five days *later, you went out on a date. And, if you're lucky tonight—*

The phone rings, and I run upstairs to answer it. "Hello?"

"Jackie, how are you?" It's Nina.

Now, is this a coincidence or a choice made by Nina to call you?

Shh.

"Fine, uh, Nina. I was just thinking that—"

"Great, great."

Sometimes I don't think Nina listens to me.

"Listen," she says, "the publisher says you haven't sent the first three chapters of the new book."

"It's not due until the end of January."

"Oh, I know that, Jackie. It's just that you sent everything for *Wishful Thinking* early, and some recent developments have changed the timetable. You see, Jackie, the reviews have been much better than the publisher expected, so now they want to put your picture on the book."

I don't know if that's a compliment or not. "Nina, why would they want to do that?"

"Jackie, dear, they're taking a novel approach on your novel." She laughs. "You have a novel novel!"

She's a lovely woman.

Shh. She might be about to ruin my life.

"Jackie, you're a white man who writes multicultural women's fiction, for God's sake. You're a rarity, and they want to make you rich!"

"I'm a rarity?"

"Yes. You're writing out of your race and sex, and that's, well, odd. You're a novelty; a novel rarity."

I knew there was something I liked about you.

Shh.

"What about that Mid-Atlantic Book Review review?"

How redundant of you to say so.

"Oh, I saw that, Jackie. Wasn't that awful? I'm working with the publisher to have it removed from Amazon. It was a personal attack by that bitch Nisi, and Amazon shouldn't have allowed it to be posted. She rarely posts nice reviews for anyone."

So, you're in good company.

"It was the most accurate review, though."

"Listen at you! Such a kidder. Look, we have great reviews from Kirkus and Booklist, and that's all that matters. So, Jackie, how do you feel about a book tour?"

This is happening too fast. "I don't."

"You will, and it's a great honor. Not every first author gets this kind of special treatment."

"But how am I supposed to write the second book if—"

"Look, Jackie," she interrupts, "if the first one takes off, and I think it will, they'll understand. I'm sure they'll extend the deadline."

I'm beginning to understand. If I travel, they'll give me more time, but if I don't . . .

"Just play the game, Jackie, and it's only for a week. And in the meantime, get some professional pictures taken, head shots in black and white and in color."

I hate this game already. "Nina, I've lost lots of weight. I look . . . gaunt."

"Oh, just ask for a little make-up and soft lighting. They can make anyone handsome with a little pancake and lighting."

I hear a beep. "I have another call, Nina. Can you hold?"

"Sure thing, Jackie."

I click over. "Hello?"

"Have you decided yet?"

It's Jenny.

She's so eager!

"No, not yet. Uh, can you hold a minute, Jenny? I'm on the other line."

"Oh, sure."

I click back to Nina. "How long is this tour going to last?"

"Only a week, Jackie. You'll be in New York when the book drops on April fifteenth; then you'll be on to Boston, Philadelphia, DC, Richmond, Charlotte, and Atlanta."

Seven cities in seven days. "Um, I have a question."

"Go ahead."

This has just popped into my head. "If I were to work with someone else on this second book—"

"Is this person cowriting it?" Nina interrupts.

"Well, no. Uh, she'll be doing some editing." I hope Diane will be up to it. I'm going to need her, or reviewers like Nisi will nail me again.

"Just thank her in the acknowledgments section, Jackie.

Listen, it was good talking to you. Let me know if there's anything you need."

Like more time to digest all this.

"I will. Bye."

I click back to Jenny, and the doorbell rings.

Sometimes life happens all at once.

Tell me about it.

"Uh, Jenny?"

"I'm still here."

"There's someone at the door. Can I call you back?"

"No, it's all right. I can wait."

So patient!

Or desperate.

I set the phone down on the top step, run downstairs, open the door, and see an older black couple dressed in their Sunday finest. Cold wind howls around me, so I invite them into the landing area, closing the door behind them.

"Thank you," the man says. "It's mighty chilly out today."

"We're from Emmanuel Baptist Church," the woman says.

Be nice. You're a Baptist, too.

I'll try to be nice.

"Yes," the man says, "and we'd like to invite you to Sunday service."

I smile. "I'm already a member at First Baptist downtown, but thanks for the offer."

The woman squints at me through some glasses. "You look familiar. Do I know you?"

"I don't think so."

She snaps her fingers. "You're Mr. Browning."

I nod.

"You taught my granddaughter, Jasmine." Her smile fades. "We were so sorry to hear about your wife and your son."

"Yeah."

"How are you holding up?" he asks.

"I'm, uh, holding."

And so is Jenny. Finish this up.

"The Lord moves in mysterious ways, His wonders to behold," the man says.

I bite my tongue. "Right." I wonder why He took my family from me. Can these two people explain that? Can anyone?

"It was God's will," the woman says.

I nod. It wasn't my will, and if I'm supposed to be made in His image, then *my* will should count for something.

He moves to the door. "We'll keep you in our prayers."

"Thank you."

I open the door, and they leave. I run back upstairs and pick up the phone. "Jenny?"

"I'm here."

Her voice has changed. It's not "cute" anymore.

"I'm sorry to keep you waiting so long, I—"

"It's all right."

Is that sadness?

"Um, I'm still thinking about selling you the car."

"Take all the time you need." A pause. "I, um, overheard you talking to those people."

"You did?"

You left the phone on the top stair, Jack, and you only have seven steps. Now is this a coincidence or a choice?

Shh.

"The Mustang is your wife's car, huh?"

"Yes."

"I didn't know that. I can see now why you want so much for it."

Say something.

I don't know what to say.

"I, uh, I'm so sorry for your loss."

Say something.

It's all coming back. The police were standing right here

on this landing that day. They were saying, "There's been an accident, Mr. Browning." Their faces were like stone—

"I, um, I'll understand if you decide not to sell it to me."

Jack! Say something!

Like what?

Anything! Just talk!

"You're, um, you're a lot like her, Jenny."

That's better.

Then why am I crying?

Because you loved your wife!

Yeah, I did. I still love her.

"I'll take that as a compliment," Jenny says, her voice brightening.

I wipe a tear. "Too much, as a matter of fact." I sit on the bottom step. "She was so alive and vibrant and . . . bouncy."

"You think I'm bouncy?"

"It's part of your job to, um, bounce, isn't it?"

"Well, yeah, but . . . I'm a lady, too."

If this isn't flirting—

Shh.

"Anyway, when you showed up today and sat . . . where she used to sit, I said to myself, yep, she belongs in this car."

"You did?"

"Yeah. But I won't sell it to you for forty-five hundred. It's not worth that much really. I'm willing to part with it for three thousand, maybe fifteen hundred down, and a hundred fifty a month for ten months."

"Really?"

"Really. I have to go to the DMV to get the title fixed. My wife's name is still on it."

"Will you go . . . tomorrow? I'm off at noon."

She's practically asking you out on a date!

To the DMV? At the end of the year?

So, you'll have two dates in one day. Dan would be proud.

"Jenny, the DMV will be a madhouse the day before the new year."

"Oh, yeah. Hmm."

"I tell you what. I promise not to sell the car to anyone else, and we'll go to the DMV together next week, maybe on the fifth or sixth, so the wait won't be as long."

Go on a busier day, Jack!

She might have to get back to work.

"You'd do that for me?"

She is hard flirting, Jack! Imagine sitting next to her for hours! Be the Sponge, Jack! Soak her up!

"You belong in that car, Jenny."

"Thank you. Thank you, Jack."

She called you by your name for the first time, Jack! She's taking this relationship to a different level!

There is no relationship.

"Uh, call me early next week to set up a time for me to meet you there, okay?" I ask.

Why are you keeping your distance?

It's safer.

"Sure, Jack. And thank you so much."

She said it again!

Shh.

"You're welcome, Jenny. Good-bye." I turn off the phone.

Aww, you like calling her by her name, too.

It's her name, isn't it?

Jack and Jenny. It has a nice ring to it.

You think too much.

One of us should! Now, was your leaving the phone in a place where she could hear what those church folks said a coincidence or a choice?

I don't want to think about it.

I think coincidence causes the choices we make. What do you think?

I think . . . *we* think too much.

33

Diane

I was stuck at the circulation desk all day, so I didn't have a chance to look up the accident involving Jack's wife and son. I know it's a nosy (and morbid) thing to do, but I can't just come out and ask a man to relive his pain, can I?

If I get to know him better, though, I will ask.

Once again, I float through my house when I get home, avoiding the cake in the fridge and vowing to make a few New Year's resolutions. One, I will lose fifteen pounds. If I could pinpoint *where* I want the weight gone, I would choose my caboose. There has to be something out there to reduce a caboose. I wonder if they sell "caboose reducers." If they don't, I'll invent them. Two, I will read all the books I'm supposed to review *all* the way through. I won't be able to review as many, but I'll feel better about it. Three, I will give Jack Browning a chance with me.

I'm going to give Jack a chance.

I'll have to tone down my cynicism some and I may even

have to compete with his dead wife for a while, but I'm willing if he's able.

But his wife is what keeps me holding back so much. During that hug, I could have held him tighter, but what if, in his mind, he wasn't really hugging me? What's that called, transference? I know the man just wants some human contact, but how can I be 100 percent sure that he's holding or even kissing just me? I have to know that he's hugging, holding, kissing, squeezing . . .

Whoo! There I go again, getting all sweaty in the hands. Should I even care? I got a hug today, and no matter what was going through his mind, I got a nice hug.

The phone rings.

It's Jack! "Hello, Jack." I didn't say, "Hi, Jack," this time.

"Hello, Diane."

"I was just thinking about you." How lame is that? I know that line was in some movie or another.

"I've been thinking about you, too."

Silence.

"Um, I sold the car today."

"That's good, isn't it?"

"Yeah, it is."

"That wasn't the car that . . ."

"No, no. We had a van."

"Oh." Shoot. I don't want to sound nosy.

"And I got another review, this one on-line."

Oh no! It posted already? That was fast! "Was it, um, was it a good review?"

"It was a fair review, the most accurate so far."

I'm holding my breath. Maybe it wasn't mine. "Uh, where can I read it?"

"At Amazon.com. Someone named 'Nisi.'"

It was mine.

"It's the only review on there so far, so *Wishful Thinking* is officially a one-star book. My agent and publisher are trying to have the review removed, but I don't care."

I do!

"At least someone actually read it and assessed it properly," he says.

She didn't actually read it, and though Jack has complimented Nisi—I mean, me—I don't want that! I want that review evaporated immediately! "What do you mean by 'fair'?"

"She basically called it a farce, among other things, and it is."

Should I tell him now? He doesn't seem too upset. But if I do, then he might ask, "Why didn't you tell me this earlier?"

I don't have an answer for that one.

I have to change the subject. "Um, how's the new book coming?"

"I haven't written a thing today. I've mainly been cleaning up the house."

I smile. The man is serious about starting over, and I'll bet his house is a wreck. "Is that one of your New Year's resolutions?"

"Not really. The house needs to be cleaned. I haven't thought about any resolutions. Have you?"

Do I tell him? "Well, you know, the usual. I'd like to lose some weight."

"From where?"

Excuse me?

"I mean, you look . . . fine."

"I have a caboose."

What in the world am I saying this for? If I read what I just said in a book . . . Maybe I've read so many of those books I'm starting to repeat their stupid lines in my conversation, and Jack's silence proves I said something stupid.

"Jack?"

"I like your caboose."

I'm holding my breath. "You . . . do?" Lord, I'm about to get horny.

"I've never said that before. Is that what you call your, um, your—"

"Booty?" Whoa, I'm using all the nasty words tonight.

"Yeah."

He can't say it. He's so shy! "I've had this thing following me around since I turned twelve, and no matter how much I walk"—or do other, unladylike things like butt crunches—"it's still there."

"But, it makes you . . . you."

"Are you saying that my booty defines me, Jack?"

"No, no." He laughs. "Your *beauty* defines you."

Oh my. Breathe, Diane. "I'm not that beautiful."

"Yes, you are. And to be honest, well, the first time I saw you, I really didn't see you as beautiful, mainly because I didn't see all of you."

I was sitting down. He didn't see the caboose that first time. A man actually likes my booty? Where has he been all my life?

"I mean, you had a nice smile and bright eyes and soft hands—*they* were beautiful. But until I saw you walking around in the reference department, I didn't realize you were beautiful all over."

I'm going to cry. This is . . . this is so unbelievable. No one has ever said that to me.

"Diane?"

"I'm here." I think. "Anyway, I want to lose at least fifteen pounds this coming year."

"And I'd like to gain at least . . . forty or so."

I smile. "I can give you at least forty."

"No, no!" He laughs. "There wouldn't be anything of you left to . . ." He stops.

Don't stop! "Left to what, Jack?"

A long pause.

"Jack?"

"I was going to say left to love, Diane."

My turn for a long pause.

"But we've only just met, and it's way too soon for me to say that, so . . . I'm sorry I said it."

"Don't be." My voice is so tiny.

"I say the wrong thing at the wrong time sometimes. It just . . . gets in my head and spills out before I can stop it."

"I'm glad you're so . . . honest, Jack."

"I'll try to restrain myself from now on."

No, don't! It's refreshing! It's new! A man who expresses his feelings and says what he's thinking! "Don't restrain yourself on my account, Jack. I like hearing these things."

Silence.

"Jack?"

"Just talking to myself some. I do that a lot. I've been holding a conversation with myself since July."

That's a bit . . . odd. Well, I talk back to books, so it's not that odd. "What do you say to yourself?"

"Do you really want to know?"

Do I want the chance to get a rare glimpse of the inner workings of a man's mind, especially one I'm starting to care about? "Sure."

"Okay, um, when we were talking about your caboose, for example."

"Say 'booty,' Jack."

A pause. "Okay, your . . . your booty."

Whoo, and my booty's warming up.

"Part of me was . . . fantasizing, and the other part of me was saying, 'But you've only just met her.'"

I catch my breath. "You were fantasizing about my booty?"

"Yes."

"Can you tell me your fantasy?"

"I could. Part of me is saying, 'Tell her now! She wants to know!' But the other part of me is saying, 'What will she think of me if I do?'"

I like the first part of him better. "So, you don't feel comfortable telling me this fantasy?"

"Overall, no." A pause. "This is a strange conversation, isn't it?"

The strangest. "A little." We're like amoebas sending out little probes or something. "I have a fantasy, too, Jack."

"You do?"

I don't, but I want to hear his, so if I tell him mine . . . "My fantasy involves your . . ." I wince. What part of him *would* I fantasize about? I like his eyes and smile, but those aren't fantasy material.

"My what?"

Pandora's box is about to be opened. "Your . . . No, I can't say it." Because I don't know what "it" is!

He sighs. "You have a voice that tells you to hold back, too?"

No, I have a voice that tells me, "Quit making up stuff!" I laugh. "To be honest—and don't take this the wrong way—but I was only going to make up a fantasy so you'd tell me yours." And now I'm being honest. Hmm. But was that too brutal? "I mean, I think about you, Jack, but I just don't think about you that way." Don't leave him hanging. "Yet."

"I like the 'yet' part."

My fingers tingle. They like the "yet" part, too. I can't believe I'm flirting so much, and over the phone! "We'll have to see how things develop . . . tomorrow night, okay?"

"Okay."

Some nice silence as I do a little chair dance on my bed.

"Will I hear from you tomorrow, Jack?"

"Sure."

"Let me give you my cell phone number." I give him the number. "Call me anytime, okay?"

"Okay."

"I'm looking forward to tomorrow night, Jack."

"So am I, Diane."

"Good night, Jack."

"Good night, Diane."

He loves my body. *I* don't even love my body, but *he* loves my body.

I don't think I'm going to need Mr. Tickler tonight.

34
Jack

*T*wo cell phone numbers in one day!
  Why do you have to be so loud?
  I'm primal, that's why. I'm supposed to urge you to splurge on your urges.
  I wish I could *purge* you.
  What fun would that be?
  I actually said the word "booty" to a woman. I'm so embarrassed. I could barely say "butt" to Noël!
  Noël had a nice ass.
  Shut up! You're talking about my wife!
  It's late, I'm tired, and though much more needs to be cleaned up—and written—I have to get some sleep. And tonight, I'm going to sleep in Noël's bed.
  And it scares the hell out of me.
  I know it shouldn't. It's just a bed that squeaked on her side, not mine. We had to "do it" on my side so we wouldn't wake Stevie. I lay on top of the comforter on my side, a little throw pillow between us, I mean, in the middle of the bed.

The little pillow was for her protection, because I have a tendency to "fly" in my dreams.

You thrash.

Shh. I don't need any company tonight.

Noël liked to spoon without us having sex—

But it often led to a good shellacking.

Cut it out! It wasn't a . . . shellacking. We were making love.

Right. You were making love so loudly that half the bed squeaked.

We weren't that wild . . . were we?

You had your moments. Remember "morning surprise"?

I liked a little "morning surprise." Those didn't happen too often, but when they did . . . I'd go in to work exhausted—

Happy.

Okay, I went in to work happy. It was so hard, at first, to face those kids knowing that only an hour ago I was—

Giving Noël a good shellacking.

Go to sleep, all right?

I look behind on the headboard and see all the flavors of candles she liked to light, like Very Berry, Vanilla Crème, Lemon Chiffon, and Honeydew. Most have been burned down to the bottom. Sometimes we only used one candle, and other times, we'd light them all. We even played this tape. . . . I have forgotten about *the* tape! I had made it for her to play in her car so she could think about me wherever she went. It wasn't in the . . . van. I wonder if it's in the Mustang?

That kind of music clashed with the Mustang. It was too romantic.

She liked it. She even brought it into the house when she was in the mood.

You went out and got it a couple times, too.

Yeah. It might be in the tape player under the bed.

With all the dust bunnies.

Don't remind me. I'll be sweeping and dusting all day tomorrow.

Why don't you see if it's in the tape player?

I don't know.

I'll bet it's there. Then you can play it.

I won't be able to sleep, not that I'm having any luck right now. Did we make love the night before she died?

It was that morning.

Yeah. It was a morning surprise.

During Good Morning, America.

I should have listened more closely to the weather report.

Let's not go over that again.

Right.

I remember that Noël had to take two showers that day, her usual long one, and a quick one after we . . . after we finished. She said there was something about the way I was sleeping that turned her on.

Your mouth was probably open and searching for flies.

Yeah. I had bed head, bad breath, and no shower at all, yet she loved me that way. She loved me that much.

She was horny, Jack.

Maybe. Maybe she was, you know, working on making a little girl. We had talked about having another child.

A boy for you, and a girl for her. The American Dream.

But it's the talking afterward that I miss most. We could hear Stevie snoring in his room—

He had your *nose.*

And we talked about . . . nothing really: her day, my day, the cost of gas, plans for the weekend, Stevie's minimilestones, what Stevie said, my writing. They were tender nothing moments bathed in candlelight, the ceiling fan cooling us down.

I hope you dream of her, Jack.

I hope I do, too.

35

Diane

It's New Year's Eve Day (what a mouthful), and I have to work. It's not so bad. There's hardly a soul in here. Everyone must be getting ready for tonight.

Tonight. I have a date tonight.

But first, I have to know more about Jack.

I use my morning break to read the *Roanoke Times* story of Jack's wife and son's deaths on a microfilm reader. I had been bracing myself for the horror of it, but the story was straightforward and detached. Jack's wife had attempted to cross a bridge over a "swollen stream" during a heavy downpour, lost control, and was swept down the creek. Attempts to revive her and her son failed, and they were pronounced dead at the scene. The story ends with a quote from some deputy: "It's always dangerous to cross through water since you can't gauge how deep it is."

The picture beside the story shows the van half out of the water.

What a horrible way to die.

I scan ahead to the next day and the obituary section. Nothing. I scan to the following day and see . . .

I know her. And I recognize her son.

I mean, I've seen them before. She was "Nice Lady," and he was "Quiet Kid." I have nicknames for many of the parents and children who arrive Saturday mornings expecting us to entertain them, nicknames like "Snot Nose," and "Mrs. Whiner" and "Super Brat." Jack's wife and son were so . . . nice. They used to come to nearly every Saturday morning reading, and both sat in the front row together, him leaning back on her legs. He was quite a giggler, his eyes focused on the book, but I could never get him to answer any of my questions. "Do you know what's going to happen next?" I would ask, looking mainly at him, and the boy—Stevie— would only shrug and giggle while the other kids shouted out answers.

I focus on her picture, and it had to have been taken at Glamour Shots. She is so pretty, with a slender nose, defined cheekbones, blond hair, and . . .

She is so much prettier than I'll ever be.

I knew looking this stuff up would depress me, but this . . . pretty picture depresses me most. What is Jack doing with me?

So, I get into a funk and watch the clock from the circulation desk in this ghost town of a library, thinking about the ghosts in Jack's life, which are now in mine. Lord, how You cross people's paths with each other. I'll bet You plan the coincidences You throw our way. I'll bet I checked out those books for Jack's son, and my fingerprints were on those books in Jack's home for six months, until he found them and brought them to me when . . . I touched him. It hurts my head and heart to think about it.

But mostly my heart.

Why me, Lord? Of all the . . . blond-haired, blue-eyed

women in this town, why did Jack choose me? Or, why did You have him choose me?

"You're deep in thought."

It's Francine, who has to be as bored as I am. "Just watching the clock."

"Do you have plans for this evening?" she asks.

"Yes."

Francine sits on the counter, something Kim says we should *never* do. "Are you going out on the town?"

I smile. "Yes." But that's all I'm going to tell you, Francine.

"Who's the lucky guy?"

I see Kim coming down the stairs from the reference section, and so does Francine, but she doesn't move off the counter. Kim eyeballs Francine, and Francine slides off the counter.

"What's up?" Kim asks.

"Diane has a date," Francine says.

"You do?" Kim asks.

I've been dying to tell someone about my date, but I don't want to share my business with the people with whom I work. I don't want my life to be the subject of gossip.

"Yes," I say.

"Anyone we know?" Kim asks.

"I doubt it," I say.

Francine raises her eyebrows. "So, what will you and your mystery man be doing?"

I smile. "I'll let you know." Not.

Kim smiles. "Is this something . . . serious?"

Just thinking of Jack reminds me of his book. "Oh, Kim, while I'm thinking about it, there's a local author who has his first novel coming out in April, and I thought we could preorder it." I pull a piece of paper from my purse with the title, Jack's name, and the ISBN and LOC numbers. I hand it to Kim.

"I hadn't heard about this," Kim says. "How do you know about it?"

Why lie? "I talked to the author."

Francine looks at the paper. "D. J. Browning. And he just . . . told you?"

I blink. "Yes, Francine." How else would I have known?

"What kind of a book is it?" Kim asks.

I read it, well, most of it. "It's an interracial romantic comedy."

Two sets of eyebrows rise.

"And it takes place right here in Roanoke," I add. "I'm sure our patrons will be requesting it, so maybe we should order at least five to ten copies."

Kim nods. "We'll need to get him in here to do a reading. When does the book come out again?"

"April." I smile inside. Shy Jack in front of a crowd where I work? I wouldn't know whether to be proud of him or scared for him, especially if other readers find his book as preposterous as I did.

"Do you have his number?" Kim asks.

Say what? "Yes."

A pause. "I'd like to call him to set up a reading."

"I can call him," I say, knowing full well that this kind of thing is in Kim's domain.

Francine smiles. "Wait a minute. He gave you his number, right?"

I nod.

"And you two . . . Are you going out on a date tonight with this man, Diane?"

Shoot. "Yes."

Then, the fluttering begins. They move in close and ask scores of questions without waiting for any answers: "What's he like?" "Where did you meet?" "Is he handsome?" "Is he rich?" "What does he drive?"

I wait for them to stop fluttering. "Look, we just met. He

asked me out, and I accepted. There's nothing more for you to know."

Well, almost nothing.

Kim squints. "He wrote an *interracial* romance, right?"

"Right." I look back at Kim, and she has her little lips pursed. Shoot. I knew I should have just said that he wrote a romantic comedy.

"He's white, isn't he?" Kim asks.

Francine looks confused. "He's white?"

Screw them. "Yes, Jack is white." As a ghost. He needs more sun.

Neither speaks for the longest time. "Well," Kim says, "I'll see about this order, and you, um, you let him know we're interested in him doing a reading. Okay, Diane?"

"Okay," I say.

Kim goes back up the stairs while Francine hovers, tapping the counter with her fingertips.

"I have some, um, things to do," Francine says, and she wanders off.

So, this is how it's going to be. Do I care? No. My co-workers are distant anyway. Let them keep their distance. "He's white?" I should have said, "He's a *man*. Now hurry up and join the rest of us in the twenty-first century."

What if I had said, "Yeah, he's a black man writing about getting it on with white women"?

It probably would have stopped Kim's little heart.

And this is just the reaction from some people I barely know. What will Mama say when she finds out?

I think I already know. "What have I told you all these years . . ."

And I think I already know how I'll respond.

He's a man, Mama, and I like him.

36

Jack

I didn't sleep much, and when I wake, I can't remember dreaming anything important.

You dreamed about lawn bowling in the mountains, Jack.

That was weird.

Maybe it's a Rip Van Winkle thing.

Maybe.

I spend most of the morning cleaning—vacuuming, dusting and sweeping, filling the kitchen trash can with dust bunnies. I even use the cooktop polishing cream for the first time, making the stove shine.

It smells like apples.

Yeah, it does.

Noël schooled you well, Jack.

I could do all this before.

Yeah, but you didn't. You were Dan Pace in the flesh with your "one of everything" mentality.

I only needed one of everything then.

But not anymore. Do you think Diane would want to eat off one plate and share the same spoon?

No. But eating off the same plate is kind of . . . intimate.

Kinky, I say.

Shh.

During my first cup of tea, I call Bandini's and find out they don't take reservations, which is good. When I ask how busy they might be tonight, I hear, "Very busy, so get here early." What's early? I asked. "Before ten."

Hmm. If I pick her up at her house at 9:30, we'll be fine.

The phone rings. "Hello?"

"Jack?"

It's my mother. I look at the calendar on the pantry door. Yep, nearly six months to the day of her last call. "Hi, Mom."

"How are you, son?"

"Fine."

"How's the writing coming?"

"Good."

"Are you going out this evening?"

"I'm going out with a friend to dinner."

A pause. "Is this friend a woman, Jack?"

"Yes, Mom."

Another pause, a longer pause. She's thinking that six months is too short to wait. She's thinking that in some cultures two years is the "proper" time for mourning.

"What's her name, son?"

"Diane Anderson. We've had lunch together once. Tonight is only our second date."

"You said she was a friend."

I roll my eyes. "Friends can go on dates, too, Mom."

A pause. "Where did you meet Diane?"

"At the library. I was taking back some books I found in Stevie's room, and that's when we met."

"Is she a librarian?"

"Yes."

I'm sure Mom has the stereotypical image of a librarian in her mind.

"She's twenty-five, Mom, and she's pretty," I say.

"Oh." I hear a door shut. "Your father wants to talk to you."

"Hello, son."

"Hello, Dad."

"Have you been keeping busy?"

I tell him about all the changes to the house, the cleaning, the trips to the Salvation Army, the sale of the car—all the things Mom never asks or cares about.

"Well, you have yourself a good new year, hear?"

"I will, Dad. You, too."

"Take care."

As I hang up, I mentally circle a date in July—for their next call. It's not that they don't care about me. They care, but they just don't know how to show it. They've never known how to communicate with me. Everything has always been so formal, so regimented, so . . . organized. And I chafed at that organization, going to a college farther away than they had hoped, majoring in a subject they thought was beneath my intellect, teaching elementary school instead of college, and marrying a girl I only knew for a few months.

The phone rings again. "Hello?"

"Hi, Jack, it's Jenny."

"Hi, Jenny."

"I know this may sound forward, Jack, but, um, do you have any plans for this evening?"

I knew she was after you!

You said it was only a crush.

I was wrong!

"Yes, Jenny, I have plans. I have a date."

That was smooth. Just "a date." Nothing serious.

"Oh," Jenny says, in a soft voice.

Tell her "maybe next weekend."

No!

Come on, Jack! You can date two women at the same time! It's not like their paths will ever cross.

Shh.

"Well," Jenny says, "you two have a good time. Bye."

Click.

Did you hear her voice? She was so sad, Jack. You should have given her a little hope!

She assumed that I didn't have a date for New Year's because I'm a widower. She assumed that I would jump at the chance to go out with her "bouncy" body. And that's all she is—a cute voice in a cute body. I'm focused on Diane now, and I wouldn't even know how to juggle two women.

But what if you and Diane don't work out?

I want it to work out.

But you're cutting off another option!

A *young* option. Diane is . . . wise for her age.

Excuse me while I stop my eyes from rolling out of our eye sockets.

You're excused.

You hardly know Diane! How can you say she's wise?

It's a feeling I have. You remember feelings, don't you?

Yes, but—

And tonight, I'm going to get to know Diane a whole lot better.

Yeah?

Not in the way you're thinking.

Right. Six months after your last morning surprise and you're not even thinking about it.

It has . . . crossed my mind, but it's way too soon.

You're not thinking about bringing her back here, are you?

No.

Good. This place is still a dump. But maybe her place . . .

I'll be picking her up and dropping her off at her place, and that's it.

What if she invites you in?

I'll go in.

What if she wants you to spend the night?

I'll . . . answer that when she asks it, but I don't think she will.

She might.

And she might not.

Well, what if she says, "Jack, please spend the night with me"? What are you going to say?

I'm going to say . . .

I bury my head in my hands.

I don't know what I would say.

37

Diane

Since we're the only three people in the library at 7:30, Kim lets Francine and me go early, telling me, "Have fun tonight, okay?"

I'm sure Kim was only being nice so I would tell her all about my date on Monday, but it was nice for someone to speak to me. The library is a quiet place, but I truly enjoy talking to patrons.

Even if I can't stand most of them.

Because I keep a clean house, there's not much to spruce up. I empty all the trash cans, dust a little, straighten this, fluff that—the usual.

Though nothing about tonight is usual.

I close the door to my bedroom, Psyche's scene coming back to me. "He's not coming in here," I say, with a smile, though it will be nice to have a man inside my house. Hmm. Will I ask him in when he gets here, or will I just meet him at the door? I could give him a tour. I'm proud of my house. I could show him my books—

I'll have to hide the advance review copy of his book, though. That would be a disaster.

I look at the closed door to my bedroom. I could hide it in there no problem, and since he's not going in there . . . At least I don't think I want him in there.

I put the copy of *Wishful Thinking* in the dryer in the laundry room. I doubt he'll be nosing around in there.

Then, I get "kitted out" for the evening. I already did my hair this morning, so it just needs a little brushing out. I put on my only formal black dress, a long one with slits up my legs and a daring cutout on my back. For whatever reason, this dress makes me seem taller. I find my only pair of spiked black heels and slip them on without hose. They still fit. Do I need hose tonight? I want to be sexy, so no hose.

I look at my toes. Hmm. I'd better put polish on them, but not black polish. I don't want to look too Gothic. I apply clear polish, and while they dry, I bathe my legs in lotion. Lord, thank You for giving me these legs. At least they're in proportion to the rest of my body. I apply a little eyeliner, pluck a few little hairs from my eyebrows, and put on some lip gloss. No lipstick tonight. I want to feel natural so I can *act* natural.

Once I am "fly," I sit in the living room wondering where we're going after we eat at Bandini's. Dancing? I haven't danced in years. I wonder if Jack can dance. Hmm. I wonder if *I* can still dance.

I see headlights shoot across the room. Someone's in the driveway. I smooth out my dress and head to the window, where I see . . . a truck? A beat-up-looking SUV. Maybe they're just turning around. Who . . . oh, it's Jack. At least he didn't drive that yellow thing, but taking me out in an SUV when I'm wearing a dress?

He's coming to my door wearing . . . a black suit with a tie and shiny black shoes. He looks sharp. I wait for the doorbell, hear it, and only then do I get just a little nervous.

I open the door. "Come in."

Jack steps through the door and looks right into my eyes.
"Hi."

"Hi."

He looks side to side, first at my dining room, where even
I've eaten only once, then into the living room. "This is
nice."

"Do you want the tour now . . . or later?"

I can't believe I just said that.

"Actually," Jack says, "I want a hug first."

This is one hugging man. I hug him gently, you know, so
I don't add more wrinkles to his suit, which hangs on him so
much. He would look sharper in that suit if there was more
of him *in* that suit.

"Thank you," he says, taking my hands and looking at
me. "You look nice."

"So do you."

He's still holding my hands. Is this where we kiss?

"You mentioned a tour."

This isn't where we kiss. This is where I take his hand
(I'm taking his hand!) and guide him through the house to
look at the living room, the kitchen, the bathroom (why'd I
take him there?), and finally the library.

"Wow," he says, but he won't let go of my hand. "That's a
lot of books."

"About as many as—" Oh my goodness, I almost said,
"as Dan Pace." I have to be more careful. "About as many as
can fit," I say.

He takes a step, his hand still connected to mine, and
uses his other hand to pull out a book. He flips it over, then
looks at the cover again. "This is an advance review copy."

I could say that I collect them, but that's a pretty weak explanation. "I review books in my spare time."

He turns to me, and he smiles. "Yeah?"

"Yeah." I step closer to him. "For the Mid-Atlantic Book
Review."

"Really." He reshelves the book. "Do you know Nisi?"

Like the back of my hand, and I'd like to backhand that heifer for writing that review! "Yeah. Not very well, though." I look at the floor. "She tends to be, um, overly critical."

He scans another row of books. "As she should be."

I release his hand so he can continue his tour. "You know, Jack, I've been thinking that maybe I could read your book, too. Do you have an advance review copy I might read?"

"You might find that it's a one-star book, too."

There are so many ironies in this situation right now. "Well, I'd like to read it."

He pulls out *Thicker Than Blood*. "Was this any good?"

"It wasn't bad."

He puts it back. "I don't have any advance review copies, but I do have the second and third drafts on my computer. I could give you a disk. Maybe we could stop by my house tonight."

He said, "my house tonight." Even my toes are tingling.

"Oh, I meant . . ." He shakes his head. "I mean, before I bring you home, I can shoot the drafts to a disk. It would only take a second."

"Sure. Which draft do you think was best?"

"The second," he says immediately. "That was before my agent and editor got hold of it."

Before they made it suck.

He exhales deeply. "Are you ready to go?"

To your house? Maybe. To eat? Yes. "I'm ready."

"I hope you don't mind the truck. . . ."

I mind the truck. I almost make another slit in my dress climbing up into the thing. It feels as if I'm in the front seat of a bus, and it rides so stiff. I feel every bump in my booty and spend most of my time holding on to a little bar above my window.

"You need a new car, Jack." I did it again! How many phrases are there with "Jack" in them?

He smiles. "Yeah, I suppose I do."

"Well, when you become a famous author, you should get one."

"*If*," he says. "I wouldn't even know what to get."

Well, whatever it is, please keep your passenger in mind. This is no vehicle for a lady wearing a sleek black dress.

We park once again on the top floor of the parking garage, because there are so many cars, and before we can even cross the street to Bandini's, we see a crowd spilling outside.

"But it's before ten," Jack says. "I called, and they said they wouldn't be that busy before ten."

"I don't mind waiting." Though, normally, I would. My wrap isn't paper-thin, but it won't keep me that warm for long.

Jack takes my hand, and we cross the street. He does it seemingly without thinking, while I know I would have to make a conscious decision to take his hand in public. On the other side, we thread through small groups of people, most with wineglasses or bottles of beer in their hands.

"Maybe they just wanted some air," Jack says.

Once we get inside, the same hostess as before smiles, takes two menus, and leads us to an empty table. She didn't even ask, "How many?" Oh, yeah. I know why. We're still holding hands.

We're a couple.

Jack lets go of my hand, helps me remove my wrap, holds my chair, and slides me in.

And my hand turns cold. It misses his hand already!

Milliseconds after we sit, Mr. Bandini appears.

Now *this* is service.

"Hello again!" he says loudly.

"Hi," I say.

"Hello," Jack says.

Gee, we're acting like old friends.

"Welcome back to Bandini's. If there is anything I can do, just let me know." He winks at me. "Is your table okay?"

Jack looks at me. "Is it?"

"It's fine." And it is. Kind of off to the side, not much traffic, nobody's back inches from mine, a white candle in a red glass holder on the table.

"Good. Enjoy your meal."

Jack leans forward after Mr. Bandini leaves. "It's almost as if I *did* make a reservation."

"Good timing."

"Yeah."

We make eye contact, and Lord help me, I'm blushing. I never blush. I may feel embarrassed, but I never feel this heat in my face when I'm embarrassed. All I said was "Good timing," and all he said was "Yeah."

"Do you want to share our meal like last time?" he asks.

"Sure."

While we eat four kinds of pasta, I see, of all things, *Lady and the Tramp* running through my head. We don't share a string of spaghetti, but we do share a bottle of wonderful red wine. Jack only sips his, which is good because he's driving, but I have three glasses.

"I'll try to get reservations at Stephen's for our next date," Jack says, swirling his wine in his glass. "Maybe when I'm a famous novelist, I'll be able to get a table anywhere." He laughs. "I'll never be famous, not even here in Roanoke."

"Oh, you never know."

He sits up straight so fast I think he's having a heart attack! "I completely forgot to tell you something."

I hope he doesn't forget much! That scared me.

"It slipped my mind," he says. "I guess I'm trying to block it out. The publisher wants to put my picture on the cover and send me on a weeklong tour, mainly of the East Coast."

I stifle my real reaction—"Are they crazy?"—and only say, "Really?"

"It's crazy."

My thoughts exactly. "Did they tell you why?"

"They say I'm a novelty. A rarity."

Jack is going to take some abuse.

"So, I have to get my picture taken soon."

I push both plates of pasta to him. "You'll need to gain some weight first, so eat up."

"Thanks."

I look at his hair just . . . sitting there. "How long have you had that part in your hair, Jack?"

He squints. "For . . . as long as I can remember. Why?"

I could be delicate, but I can't. The wine won't let me. "Why don't you change your hairstyle?"

"To what?"

I look at all that fine, blond hair. "Can I be blunt?"

He smiles. "Sure."

"You're a twenty-first-century author with an early twentieth-century hairstyle. You look like old pictures I've seen of F. Scott Fitzgerald."

He wipes his lips with a napkin. "At least I'm in good company."

"You'd look better if you, I don't know, spike it up, make that part disappear, cut it even shorter. Something." I lean forward. "I like a man with short hair. We could get you some gel."

He nods. "I'll . . . get some gel." He looks into my eyes. He's always doing that, and while at first it made me paranoid, now it makes me feel . . .

Nervous. It makes me feel nervous when a man looks into my eyes. What's he trying to see in them? And why don't I see anything in them when I'm applying some eyeliner?

"Maybe you should go with me when I go to the photographer."

I look away. "Oh, I don't know about that."

"You have nice eyes, Diane, and I'm sure they see things I can't see."

I look back at him.

"I mean, I'm sure you can make me look better for this picture."

"I can try."

He looks down at his plate. "Good." He leans back in his chair. "I can't eat another bite."

I look at a clock over the bar. It's a little after eleven. "What's next?"

38
Jack

Yes, Jack, what's next?

Shh. I'm still thinking about what she said about my hair.

Don't give it another thought. She was only making a suggestion.

Noël liked my hair.

So does Diane!

But . . . putting gel in my hair?

Dan would do it.

Dan would do anything to get into a woman's drawers.

It's "draws," Jack.

Whatever.

"Jack?"

I look up at Diane. "Just thinking."

"So, where are we going?"

I toss my napkin on the table. "We are going for a little ride."

She hates the truck, remember?

"Just a short ride, I promise, and I'll try not to hit any pot-holes."

She smiles. "Good luck in this town."

I pay for the check, help Diane with her wrap, take her hand, and we leave Bandini's, weaving around an even bigger crowd than before. The air is cold and crisp, but I guess these folks don't feel a thing, champagne bottles in abundance, several corks popping as we move by and cross the street to the parking garage.

Where are we going, Jack?

I don't know.

Diane's eyes are sparkling, Jack. She must not be a drinking woman. You know what that means. . . .

It means that I will take care of her.

We squeeze into an elevator filled with rowdy people, many openly drinking from wine and champagne bottles. I pin myself to a side and pull Diane close to me, her . . . caboose pressed hard against me.

We like this.

Yes, we do.

You have your hands around her stomach.

So soft!

She's backing into you, Jack. There's room in front of her, and she's—

"Are you okay?" I whisper in Diane's ear.

"Yes," she says, and she pulls my arms around her more tightly.

She likes this, too.

It appears that she does.

We get out with several other couples on the top floor, and before I realize it, my hand is pressing on the beginnings of her caboose! I draw it back quickly, hoping she didn't notice.

She noticed.

I was aiming for the small of her back!

Right.

I open her door. "Um, sorry about that, I was just—"

She puts a finger to my lips. "You don't have to explain." She gets in.

"No, really, Diane, I was just trying, I was aiming for your back."

She bites her lip in the sexiest way. "Your hand went where it wanted to go, Jack. And anyway, how do you know that my booty didn't reach up and grab your hand?"

Can she do that?

Maybe she can!

I take several cold, deep breaths before getting in the truck, and when I do get in, I'm almost hyperventilating.

"Are you all right, Jack?" Diane asks.

"Yes."

"What are you thinking?"

I start the truck. "You don't want to know."

She keeps me from shifting into reverse. "Yes, I do."

I rev the engine a couple times and turn the heater on low. "Okay, here goes. I like the feel of your booty." Her hand drops from the stick shift. "You wanted to know."

She settles into her seat and puts on her seat belt. "Well," she says, "I like the way your hand felt on my booty."

I rev the engine again. "It was an accident, I swear!"

"Accidents happen."

I let the truck idle, and though I try not to let it show—

It's showing, Jack. She's noticing.

You heard what she said.

She was talking about your hand accidentally touching her booty, that's all. Don't go overboard on this one, Jack. You're having a good time.

"I'm sorry, Jack," Diane says.

"It's all right," I say. "I have to be less sensitive."

"No, I shouldn't have said that."

I sigh. "It's okay, Diane. Really."

Shit. I really know how to ruin a mood.

Shit happens. Relax. Go for a drive.

We leave the parking garage and join a light flow of traffic going from Campbell Avenue to Williamson Road to Franklin Road. Without thinking, I turn on Third Street, passing First Baptist, a sign announcing: "New Year's Eve Service 11 P.M."

"It's been so long since I've been to one of those," Diane says. "I used to go every year when I was a kid."

We stop at the stoplight on Luck Avenue. "I haven't been to church since the accident."

You said that word this time.

And maybe if I say it enough, it won't bother me anymore.

"You should go," Diane says.

The light changes, but I don't move. "Can I go now?" I point back at First Baptist. "I'm a member there."

Diane sits up straighter. "If that's what you want to do."

A horn sounds behind me, and I turn left on Luck, drifting to the curb to let the car pass. "I don't want to, but I know I should. But, we're on a date, and we should be going somewhere to celebrate or dance or do whatever it is people do on New Year's Eve."

She touches my hand. "You drove this way for a reason, Jack." She looks out her window. "And it seems as if we've found a parking space. You also promised to take me for a walk."

She has a good memory.

Yeah.

I turn off the truck. "We don't have to go in. We'll just . . . walk over there."

"Okay."

I get out of the truck, open her door, take her hand—

Kiss her!

What?

Kiss her, Jack!

Why?

For being so understanding! For looking so nice! For

*feeling comfortable enough to tell you that your hairstyle
sucks!*

I look into her eyes. "Diane, I . . . Thank you."

She steps closer. "For what?"

She's waiting, Jack.

"For understanding, and for—"

Diane kisses my cheek. "Let's go for a walk, Jack."

She kissed you! She kissed *you* because *you* can't get
your shit together!

I take Diane's face in my hands and kiss her firmly on the
lips.

Tongue! Use the tongue!

No.

I pull back, her warm face still in my hands. "Let's go for
that walk."

We walk hand in hand across Luck and up Third Street,
weaving around a telephone pole, smiling, listening to honking horns colliding with the strains of the organ music inside.
We stop at the bottom of the steps to the main sanctuary, and
I slip my arm around her shoulders.

"Are you cold?" I ask.

"A little."

Get her out of the cold, Jack. Take her home.

"We could just . . . sit in the back for a while."

She nods. "I'd like that."

We start up the stairs.

*You're taking her to church? On a date? On New Year's?
Are you out of your mind? What if Noël's parents are here?
They're members here, too!*

I open the door and see . . . candles everywhere, at the
base of every window, and in the hands of nearly everyone
inside.

"It's beautiful," Diane whispers.

*Think of all the candles you can be lighting back at her
place, Jack! Don't go in!*

We step into the foyer, the door shutting behind us, and

Mr. Highsmith, one of the regular greeters, hands each of us a small candle. A children's choir is singing "Silent Night." Stevie used to sing in that choir. I feel a tug on my hand.

"Let's go in, Jack," Diane says.

You don't want to go in there, Jack. The last time you were here, there was a funeral with two caskets. One big, and one small. Don't you remember?

Wait for us outside. We won't be long.

39

Diane

Jack's taking lots of big steps tonight.

Okay, we both are. I kissed him first. Yes, I took the initiative. But his kiss back to me . . . my lips are still buzzing. We were in liplock and in eyelock, and if he kisses me every time like that—I intend to get *many* more later—I won't be able to talk to anyone without adding the letter *Z* to every word.

We light our candles using a huge candle sitting in the first window, and now we're in the back row of the church holding hands and listening to the singing of several choirs. I try not to look at Jack's tears, focusing instead on my candle, the music, our hands laced together, the kiss, and the fact that there are a few black folks in this church. I wish I could help Jack more, but this is something he has to do on his own. I was raised to believe that when you go through any tragedy, no matter who is there to help, you go through that tragedy *alone,* and only *you* can work it all out. Jack's working it out, and though this isn't what I expected would happen tonight, I'm glad I'm here.

Lord, he loved his family, I pray. *Please let him have some love left over for me. Amen.*

At midnight, in addition to car horns honking outside, we hear all the choirs singing "Joyful, Joyful We Adore Thee," and I get severe goose bumps, especially when they cut out the piano and organ and sing it *a cappella*. We're not kissing at midnight, a tradition I've never had happen to me, but our hands are kissing. In fact, they're getting downright nasty with each other. As soon as the song ends, we hear the benediction, blow out our candles, and leave the pew. We don't speak to anyone on our way out, but Jack smiles and nods to several people, and the whole time he has his hand in the small of my back.

I can get used to this attention, oh yes I can!

And when we get inside the truck, *I* kiss *him*, holding his face in my hands. "Thank you, Jack."

He turns and starts the truck. "For crying during church?"

"No. For loving your family."

More tears form, but he blinks them away. "Yeah." He turns on the heater and revs the engine. "Where to?"

"Wherever you want to go, Jack," I say.

He nods. "We'll go to my house, then, so I can make you a disk."

"Okay."

Though it's dark when we get to Jack's split-level house, I can tell his house had lots of love in it. There are four huge flower beds hugging the house, the dirt dark and the flowers gone now, but flower beds have always been signs of love to me. Anyone who can tend the earth and cultivate color has to have love for other people, which is why I know my daddy loves me. And if she died in July—and I'm sure those beds were bursting with color then—Jack had to have tended them, even cutting them down in the fall during his most acute grief.

Jack parks in front of the house, because the Mustang is still in the driveway, and we walk past a square flower bed in the middle of the yard. He said he sold that car, but that car is still here. I don't bother him about it. "What grows here?" I ask.

"Tulips in the spring," he says, "and whatever we could find cheap at Home Depot after that. Sometimes pansies, sometimes whatever was most colorful."

He leads me to a small concrete porch covered with brown carpeting. Everything about this house is brown, from the dark brown shutters to the light brown siding. "What about these beds along the house?"

"Daylilies, hostas, roses, mums—you name it, it will come up."

He opens the door, and we go in and stand on the landing, lit up by a beautiful glass lamp hanging from the ceiling.

And it dawns on me that I am in a dead woman's house.

This is *her* house.

Oh, I know it's Jack's house, too, but from the second I see neutral white carpeting on the stairs, white walls, and modern, overstuffed furniture in a room downstairs, I know I'm in *her* house.

"Pardon the mess," Jack says, turning on a light and leading me downstairs.

But I don't see a mess! It's like a museum. A cream L-shaped sectional sofa hugs the far walls, two large framed pictures of flowers centered over each section. The sofa faces a wide-screen TV, a stereo system, and a bookcase holding . . . kid's videos and DVDs.

Ouch.

"Um, sit anywhere you like," Jack says, going to a white computer workstation under a long window. "This will only take a minute."

"Is that where you write your books?" I ask. I'll bet the sun shines in here all day.

"No," Jack says. "This is Noël's computer. My, um, office is down the hall."

Noël's computer. I want to tell him that it's *his* computer now, but I don't.

I sit in a rocking recliner, drinking it all in. This room is huge. I'll bet his son was tearing it up down here. I see a few tiny white Legos here and there, and it makes me sad. I don't know what I'm supposed to feel, but it's kind of scary.

And my bladder is feeling full.

"Um, Jack, may I use your bathroom?"

He turns to me. "Um, the upstairs bathroom is the cleanest. Just go up the stairs, turn left, second door on the left."

I go upstairs, turning on a hall light and seeing . . . pictures, a whole wall of them dedicated to Noël and Stevie. There's only one family portrait, with Jack standing behind Noël, who is holding Stevie as a baby . . . and that's the only one of Jack. He was so much more handsome then! I mean, he had a full face, a tan, and some substantial arms and chest. Lord, why does death suck so much life out of the living? Jack must have taken most of these pictures. Noël and Stevie at the beach. Noël and Stevie at the zoo. Stevie alone on a swing. Noël in her garden. I try for the life of me to, you know, superimpose myself into these pictures, but I can't.

I glance into a living room where an overly decorated Christmas tree stands in front of a bay window. There isn't room for even another strand of tinsel, but it's beautiful and beats my Charlie Brown tree to death. Jack still put up a tree, after all that has happened to him, yet . . . there aren't any presents under it. Oh, I'm sure he got some. He just put them away.

I count two doors down and enter a bathroom that definitely says "female." Fluffy rugs in sky blue and orange pastels, matching toilet lid cover, seashells on the wallpaper, fish swimming across the shower curtain and matching window curtain, and blue and orange towels of every shape and size hanging off hooks and bars. The off-white marble sink is spotless, a huge orange candle in the corner, an orange soap dish holding an unused bar of Dove, a sky blue tooth-brush holder—

Two toothbrushes, one long, one kid sized. Two tubes of toothpaste, one Crest Dual Action Whitening, the other Crest Sesame Street. This is *their* bathroom, and Jack hasn't changed a thing or done a thing in here. No dust on the sink base, though. He cleans up in here but leaves their tooth-brushes and toothpaste?

I hike up my dress, drop my panties, and sit on the toilet, looking at half a roll of toilet paper. They used this same roll, I'll bet.

This is awkward, and I'm having trouble peeing. I'm sit-ting in *their* bathroom, where Noël gave Stevie baths; where Noël showered or took a long, hot bath; where Noël *sat* and did her business. I try not to look into the large mirror above the sink, because I'm afraid I'll see her ghost.

This is creepy.

I finish, wipe, flush, and hesitate before picking up the bar of Dove. No one has ever used this. It's just for show, and for some reason, if I use it, I'll be desecrating this "shrine" to Noël and Stevie. I'll bet there are even some toys on the ledges of that tub behind that curtain. I just can't desecrate anything in here.

I leave the bathroom and stare at two closed doors. I don't open them. One has to be Stevie's room, the other Noël's. I go instead to the kitchen, flip on a light—hey, this is *nice!*—where I use some Softsoap to wash my hands and dry them on a dark blue towel. This isn't what I expected at all. I ex-pected a sink full of dishes, garbage spilling out of the can, a table crawling with crumbs and a colony of ants, and a streaky floor. Instead, it's like a picture from *Better Homes and Gardens* in which everything gleams and shines.

I *love* this kitchen! My own kitchen is cramped, but this one has some space to move from the sink to the stove to the fridge to the microwave on its own cart. I marvel at the cabinet doors of frosted glass, the window treatments matching the wall border exactly, all the pots and pans hanging—

"You're in my favorite room," Jack says behind me.

"It's nice," I say. It's more than that, much more. This is the heart of Jack's home. This is where Noël's heart beat most.

He opens the fridge, and I look inside. Jack . . . drinks a lot. And such a variety!

"I wish we had some more of that red wine," he says, grabbing a bottle of . . . is that eggnog? With Santa on the bottle?

"I'm fine," I say.

He puts the bottle back. "Me, too." He hands me the disk. "I hope you have Microsoft Word."

I look at the disk, "second draft" written on it. "I do."

"I could make you some coffee or some hot tea."

And I could do the same for him at my place. "I'm okay."

"All right." He leans against the fridge, and that's when I notice it's completely clear of all those magnetic doodads people put on them. "Um, I'd give you a tour, but . . ."

"It's okay." I've already kind of taken one. "But I want to see where you write."

He takes me downstairs past three closed doors to the end of the hall. He stands aside so I can enter. . . .

What is this place? This is where a writer writes? This is an office?

"It's kind of . . . crowded," he says.

"Crowded" isn't the word. "Shoehorned" would be better to describe this library/office/dumping ground.

"You write in here?" I ask.

"Yeah."

"Doesn't it make you claustrophobic?"

"Sometimes. Sometimes I take my laptop to the kitchen and write."

To be nearer to Noël's heart. I turn sideways so I can navigate between a TV stand with no TV and the edge of a . . .

bed? There's a bed under all those papers, files, and Post-its. I look up at some seriously sagging shelves. The man is well read.

"You have quite a collection, Jack." I look at his desk and see even more pictures of Noël and Stevie. "Is there, um, some kind of organization here?"

"No," he says. "But I kind of know where everything is."

I shimmy past the bed/open-air filing cabinet to his chair and take a seat. "So, this is where you sit."

He comes up behind me. "Yep."

"Is this where you wrote *Wishful Thinking*?"

"Yes."

I can now see better where and how Dan Pace lived. "Is your book kind of autobiographical?" I ask.

"Yeah," he says. "Most of the places are where I used to live. Dan's apartment, for example."

I play dumb. "Dan?"

"Yeah, my main character, and he's quite a character. He lives in a one-bedroom efficiency like I used to."

Which means that Jack . . . had a king-sized bed in that little apartment. Is there a king-sized bed upstairs right now?

"I don't know how you do it," I say, swiveling as far as the chair will go, almost facing Jack. He needs a new chair. "I would go crazy down here."

"I'm used to it." He gives me his hand. "I'd better get you home."

I hold his hand with both of mine. "No rush."

He sighs.

"Unless this is too awkward for you."

He nods. "I, uh, I need to get out of here, maybe get another efficiency. This is too much house for one person."

I don't know about that. I still think three people live here. "Was this your first house?"

He nods. "First and last, I used to think."

It still might be. I'd have to remove most of the pictures first, of course, and this room has to be tipped on its side and emptied, but . . . I can see myself in this house. I'd definitely stand out with all the whiteness in here.

I pull myself up to him, draping my arms around his shoulders. "Well, if I were you, I wouldn't sell it. It's a beautiful house."

"Thank you. I like your house, too."

"It's not nearly as big as this one, or as modern."

"I like old-fashioned things like hardwood floors and real wood furniture." He looks down. "Your house says quality and craftsmanship."

I smile. "My furniture says secondhand at a yard sale."

"You have good taste."

"Thank you. Um, would you like to take me home now?"

"Yes."

"Will you come in for some coffee? I make a mean cup of coffee." With a coffeemaker I've been using since college.

"I'd like that."

But when we get to my house, and I let him in, I have no intention of making any coffee. I close my door and lock it, and then I lock lips with Dan until we're both on my sofa pawing at each other. I get his jacket and tie off quickly enough, but there are too many buttons on his shirt—

He pulls away, breathing heavily, but not nearly as heavily as I am.

"What's wrong?"

"I, uh, I haven't been with anyone else."

I sit up, letting the slits in my dress keep on revealing my legs. "You mean, since . . . Noël died?"

"No. Since . . . ever."

I don't know what to say at first. I mean, what do you say? Do you say, "You were a virgin when you got married?? Do you say, "I like a faithful man"? Do you say, "I find this hard to believe, Jack"?

Or, do you believe it and say nothing?

Not only did he lose a wife; he lost his first love *and* his first lover. And here I am, on my reading sofa, ready, willing, and able to be his second. It's not as special as being his first, of course, but I've been waiting long enough! I'm sitting on the sofa where I have had many wicked fantasies that sent me running to my bedroom for some privacy and buzzing under the covers. If only I hadn't had trouble with all those buttons!

I straighten out my dress, pulling a sleeve back to my shoulder.

"It's not that I don't want to, Diane. Really."

From the way he, um, grew down there, I believe it, too.

"It's just . . . I'm . . . I'm not ready. I know that sounds cliché."

A man whom I was about to let be my first . . . isn't ready to *be* my first? This is definitely a first. "I understand, Jack."

"You do?"

I nod.

"Well," he says, "I wish you could explain it to me."

Now what do I say? "Noël, um, she was your first love."

He nods.

"And, uh, you still love her."

He nods again.

Shoot. I'm in competition with a dead woman. It's as if *Wuthering Heights* has broken out in my living room. "And you still love her enough . . . to remain faithful to her."

"Yeah." His eyes are tearing up again. "Yeah, that's what I'm feeling." He turns to me. "It's not fair to you, though."

True. "We'll have to take it slow then."

"Thank you." He sighs. "I'm a mess, aren't I?"

I slide next to him, putting my head on his shoulder. "Yes, Jack, you are a mess."

He laughs a little. "I'm sorry, Diane. I thought I could . . . let it all go." He kisses my forehead. "But I can't."

"We have time," I say. "I'm a patient woman."

He kisses me tenderly. "You're one of a kind, Diane Anderson."

"You're pretty unique yourself, Jack Browning."

And then . . . we snuggle, not speaking, for a few hours, just sharing each other's company—and warmth—occasionally kissing, squeezing, smiling, sighing . . . until I fall asleep.

And when the sunlight wakes me on the sofa a few hours later, Jack is gone.

40
Jack

*W*hy *did you leave? She wanted you to stay!*

I couldn't stay. I can't stay.

Grandma Ella would say "can't" really means—

I *might* stay someday. Just not today. This is all too soon, too soon. It feels like I'm cheating.

You're not.

I know I'm not. It just feels like I am. I'm not done being faithful, okay? We went out to eat, went to church, kissed a bit—

You two were doing some grinding on that sofa, too. Don't forget that.

I almost lost control.

You're human, Jack.

I know.

And she seemed willing, right?

She was so soft, so . . . *there.*

Is Diane who you're thinking about right now in Noël's bed?

No.

Then turn off that tape!

I had found the tape in the tape player under the bed, cued up to "Right Here Waiting" by Richard Marx. *That's where I am, Noël,* I was thinking, *just oceans apart from you.* "All I Want Is You" by U2 made me think of the promises I had made to her, from the cradle to the grave. Billy Ocean's "Suddenly" didn't give my life any new meaning, Jim Croce's "Time in a Bottle" reminded me that my box of wishes is empty, and now . . .

Turn it off, Jack.

But it's "Back in the High Life" by Steve Winwood.

Then do as the song says and let the good parts last.

What good parts?

It's supposed to be a happy song, Jack! You're supposed to be drinking and dancing. Aren't you listening to the chorus?

I only hear the verses.

The song fades out and fades in to Phil Collins's "In the Air Tonight."

Please, turn it off. Get some sleep.

No.

This song always depresses you.

I know.

Then turn it off!

No . . . Here come the drums—

Don't—

"The hurt doesn't show, but the pain still grows . . . ," I sing, and then I sit up and play the "air drums."

I need a drink.

No, Jack.

Am I hearing myself correctly?

Yes.

But you're Dan Pace. You're the party animal. I thought for sure that *you* would be thirsty.

Now isn't the time. Rest.

But it's a brand-new year! Drinking is the thing to do on New Year's Day!

Don't.

Why? Are you afraid I'll drown in my memories?

No. I'm afraid you won't want to make new ones.

Oh, shut up.

I go to the kitchen, grab a full bottle of Boone's Farm Melon Ball, and down half of it in one gulp. Then I make a toast: "Okay, then. Here's to *no* memories."

41

Diane

I wake up alone.

I'm used to it, so it doesn't bother me that much. At least he locked the front door after him. And he did leave the disk on the kitchen counter. At least I have that.

"Happy New Year, Diane."

I stretch and wander into the kitchen, start the coffee-maker, and look at my tiny kitchen. There's only room for one cook in this kitchen. I can stand right here on this tile and almost touch everything—

Okay, it bothers me.

Shoot.

I wanted to wake up with him. I wanted to cook him breakfast in this tiny kitchen. I wanted to spend the first day of the brand-new year with him, reading his book while he . . . What would he do? Hmm. I would have sent him home for his laptop, and he could be writing his next book while I'm reading the first. We could have had lunch together. We could have maybe even watched the Rose Bowl parade or even a football game or two. We could have, I don't know, had dinner at his place— Wait, there was no food in the fridge. Well, we would have driven around and found something at maybe a convenience store.

I miss him.

He should still be here.

I shouldn't have fallen asleep, but I felt so . . . something I've never felt before. I felt needed, wanted, cherished. I felt . . .

Lord, I felt *home*.

I pick up the disk. "Looks as if it's just you and me."

I take my cup of coffee to my library, taking sips and nodding to myself, and boot up the computer. He just needs more time, that's all. He'll come around. I mean, he practically stayed the night, right? He knows a good thing, and I am a *good* thing. And next time—and there *will* be a next time—he'll stay even longer, maybe even the whole night. And one day, when we least expect it, we'll be in my bedroom . . .

I should have opened that door on the tour, you know, to give him ideas.

I double-click the Word icon, then load "WT," the only file on the disk. And then I start reading the screen with a new set of eyes.

And I get an eyeful.

What I read hardly matches the advance review copy. Dan is so much more endearing and much less of a pervert, Ty is softer and not nearly as rugged, and though they still bump into each other before that teacher conference, it's so much more romantic . . . and realistic. Pat the freak and Mike the gay guy don't even make an appearance, and I get a clearer glimpse of Dan the teacher—*and* Jack the man:

. . . I'm a grumpy man who stayed up late pounding nails into boards. I leave a message with the real estate company that owns the Cube to replace my door—"steel preferred," I tell them. There's just not that much wood left to nail into anymore.

As whipped and tired and grumpy as I am, I still manage to muddle through traffic to Monterey, and on a whim—and because I really don't have a lesson planned—I have my first class redesign then rearrange the room. And, of course, the principal, Mrs. Wine, chooses the moment we begin scraping desks noisily around the room to enter, settle her rump behind my desk, and start taking notes for my preliminary evaluation.

I'm in trouble.

The students decide they need to be able to see me and each other (not always a good idea), so they design a room arrangement that can best be called "the wagon wheel." The desks are "spokes" radiating from a circular "hub" (me) in six directions. One of the spokes can't be completed because my desk is in the way. And because my students and their education come first, I ask Mrs. Wine to get up from my desk.

Oh no he didn't! I'll bet all this really happened, too.

"Pardon me?"

"We need to move my desk to complete the spoke, Mrs. Wine."

A full minute later, the monolithic Mrs. Wine extricates herself from my chair and hovers nearby. "Hovers" is probably the wrong word. She, uh, wobbles nearby. The faculty really needs to buy her one of those electric scooters to get around.

Once the last spoke is finished, we slide my desk into a corner where only skinny me could possibly get into my chair.

Mrs. Wine, then, has to stand and sway.

She is not pleased.

"Okay, class," I say from the hub, "I need someone to give us a review of what we covered Monday." Mainly because I can't honestly remember myself. The kids don't call me "Mr. Space" for nothing.

Dan is *definitely* Jack here. I wish the book coming out in April had more of him in it, too. Why do editors cut out reality in favor of sensationalism? Not all books have to be complete escapes from reality!

Kendra raises her hand. "We were talking about the Greeks."

We were? Hmm. "And what did we learn about the Greeks?" No hands, not even Kendra's. Help me out here, kids! "Tony,"—the student who usually has his hand raised more than Kendra does—"what did we learn about the Greeks?"

"I was absent Monday, Mr. Pace," Tony says.

I wince. I should have known that! "Raise your hand if you were here Monday."

Eighteen of thirty hands drift into the air. I zero in on Angie. "Angie, what did we learn about the Greeks?"

Angie shrugs.

"Kevin?"

Kevin shrugs.

"James?"

James takes a deep breath, and I hold mine. Yes! I taught them something! James exhales loudly and says, "I dunno."

I'm in serious trouble. Because I'm standing in the middle of the hub, I can't get to the board to write anything without half the wagon wheel having to turn completely around.

"Um, did I tell you any stories?"

Thirty heads shake back and forth. Wait, only eighteen of you were here! How could all of you be shaking your heads?

I will never be a teacher. There's entirely too much drama!

"So I didn't tell you the story of . . ." Think! I look at Mrs. Wine, her long, stringy hair plastered to her head like a squid with tentacles curling up at the ends and resting on her more than ample bosom. "Medusa?"

Perfect!

"Who?" Kendra asks.

I am now in my element. Teaching history to me is really telling stories in the past tense about the past.

"Medusa was a gorgon."

"A what?" Kendra asks. She loves to ask questions, and at times, I think she's the only one in the class listening.

I spell "gorgon" for them, but only some of them write it down. "A gorgon was a monster with snakes for hair whose look turned the beholder to stone." Lots of blinking. Hmm. "Beholder" isn't in their vocabulary. "That means, if you looked at her, Angie, you would turn to stone."

"This isn't real, then," Angie says.

"You're right, Angie," I say. "This isn't real. It's a myth. Do we all remember what a myth is?" Please, for the love of God, please nod your heads!

But we all don't remember what a myth is because I didn't tell them what a myth is on Monday, and Mrs. Wine is writing furiously, and I look like a fool, and—Ah, screw it. If you're going down in flames, at least have some fun.

"Then I must have made a myth-take," I say.

"Boo," I say aloud. But it's cute.

No one giggles.

"Thith ith information that you're myth-ing." A few smiles. "We must put this myth-ing information about myths in your notebooks, no myth-ing around."

I go to the board and write "Greek Mythology," then return to the hub. "Mythology is a collection of stories that have been passed down by word of mouth for hundreds, even thousands, of years. Most myths have supernatural beings, monsters, and powerful heroes in them. One Greek myth is about Medusa."

I pause and cut my eyes to Mrs. Wine. A few kids notice and smile at me. They understand.

"Medusa was one of three sisters, but only Medusa was mortal, meaning that she was somewhat human."

The same could be said for Mrs. Wine. I think there's a human being in there somewhere.

"Perseus is our hero in this story. It is his task to kill Medusa, but if Perseus looks at her, he'll be turned to stone. How can Perseus kill Medusa without looking at her?"

For the next few minutes, my students give me every possible method from throwing a running chain saw at her to dropping an atomic bomb on her.

Time to refocus.

"This myth is over three thousand years old. All you have to kill Medusa are some armor, a sword, a shield . . . and some magic."

Mrs. Wine coughs—or is she gasping?—and toddles out of the room, and the class and I relax.

"Whew," I say, wiping imaginary sweat from my forehead, "it's about time she left. I was scared she would turn me to stone!"

Those kids will never forget the story of Perseus and Medusa.

Jack had to have been a wonderful teacher. I wonder if he misses it.

Later, however, at my evaluation conference, I have to look Medusa in the eye as she rags my ass.

"Absolutely no organization, Mr. Pace. None. Your lesson was sheer bedlam. . . . "

Like that "office" of his downstairs. It's not "bedlam," but it's getting close.

My God, she can blather, can't she? Does she use that Botox stuff? Maybe she secretes it naturally, her face is so tight. Her ears must have little hands holding them onto her face.

HAAAA!

"And you must re-rearrange your room to something that resembles an approved diagram from *Instruments for Instruction*. . . ."

Is "re-rearrange" a word? How does she get her hair to loop up at the ends like that? The rest of her body doesn't defy gravity, so how can her hair?

HAAAA! Jack, I mean Dan, has a wonderful sense of humor. Why did the editor cut out so much of his humanity?

"As you know, this is the year during which either you earn tenure or we'll have to let you go. . . ."

This is my last year here anyway, Medusa. There's nothing to keep me here in Roanoke, no one to keep me here. I have no friends, only colleagues. I am the oldest member of the single's Sunday school class I sometimes attend when I'm looking for someone a lot purer than me. Yeah, I'm trolling for purity, but I'm sure not the right man for a righteous woman.

So, maybe this was before he met Noël. That means . . . that *she* kept him from moving away. If it weren't for her, I wouldn't have ever met him.

"Your handwriting is atrocious. I'm surprised they can read anything you put on the board. And lisping? Really, Mr. Pace. I know you can enunciate better than that. And why begin with that horrible, violent story? I'm sure I'll get phone calls this afternoon from parents who are up in arms. . . ."

I have to face facts. The tread on the boots of my life have gotten thin, my laces are frayed, I have scuff marks, even gouges. I could maybe get a retread on life, get that new-hiking-boot smell. It wouldn't take much to start over. I'd just load up my books in a little U-Haul trailer and go on a one-way trip to where snow is snow and not this ice storm stuff, where Ansel Adams skies take my breath away daily.

I wonder if he's thinking these very things right now. I have to call him, but I'm afraid to. Maybe later.

"And bringing magic into your lesson? I thought I was very clear about any reference to magic for this grade level. . . ."

Maybe Alaska? I've had plenty of offers from school systems in Anchorage. Six months of darkness . . . That would be magic. It would move me closer to Dysfunction Junction (San Francisco), but then I might be able to help my sister.

His sister? She didn't appear in the first book.

"Are you following the Standards of Learning, Mr. Pace? I hardly think so. And another thing, Mr. Pace, I know you know we have a dress code here. . . ."

I'm too much of a free spirit, I guess. Maybe I'll be a mountain guide, an American sherpa, or I'll work at a wilderness camp for kids. Despite what Medusa says, I can probably teach anywhere because male elementary teachers are in demand. So are male administrators. Nah. I'd have to get a suit, a tie, and an attitude. I'd quit and work at Blue Ridge Outdoors before that ever happened.

"Do you understand everything I've said to you today, Mr. Pace?"

Is she talking to me? I squint at her. She isn't talking anymore, so it must be my turn. "Uh, yes, Mrs. Wine."

"I'm marking 'needs improvement' for your overall preliminary evaluation."

I nod.

"Sign here."

I sign the form, nod again at Mrs. Wine, leave the office, then drift down the hall to the cafeteria. Watching students play "chew 'n' show" always makes me forget just about anything horrific.

"Mr. Pace?"

I look at Laverne, one of the lunch ladies, polishing the table in front of me. "Yes?"

"Don't you have a class to teach?"

"Oh, yeah." The bell has rung. The cafeteria is emptying. Thirty fourth-graders are sitting in a wagon wheel waiting for me to introduce them to Greek mythology and a lady with snakes for hair.

I am always late for class, and the kids think it is so cool.

I know I would have liked *this* version of the novel much better. This is four-star material at least.

"The man can write," I say to my library. "If they will just *let* him write."

I have to call and compliment him. I dial his number, and it rings ten times before he answers.

"Hello?"

He sounds sleepy.

"Jack, it's me, Diane."

"Hey."

Hey? "Um, I've been reading your real book here, and I just wanted to tell you how wonderful it is."

"Thanks."

"I, uh, I didn't wake you, did I?"

"Nope. Haven't been to sleep."

"Oh." So, what has he been doing? "Are you watching any of the games?"

"Nope."

Nope and hey? What's going on here? "Are you writing, then?"

"Nope."

Another "nope" and I'm hanging up. "Is anything wrong, Jack?"

"Nothing this eggnog can't cure."

He's drunk. The man left me on my nice soft sofa, went home, and got drunk. "I'll, uh, I'll let you go, then."

"No, no, don't hang up yet."

"Why?"

"I've been meaning to tell you about the new book."

"But you're not writing it."

"It's in my head, and you're still in it."

In his head or his book? I don't say anything. I might confuse him.

"Anyway, Arthur and Diana . . . Her name is Diana. I hope you don't mind."

I smile, despite Jack's drunk voice in my ear. "I don't mind."

"Well, Arthur and Diana will meet in the library where

he's researching his family tree, and she's helping in the gynecology room."

"The what?"

"You know what I mean. I overheard you at the library that day. That old man gave me the courage to talk to you."

"He did?"

"Yeah. I was afraid to approach you."

Alcohol—the greatest truth serum. "You were?"

"Uh-huh."

Silence.

"Jack?"

"Hmm?"

I have to ask while he's being so excessively honest. "Did you want to make love to me last night?"

"Yep."

That was a quick answer. "Then what stopped you?"

"I told you why."

"Tell me again."

"Okay. I still feel married to Noël, and if I had made love to you, I would have felt guilty about it."

I blink.

"Not guilty about making love to *you*—not at all. You're beautiful. It's just that I would have felt like I was cheating on Noël, you know?"

No, I don't know. "Well, thanks for telling me that, Jack."

"Sure thing."

"Um, do you still want to see me?" I sound so desperate!

"I still want to see you."

Whew. But I have to be sure. "To help you get over her?"

"Yep."

My heart sinks. "That's all?"

"No, I mean, I don't know. We're just starting out, you know? It's like I'm riding a bike for the first time all over again. I want to go, my body wants to go, and your body seems to want to go."

It does. It still does.

"But I can't seem to make the pedals work, you know?"

"I think I understand, Jack."

"So, we can take it slow, just like you said, right?"

Despite my better judgment, I say, "Sure. Sure, Jack. We'll take it slow."

42
Jack

Well, we should take down the tree. It's time to put the tree at the curb for the wind to send the tinsel into our neighbor's lawn.

You just hurt her, Jack.

No, I didn't. She's a big girl.

She cares about you.

I know, I know.

Call her back and apologize.

I'd rather take down the tree. It has too many memories hanging on it.

You'll save all the ornaments, won't you?

What for? They'll only open the wound again next December. And anyway, I thought you wanted us to have a new life.

Call Diane. Apologize. Have her help you with the tree.

But I'm drunk.

Then sober up! Stop drinking. Take a long walk. Take a shower. Drink some coffee.

Maybe I'll just . . . sit here for a while. . . .

When I wake up hours later with a Kris Kringle hangover, I check my messages. Diane has called several times, and Noël's mother, Sandra, has called once. Why would she be calling me?

I dial Sandra's number. "Hi, it's Jack."

"How are you, Jack?"

"Okay."

"I'm calling about Noël's and Stevie's clothes. I'd like to take them to Goodwill."

Sandra is still in mourning, too. "I already took them all to the Salvation Army."

"Oh. That's good. Uh, good, Jack. Do you still have all those photo albums?"

"Yes."

"What about the pictures in the hallway?"

Where is this going? "Yes, they're still up on the wall."

"Well, if you decide to take them down, please keep me in mind."

Why would I take them down? "I will."

"Um, who was that woman you were with at church last night?"

This is *really* why she called. "She's a friend who's helping me write my next novel."

"She's, uh, just a friend?"

Though it's none of her business, I say, "Yes, Mrs. Wilcox."

"Well, uh, don't you think you could have had a little more respect for Noël and Stevie than by showing up at the church like that, even with just a friend?"

Geez, my head is on fire and now this. "What is it you're trying to say?"

"I mean, really, Jack, a black woman?"

Ah. Now I get it all. "Mrs. Wilcox, Diane—that's the name of my good friend—Diane and I have just started dating."

"You're . . . dating?"

"Yes. And it is out of respect for Noël and Stevie that I go on living, as they would want me to."

"But with a black woman? How do you think Noël would feel if—"

"Noël's dead, Mrs. Wilcox, so I don't think that matters much to her."

I hear Mrs. Wilcox crying. "You're ruining her memory, Jack!"

I close my eyes. "I could never do that, and I will never do that. I still love your daughter very much. I just need . . . to get on with my life without her."

"And this . . . black woman is going to do that for you?"

"No. This *woman* is going to do this for me."

Mrs. Wilcox hangs up.

Maybe I was too harsh.

You were.

But she focused only on Diane being black!

Jack, if you had dated another blond-haired, blue-eyed girl, Mrs. Wilcox would have had the same reaction.

I don't know. She kept saying "black" as if it were a curse.

Mrs. Wilcox is still healing, too. You and Diane have to be a shock to her.

Yeah. Maybe I should have let Mrs. Wilcox take the clothes back.

No. It was your job, not hers. You could go visit their graves, though, you know, to make sure they're being tended properly.

I'll take them some flowers in the spring.

You could . . . take Mr. Bear to Stevie.

Not yet.

I throw some water on my face and try to brush the sour eggnog taste from my mouth. Then I call Diane to apologize, but she doesn't answer the phone. I wait for the beep and leave a message: "Diane, I'm sorry about leaving you last night and I'm sorry for . . . for drinking myself to sleep today. Please call me back."

I hang up, staring at the tree.

And then I get the ornament boxes from downstairs.

43

Diane

Let's take it slow, he says.

Let's take it *silent* is more like it.

I called him *four* times, and he didn't answer because he was stone drunk. When he wakes up, he calls me to apologize. I could have picked up, I could have talked to him, but I'm too angry. He could have *known* me—in the biblical sense—yet he would rather drink until he passes out. That's hard for my self-esteem to take.

The phone rings for the third time. I check the Caller ID. Jack again. I don't pick it up. After it stops ringing, I wait a minute until the "message waiting" light starts flashing. I dial for my messages and hear, "Diane, will you please come over to my house and help me take down my tree?"

"No," I say aloud.

Though it's more reasonable than the second message he left. He actually wanted to know if I would go out with him for ice cream! On New Year's Day! What kind of a . . .

I like ice cream, mind you, but I'm still mad at him. It's

also far too cold, and I doubt that anything's open. We'd probably end up at some convenience store and pay way too much for a pint of Ben & Jerry's.

I like Ben & Jerry's, but . . .

No. I am going to be strong, and he had better come stronger and with better messages if he expects me to speak to him again.

Hmm. I could call him back to tell him no. That would be the proper thing to do. Just, and politely now, tell him he's crazy for asking any woman out for ice cream on New Year's Day and for asking any woman to take his Christmas tree down.

Wait. Hold on, Diane. Jack is asking *you* to help him take his Christmas tree down. Who else has *ever* helped him do that? Noël. Okay, she's not around anymore, you're in his life, and if you want to *stay* in his life, you're going to have to take her place . . . even for something as simple as this.

I dial Jack's number, and it rings ten times before I hear, "Leave a message at the beep."

I hang up.

Oh, now *he's* screening his calls and waiting for *me* to leave a message. Well, I'm not going to give him the satisfaction. I've heard of people playing phone tag, but message tag? No. That's not a game for me. I don't play games.

Okay, I didn't answer the phone when I could have, but . . . I'm allowed to be mad. I'm allowed to be hurt. I'm allowed to be stubborn. I am the wounded party. He is the one who has to grovel. He is the one who has to—

The doorbell rings.

I jump up and look through the drapes.

It's Jack, and he's holding a pint of ice cream.

Part of me says, "Girl, he's only using the ice cream to lure you back to his house to work on that tree," and the other part of me is saying, "He's so sweet!" I look more closely at the ice cream. Häagen-Dazs. Chocolate. Oh my.

The doorbell rings again.

I tell the first part of me to shut up and open the door.

Jack holds out the pint of ice cream to me. "I'm sorry, Diane."

I pull him inside, the ice cream still between us. "Did you already take down your tree?"

"No."

I look at the ice cream. "Is this supposed to seduce me into coming back to help you?"

He laughs. "No." He looks into my eyes that sexy way of his. "It's only for seduction."

My mouth is a tiny little *o*.

"I hope you like chocolate. The vanilla looked a little old in that—"

I slam my body into the ice cream and into him and into the door until it finally shuts. He tries to move the ice cream from between us, but I keep that pint firmly between my titties. "I don't have any bowls, Mr. Browning."

"You don't?"

I do, but . . . "No. How on earth are we going to eat this ice cream?"

He looks down at the ice cream. Or my titties, I don't know! "It could get messy."

"It could."

He lets go of the pint and reaches around me, his hands sliding lower and lower until . . . Oh, yes, a man's hands are handling my booty like a booty should be handled!

"It might . . . melt all over us," he says as he cups my caboose and lifts me almost off the ground.

"It sounds . . . yummy," I say.

And after that, we rip each other's clothes off and have ourselves some "Exploratory Foreplay Sundaes," and we don't need whipped cream, wet walnuts, strawberries, pineapples, or even a cherry on top. I have a Jack Sundae, he has a Diane Sundae, and I have never tasted anything so good!

And right there on the floor of my kitchen! His hot tongue licking the ice-cold ice cream off my seriously hot body in every possible place on the cold linoleum floor is almost as good as me doing the same to him. When all the ice cream has melted, we do a little "mud wrestling" in my tiny little kitchen until I'm sitting in his lap with my legs locked around him, wanting all the while for Jack's "banana" to complete my sundae. All I have to do is lower myself maybe an inch, and I will have a man inside me for the very first time.

"I need a bigger kitchen," I pant as he licks on my neck. Why did I just say *that?*

He kisses me and laughs. "It's big enough."

"I'm all sticky." I look down at his . . . Johnson. "And so are you."

There is a moment of silence as we look from his . . . stuff—I don't want to use the D-word—back into each other's eyes.

"Jack, I'm . . . I'm a virgin."

"Whoa," he says.

"Whoa as in stop, or whoa as in . . . whoa?"

He hugs me tightly, and my nipples are so hard I'm afraid I'll cut him. "Whoa as in *both,*" he whispers.

"Yeah?"

He wipes a smudge of something from my cheek. "Diane?"

"Yes?"

"Diane, I need you, and I hope some small part of you needs me."

I bite my lip. "A large part of me needs you." Oh, God, what is this feeling? My whole body is warm, and my eyes are filling with tears—but I'm not crying. I'm looking, not staring, into a man's eyes whose face . . . is covered with chocolate ice cream. Yet . . . could this be . . . "All of me needs you, Jack."

"Good." He kisses me on the nose. "Good, because I want this to last."

I'm not sure what he means. "Want what to last?"

"Us."

There's that warm feeling again.

"We met, what, two weeks ago, and I'm just getting over my wife. I never thought I'd ever get over her but you . . . you came into my life."

Oh, the tears.

"And I don't want you to think that this is all I'm after, Diane, though I want it really, really badly."

We both look down. Yep, he still wants it badly.

"I want something . . . permanent with you, something lasting . . . something forever."

Cold feeling all the way to my toes. What's this? Where'd that warm feeling go? "And you can say all this after only two weeks?"

"Yeah, I know it sounds crazy, I know, but . . . my son's books, those overdue books, brought us together. It's as if we're . . . meant to be, you know."

My eyes are drying up. This sounds so much like a crummy romance novel! "I'm not sure. I mean, I don't know if I feel the same way, Jack."

He looks away, but I turn his head back to me with a sticky hand.

"I mean, about this, yeah, we might be rushing this, though I've waited a long time for this." I smile and look down. "This is as close as I've ever been, Jack, and all I have to do is move a few inches, but"—I search his eyes—"Do you really want me that way?"

"Yes."

He wants me that way. No one has wanted me that way. The warm feeling creeps back through my body. Whoa. "Look at us. If you put our situation in a novel—"

"Reviewers would say it's preposterous."

Oh, he had to use Nisi's words.

"So," I say, "what do we do next?"

"You mean, after our shower?"

Oh, I'm a-tingling now. "Yeah, after our shower."

"Well, we date." He smiles. "We see each other, we go together, we talk, we go steady."

I giggle. "We do all that?"

"I don't know what people call it these days."

I like the way his eyes dance when he's babbling. "Go on. What else?"

"We go out to eat and go to the movies and go window shopping and attend concerts and go to shows and sit next to each other in church and . . . and you help me write a better book."

"All of that?"

"Yes, Diane. We become a team." He takes my hands in his. "I guess I'm saying that I want you to be my girlfriend, Diane. I know that sounds weird. I mean, I could call you my lady friend or woman friend or significant other—"

"Or main squeeze or old lady," I interrupt.

He squeezes my hands. "Or I could just call you Diane."

God, I'm blushing again, and he only said my name!

"And maybe in a few months, or years, who knows? Maybe we can take the next step."

Oh, Lord! The next step! Why is this a better feeling than wanting sex? I'm beginning to feel . . . hope and joy . . . and maybe love. But will he want me that way if he finds out—

"Jack, I write reviews for books under the name of Nisi."

He blinks but doesn't stop smiling. "You . . . do?"

"Yes, and I read an advance review copy of *Wishful Thinking*, I didn't like it at all, and I posted that horrible review." He starts to speak, but I growl, "I'm not finished."

He nods.

"But since I've been reading your second draft, I realize that *Wishful Thinking* wasn't the book you wrote. What I've been reading today has been wonderful. It's so romantic and loving." I smile. "Kind of like this moment."

I said "loving." I didn't say "love."

"Look, Nisi," Jack says, "your review helped me."

"It was unfair and cruel."

"No, it was honest. That's why you need to help me edit this next book into something you like. I need your critical eye. I want the character to be you, and it can't really be you without you . . . or something."

I can't believe he's not mad. "Jack, I trashed your book without even reading all of it."

He shrugs. "I had trouble reading it, too."

"So, you're not mad at me?"

"No." He nuzzles my cheek with his nose. "Why would I be mad at someone with an honest heart and a critical eye?"

This man is too amazing for words! "What if . . . what if I don't like some of what you're writing . . . about me?"

"You'll tell me, and I'll make the changes. And in the next few months, I'm sure we'll make changes to the changes."

Changes to the changes. For some reason, I like the sound of that.

"Now, you need a shower," he says.

"Just me?"

He smiles and looks at his arms and chest. "I kind of like this color on me. Maybe I'll smear myself with ice cream for my professional photograph."

I put my arms around his neck and pull his eyes to mine. "I'd rather you smeared *me* all over you."

"I kind of already have," he whispers.

"Good point," I whisper.

"So, Diane, I want to be your boyfriend. Will you have me?"

"Yes." Baggage and ghost wife and all.

I think I have myself a man.

44
Jack

Don't let her read that rainbow mess.

Why?

It's too . . . girly. It's not womanly enough.

I'm sure she'll tell me.

And, definitely don't let her read those background chapters about your family. They'll scare her away because they're too strange.

Well, I'm strange.

"Your lips are moving again," Diane says, from the sofa downstairs in my house a few hours after we had showered and cleaned her kitchen.

"Just arguing with myself," I say.

"You do that a lot."

"I have a lot to say to myself."

Especially during that shower.

Shh. Diane's waiting.

When you kept saying, "Oh, I've missed a spot. Here's some more chocolate"—that was slick, Jack, and so was she.

Yeah. Now leave me alone so I can connect this laptop to Noël's printer.

You spent forever on her legs.

Please, I need to concentrate.

"Hurry up," she says. "Give me something to read quick, or I'll have to turn on the TV and watch a football game."

I finish the connection, print it out, hand her "that rainbow mess," and kiss her on the lips. "Be cruel, be mean, be—"

"Be quiet," she says. "Go write some more."

I return to Noël's desk, insert a new page on the screen, and stare at the flashing cursor in front of me. Okay, let's write that scene at the library—

"How old is Diana supposed to be?" Diane asks. "She sounds so young and naïve."

"I was hoping . . . twenty-five."

"She sounds like a teenager, Jack."

I swivel in Noël's chair. Diane wouldn't let me write down the hall in my office because she refused to make room on the guest room bed. "She doesn't sound romantic to you?"

"She sounds sixteen, and is this a prologue? It's reading like a prologue."

She's right. "That's a good idea."

"Is she going to be your only narrator?"

She should be. "I have been experimenting with third-person omniscient—"

"For a romance? How boring."

You wanted her opinions.

Yes, I did.

She's right, you know.

I know.

"And this green card idea has been overworked. If she is a black woman and she's going to hook up with a white man, why would she even consider a foreigner?"

She is sharp!

I have an answer for this one.

"I'm just trying to show that she's open to all colors." I smile at Diane. "I got the idea from something Maya Angelou wrote."

"Hmm," Diane says. "Well, couldn't this be a poem she writes instead of her thoughts? We'd have to edit out all the naïvete, of course."

I hadn't thought of that. "We could."

"Do you have a character sketch of her handy?"

I walk over and sit next to her. "But you're her."

Diane rolls her eyes. "Like I said, do you have a character sketch of her?"

"No."

"No?"

"No."

She shakes her head. "Well, you're going to need one. Get some paper."

45

Diane

Jack the writer doesn't take up for himself enough. This prologue isn't bad, but I'm reading it as Nisi would. At least he's open to new ideas and my suggestions.

He returns with one of his trusty memo pads. "Why do I need a character sketch when the character I'm sketching is you?"

"One of us has a job and won't be around all the time."

"True." He rubs my leg. "I could call you . . . often."

"I'd like that, but . . ."

He stops rubbing my leg.

"That doesn't mean you have to stop rubbing my leg."

"Oh." He rubs my leg again, reminding me of the way he washed it in the shower and later as he rubbed in all that lotion. *Heaven.*

"Okay, let's start with the physical features." You know, just to see what he *really* thinks about my body.

He starts writing.

"Out loud, Jack."

"What's the paper for?"

Hmm. "You'll see." I have an idea.

"Okay . . . five-six—"

"Seven," I correct.

"I was close."

"Weight?" And he had better guess low or else.

"One-twenty."

I smile inside. "You are correct." If I cut off one of my legs. "Eyes?"

"Beautiful." He starts nibbling on my ear.

"Stop."

"I'm investigating your ears."

It gives me chills, but we aren't getting anything done. I push him back gently. "What color are my eyes?"

"Light brown with dark specks."

He knows my eyes. "Complexion?"

He doesn't answer right away. "Well, some parts of you are beige, others tan, others brown, others dark brown. You don't, um, have any one color. To me, anyway. And, I'm sure there's still some chocolate ice cream on you somewhere. We may have to take another shower."

I like the way this man thinks, but . . . "You can't put all that in a quick description, Jack."

"So, it won't be quick." He smiles. "I'll just have Arthur go really slow up and down her body while he explores all the sexy aspects of her color." He kisses my neck. "Just as I did in the shower."

Whoo! "You'd better write that one down."

I give him time to make his notes, all in capital letters, for some reason. At least they're legible.

"What's my favorite song?" I ask when he's done.

"You tell me," he says.

"Guess." I'm curious.

He looks me up and down, and I like it. "How about Stevie Wonder's 'Something about Your Love'?"

I blink. "That's so old school, Jack. She's supposed to be

twenty-five. Why not something by India Arie or Alicia Keys or even Mary J. Blige?"

He writes it all down.

"What's my favorite . . . meat?"

He hesitates. "Beef?"

I gasp. "You think I'm a heifer, Jack?"

"No, no. I was trying not to stereotype you with chicken or ham."

"I like chicken and ham."

He writes it down.

"And pork chops with pinto beans is my favorite meal."

He writes that down, too.

"What's my favorite vegetable?"

He sighs. "Potatoes?"

"Jack! Do I look like a beef and potatoes woman?"

"I'm trying not to offend."

I do like potatoes most, but Diana will like . . . "Corn on the cob."

He writes it down.

"What's my favorite . . . fruit? And think out loud with your answer, okay?"

He leans back on the sofa. "An apple has some symbolic value, forbidden fruit, that kind of thing. And so does pineapple, since you have to cut off the surface to get to the sweetness." He debates with himself for a few seconds. "Okay, pineapple."

"I like peaches," I say.

"Oh."

Twenty minutes later without any "corrections" from me, Jack tells me that Diana is the all-American black woman who loves the fall, drinks Coke, snacks on Chex Mix and Reese's Peanut Butter Cups, doesn't watch TV, and thinks *Casablanca* is the greatest romantic movie of all time.

I am so glad I'm here to correct him.

"First, I love the spring. I love it when the world comes back to life. Second, I'm a Pepsi girl; Coke makes me burp.

Third, I can eat sour cream and onion Lay's potato chips all day, and those peanut butter cups give me gas. And, I don't have a favorite movie, because I think they're all so unbelievable."

"I was way off."

True, but how would he know? "Okay, I want you to list any pet peeves you think I have."

He nods. "Funk in any form, long hair on a man, long or dirty fingernails on a man, rude people, men who don't make eye contact, fake people, men who talk to themselves, men who hesitate too long before answering, unreal books . . ." He takes a breath. "Any of them wrong so far?"

Not a single one! "Why do you think I have so many pet peeves?"

He smiles. "I'm right, though, . . . right?"

I laugh. "Add one more: a man who thinks he knows everything about a woman he's seeing. There is no way you will ever truly know me."

"I'd like to try."

"And I'll keep you trying." I get an idea. "As long as you . . . bring me lunch every day for the next, oh, four months."

And if he has any sense, he'll bring pork chops and pinto beans at least once a week.

46

Jack

So, in between a long day at the DMV with Jenny—

You know, Jenny's pretty, but when you spend two hours at the DMV with anyone, that beauty fades in a hurry.

Having to show that death certificate was hard.

You managed.

And then later watching Noël's car drive away—

It's a good thing you're having Jenny mail the checks.

And taking Diane Chinese food just once to know that she doesn't like Chinese food at all—

She liked the fortune cookies, though. "You have tremendous charisma" was yours, and she added "in bed."

And writing like I've never written before—

Don't forget trading in your truck for a Honda Accord.

That, too.

Diane likes it.

So do I.

In between all that, I get to know Diane so much better. We go for rides in the Accord. We go to movies at The

Grandin Theater, an old-time movie theater; sit in the back; eat popcorn; and make out like teenagers.

She even liked Casablanca.

What I let her see of it.

Diane even "calls in sick" or "gets sick at work" so she can have more time to edit my book.

And give you more time to explore her body.

I like exploring.

You're so much like Dan Pace now.

Just without all that imaginary sex.

Come on, Jack. Diane is all over you like brown on rice.

It's nice to be wanted like that.

It's nice to want someone else like that.

As spring arrives in Roanoke, our relationship grows. I love working together with her. I love hitting every "ethnic" restaurant in town, though Bandini's is still our favorite. I love when she cooks for me after a long day at the library. I love cooking grilled cheese and tomato soup for her. I love snuggling with her in front of the TV, which we never turn on. It's all been so . . . intimate.

Our book, though Diane insists she's only the "first editor," is titled *A Single Touch*, and so far, my editor loves it. I've sent Trina six chapters, none with a single sex scene or foul word in them, yet she says, "This is so cutting edge!" It isn't—it's just real, normal life—but that gives me incentive to keep writing more. Both Nina and Trina had me redo my professional photograph because I was still too skinny in January, and the final picture has me with a fuller face and gelled hair.

It makes you look younger.

Diane says it makes me look "cute."

And you do.

Now everything is building up to the tour, which is only one week away. I've been interviewed in the *Roanoke Times* and on local radio, and the *Times* wrote a complimentary review of *Wishful Thinking*, focusing mainly on Roanoke's more "colorful settings." I've set up one signing downtown at Cantos Booksellers for the end of April—

The phone rings. It's been ringing off the hook for the last few weeks, and not all the calls are from Diane.

"Hello?"

"Jackie, I have some good news!"

Nina. "Yes?"

"*Wishful Thinking* is already out, and Amazon has already started shipping."

"That's great." I think. "But if they've already started shipping, won't that affect my New York sales?"

"So Amazon jumped the gun. They usually do. But sales via Amazon.com are a teeny, teeny, *teeny* portion of the pie. Not to worry."

Who says "teeny" three times to make a point?

Shh.

"But won't that give all sorts of crazy people time to post reviews on-line before New York?"

Nina and Trina had been unsuccessful in getting Nisi's review removed, but Diane had written another—and under her own name—that gave the book four stars, to even it out some.

She was basing her review on the rough draft, though.

Who's going to know?

"Don't worry, Jackie," Nina says. "It's selling, and that's all that matters."

It's selling!

Yeah, it's selling.

Nothing can harm me anymore.

47

Diane

It has been so nice to have a man, and I couldn't have picked a better one. Jack is devoted to all phases of my life: my job, my meals, my house, and my body.

Especially my body.

It's like I have an addiction for his hands on me. I used to consider that sort of thing perverted, but not anymore. It's a necessary part of my life now. I feel so cold where he isn't touching me . . . so I make him touch me all over a *lot*. I wish he had more hands.

My own hands seem . . . nervous. Maybe it's the anticipation of using them on him. I still play solitaire in my spare moments, looking always for red jacks, and I only review one book at a time now, turning the pages slowly and reading them all the way through. I have still found quite a few clunkers, but . . . I won't give any book one star anymore, mainly because they've kept my mind and hands busy.

What do I like most about Jack? He makes me feel sexy. I've never felt sexy before, maybe because of my profession, maybe because of the way I was raised in the church. I've been called "cute," but I've never been called "sexy." He comments on my body as being "so soft," "so firm," "so tender." He touches my skin and says, "Delicious." As a result, I'm starting to give him more skin to touch, leaving a button undone, a leg uncovered, my neck exposed at all times. I'm even scenting myself in places I never used to scent and paying complete attention when I shave to get every tiny hair. I'm not wearing anything too low cut—yet—and I'm not wearing hip huggers (I have too much hip to hug), but I do have a full set of push-up bras that make my girls rise to the occasion.

And now I am *damn* sexy for a librarian.

Francine and Kim are warming up to the idea of "Jack and Diane," though it hasn't been easy. At first, they stared and shot each other those "knowing looks" white women are famous for: pursed lips, raised eyebrows, slight shake of the head. But once they saw a real, normal romance up close, they warmed up to the both of us. Oh, except for when Jack brought me Japanese food for lunch. That's not my cup of tea. Uncooked fish is not in my culinary repertoire, and it sure stunk up the circulation desk. Maybe Jack likes sushi because sushi smells like . . . Hmm.

I like a man who likes sushi.

A *lot*.

Now, not everything is perfect. Jack is, well, tardy all the time, and he has this habit of "zoning out" for minutes at a time while I'm talking to him. It's as if he gets lost without even moving. It's hard to explain. He's there one moment and gone the next several moments. His eyes don't glaze over or anything as obvious as that. He just . . . disappears . . . though he's sitting in front of me at a restaurant or lying next to me on the sofa or even talking to me on the phone. At first, I thought it was extremely rude, and I still sort of do. It's not that he isn't listening; it's well, it's annoying! I must say, "Earth to Jack" at least once a day. No wonder he made

Dan Pace such a space cadet. I ask him to tell me where he's been, and he shakes his head, blinks, and says, "What?"

I wonder if all writers are this spacey.

Because of his inattention, I doubt that Jack will ever pick up all the hints I've been dropping about selling my own house so I can move into his house when we get . . .

Yeah, it's getting close to that. Whenever we go to the mall, I make him linger longer and longer at jewelry stores. He's already gotten me a necklace and some earrings, "just because," he says, and he blew me away at Valentine's with *two* dozen long-stemmed roses, a Victoria's Secret gift certificate, and a box of Russell Stover chocolates. He made the biggest deal out of those chocolates, for some reason. They were all right, nothing special. He just couldn't understand why I didn't eat any of the ones with nuts.

I couldn't yet tell him that nuts, um, well, they sort of curl up in my intestines and constipate me. I am not a nice human being when I'm constipated. We've come a long way in our relationship, but that information is a little too delicate to tell him about right now.

I wish all this book mess wasn't taking his attention away from me. I know the tour is only for one week, but . . . I'm afraid.

I'm afraid a whole bunch of Nisi's are going to show up at one of his readings or signings and try to ruin him.

There are so many haters out there who have already posted mean-spirited, "white-men-can't-write-about-black-folks" reviews at Amazon.com and at other sites on-line. One fusses that Ty is dark skinned, and "What about us fine light-skinned sistas?" And I'll bet if Jack had made Ty light skinned, someone would be crying, "What about us dark-skinned sistas?" Another cries, "This is another example of the Man getting over on us and taking our money." Yet another screams, "What about black writers who aren't getting published because of this travesty?!!"

Yeah, my word "travesty" is coming back to haunt me. Fortunately, my review has moved down the Web page, so it isn't the first one people read anymore.

But Jack takes it all in stride, shrugging his shoulders and letting all that hate roll off him. He'll look at a review like, "Browning can write, just not about black people," and he'll take it as a compliment. "See," he'll say, "I *can* write."

And what he's writing now . . . Oooh, those haters are going to eat every single one of their words, and I can't wait. He is writing about something that really happened—and *is* happening—between an average sister (neither too light nor too dark for those still hung up on color) and an average white man. They can't possibly find fault with so much truth!

But in the back of my mind, I can't help but worry that folks will have trouble even with the truth. And it's scary, but if Jack were black, he probably would be getting as much if not more abuse from black male reviewers for having an "African queen mess with Uncle Cholly."

Today, while Jack waits for the dealership to finish his car's first checkup, I'm home waiting for him, preparing a field green salad with boiled eggs and bacon. I've become kind of domestic, I guess, and it isn't so bad. Although we eat out a lot—and *he* eats a lot—we're both minding our weights. I've lost ten pounds, and he's gained twenty, so I have more of him to hold on to.

The phone rings. It must be my "Boo."

"Hello, honey," I say.

"Honey?"

Oops. It's Mama. And the closest holiday was April Fools' day last week. I hope nothing bad has happened. "Hi, Mama. Is everything okay?"

"No, everything is not okay."

I swallow hard. "Is Daddy okay?"

"Yes, yes. What's not okay is what's sitting in my hands. I just bought your boyfriend's book."

My shoulders sag. Contrary to what I used to think, some phone calls *can* be life changing, and this is probably going to be one of them. It was bound to come out sooner or later, but why today? I was having such happy thoughts while making a simple salad for my Boo!

"Did you hear what I said?"

"I heard you, Mama."

"Dee-Dee, why didn't you tell me he is white?"

Because I was afraid of *this* reaction. "You never asked."

"I shouldn't *have* to ask."

True. "Well, it's none of your business, Mama. I had my reasons."

"And what were they?"

I don't want to get into this, but . . . "I knew you wouldn't approve."

"So if you knew I wouldn't approve, why did you ever get mixed up with this man?"

"I'm not 'mixed up' with this man, Mama. In fact, my life makes a whole lot more sense *because* of this man."

A millisecond of silence, and then . . . "Well, I've been telling everybody, and I mean *everybody,* for the last three months that you were dating a fine *black* author, even Imogene Blakeney. Dancing with that white boy was one thing, but dating a white man . . . I may have to change my church membership now."

"You're overreacting, as usual, Mama."

"Child, why did—"

"I'm a grown woman, Mama," I interrupt. "I'm no child anymore."

A whole second of silence. "I don't understand you anymore, Dee-Dee," she says finally.

Time for a little payback. "But you understand Reesie perfectly, huh?"

"What does Reesie have to do with any of this?"

Time for some brutal honesty. "Mama, Reesie has been nothing but a *ho* since she turned thirteen."

A gasp. Good. Gasping is good for Mama's circulation. "What did you say?"

"Reesie is a trifling ho, Mama. It's true, and it's about time you faced the truth."

"But she's your sister!"

"I know that, Mama, but she is *bad,* and she's been bad since the day she was born. I am the good girl in our family, and yet you treat me like shit."

Another gasp. "I have done no such thing!"

"Mama, Reesie slept around and got pregnant with three *different* boys, and the last boy was barely eighteen. She was robbing the damn cradle. She has three baby daddies for the Qwans, she sponges off you and Daddy, she's never held a job for more than a week, and she and the Qwans treat *you* like shit. And you just sit back and take it."

"I will not listen—"

"Yes, you will, Mama. I've been good. I graduated high school with honors while Reesie barely got her GED. I finished college with honors, and I doubt Reesie can even spell 'college' on a consistent basis. I'm not waiting on any *boy* for some diapers. I have a *man.* And, despite what you think, I'm still holy."

"I don't believe that for one minute."

"Mama, believe it. I am still a virgin, something Reesie hasn't been able to say since she was thirteen."

Another gasp. Shoot. Everybody in the church knew about it, and I'm sure Mama knew, too. Mama has been living a life of denial for far too long.

And so have I, in a way. But, I have to hear "I do" first.

"Mama, I want to sleep with Jack in the worst way." That didn't sound right, but does "in the *best* way" make any more sense? "I want to, but he's not ready."

"What?"

"His wife and son died last July, he has been trying to get his life together, and I'm helping him. There have been times when I have been tempted"—just about every time we're together!—"but I've resisted that temptation, I've been good, and all you can tell me about is the shame you feel for me dating a white man. It's fucked up, Mama."

The loudest gasp. Mama is getting a phone workout today. "I didn't raise you to talk that way!"

"You're not even listening. I don't know if you've ever really listened to me."

"I hear you just fine, you and that . . . guttural language."

"Guttural? You say the word 'titties' all the time!"

"Well, that's what they are!"

I sigh. "Mama, you hear me, but you're not listening. You're not *feeling* what I'm saying. I like Jack, and I may even love him. He's a good man, a decent man, a kind man, a quiet man. He reminds me of Daddy in so many ways. He just happens to be white. There is no shame in any of this, Mama. None. You should be proud of me for keeping my virginity this long, proud of me for graduating college, proud of me for having a good job, for not sponging off you, for not filling your house with Qwans, for still keeping my faith."

"Reesie still has her faith."

"Oh, Mama, this isn't about Reesie, and you know that girl cries 'Oh, Jesus!' to any black boy who will buy her kids Pampers or shoes. When are you going to be proud of me?"

Silence.

"Mama, answer the question."

"You're just dating him, though, nothing serious?"

"We are *getting* serious. We can go to the next level at any time."

"Engagement?"

I roll my eyes. "Don't worry, Mama. We won't put our engagement picture in any of the Indianapolis papers." Or even any Roanoke papers, for that matter. It's not that I wouldn't want anyone to know. I just prefer our relationship to be low-key because I believe true love does not have to be advertised.

That thought was *such* a cliché! Maybe the words in those books I've been trashing have been telling me the truth, and I've not been listening.

After some static-filled silence, Mama yells, "But you barely know the man!"

This is kind of true. Hmm. I know next to nothing about his family, and Jack never talks about them. "Look, Mama, I know what I like, and you know how picky I am. I *want* this man. I want to have a little ring on my finger that says I *belong* to this man."

Whoa. Did I just say that? I did. Do I want Jack that much? I do.

I do. Two little words I want to say in front of a church holding on to Jack's hand.

"I . . . I don't know what to say."

"Just . . . don't say anything negative about him or me or *us* until you get to know him."

Silence. "He'll probably want to start up another family."

"And that's wrong?"

"I didn't say it was wrong. I just said—"

"Mama, *I* want to start a family. *I* want a child. If he happens to be my husband and father of my child, that's perfect." Perfect . . . a bookworm and a writer hook up and have kids who are genetically predisposed *not* to watch TV! It would be so . . . old-fashioned. Hmm. But we wouldn't have a cable bill.

And that would be so cool! "Cool" is one of Jack's words, and though I don't ever say it, I'm starting to think it more and more.

"He isn't right for you, Dee-Dee."

My turn to gasp. "How can you say that? You haven't even met him!"

"I'm looking at him right now. What's up with his hair?"

I take a deep breath. "Mama, why do you have to be so skin-deep about everything?"

"Skin what?"

"Skin-deep. You only look at the surface of people. You look at Reesie, and all you see is an angel, when Reesie is really the devil in a short dress with tattoos over both her titties. You even think that the Qwans are angels as long as they've had their baths."

"I don't think—"

"And that picture doesn't do Jack justice," I interrupt. "He was skinnier when that picture was taken. He's filled out just fine since then."

"But blond hair and blue eyes? And he has a nose sharp enough to open a tin can!"

His nose is kind of . . . severe, but . . . "I like his nose."

"And does his hair stick up like that all the time?"

"It's called gel, Mama, and it was my idea. It makes him look younger." Though when Jack puts it in, it makes him look like a Marine or a blond Chia Pet.

"Well, he isn't that handsome, not nearly as handsome as your father."

My daddy *is* a handsome man, but . . . "Jack is handsome *to me,* Mama, and that's all that matters. By the way, what does Daddy think about all this?"

"He's as confused as I am," she says quickly.

I doubt that. "Let me speak to him."

"He's out in the garden."

"Well, go get him."

"I don't want to bother him right now."

Which means that Daddy isn't nearly as outraged as Mama. That's a good sign. If Daddy were really confused, all three of us would be talking right now.

"So, what does Jack do other than write?"

What's she fishing for here? It sounds like a normal question, but coming from Mama, it could lead to more trouble. "He used to teach fifth-graders."

"*Used* to teach?"

"He's taking a year off to mourn." I don't know whether this is completely true or not, but Mama has to respect a man who teaches and properly mourns.

"Oh, it sounds like he's doing quite a bit of mourning while he's running around with you."

I want to scream, but I don't. "It's been almost nine months since his wife and son died, Mama."

"But he started messing with you back in December. I'll bet he really didn't love his wife that much."

I have a feeling that Jack will always love Noël, and I'm okay with it. I'm beginning to believe that God, who *is* a God of love, can sometimes provide *two* "loves of a life-time."

"Well, does he have a lot of money at least?"

I growl. "Oh, Mama, when will you grow up?"

And I hang up on her.

Hmm. That wasn't a very grown-up thing to do. It felt good, though.

The phone rings seconds later. "Hello?"

"Your daddy and I are coming to visit—"

"What?" I jump off the sofa.

"And we'll be staying with you, so he'll have to stay somewhere else."

If Mama ever stops assuming things . . . then she wouldn't be my mama. "Jack has his own house, Mama, and he has never spent the night." He has come close, but he usually leaves before sunrise. I watch him go sometimes, seeing his white body disappear into the darkness.

"Well, we are going to meet this Jack Browning."

This could be tricky. "When are you coming?"

"This weekend."

This weekend? Jack and I had plans to drive up the Blue Ridge Parkway Saturday before he went on his tour. Hmm. We can still do that . . . *with* Mama and Daddy in the back-seat? Well, I guess I have nothing to hide anymore, so I say, "Fine."

"Fine?"

"That's what I said—fine. How long are you staying?"

"Um, well, we'll decide when we get there."

"Fine."

"Fine?"

"That's what I said."

Silence, this time for five whole seconds. "Okay, we'll see you this weekend. Good-bye."

"Good-bye."

I slam the phone down and return to my field greens. If Mama and Daddy arrive on Friday, they'll be too tired to do anything, and I'll keep Jack away from them. A tired Mama is a dangerous Mama, and a tired Daddy usually gives in to a tired Mama. Then on Saturday . . . I'll work in the morning. Yes. I'll do the children's reading. They might come along with me, and they might not. Maybe they'll just putter around in the house and get really bored. We'll all drive up the Parkway in the afternoon, then out for dinner to Bandini's, church Sunday morning—yeah, and at *Jack's* church, so Mama will feel the most uncomfortable—and by Monday, when I'm at work all day and Jack's gone to New York, they'll be so bored they'll leave.

Four days tops.

48

Jack

I'm getting so used to visiting Diane that I'm starting to wave at her neighbors.

You've made yourself at home. Even the neighbors' dogs don't bark at you anymore.

Yeah.

You even check her mailbox and take her trash to the curb without thinking every Sunday evening.

I am a gentleman.

Pretty soon, you'll be washing her windows and cleaning leaves out of her gutters.

Those bushes could use some shaping, and those two trees need to be cut away from those power lines.

You practically live here already. Why not make it permanent?

Oh, I don't know.

All it would take is a little paint on the mailbox. Simply change "Anderson" to "Browning."

Or simply add "-Browning."

Anderson-Browning? Diane seems old-fashioned enough to take your last name.

The world is changing. And anyway, for any of that to happen, it will take a ring and a wedding.

Of course. You're, uh, you're not thinking of tying the knot again, are you?

I don't like that phrase. I prefer "joining in marriage."

It means the same thing.

"Tying the knot" has a somewhat negative connotation.

"Earth to Jack," Diane says, after sipping her coffee on the sofa next to me.

You're on the sofa, you're sipping coffee, too, you've just finished a delicious salad, Diane has been saying something about . . . working Saturday morning—

I know where I am.

I look at her. "Sorry."

She sighs.

She does that a lot when you're thinking to yourself.

I know.

"Can I ask what you were thinking about?" Diane asks.

She knows you weren't listening, so don't even try to say, "I was listening," because then she'll ask you what she was talking about, and since you have no clue, you'll be wrong, she'll get mad—

"I was thinking . . ."

Be careful. If you bring up the mailbox and she's not ready to hear it . . .

I sigh. "I was thinking about selling my house."

You're in trouble now.

No, I'm not. I didn't bring up the mailbox.

You should have said you were thinking about her eyes— or her thighs. Something noncommittal like that.

Shh.

"Where will you live after it sells?" Diane asks.

See, I told you. Now, you'll have to tell her what you were really thinking.

"Um, well, Diane, I . . . I was hoping to live . . . here." I pat the sofa.

"On my sofa?"

She's funny.

I think she's being serious.

"Uh, no, I meant . . ."

Diane slides closer, taking my coffee mug from me and setting it on the coffee table. "You'd like to move in with me?"

You could have even talked about the weather, but no, you had to say, "I was thinking of selling my house." And then you tell her you want to stay here? Pitiful, just pitiful.

"I want to . . . get away from those memories, um, permanently, and, uh, I like your house."

The first part—okay. A reasonable explanation. The second part? "I like your house"? Man, what about the woman who lives in this house?

"And," I continue, "and I like the way I feel at home in this house."

Diane bites her lower lip, her eyes getting so wide. "And you like the way *I* feel in this house, too, don't you?"

Oh no, Jack. She's warming up. When she does that lip thing—

Shh. I'm trying to think.

"Diane, I like the way you feel anywhere."

"Uh-huh." She licks her lower lip.

And now the licking of the lip thing. Jack, you're in more trouble now than you've ever been before. Be careful what you say next. Or better yet, kiss her and keep kissing her until the conversation fades away from her memory. Start, you know, grabbing on her, rubbing her feet—she loves that, you know—and then—

No.

You're not ready for this, Jack.

Hmm. Maybe you're right.

I lean forward to kiss her, but she pulls back out of range.

You only leaned. You should have lunged!

"What were you saying about my house?" she asks.

She's on to us. It's as if she can read our minds!

Are my lips moving?

No. It's a woman thing. Noël had it, too. She could read you like a book, and right now, you're giving Diane too much to read!

I take Diane's hand. Such a nice hand, a soft hand, a many-colored hand.

A sweaty hand! Oh no! She's expecting the question! You've set her up, and you can't let her down. You even have her hand in yours! This is a classic "Will-you-marry-me?" moment! Let go of her hand. Stand up. Walk around. Leave. Do something rude. Rub her toes! Get her mind off it!

No. This is a hand that I've grown to love. It's a caring hand, a helping hand, a strong hand.

"Earth to Jack," she says.

Well, go on. It was bound to happen sooner or later. Just don't talk her to death.

"Diane Anderson." I look from her hand to her eyes. "I want . . ."

You're doing fine.

"I want you . . ."

Just a few more words.

"I want you to be . . ."

Finish the sentence!

"Happy."

What the—?

Diane squints. "I am happy, Jack, happier than I've ever been."

I nod. "That's good, that's . . . good. I'm happy, too." I smile.

Oh, this is going so well. Happy?

Shh.

I look out the window. "I was thinking . . ."

And we both know that this is a dangerous thing for you to do.

"I was thinking that we could . . ."

"We could what?" Diane asks, her voice almost a whisper.

"We could . . . maybe . . ."

You don't say "maybe" when you're proposing! You can't leave any room for doubt!

"Um, I was thinking that we could work . . ."

Huh?

"We could work out in the yard this weekend."

You have got *to be kidding!*

Diane's eyes pop. "What?"

"I could trim the bushes and cut back those trees, and maybe we could plant some flowers. . . ." I look at her, and she's blinking. I look at her hand.

Gardening? You're talking about gardening *when she's expecting— What in God's name are you talking about?*

"I mean, we've been . . . growing together these past few months, and planting plants, working with plants, the whole planting process . . . it's like a metaphor, you know?"

You have really *messed this up, Jack. And if you use any form of the word "plant" again, I'm going to scream. Diane looks as if she might already be screaming in her head!*

"I want to . . . put down new roots, Diane."

Better. But you might be working that extended metaphor a little much.

I look into her eyes. "I want to . . . plant flowers with you." My eyes are starting to tear up. "Do you understand?"

Diane's eyes stop popping. "I think I do."

"I want to . . . to make the front of your house *our* house. I want to get out of the car every day and say, 'Those are the flowers Diane and I planted.' I want people to know that *we* planted them together."

"I want to garden with you" is not the same as "I want to marry you," Jack, but . . . I get it. It makes sense.

"In a roundabout way, Diane, I'm asking you . . . if you'll have me . . . to be . . . your husband."

Finally. How do you feel?

I feel . . . weightless.

You're not, you porker. You've put on twenty pounds in four months!

Diane nods and blinks away her own tears. "I'll have you, Jack." She laughs. "To be my lawfully wedded gardener."

Oh, now she's extending the metaphor! You two are made for each other. But, um, doesn't it strike you as odd that neither one of you has used the L-word yet?

We don't have to say it. We feel it. We know it.

Well, you know a woman likes to hear it every now and then. I mean, you've just asked her to marry you, right? You might want to, you know, slip it in somewhere.

"I wish I had a ring to give you now. I mean, I didn't expect to be saying any of this today. It just . . . it just felt so right." I grip both of her hands. "I want to marry you, Diane." And now is the time. "And I love you."

She pulls me to her, rubbing her soft, tear-soaked cheeks against mine. "I want to marry you, Jack, and I love you, too."

That's better. A little out of order, but . . .

"But we need a ring," I say, hugging her close.

"No, we just need the memory of this moment."

Yeah, your arms circling her, her arms circling you. Those are the best circles, and you can run around in them all day and not get tired. You need to write all this down later. "The memory of this moment." Lots of Ms. "Mmm" sounds are good. But make sure you put "I love you" before "I want to marry you." Your readers might have a problem if you get them mixed up.

Shh.

I kiss her lips tenderly and wipe off several of her tears with my fingers. "I want other people to know." I check the watch Noël gave me. Though the watch reminds me of Noël, it's becoming just a watch I wear so I'm not as late. "We have time to get out to the mall."

She wipes her eyes with her hands. "Maybe we should . . . wait."

"What for?"

"Well"—she takes a deep breath—"my parents are coming in this weekend."

"Cool."

She smiles. "Cool?"

"I have to meet them sometime, don't I? And it will be perfect. They'll see us as an engaged couple, and we can all sit down and talk about plans for the wedding. It'll be up in Indianapolis, right?"

Diane doesn't speak for several long moments.

She's not usually this quiet. Back off the wedding talk.

Why?

Her parents are coming to meet you, *Jack. One shock at a time.*

Shock? What shock?

You're white, Jack.

Oh yeah. But . . . so?

It might matter to her parents.

It doesn't matter to mine.

Because they're from northern California now, Jack.

Oh yeah.

"You're worried about what your parents will think of me," I say.

Diane nods. "I already know what my mama thinks. She saw your picture on the book cover, and she's not too pleased."

I shrug. "She will be. Once she sees how happy we are together, she'll—"

"It's not that easy, Jack," Diane interrupts.

"Why not?"

Yeah, why not?

She grips my hands. "I think Mama is coming down here to . . ." She shakes her head. "Let's put it this way, Jack. My mama is probably coming down here to start some trouble."

"Why would she do that?"

Yeah, why would she do that?

Stop echoing me.

Sorry.

49

Diane

I don't want to talk about my mama at a time like this! I've just been unofficially engaged (without the ring) in my own living room, and a man has just said "I love you" to *me* on my own sofa. This wouldn't play well *at all* in a movie where the hero is supposed to propose at some fancy restaurant or on some beach as the sun dissolves into the sea or in front of a crowd of his and her family and friends. And that "I love you" thing? We should have said it a couple *hundred* times before this moment and only *meant* it now.

We are doing everything so backward!

"We talked on the phone earlier today, and, well, I said some things"—I actually cussed at my mama!—"and then she said some things. . . ." I frown. "It wasn't very pleasant."

"Then we'll have to make their stay here as pleasant as possible, her stay especially nice."

Not if I want them to leave quickly, we won't!

"You were saying something about Saturday morning,"

he says. "Are you planning to work the day after they get here?"

"Yeah, hopefully so they'll get bored and leave."

He knits his eyebrows and squints. This means he doesn't understand. The first few times he did that I had wondered if he had gas. "I was hoping we could drive up the Parkway in the morning to beat the traffic and later have lunch at Bandini's."

"What about Saturday night?" He's not leaving me alone with my parents on a Saturday night!

"Well, I'll have some packing to do, and I thought you'd want to spend some time with your parents. When's the last time you saw them?"

That isn't the point. "It's been a while, but . . ." I sigh. "All right. We'll . . . go up Saturday morning."

"Good." He smiles. "We're getting married."

I force a smile. "Yeah."

"Up at your church in Indianapolis."

I frown. "No."

"Because . . ."

"Because . . ." Because why? I wouldn't mind standing in front of those people. They know me. They know I can wear white. But wearing white *and* marrying a white man? I don't know. "Because it would shame my mama."

"Would it shame you?"

"No," I answer quickly. "Not at all."

"Hmm."

"Hmm?"

He nods. "Hmm."

Either he understands or he says "hmm" to make it appear that he understands. I slide my legs around him, my hands around his neck, and I realize I need a bigger sofa. "So . . ."

"Hmm," he says again.

"What are you thinking?"

I brace myself for another convoluted tale. Somehow, he went from working in the yard to asking me to marry him. He's such a storyteller. At least his tale ended happily.

"I can't marry you at my church," he says.

That was direct.

"I'm sure it's not proper form to marry two different women in the same church so few years in between, especially since it's Noël's family's church."

I wouldn't feel comfortable there either.

"What about your church here in Roanoke?"

I shrug. "They hardly know either of us because we've been alternating between yours and mine."

"Hmm."

Maybe "hmm" means he's making a decision.

"Then let's make your church our church."

First, my yard is *our* yard and now . . . "Cool," I say.

He blinks. "You said 'cool'?"

I nod. "It is cool. New beginnings all around." I cringe. "We'll probably have to take a couple's class."

He laughs. "Where they teach us how to be a couple?" He rubs my foot. "I think we already know how to do that."

I put my other foot in his hand, and he rubs it as well. "I think they'll teach us how to have a holy marriage." And this time I cringe inside. The Bible tends to be, well, sexist when it comes to marriage, with the woman taking second place to the man. I know I can love Jack, but can I *obey* him? That's stretching the limits of everything I believe. "I suppose the class is required if we want to get married there. We may even have to become members."

"Fine."

"Just like that?"

He nods once. "Just like that." He squeezes each individual toe, and I squirm with delight. "If I were to, say, buy a ring sometime this week, what size should it be?"

I want this ring so badly, but . . . "Let's hold off on that until my parents leave and you come back from your tour, okay?"

Yeah. I'd be waiting for that engagement ring for almost two weeks. But, I've waited this long, so . . .

"One shock at a time, okay?" I say.

He sighs. "Okay."

I put my head on his chest. "Size seven, round diamond," I whisper.

"What was that?"

I know he heard me. "Nothing." I mean, he can give it to me anytime, right? I just won't *wear* it when they're here.

We cuddle for a long while, occasionally kissing, occasionally squeezing, but mostly . . . just cuddling—and talking about *his* parents.

And I learn that his parents are, well, weird.

His father, Arthur Davis "David" Browning, and his mother, Maryanne "Annie" Berry Browning, have had a dysfunctional (yet enduring) romance.

"Dad was born in Delaware, first son of the five children of Grandma Ella and the Reverend Jack Browning," Jack begins. "He lived in north Philadelphia, where he became an athletic schoolboy legend of the gridiron."

I try not to giggle at Jack's choice of words. He sounds so much like a movie narrator.

"Dad's attempts at being a star in baseball were thwarted one cold, Philadelphia day. With the legendary pitcher Robin Roberts in attendance, Dad pinch-hit late in the game after riding the pine. He lined a clean, crisp single to left, then ran himself literally into the ground on his way to first base. His legs, inert for six innings, just wouldn't work. The left fielder threw him out at first base."

I don't know much about baseball, but that doesn't sound good.

"On the football field, however, Dad was amazing, quarterbacking the Abington High School Ghosts to many victo-

ries and playing halfback for the Wheaton College Crusaders."
Jack pauses. "They're called 'The Storm' now."

"To be politically correct?" I ask.

"Strange name for a Christian college, though. Anyway,
Dad earned all-American honors and a picture in *Sports Illustrated*."

"Yeah?"

He nods.

"Are you athletic?"

"I used to be," Jack says. "I played baseball mainly."

I learn that Jack's father had studied criminology and as-
pired to be a detective, but a ride-along with the Chicago
vice squad quickly put that out of his mind.

"Dad was a bit of a prankster in college. He and his team-
mates once carried a Volkswagen Beetle, owned by a particularly difficult history professor, into the faculty cafeteria.
He had even led an aged horse into the office of an evil
Greek professor, who had failed half of the starters from an
undefeated team, causing them all to take summer school. It
was June, it was hot, and the professor was on vacation."

Nasty!

"The horse died, and the building had to be fumigated."

"That really happened?"

Jack nods.

I thought that sort of thing only happened in the movies.

"Because Dad went to college on the GI Bill, he owed his
soul to Uncle Sam and served his tour of duty at Fort Bliss,
just outside of El Paso." Jack smiles. "And that's where he
met Mom."

From Delaware to Philadelphia to Illinois to Texas. Jack's
dad certainly got around.

"Mom was the third of four children born to Ree Theus
Berry, a bilingual high school business education teacher,
and Jefferson Davis Berry, a lieutenant in the United States
Army. Grandpa Jeff, given the choice between being sta-

tioned in Pearl Harbor or Panama in forty-one, chose Panama, where Annie was born." He looks at me. "Otherwise, I might not be here."

"I'm glad you're here."

"Me, too." He looks at the ceiling. "Grandpa Jeff spent two years in the Italian campaign, then spent the rest of his life trying to forget the Italian campaign, running a grocery store and drinking rye for breakfast. Mom, who learned to drive at the tender age of eleven, graduated from Texas Western, which is now called UTEP, in three years and was a virtuoso viola player."

His parents are a football star from Philly and a viola player from west Texas. Wild!

"In sixty-one, Dad, an eraser-headed second lieutenant, attended church in El Paso with his buddy Pete, a red-faced Irishman who wanted Dad to meet 'his girl'—Annie Berry."

"Your daddy stole your mama from someone else?"

Jack nods. "From the moment Dad's and Mom's eyes locked, it was love at first sight. Mom quickly gave Pete the boot, and only thirty days after knowing each other's names, Dad asked Mom to marry him."

And I thought that Jack and I were moving fast!

"Mom, naturally, said no."

As any woman would have . . . wouldn't she?

"Rebuffed but not disheartened—"

I start to giggle.

"What?" Jack asks.

"'Rebuffed but not disheartened'?"

Jack shrugs. "I read the thesaurus a lot as a kid."

Poor kid!

"Dad continued to pursue Mom for the next three months, writing her long letters—in all capital letters."

So, that's where Jack gets his handwriting.

"I remember finding one of those letters in a cigar box, of all places; Dad doesn't smoke. It read something like,

'Annie, just being with you is heavenly, whether we're washing dishes or just picking the meat off the chicken bones after a meal.'" He laughs. "My father has a way with words."

And despite the "chicken bones" line, it's kind of sweet.

"So, four months after they first met, Dad went to Grandpa Jeff and asked for Mom's hand in marriage. Grandpa Jeff sized up Dad and asked, 'What about the rest of her?'" Jack smiles. "Dad said he wanted the rest of her, too."

This is so . . . quaint!

"They were married in El Paso, and he drove her to Aylen Lake, Ontario, Canada, the first time she had ever been north of Oklahoma, for their honeymoon."

I'm beginning to think I need a map to understand all this!

"On this honeymoon, they played Monopoly, and when Mom won, Dad, after upsetting the board first, decided to let Mom run their finances for the rest of their marriage, something he tells me was the best decision he ever made. Mom ate fish for the first time, used an outhouse for the first time, and almost cleaned a smallmouth bass for the first time, too." He sighs. "I'm not boring you, am I?"

"No." This is all so . . . odd.

"After my sister Jeannine was born—"

"You have a sister?"

Jack nods. "Two, actually. Jeannine's a year older than me. She lives out in Los Angeles, and Jessie, who lives in Atlanta."

Four months I know him, and I really don't know him. "Go on with your story."

"So, after Jeannine was born, they all moved to Philadelphia. Dad approached Westinghouse, General Electric, and the Aluminum Company of America, Alcoa, and said: 'What can you do for me?'"

That's cocky.

"Dad entertained offers from all three but settled on

Alcoa. So, while I was being born, Dad was taking the return train from Manhattan and the World Trade Center back to Philadelphia."

That's *quite* a daily commute!

"So, where are they living now?" I ask.

"North of San Francisco somewhere," Jack says. "I've never visited them there." He drops his chin. "And we don't, um, talk as much anymore."

"They know all about me, right?"

He nods. "I sent them an e-mail. That's how we talk most these days." He starts to massage my back. "Platinum or gold?" he whispers.

"What?"

"Platinum or gold?"

We go from his family back to the rings? I guess he doesn't want to discuss them anymore. "What do you think?" I ask.

He kisses my neck, and then . . . we attack each other until we fall off the sofa, continuing our clothed grinding in between the sofa and the coffee table, spilling the coffee and panting and—

I *definitely* have to get a bigger sofa! And softer carpet here! I'm getting rug burns through my clothes!

Sometime after who knows when—because suddenly time doesn't matter as much to me anymore—Jack gets up to leave. I kiss him three times. "Those kisses are for those three little words you said to me."

He pulls me to him . . . and squeezes my caboose three times! The nerve!

"What were those for?" I ask.

He puts his lip near my ear. "Those were for these three little words: I want to make love to you."

I count the words in my head. "That was seven."

"I know." He squeezes my caboose four *more* times, powerfully and with more ferocity than ever before. "And now you know that I can't count. I'm terrible with numbers. Now, did you whisper six or seven?"

I squeeze his caboose once, digging my nails in. "Seven."

"Hmm."

"Round diamond."

"Ah."

I wince. "Ten carats."

He blinks. "Ten?"

"Ten." As if *that* will happen!

He nods. "Ten it is."

I pat his behind. "I was kidding."

"I wasn't."

I sigh. "Kiss me and get out."

He kisses my nose. "Let me get this straight. You're a size ten, square diamond, platinum, seven carats."

"Go home, Jack."

His eyes soften. "I am home, Diane." He cocks his head at the door. "That other place is just temporary. This is where I want to be."

"This is where I want you to be." And then I start laughing uncontrollably. This is all *so* corny! And yet, I know in my heart that I'll be reading it in Jack's next chapter of *A Single Touch*, every word, every gesture, every squeeze. When I recover, I hold Jack's jaw in my hands. "Please don't put any of this in the book."

"I intend to."

"Oh, come on, Jack! Let's keep some of our lives private."

"No."

"Please, Jack?"

"Hmm . . . I'll think about it. I won't put anything about my parents in there."

"Why not?"

"Who would believe it?"

True.

He hugs me. "I'll be up all night writing."

"Not about this conversation, right?"

He nods. "I won't put any of this in our book."

"Promise?"

He crosses *my* heart, and the girls perk up. "Promise." He turns to go, but I grab his arm.

"What will you be writing all night about, then?"

He winks. "Our first night of passion."

"You're going to put a sex scene in *our* book?" Mama will hate us more for sure!

"Call it . . . my *plan* for our first night, then. I'll even let you edit it to your satisfaction."

That could be fun. "Will there be . . . ice cream?"

He looks up. "No. Scented oils, I think. And candles. And a foot massage followed by . . ."

I'm warming up just hearing about it. "Followed by what?"

"Followed by some serious boot knocking."

"Huh?"

He pulls me to him. "I'm going to knock your boots so long they'll end up in Tibet, and some sherpa is going to trip over them and smile because he knows in his Tibetan heart that someone is getting a good boot knocking."

I'm speechless. Mild-mannered Jack *is* Dan Pace when the sun goes down.

"And tonight, I'm going to go on-line to explore all the positions of the *Kama Sutra*." He smiles. "This is going to be a very long chapter."

I'm still speechless.

"And even if it doesn't get into the book, it *will* get into your head."

It already has! My upper lip is sweating! "Um, size seven, gold, round diamond, you decide the number of carats."

He rubs on my caboose. "You just make sure you have your boots ready to get knocked."

I'm nearly out of breath! "I'll, uh, I'll shine them up for you."

His eyes change, softening back to the Jack I love. "You already shine, Diane Anderson."

Oh, that's so sweet!

"And I intend to polish you until the sun and moon get jealous."

And that's so nasty!

"And yes, I'm putting those two lines in my next chapter."

Lord, I'm sorry, but this man is making me horny. Please make him go!

He kisses me tenderly, hugs me once, winks, and leaves me . . . with wet panties. If he can *talk* me into it, just imagine . . .

Lord, shield Your eyes for about an hour, okay?

And please let me have some fresh C batteries somewhere in this house!

50

Jack

*B*ig *day, eh?*
Another giant step.

How could you sleep after you wrote out that sex scene?
I had nice dreams, didn't I?

The best.

I find an empty box in the laundry room and trudge up the stairs one final time with Noël and Stevie's eyes staring at me from the wall. I start with the family portrait.

That only took one take. Stevie smiled right on cue, even though all those other kids in line were wailing like banshees.

I put the portrait in the box. The next is Noël in her garden. She was the brightest flower in that garden.

And she smelled the best, too.

I put her picture in the box. I try not to think as I remove the others, but it's hard. It's as if I'm taking down life itself, and the memories won't let me be. Stevie is dancing in the surf at the beach, unafraid of the waves, while Noël's face outshines the sun in an eternal smiling laugh. . . .

Noël's mother would like these.

Yeah. I'll drop them off at her house while I'm out today.

What about the ones in your office?

Them, too.

You'll need a bigger box.

I don't have a big enough box . . . for all these wishes.

Steady now.

I'm not crying. Just remembering.

What about the photo albums?

I have to hold on to something. I'll keep them. In storage.

What about . . . the ring?

The one I'm planning on buying or . . . *that* ring?

The one in your pocket, Jack, the one you roll around in your fingers when you're nervous, the one you keep in your pocket on dates with Diane, the one you put on the dresser before you go to sleep, the one—

I know which one. I'll take it to a pawnshop.

You should have buried it with her.

I know.

I drive first to Noël's childhood home, a Cape Cod in southwest Roanoke with a huge backyard now full of red and yellow roses. Roses must be Sandra's therapy. They take lots of careful tending. After parking at the curb, I walk to the front door and hesitate before I ring the doorbell. I count to ten. No one arrives. I put the box on the welcome mat.

You should stay and talk to her.

We've never had much to say to each other that didn't involve Noël and Stevie, and here they are all boxed up. I'll just leave her be.

On the way back to the car, I look up at Noël's window one last time. She had looked out at the world from that window for nearly twenty years before I gave her other windows to look out. And the last window she looked out of was the van's. . . .

Think about something else.

I squint at the sun peeking out of a cloud. And now she and Stevie are looking out of heaven's window on me.

That's better.

I stop at the first of several pawnshops I come to on Williamson Road, only a few blocks from Hooters, which is a strange placement for a pawnshop.

Hey, if you really like their wings, you might need to pawn something.

I hand my ring to the pawnshop owner, a bald man wearing a lime green tank top and sitting on a stool. "How much?" I ask.

The man weighs it in his hand. "Thirty."

It cost close to $900!

I shake my head and put out my hand. "Thanks anyway."

Three more pawnshops later, I still have the ring, fifty dollars the best offer. I put it back in my pocket and head to the mall and Kay's, where Noël and I had bought our rings five years ago.

You sure you want to go to Kay's? There are four other jewelry stores in this mall.

I'm sure.

While the salespeople wait on other customers, I stroll through the store, looking at all the possibilities. I've already gotten Diane a necklace and some earrings. What's left?

A toe ring.

A toe ring? Here, at this fine, upscale jewelry store? How would they even size it?

That one says, "One size fits all."

I doubt that. And what are those dangly things?

"How may I help you today?" A tall flaxen-haired woman stands in front of me, looking down at those dangly things.

"What are they?" I ask.

"They're for piercings," she says.

Kinky. Ask her where!

No.

I straighten and look at a poster behind her of a white woman showing off a stunning diamond ring to a white man.

Even jewelry store posters separate the races.

Yeah.

"I'm here to buy an engagement ring. Round diamond, gold band, size seven, one carat or more."

You remembered!

In a flash, she whips out a glossy C's booklet. "Let me tell you about diamonds."

"I've, uh, done this before. I'd like the highest-quality diamond that you have between one and one and a half carats."

She closes her booklet. "Certainly, sir."

Oh, now *she calls you "sir."*

Shh.

"Are you sure about the round cut? We have Marquis diamonds that are just stunning."

I don't want to put Noël's diamond on another woman's hand. "She prefers round."

"Okay."

I look at row after row of gleaming diamonds, afraid to touch them lest my fingers mar their brilliance. "That one," I say, pointing to the one that hurts my eyes the most.

She removes the ring from the velvet cloth, turning the price tag to me.

With tax, that will come to . . . five digits!

"This one is one-point-five with—"

"I'll take it," I interrupt, taking out my checkbook. "Is it a size seven?"

She slides the ring onto a long metal rod.

I hope they clean that thing occasionally.

"It's a seven," she says. "Would you be interested in an extended service plan?"

While she rambles on and on about the benefits of the

"ESP," I think back to the first time I bought rings here. We added ESP to our rings, but we never brought them in twice a year to get them checked and cleaned, because Noël preferred to clean them more often at home.

"Sure," I say when she's done.

She smiles. "Okay. I'll just . . . ring this up then."

She's ringing up a five-digit ring. I'll bet she didn't expect to do that today. She just sold a five-digit ring in five minutes.

I start writing out the check.

You may have to go back to work soon.

Yeah.

First the Accord, and now the ring. I can still see the salesman's face at the dealership. When you said, "Just throw in some floor mats," he smiled. But when you wrote the check—

His eyes nearly burst from their sockets.

Kind of like this lady here, huh?

"Okay, we're all set," she says, displaying the ring one final time before snapping the black velvet box closed and putting the box into a small gray bag.

I give her the check and my driver's license, for good measure.

"Do you have an account here, sir?"

"No," I say, taking the bag.

"Would you like me to set up one for you and your fiancée?"

So you can make this lady's day again and again.

And Diane's, too. Hmm.

"Not today, thank you," I say. "But I'm sure I will in the future."

I put the bag in one pocket and still feel the weight of my own ring in the other.

Now it's time to surprise Diane, right?

Not yet.

I drive to Evergreen Cemetery, and after sitting in the car

for several agonizing moments, I get out and go to Noël and Stevie's graves.

You're doing the right thing, Jack.

The graves, festooned with freshly cut red and yellow roses, look immaculate, the marble a mirror to the dark green grass below. I crouch and touch the *S* in Stevie, wishing I had brought Mr. Bear.

Another time. Mr. Bear is too good of a listener to leave out here with no one to listen to.

What do you say to dead people who are still alive in your memory? I'm sure they already know my intentions. Why am I here?

To talk to them.

"Such a peaceful place," I whisper. "Um, I'm sure you already know that I'm planning to remarry." My voice catches. "It doesn't . . . it doesn't mean that I don't love you anymore."

Love is infinite.

"I know I'll see both of you again."

In the infinite.

"And, uh, Stevie, I'll be sure to make you some brothers and sisters to play with in heaven."

You're crying.

As I should be. "Noël, honey . . ." Oh, God, this is so hard! "You'd like her, Noël. She's down-to-earth and exquisitely patient with me, like you were." Why is this so hard?

Say good-bye, Jack.

"I'll . . . I'll try to visit more often, but . . ." I bow my head. "It's been so hard without you two, so hard."

You've made it through, Jack.

"I'll always remember you two as happy. Always."

Say good-bye.

I take my ring from my pocket, pushing it into the soil until it disappears. "Good-bye."

Go see Diane.

Not yet.

Then rest here a while. Feel the peacefulness of this place.

I'm done resting. I need to go to the grocery store.

For Kleenex?

No. For something much better.

51

Diane

Even though I'm working the circulation desk, I'm smiling because . . . I'm engaged!

I *am* engaged.

I am engaged to be *married.*

I now *officially* get to think this. I just wish I could *say* it to someone. I can't tell anyone here. If Mama and Daddy come in Saturday morning, Francine and Kim will bust me out. Kim might start interrogating me today, though, because I have let every single fine slide. I am a genuinely, totally happy librarian working the circulation desk.

The patrons must think I'm crazy! I need to settle down . . . but I can't!

I'm engaged!

I could be thinking about Mama and how she'll try to dismantle us this weekend. She'll probably pick with me and with Jack here and there and make lots of strange faces, looking for what she thinks will be the wedge that drives us apart. She's sitting in the backseat for sure on our drive up the Parkway. I might use the vanity mirror on the visor to spy on her. Daddy will probably fall asleep or just sit back there humming while Mama fumes.

I look at the clock. Twelve-fifteen already? Lord, time sure does fly when you're engaged.

And I ought to know, because . . . I'm engaged!

And in fifteen minutes, I'll be an *engaged* woman sitting down to eat an *engaged* woman's leftover salad and a peach, marveling at an *engaged* woman's flatter stomach . . . and sighing at her empty finger. Two weeks. I can wait two weeks. I *know* I'm engaged, and that's all that really matters.

Though a ring *would* look nice—

"Hi."

I look up. "Jack?" How did he sneak up on me?

He pulls a long flower box from behind his back. "For you."

I blush. "For me?"

"For you."

"Just because?"

He nods.

I untie the ribbon, open the box, and see . . . lots of orange. "Carrots?"

"Count them," he says.

I count . . . ten. I roll my eyes. "Ten carrots. Funny."

He touches my hand. "Open the card."

The card is a little . . . lumpy? I pull out the flap, and a ring—*yes!*—slides out into the palm of my hand! Lord, forgive me, but *damn!* I close my hand. "You didn't."

"I did."

I open my hand to make sure it's still there. *Damn, that's a diamond!*

"Put it on."

"But, Jack, I said—"

He strokes the back of my left hand. "Put it on, Diane."

I look up at him. "You're supposed to do it."

He takes the ring from my palm—*give it back!*—and

slides it gently onto my ring finger. It slides on just like golden butter, and it fits like a dream! I am never taking this off. Never never never—

Oh no. Here comes Kim bouncing down the stairs. I drop my left hand under the counter. "Hi, Kim."

Kim stands next to Jack, putting her hand on my man's arm! "Jack, it's so good to see you." She'd better not—She squeezed his arm. Why does she have to touch people like that? "What have we brought Diane for lunch today?" She looks at the carrots. "Carrots?"

"For my salad," I say quickly. "I told you I only needed one, Jack."

Jack throws up his hands. "I'm such a scatterbrain."

Kim taps the counter. "Francine will be down in a jiffy." She squeezes Jack's arm *again* and wanders off. He's mine, you wench! Go feel up some homeless man's arm!

I look up at Jack. "But I don't want anyone to know yet."

"I know you don't." He tries to look over the edge of the counter to see the ring, but I hide it farther in the shadows. "It looks good on you, what I saw of it."

I look down, and there it is, shining in the shadows. "Did you bring a peeler for the carrots?" Which is a *stupid* question to ask when I have this ring!

"No."

"Then how am I supposed to— Oh, here comes Francine. Act natural."

Jack leans on the counter, his chin jutting high into the air.

"With your chin down, Jack."

"Oh." He drops his chin.

Francine comes over and looks at the carrots. "Some lunch," she says.

I stand, my left hand sliding under the box. "Best lunch I've ever had," I say, then carry the box around the counter to Jack.

Francine takes my seat. "Has it been busy down here today?"

I look at Jack, and he's looking at me like he was last night with blue-eyed animal passion. "Uh, yeah, pretty busy."

But not nearly as busy as we're going to get when we get to my house!

"Um, Francine, I'm not feeling very well."

Jack nods.

"I'm going to take the rest of the day off. You'll tell Kim for me, won't you?"

Francine looks at me with a pursed-lip smile. "Sure, Diane. I'll tell her you're sick—*again*—but you owe me another one."

I'm almost out of breath by the time we get to my car. "Follow me home, okay?"

He grabs my caboose right there in the library parking lot! But instead of getting angry about it, I get right horny and make a sound something like "ah-uh-huhnnnn." I have never made this sound before in my life!

"I'll race you," he says.

"You're on."

Some race. I hit every single light on the way home, and Jack is standing beside his car in the driveway. I park behind him and smile because . . . now he can't escape because my car is blocking his.

When we get inside, I take his hand and march him directly to my bedroom.

"We might do something we shouldn't," he whispers, his breath so hot on my neck.

"That's what I'm hoping for. . . ."

Several frenzied moments later, zippers and buttons flying, we're in bed hugging and squeezing and kissing and touching and feeling and—

He stops.

He just . . . stops.

"What's wrong?" I ask, pulling him on top of me.

"I, uh, nothing's wrong, Diane."

I pull him as close as I can, and . . . oh yes, he's ready! And I'm ready, too. I hope. "Then why'd you stop?"

He rolls off me and gets out of bed, sweat glistening on his chest. "Diane, I'm practically a virgin."

What? "So?" I reach for him, taking a moment, you know, to look at my ring again. So many sparkles!

"So . . . I want our wedding night to be glorious."

"It will be, Jack. I know it will be." I rip off the covers and sit on the edge of the bed. Though, technically, a man who fathered a child isn't a virgin, but I don't want to discuss any of that. "But doesn't the first time, um, hurt?" And won't it make me bleed? Hmm. I don't want to discuss that part, either. "If we do it now, I'll be, um, more ready on our wedding night." I just said "more ready" instead of "readier"? Sex must make your grammar go all to pieces.

"I went to my wife's grave today."

And now, my plumbing down there has completely dried up.

"I hadn't been there since the funeral."

I pull the comforter around me.

"I, uh, I left my ring there, and, uh, before that, I dropped off all those pictures, the ones in the hall? I took them to Noël's mother." He kneels in front of me. "I'm not in my right mind today, Diane, not for this." He looks down at his stuff, and he's still right rigid. "My, um, appearance to the contrary."

Jack has had quite a day, quite an emotional day. "You want me though, right?"

He nods. "I dream about you, Diane, and we, um, we really go at it."

I smile. "Yeah?"

"You, um, you're pretty voracious in my dreams."

"I can't get enough of you, huh?"

"No." He laughs. "And I wake up exhausted."

I pull him to me. "I have a feeling we'll both be waking up exhausted a lot."

"I'm sorry about this, Diane. I keep—"

I put a finger to his lips. "You don't have to explain."

"I want to, God knows I want to."

I look down. "I can see that." And, so can God. I immediately feel guilty and cover up more of my body. "Did you, uh, did you write out our love scene?"

"Yes," he says.

"Well, where is it?"

"I'll have to e-mail it to you."

I lick my lips. "Is it hot?"

He nods.

"Is it nasty?"

He nods.

"Is it downright vile?"

He smiles. "Let's just say it's . . . involved."

"Hmm. I like an intricate plot." I sigh. "Jack, we have to get married soon, okay? I'm aching for you."

He frowns. "Me, too."

I run my fingers through his hair. "Come on. Let's take a shower or something."

"You're not mad?"

I close my eyes. "No. I'm still horny, but I'm not mad."

"I'll make it up to you."

I kiss his forehead. "I know you will." I look into his eyes. "For the rest of our lives, right?"

"Right."

I stand, but he doesn't, his face millimeters from my stomach, and he starts kissing me hard, his hands gripping my caboose so tightly. I start to pant almost immediately. "Is . . . is this in our love scene?"

He nods his head, but he doesn't stop kissing on me.

"Do I . . . I scratch the back of your neck?" I dig my nails into his neck as he nods. "Do I start to moan?"

He nods his head, his nose rubbing just below my belly button.

And in a moment, I'm moaning . . . and groaning . . . and lying back on the bed . . . and gripping the comforter.

"Jack?"

He doesn't answer, but I don't want him to. He'd have to use his tongue to speak, and I only want him to keep on doing . . . oh, Mr. Tickler, you're about to be replaced. . . .

"Keep talking to me, Jack, just keep talking to me. . . ." And right as I'm about to get my happiest happy on, I think, *I am going to save a fortune on C batteries!*

Jack *almost* spent the entire night with me, but it's just as well he left as the April sun started to warm up the horizon. If he had spent another second with me, I probably would have died. My death certificate would have read: "Death by Orgasm."

I would have died happy, but the mortician would have had quite a time getting my mouth to close again.

And now this . . . *sex* scene in front of me. It's not a love scene at all. This is far too erotic. I didn't make it through the first page as the other pages were printing out before I started to sweat. Jack could be writing erotic fiction under another name and making lots of people sweat. He has such a vivid imagination, and while I read, I ride the whirlwind.

And I'm horny again.

I can't go to work at a library horny! So, I call in sick—luckily, Francine answers the phone—and just sit around my house naked until I realize something: Mama is coming tonight.

I have some stuff to hide.

And you can't be sneaky when you're naked. I throw on a robe and flutter around the house, straightening, dusting, and wondering how to hide things that will give Mama a heart attack.

I can't leave these pages in the house. Mama will snoop around, find them, and die. And what will I do with this ring? And what will I do with Mr. Tickler, whose days are surely numbered anyway? Where *won't* Mama look? Think!

I could take it all to Jack's house.

No. You don't take Mr. Tickler to your fiancé's house. He might get jealous.

I could put it in the glove compartment of the car. No!

The freezer behind the ice cube trays? Yuck!

Bury it in the yard? For the neighbor's dog to dig up? Never!

How do you hide a vibrator from your mama?

Hmm. I look around my bedroom first. I could put it under the mattress in the middle, but they'll be sleeping in here while I sleep on the sofa! What if it turns on in the night? Mama might actually like it, but . . .

Oh, man, and I have to wash these sheets, too! They are so funky and—

The trunk of my car! Yes, in the trunk under the spare tire. I don't care if Mr. Tickler gets a little greasy. Oh, and I should remove the batteries first. One bump, a little hum, and then Daddy's tearing the car apart looking for the problem.

Vibrator problem: solved.

As long as I don't have a flat tire.

The pages . . . I can hide them in plain sight in my library. Just stick them in a book . . . that Mama has already read? Hmm. That might work, but . . . No, I'll just burn them. I can print them out again after Mama and Daddy leave.

Nasty-ass sex scene problem: solved.

That only leaves this . . . glorious ring. I should simply wear it with pride, and I've already vowed never to take it off. On the other hand, I'll be wearing it for the rest of my life, so a few days won't hurt. I slide it to the middle of my finger, but I can't make it go any farther! *It* doesn't want to come off, either! I slide it back down. I'll just . . . I'll just make that decision when the time comes.

I look at my alarm clock. Shoot. I'll have to make my decision in less than six hours; their flight arrives at 6:45.

I know I'll make the right decision. Until then, I have to air the funk out of this place. I look back at that naughty stack of pages.

Okay, one more time. I'm young. I can handle it.

And before I set it on fire, I know it will set *me* on fire.

52

Jack

We're cleaning the house again?

We'll have to sell it when I get back from the tour.

What if it sells before the wedding?

I'll move into a hotel or something.

What about your stuff?

I'll store what Diane wants to keep and sell or give away the rest.

You think you have an answer for everything.

Lately, I do have an answer for everything.

The phone rings. "Hello?"

"Hi, Jack, it's Jenny."

I look at the calendar. She doesn't have a payment due for another three weeks. "Hi."

"Um, I was cleaning out the car, and I found something jammed under the seat belts in the backseat."

"What?"

"It's a little bracelet that says, 'Daddy is the best.'"

The bracelet. It was something Stevie made at school,

one for each of us. I wanted to bury it with Noël, but her family wouldn't have it. But how did that bracelet end up in the backseat?

You don't remember?

No.

"Do you want me to swing by and give it to you?"

"Uh, sure. And, uh, just leave it in the mailbox if I'm not here."

Where else would you be?

True.

"Okay. I hope to see you."

She hopes to see you.

I've got too much to do. I have to clean this house before the tour because I'm sure I'll be too bushed to do it when I get back. I have to do some laundry, pack, check the flight information—

Don't forget your day with Diane's parents tomorrow.

I'm not worried.

What if they don't like you?

I'm not marrying them.

True, but . . . what if?

They'll like me.

The phone rings again. "Hello?"

"Jackie, there may be a change in plans."

Don't you hate it when Nina calls you that?

There are worse things.

Like little bracelets.

Shh.

And how they mysteriously end up in the backseat of a car.

Be quiet.

"The publisher seems to be backing off your tour."

As it should.

"Negative publicity is hurting your sales."

As it should.

"They'll probably want more of your new book now, and whatever you send them, make it something juicy."

Just send the sex scene.

But it's not connected to the chapters I've sent so far.

As if they'll even notice.

True.

"Uh, thanks for warning me about all this," I say, "and, by the way, Nina, I'm engaged."

"You are, Jackie? Congratulations! What's her name?"

"Diane."

"And when's the wedding?"

Good question.

Soon. Another couple of millimeters yesterday, and . . .

"We haven't decided. I'm meeting her parents tomorrow, so maybe I'll have a better idea of when by Sunday."

"Well, that's great, Jackie!"

"Um, Diane's black."

Why'd you say that?

To see how she'd react.

So you can sponge up her reaction.

Precisely.

"Is she the one helping you with this new book?"

Strange reaction.

"Yes."

"I'll call you right back."

That was weird.

Nina was speechless.

I hear a familiar horn outside. Jenny's here.

In the car where she found your bracelet in the backseat. Don't you remember?

I'm trying to forget Noël, and then this happens.

"Mommy *is the best,*" she had said, and she tore off your bracelet, then she ripped off all her clothes, and—

We were trying to be kinky.

Doing it in the backseat of a car in your own driveway?

It was late at night, Stevie was sound asleep in his bed, we turned all the outside lights off, there wasn't a moon, and it was—

The phone rings again, and so does the doorbell.

All at once, this life just seems to happen.

Yeah.

"Hello?"

"Hey, baby."

Diane. She had called me "baby" a lot last night. "What's up?"

"Not much, just cleaning up a bit before my parents get here. Did you get any rest?"

I go to the door. "No. I've been cleaning up here, too." I open the door, step outside, and hold a finger out to Jenny. Jenny nods.

"Do you miss me?" Diane asks.

"Of course."

"I've been reading our scene."

I smile. "Yeah?"

"And I wish I hadn't. It's keeping me from cleaning the house!"

Jenny hands the bracelet to me. It's so light. "Daddy is the best," it says. But that night in the backseat, *Mommy* was the best—

"Jack?"

"Oh, sorry." I hear a beep. "Uh, Diane, I have another call. It's probably my agent. Will you hold?"

"On to what?" she says, laughing. "I'll hold."

I click over. "Hello?"

"Jackie, they just love the idea of you traveling with your fiancée. Would she be willing to go along?"

This is an interesting turn of events.

"Um, she's on the other line."

And Jenny is still standing next to you! She looks good, too, all freckly and tan and cute.

"Well, Jackie, why don't you ask her?"

I cover the mouthpiece and smile at Jenny. "Thanks for bringing this by, but I'm really busy."

"I understand," Jenny says, backing away down the sidewalk. "It's good to see you, Jack."

"It's good to see you, too, Jenny."

I'll say.

"Nina, will you hold?"

"Sure thing, Jackie."

I watch Jenny get into the car and go back inside the house.

I click back to Diane. "You're not going to believe this. The publisher wants you to go on tour with me."

"What?"

"They want you to go on tour with me."

A moment of silence. "They need me to help your book sell, huh?"

I hadn't thought of this. "Yeah, I guess so."

Some more silence. "I'll have to think about it, Jack. That's an entire week of my vacation, and I only get two weeks a year. I mean, I took off half a day yesterday and all day today to get ready for my parents. There won't be much left for our honeymoon."

"True."

"I'll think about it, okay?"

"Okay. I love you."

"I love you, too. Bye."

I click back to Nina. "She says she'll think about it."

But what's up with Jenny? She's just sitting out there in the car.

"Look, Jackie, they want an answer now."

Is Jenny having car trouble?

"Uh, Nina, is tomorrow okay? Diane needs some time to think about it."

"Convince her, then, Jackie. It will be fun, and it will be all on the publisher's tab. We can get you two of the finest suites in every city."

With king-sized beds, stocked minibars, and Whirlpool tubs?

Shh.

"Like I said, I'll have to let you know tomorrow. I have to go. Good-bye."

I turn off the phone, go outside, and approach Noël's—

Jenny's.

Right.

I approach Jenny's car. "Is everything all right?"

Jenny looks up. "Yeah. No, I mean, well, not really. You see I've been trying to work up the courage to say something to you, but every time I'm about to, I just . . . freeze up."

She's going to ask you out.

No, she isn't.

"It's not a cold enough day to freeze up," I say.

Jenny laughs. "Yeah, I guess it isn't." She looks at the steering wheel. "I've, um, I've read your book, and, well, Dan sounded so lonely, and I just thought maybe, you know, you might like to go out with me sometime."

What did I tell you?

This isn't happening. This *doesn't* happen.

At least to you.

What do I say to this?

The truth usually works.

"Um, Jenny, I'm engaged."

She sucks in a quick breath. "Oh."

Say something.

What?

She seems hurt. Make her feel better.

"Um, but if I weren't engaged, I would definitely go out with you."

She turns to me with a bright smile. "Yeah?"

Say more.

I don't want to lead her on.

Then have a conversation. Be her friend.

"So, uh, what did you think of the book?" I ask.

"Well, it's kind of . . . kinky, you know?"

I blink.

I'm blinking, too.

"Did you really get dumped for another woman?"

I smile. "Yeah, in college."

She giggles. "You're kidding!"

"I wish I were."

And her name was *Beth. I wonder if she has read your book, too.*

"Well, um," Jenny says as she starts up the Mustang, "give me a call sometime, you know, just to talk. You still have my card, don't you?"

I nod, even though I've already tossed the card.

Who else would *you call? You don't know anyone.*

"Um, good-bye, Jenny."

"Bye."

She drives away. I feel pulled in so many directions right now. Nina, my publisher; Diane; Jenny; and this . . . bracelet.

Daddy is the best.

Yeah.

Big daddy is the best, too.

Shh.

I put on the bracelet and immediately call Diane. She answers on the first ring. "Diane," I ask, "how many children do you want?"

53

Diane

What a question! "How many are you planning to give me?" And he said *children*, as in more than one. Where is this coming from all of a sudden?

"How about . . . seven, one for every day of the week."

He has to be joking. "Let's start off with one and see how that goes." A cute little brown-yellow . . . girl. Named . . . Tawny, or something colorful like that, who will *never* hang out with the Qwans. "What brought this up?"

"The girl I sold the car to found a bracelet Stevie made for me. She just brought it by, and I'm wearing it now. It says, 'Daddy is the best.' Anyway, it popped into my head that we haven't discussed children yet."

She's owned that car for four months now, and she's just *now* finding this bracelet? "Um, what would you like to discuss?"

"How many children, for starters, and how soon?"

I *have* to be ripe. He *has* to be ripe. And if we get married within the next few months, this time next year I'll be having a baby. "You miss being a daddy, don't you?"

"Yes."

I smile up at God. *Thank You,* I pray, *for blessing me with a man who wants to be a father.* "Well, I want you to be a daddy as soon as possible, then."

"Yeah?"

"How about . . . we have a baby girl one year from now?"

Silence.

"Jack?"

"Sorry, just doing some math. That would mean we'd have to have an August wedding."

My hands shake a little. So soon! "Yes," I say, and the shake is now in my voice, "we'd have to get married in August."

"Cool."

Whoa. An August wedding in Roanoke? It will be ninety-five degrees with humidity over 60 percent. That would be such a sweaty wedding, the flowers will wilt, and someone will faint. . . . "I, uh, I have so much to do around here. Is that the only reason you called?"

"Yes."

"Well, I'll, uh, call you later tonight after my parents arrive."

"I'll be here."

Where else would he be? "See you later . . . Daddy."

"Bye . . . Mama."

Lord, that is a powerful title.

And two hours later, I am waiting for the powerful little lady I call Mama. Her flight is late, because the flight from Indianapolis to Pittsburgh was late. Flights to Roanoke are always late. They set some sort of record for most late flights in a row a few years ago. Mama will be pissed. Daddy, though, he won't care. He'll probably sleep all the way here, sleep all the way to my house, and go to sleep before ten, leaving just me and Mama to . . .

I shudder. I will have to give Daddy lots of coffee when we get home.

I spend the next hour admiring my ring. It's a big stone, but it isn't gaudy. It's a simple circle of light, a beacon of hope, a glittering dream.

And it's *mine!*

But the second they announce the arrival of the Pittsburgh flight, I rip off that glittering dream and put it in a zipper pouch inside my purse. Sorry, Jack, but I'm not ready for that kind of drama.

I meet them as they come out of that moving tunnel thing, and though I told myself not to ask, I ask, "How was your flight, Mama?"

Mama looks ragged, and Daddy looks like an unmade bed. "Rough," she says. "Just get us to your house."

Daddy gives me a hug. "You look good, Dee-Dee."

I hug him back. "So do you, Daddy."

"Do you have a lot of luggage?" I ask.

Daddy only nods and cuts his eyes to Mama.

Oh . . . joy.

I somehow manage to fit *six* suitcases into the trunk of the Hyundai (after a tiny little tense moment worrying about Mr. Tickler getting crushed to death), and we speed to my house in complete silence. I know Mama is just warming up her drama batteries, but that's okay with me.

My batteries are good and ready, too.

While Daddy brings in the luggage, Mama tours my house on her own with me trailing behind. I hear an occasional "um," an "uh-hmm" or two, and an "oh." The "oh" was for my bedroom.

"Is this where you two fornicate?" she asks.

"No, Mama." It's where we *almost* fornicate.

"Uh-hmm." She smooths out a wrinkle on the bed. "You sure used enough air freshener to cover the smell."

I don't answer. The less I say, the less she feels she *has* to say.

Daddy drags the suitcases into the bedroom. "I like your place, Dee-Dee," he says as he sits on the edge of the bed. "When are we going to meet Jack?"

I smile at the mention of Jack's name. "He'll be by tomorrow morning." I turn so I can't see Mama's reaction. "We're all going to drive up the Blue Ridge Parkway tomorrow."

"Yeah?" Daddy says. "It's a pretty drive, huh?"

"Yes."

I hear Mama cough.

Daddy chuckles. "Hope you don't mind if I . . ." He looks at the bed.

Daddy! Please stay awake! "You must be tired," I say instead. "Um, good night, Daddy." I kiss his cheek.

He pulls me close for a hug. "If your eyes dance anymore," he whispers, "they're going to leave your head."

I step back. "Get some sleep, Daddy."

"I will."

Mama and I leave the room, closing the door behind us. I follow her to the kitchen, where she turns and faces me in front of the stove. "You haven't done much with this place."

Here we go. "I haven't had the time." Or the money.

"Right." She opens the oven and peers in. "Where do you two plan on shacking up?"

Good thing I cleaned the oven. "Here."

She lets the oven door shut with a bang. "Here?"

"Yes."

"What kind of man—"

I wave a hand at her. "Don't start." I take a seat at the kitchen table. "His house has ghosts, Mama. He wants to start over someplace new."

She squints at the ceiling, focusing on a cobweb I missed. "This place isn't new."

"It's new to him," I say. "And we'll be planting flowers soon."

She drifts to the sink. "You should have already done that last fall."

"I know. We'll just be planting some annuals for now."

She smiles. "Really? Only annuals?"

I don't respond. Mama won't have annuals in her garden at all, because they aren't permanent enough. There must be a couple thousand bulbs in her flower beds back home.

The phone rings, and my pulse races as I leap out of the kitchen and head to the living room to answer it. It's Jack! "Good timing," I whisper.

"Yeah? How are things going?"

"Mama's just getting warmed up," I whisper. I walk to the far window. "I miss you."

"I miss you, too. How early should I arrive tomorrow?"

"I'll be serving breakfast at, oh, seven-thirty, so please don't be late."

He laughs. "I'll set my alarm for six."

"Good."

I feel more than hear Mama's presence in the room.

"I'll see you in the morning," I say. "Good night."

"Good night, Diane."

I turn off the phone and turn to Mama, who has made herself comfortable on what later will be my bed.

"He's a man of few words," she says. "You two will have a quiet house."

I sit at the other end of the sofa. "*We* had a quiet house." Before the Qwans arrived, that is.

"Hmm."

I see her cover a small yawn. "You must be tired, Mama. Why don't you get some sleep?"

"I'm fine."

Shoot.

"I could use some coffee, but that coffeemaker in there has to be cleaned first."

"It is clean." I think. Have I ever cleaned it?

Mama shakes her head. "I'll take some tea if you have any."

I force a smile and go to the kitchen, hoping I have at

least one decaffeinated tea bag left. All the excitement today has me wired, but I am so tired! I can't argue effectively with Mama if I'm about to fall asleep!

I bring two cups of Lemon Zinger into the living room, placing the cups on the coffee table. Mama takes a sip and raises one eyebrow. "Is this herbal?"

Shoot! "Yes."

"Is this all you have?"

Lord, forgive me, but . . . *damn*! "I thought you would like it, Mama, since it's getting so late."

"There are a lot of things you thought I would like," Mama says, putting down her cup. "And this is yet another."

"Mama, I don't want to discuss—"

"I know, I know," she interrupts, with a lazy smile. "We have plenty of time."

Yeah, *six* suitcases' worth.

As I hear the ticking of my monkey clock, I have never wanted the sun to rise faster in my life.

54

Jack

To gel, or not to gel. That is the question.

Go natural, and maybe you'll act natural.

I always act natural.

Just don't try to act too white.

It's kind of in my genes, you know.

Just . . . be careful.

I will.

After donning jeans, hiking boots, and a green sweatshirt, I get into the car at precisely 7 A.M. and drive to Diane's, parking behind her car at seven-fifteen. I see a tall black man in the yard, his skin Diane's delicious color, and he wields some shears as he trims the hedges. I get out of the car, and when I shut the door, he turns.

"You're Jack," he says.

"Yes," I say.

He removes some heavy gloves as he comes over to me.

Those shears look sharp!

Shh.

He extends his hand, and I shake it. "Bill Anderson."

"Nice to meet you, Mr. Anderson."

He waves the shears in the direction of the bushes. "Just tidying up a bit."

I point at the tree branches hiding the power line. "I had planned to cut those back soon. The power company will come out, but they do a lousy job."

Mr. Anderson nods. "I do my own, too."

I look at the empty flower beds. "Diane and I will be planting some flowers soon."

He nods. "Good soil around here."

Now what?

"Um, how was your flight?"

That was lame.

"I slept most of the way, but it was long."

"Yeah."

Change the subject.

"Well, we have a beautiful day to go up the Parkway," I say.

He nods.

"Uh, did you bring a camera? There are plenty of over-looks and lookouts on the Parkway."

"I sure did." Mr. Anderson turns slightly, and my eyes follow his to the window where—

That's Diane's mother.

She's pretty.

Everywhere except her eyes. Jack, you are being eye-balled to death.

I know.

"Is that . . ."

"Uh-huh," Mr. Anderson says. His eyes dance back to mine. "That's Diane's mama."

I decide to be blunt. "Are her eyes always that . . . locked and loaded?"

"Uh-huh. Just try to stay out of her beam." He laughs. "So, do you plan on marrying Dee-Dee?"

"Yes."

"Have you bought her a ring?"

She isn't wearing it. Why isn't she wearing it?

Should I lie?

She must have a reason.

Well, I don't like it.

"Uh, yes. I presented it to her Thursday."

He looks at his feet. "I knew she had one. She kept looking at her hand last night." He looks at Mrs. Anderson and smiles. "But I know why she isn't wearing it."

"Yeah."

He puts his hand on my shoulder. "My condolences on your family, Jack. I don't know how I would have reacted if it had happened to me, but I know it would have stopped me in my tracks."

"It, um, it almost stopped me."

He nods. "Do you love my daughter?"

"Yes, sir."

"Hmm. She's precious to me, too. She never needed much tending, and she's kind of a wildflower at heart—and picky! I never met a more picky child."

"Um, Mr. Anderson, I want to marry your daughter. Do I have your permission?"

That took guts! It makes you appreciate your own daddy more, doesn't it?

Yeah.

Mr. Anderson smiles. "Yes. Of course, my word isn't worth nearly as much as . . ." He cocks his head toward the window, but Mrs. Anderson isn't there anymore. He squints at my hair. "Let me tell you, Jack, it's a good thing you aren't wearing that stuff in your hair today."

"It was Diane's idea."

"Her mama thinks it's girly."

I'm scared of Diane's mama now.

Me, too.

"Um, do you have any advice for me in dealing with . . ." I cock my head toward the window.

"Take lots of deep breaths," Mr. Anderson says. "I have developed some mighty big lungs from all the deep breaths I've taken during thirty-five years of marriage."

"I will."

"And say as little as possible."

That shouldn't be too hard.

"And try to keep a neutral face like this." His smiling face turns, well, neutral, with neither a smile nor a frown, his eyes dead ahead. "She reads faces. One little curl up or down with your lip and . . ."

"Neutral," I say.

He pats my arm. "Just be yourself, Jack."

You're good at that.

He claps some dirt off his gloves. "Well, we'd better be getting inside. Diane has breakfast going."

I take a deep breath, hold it, and let it out slowly. Then I put my best neutral face on and follow Mr. Anderson into the house.

55

Diane

I'm nervous, my back hurts from a night on the sofa, and I'm grumpy because Mama is doing none of the cooking but all of the criticizing. "Those eggs aren't hard enough," she had said. "You aren't going to serve that limp bacon, are you?" she had asked. "Those hash browns look raw," she had said.

We should have eaten at IHOP.

And when Mama had told me, "He's here," I had nearly dropped the serving platter.

But once I had realized that Jack was talking to Daddy, I relaxed. Daddy seems to be okay with Jack, and he makes a better welcoming committee than Mama does.

God, please bless everything about this day, I pray. *And keep Mama's mouth in the hollow of Your hand.*

When the front door opens, I yell, "Breakfast is ready!"

I plan to fill Mama's mouth with food before she can fill it with venom.

Jack strides into the kitchen like he owns the place—with no gel? He looks okay, but he needs another haircut. "Good morning," he says.

"Good morning," I say. We're so domestic!

Then he kisses me on the cheek right there in front of Mama!

"Good morning, Mrs. Anderson," Jack says, while I try to recover. "It's a pleasure to finally meet you."

I look sideways at my parents. Daddy is smiling, but Mama has her stone face on.

"It's, uh, it's a pleasure to meet you, too, Jack," Mama says, in her formal, "I'm-so-sorry-for-your-loss" funeral voice.

"Well," Daddy says, "let's eat."

Thank you, Daddy.

Then we sit . . . and eat. No one is talking. All I hear are forks hitting plates and sipping sounds. Somebody break the ice!

And, oh, Jack don't— He's putting ketchup on his eggs and hash browns. He couldn't just put a little dot of Texas Pete on his eggs like Daddy. I'll hear about this later. And don't— Lord, my man loves his sugar, but four heaping tablespoons in his coffee? And why did he wear that thread-bare sweatshirt? It has to be as old as I am!

I see Mama starting to speak several times, but her mouth only opens and shuts. She's as speechless as I am, and we both just tear at our bacon.

"Dee-Dee," Daddy says with his mouth full, "everything is delicious."

"Yes," Jack says with *his* mouth full, "delicious."

I hope Mama is seeing what I'm seeing: two grown men behaving almost the same way at the breakfast table. Maybe it's a man thing.

Daddy swallows and wipes his lips with a napkin. "And Jack here tells me he got you a ring."

Oh . . . no.

"Where is it, Dee-Dee?" Daddy asks. "I want to see it."

I can't look at Jack or Daddy or Mama. Is anyone breathing besides Daddy? I know I'm not. Oh, Lord, and now Mama is the last to know! I'll never live this down.

"Excuse me," I say, and I get up from the table, go to my purse, take out the ring, slide it on—I've *missed* you!—and walk back into the kitchen, showing it to Daddy first, though the gleam crisscrosses the kitchen as I do.

"My, my," Daddy says, holding my hand and admiring the ring, "that's a fine-looking ring. Look, Rachel. Isn't that nice?"

Don't look at Mama, don't look at Mama, don't look— I look at Mama. Her eyes—I catch my breath—are little brown dots of death!

Mama never looks at the ring, holding me in her eyes with all that death. "Yes, it is a nice-looking ring."

I brace for, "Why weren't you wearing it last night?" It *should* come. That's something Mama should say while blinking those brown dots of death at me. But, it never comes.

"So," Daddy says, grabbing the last slice of bacon, "when's the happy event going to take place?"

Don't answer, Jack, please don't—

"August," Jack says.

Mama still hasn't spoken, but her eyes are speaking volumes. They're saying, "I have *not* been happy; I *am* not happy; I will *never* be happy."

And this makes me unhappy.

Lord, make her speak or something! She's winning this argument without saying a single word! Oh, yeah. I asked You to control her mouth. When have You ever listened to me?

"Well, congratulations," Daddy says. "Where will the wedding take place?"

I catch Jack looking at me, but I don't lock onto his eyes.

I'm focusing on a speck of egg, hoping that it's a magic speck of egg that will miraculously whisk me to another dimension in time.

"Here in Roanoke at Diane's, I mean, our church," Jack says.

And that ruins all sorts of Mama's dreams now. She had to be counting on marrying off one of her daughters in her church.

"And where will you two settle down, Jack?" Daddy asks.

"Here," Jack says. "I'll be selling my house as soon as I can. . . ."

While they talk about Jack's house and interest rates and housing slumps and all the other things involved in selling a house, Mama and I try not to stare at each other. I think she's staring at a burned piece of hash brown. Eventually, Daddy and Jack get up and leave the table to "get some fresh air," according to Daddy.

Yeah, the air in here has gotten pretty stale pretty fast.

"Mama, are you going to say something—anything?"

Mama shakes her head. "Oh, I'm just listening today, Dee-Dee. You accused me of not listening, so I plan on just *listening* all day long."

She's not fighting fair! "Well, your silence was rude."

"How can silence be rude?"

Silence in a library isn't rude, because I expect it. But unexpected silence from your mama after all these little bombshells *is* rude.

"Your father and Jack were having a conversation, Dee-Dee, and it would have been rude to interrupt."

I hate it when she's basically right. "I can tell you wanted to."

Mama leans back, her coffee mug in her hands. "Would it have made any difference?"

"No," I say quickly.

She shrugs and hums a little. "So what does it matter

what I think? I mean, if you're ashamed to wear his ring, who am I to judge?"

Finally, we can have an argument. "I'm not ashamed to wear it."

"You didn't have it on last night."

"I didn't want to shock you."

She lets out a "tsk-tsk." "Oh, child, it's *way* too late for that. And if you don't want to get married in your home church, well . . ."

"But I do! But I wouldn't if it would embarrass you."

She blinks. "Why would I be embarrassed?"

Shoot. I walked right into that one. Never make a statement to your mama that she can turn into a question. "Think of the shame."

She looks away. I knew it!

"Anything else, Mama?"

She looks at me. "What do you mean?"

I feel like rolling up my sleeves and throwing hands with her. "Go ahead. Lay it all on me."

She sniffs a laugh. "I have nothing to lay on you."

Yes, she does. "What about the way Jack ate?"

"All men could use some manners, your daddy included today, for some reason. Both of them ate abominably."

That didn't work. "What about the way Jack's dressed?"

"So he doesn't iron. Your daddy hasn't ironed a single thing since we've been married."

Hmm. "What about Jack's general appearance?"

Her lips twitch. Here it comes. "Well, of course, he could be darker."

I close my eyes. "I'll take him to a tanning booth. Will that help?"

Mama laughs. "Not in a million years, but what does it matter to me? I'm only your mama. You do what you want to do. You have your own life now. You go on and live it."

Lord, this drive up the Parkway is going to suck!

* * *

While we drive, the only thing warming up is the weather. Daddy and Jack talk our ears off, mainly about the car, the next overlook, the last overlook, the way the fog burned off, the way the buds on the trees lean into the sun, and the lack of traffic. I should have put Daddy in the front seat so he wouldn't have to shout. Mama stays inside the car the entire time, and no amount of Daddy's coaxing for a "family picture" will get her to budge. On overlook number seven—I've lost count—I pull Jack aside.

"Can we go back now?"

"Your mom's not having a good time?"

"No."

"We can go back." He winks. "Maybe Bandini's can warm her up."

"I hope so."

But Bandini's, and Mr. Bandini in particular, can't get Mama to open her mouth for anything but her spaghetti, which she pushes around on her plate. Daddy, Jack, and Mr. Bandini, though, don't even seem to notice, carrying on as if they were old buddies. Mr. Bandini even pulls up a chair!

And they're beginning to piss me off! Can't they see how miserable Mama and I are?

On the way back to my house, Jack whispers, "Have you decided about the tour?"

As a matter of fact, I have—just now. "I'm not going."

"What's that?" Daddy asks.

Jack, you'd better not—

"My publisher wants Diane to go on tour with me," Jack says, "but if she takes a week off now, that would cut into the time we could spend on our honeymoon."

That's not the reason, Jack! It's the lady behind me boring holes through my seat with her eyes! It's the way you and Daddy have been ignoring the silent argument Mama and I are having!

"Where are you going on this tour?" Daddy asks.

And they're off again. At the mention of any city, Daddy tells a story, and Jack is driving ten miles under the speed limit so he can hear all the stories. Just get us home!

When Jack stops his car behind mine, I jump out and head straight for the house, fumbling with my keys at the door. I just want all this to end!

"Next time you visit, there will be flowers here," Jack is saying.

Where is my damn house key!

"And Mrs. Anderson," Jack says, "maybe the next time we'll have more time to talk, just the two of us."

Oh, no, Jack, don't tell her that! That's just the opening she needs to—

"What's wrong with right now?" Mama asks.

I drop my keys and kick them toward the edge of the porch.

"You're right," Jack says. "We could go for a walk."

I look down to snatch up my keys and see . . . Jack holding Mama's hands? He's touching the beast with X-ray eyes?

"A walk will be fine, Jack," Mama says. "I've been sitting for far too long."

I turn as slowly as I can. Daddy's eyes are dancing, Mama's nodding, and Jack is smiling.

And I'm shaking. I drop my keys again. What I said earlier about people having trouble with keys in the movies— forget that. My hands are so sweaty right now I couldn't use one hand to hold on to the other.

"Uh, Diane," Jack says, "we're going for a little walk."

"Okay," I say, in a tiny voice.

Mama looks hard at me. "See you around, Diane."

She never calls me that! What does it mean? Is this some new code?

Then Mama *links* her arm in Jack's and walks away!

I look at Daddy. "Daddy, I'm—"

He gives me a hug. "Jack can handle himself."

"I know, it's just—"

"Shh, shh, Dee-Dee," Daddy says, picking up my keys. "It will be all right."

Oh, God, I hope so!

56

Jack

Do you know what you're doing?
I think so.

This woman could be dangerous!
I'm just trying to be friendly.

Friendly? This is crazy! You should only deal with dangerous people under controlled conditions. Diane should always be nearby!

Diane's mother is the only one who seems to have a problem with us. Diane's father has already given me the green light.

While her eyes have been screaming, "Stop!"
Yeah. They're spooky, huh?

Mrs. Anderson and I walk arm in arm for a block or so, and I can't think of anything to say.

To her.

I'm glad you're here to talk to. In fact, if it weren't for you these last eight months, I don't know—

"Tell me about your wife," she says suddenly.

We weren't expecting that question.

What do I tell her?

Be Emerson about it. "Speak the truth in words as hard as cannonballs."

Okay.

"Uh, Noël was amazing. She was sunny, happy, the best mother, a great cook, hardworking, shy. . . ."

You're babbling.

Just making a list.

You didn't say "sexy."

Just making a careful list.

"Was she your first love?"

I smile. "Yes. She swept me off my feet."

Why tell her that?

If she hadn't, my feet would have walked out of Roanoke a long time ago.

"Tell me about your son."

She's asking questions Diane hasn't asked.

Maybe she's asking on Diane's behalf.

"Stevie took after his mother mostly. He was happy, quiet, curious like me, loved to draw . . . I miss him." I stop walking. "And I miss her, too."

Mrs. Anderson nods.

"I don't miss her as much because of your daughter, but . . . I thought Noël was my soul mate, you know?"

You're revealing too much.

I'm being honest.

"And to lose her and Stevie in the same day . . ." I sigh. "I thought my whole world had ended."

We continue walking a little farther past some ranch houses, their yards full of pansies and daffodils.

"What attracted you to Diane?"

Try not to be too honest here.

I will.

"First, it was her hands."

"Her hands?"

It does sound kind of kinky.

"Her fingers, actually."

Now that's kinky.

"Diane touched the palm of my hand when she gave me some change at the library. No one had touched me like that since the funeral, and I took it as a sign from God."

You didn't then.

I do now.

Mrs. Anderson stops walking and drops her hand from my arm. "She gave you change at the library?"

"I know it sounds crazy, but . . ."

She blinks several times. "She . . . touched you while giving you change?"

"Yes."

She closes her eyes. "Go on. What else do you like about Diane?"

She thinks you're crazy.

"I'm glad Diane is so patient. I'm kind of spacey."

You're telling me.

Shh.

Mrs. Anderson opens her eyes. "So far, we have fingers and patience. What else?"

I smile. "I like her smile, her eyes . . ."

The way she moans.

Shh.

"Her honesty . . . and her faith."

Yes! Great point!

"I, uh, I hadn't been on good terms with God since the accident, and Diane helped me to talk to Him again and return to church. That's where we went on New Year's Eve."

She blinks again. "You took Dee-Dee to church on New Year's Eve?"

"Yes."

Mrs. Anderson laughs. "Cheap date."

She laughed!

And it was genuine.

Was it?

I hope so.

It could be one of those crazy people laughs.

It sounded genuine to me.

"Yeah, I guess it was a cheap date, but it was an important date, Mrs. Anderson. Diane has helped me to live again, and I'd like to share the rest of my life with her."

That was good.

That's how I really feel.

"So, you're not just using her to help you write your next book?"

She's shrewd.

"She's helping me to write it, yes, but, no, I'm not using her."

"Hmm." She takes my arm again. "You wanted her to go on this tour of yours, though."

"At first, yes. I miss her when we're apart."

"And now?"

"I miss her now, too."

That wasn't what she was asking!

Oh!

"No," Mrs. Anderson says, "I meant, do you want her to go with you now?"

I sigh. "It doesn't matter whether I want her to go or not. She has already decided not to go."

"And you're not going to try to change her mind?"

I shake my head. "I wouldn't even know how to start."

Mrs. Anderson laughs. "That's true."

Another laugh! And is that a smile?

Her eyes aren't . . . killing me anymore.

She might just be setting you up, Jack. Be careful.

We walk a long, silent distance, circling the neighborhood once and not doing anything more than commenting on flowers, landscaping, why people use tacky lawn ornaments, and which shutters need to be painted.

This is going well.

Yeah.

I'll bet Diane is going crazy.

Yeah.

"And you really want an August wedding, huh?" she says as we get to Diane's driveway.

"I'd marry her tomorrow if I could," I say, "but I can wait until August."

Mrs. Anderson turns and waves at Diane, who looks at us from the living room window.

Diane doesn't look too happy. Wave or something.

I wave and smile.

She's not waving back. Check out her eyes!

Are her eyes killing me . . . or her mother?

Mrs. Anderson turns to me. "I don't think Diane can wait, Jack."

Hmm?

My thoughts exactly.

"I think *she* thinks she has waited long enough," she says. "What do you think?"

I'm still stuck on "Hmm?" How about you?

I'm stuck on all the "thinks."

"I think . . . that I'll, uh, I'll have to ask her."

Mrs. Anderson smiles. "I know my daughter. At least I think I do. She's changed a lot since she came down here. But something tells me that there won't be an August wedding. In fact, something tells me there won't be a wedding at all."

How does she know this?

I'll ask her.

"How do you know all this?"

Mrs. Anderson looks around the yard. "You two need to put up a bench out here somewhere so us old folks can sit down."

"We could sit on the steps."

Mrs. Anderson frowns. "I might not get up again. Those

are some low steps." She looks up at Diane in the window. "And I don't want to be overheard."

She's sneaky.

"I could bring out some chairs from the kitchen."

Mrs. Anderson nods. "Do that." She smiles. "I'll be waiting under that oak tree over there."

As I walk into the house, Diane stops me. "Is everything all right?"

I smile, then kiss her on the cheek. "Yes." I step around her, go to the kitchen, and take two chairs.

"What are you doing?" Diane asks.

I hold up the chairs. "Um, getting some chairs. Your mom must be tired. She says we need to put a bench outside, and I think it's a good idea."

"She could come inside," Diane says forcefully.

I shrug. "Um, we're not through talking."

"You're not?"

I shake my head.

"Well, what are you talking about?"

I kiss her lips. "You." I move around her, holding one chair in front of me, one chair behind. When I get to the door, I turn to Diane. "Could you open the door, please?"

She rushes around me and holds the door as I move outside. "Um, how long do you think you'll be?"

"I don't know."

She shoots a look at her mother. "Should I worry?"

I shake my head. "No. But . . ."

"But what?"

I put down the chairs and take her in my arms. "August is far too hot for a wedding, don't you agree?"

She blinks. "What are you saying?"

I turn and smile at Mrs. Anderson. "I'm not saying it. *She* is."

More blinking.

Maybe she has something in her eye.

"I had better not keep her waiting."

Diane only nods. "Kiss me first."

I kiss her.

"I'll, uh, I'll be inside waiting," she says. "Don't keep me waiting too long."

I shrug. "It's not up to me."

"Just . . . hurry, okay?"

"Okay."

I pick up the chairs and return to Mrs. Anderson, setting hers on a level space and mine on a somewhat level space under the tree.

Try not to rock.

I'll try.

"I've flustered her, haven't I?" Mrs. Anderson asks.

I nod. "She seems worried."

"She should worry after worrying me to death for the past few days." She leans forward. "I've always liked you, Jack. I want you to know that."

Hmm?

"The way she talked about you since December, just the way her voice sounded so happy. It had . . . music in it, you know? It made me like you. It made me happy that she had finally found someone who cared about her almost as much as I did."

Hmm. She's using past tense.

I hear it.

She leans back. "But . . . when I saw your face for the first time on that book, well, things changed."

Is it getting darker out here or what?

Shh. The sun is just going down.

Mrs. Anderson shakes her head slightly. "But things only changed for me," she says softly.

What do I say?

Saying nothing seems to be working.

She looks up, her eyes soft like Diane's. "I wanted to hate

you, Jack, but it was too late, and not just for Diane. She has already made her choice. I had . . . accepted you for four months before I knew you were . . ."

Should I say it for her?

Silence is golden.

"So I should keep on accepting you." She shrugs. "I mean, I liked you then, so why shouldn't I like you now, right?"

Do I answer?

Just nod.

I nod.

She looks around us. "You could put a nice flower box around this tree, you know, put some tulip bulbs down this fall, and they'd be blazing red come spring."

"That's a good idea."

Ooh, smart. Always agree with your future mother-in-law.

"And that third bedroom in there needs a lot of work," she says.

Hmm?

"I'd put carpet down in there and paint the wall a nice pastel color. It's far too wooden and white for a nursery."

Hmm. Does this mean—

Shh. She's not finished.

She looks at her hands. "And maybe this time next year, I'll have a grandbaby to hold on an evening like this. We'll just sit out here—on a bench, don't forget the bench. We'll just sit here and admire the tulips."

"I'd like that, too."

She nods. "Not as much as the woman in there. She reminds me of me when Bill and I first started out. We, um, we eloped, but don't tell Diane. She doesn't know."

You're going to tell Diane, aren't you?

I don't know if I should.

Mrs. Anderson laughs. "I'm feeling so *old* these days. My baby is in love." She reaches out and grabs my knee. "An

August wedding is out of the question, Jack. I don't know how or where, but you two have to get married as soon as possible."

Are you catching all these hints?

Like a can of corn bloop to center field.

"If *I* were to elope today, I might go to . . . Jamaica." She drops her eyes. "Bill and I honeymooned in Kentucky, not that I saw much of Kentucky during that time, but Kentucky is not Jamaica. I've always wanted to go there. It's not too hot this time of year, not too cool, just quiet, beautiful, isolated, natural. I'm trying to get Bill to consider going there on our fortieth anniversary, but . . ."

That wasn't a hint.

That was a line drive.

"It wouldn't bother you," I say, "if we didn't get married in your church?"

She sighs. "No. And I suppose it wouldn't bother me if you *did* get married there. It's just"—she scrunches up her lips—"I would feel uncomfortable."

"I understand."

"Not because you're . . . white."

She said the word!

I heard.

"But because most of the fools in my church would see you *only* as white." She smiles. "They don't know you like I do."

I lean forward. "Um, how does one elope?"

She smiles. "You want her badly, don't you?"

I nod, blushing.

"Maybe you could get married on your tour."

"But she's not going."

"Jack, Jack, Jack," she says, her eyes dancing, "she'll go."

"How do you know?"

"I know. You'll get a phone call later this evening, I promise."

How can she be so sure? Ask her!

"How . . . how can you be so sure?"

"I'm her mother. I can convince her of anything, but you have to do your part. Let me tell you how we're going to do it. . . ."

57

Diane

I hate my mama.

Okay, I don't hate my mama—much—but she's keeping Jack away from me for far too long, and the more I check on them at the window, the longer it seems to get!

"A watched pot never boils," Daddy says as he leafs through the newspaper on the sofa.

"She's doing this on purpose." I sit next to him in a huff.

Daddy folds the newspaper in half and sets it on the table. "I'd be more concerned if it was a short conversation. They've been at it for almost an hour. Maybe she's liking what she's hearing."

"But Jack isn't doing any of the talking! His lips aren't moving! All he's doing is nodding and rocking in that chair. Why does she have to be so . . ." Is there even a word?

Daddy puts his arm around my shoulders. "Your mama has been *so* . . . ever since I met her. It will all work out. You'll see."

I lay my head on Daddy's arm. "You like him, don't you?"

"He's a fine man, Dee-Dee."

"But, if you like him, and Mama loves *you,* why doesn't Mama like Jack?"

He squeezes my shoulder. "I think she does. You should have heard her singing his praises everywhere she went back home."

I cross my arms in front of me. "Until she saw his picture."

"Well, he is a bit white."

I smile. "He doesn't glow or anything."

"Girl, you'll never need a night-light."

I punch him playfully in the chest. "He's not *that* white." He has some dark patches . . . in special places.

The door crashes open, a chair preceding Jack, who drags the other chair behind him down the hall to the kitchen. Mama comes in looking . . . solemn? Oh no! Did it end badly? She, too, goes down the hall.

Daddy removes his arm from around me. "Something's up," he whispers.

Oh, God!

Jack comes into the living room, his hands in his pockets. "I, uh, I have to go pack."

I stand. "I'll walk you to your car."

He shakes his head, and he won't even look at me. "That's okay. Um, your mother wants to talk to you."

I sigh. "She can wait."

Jack's eyes flit up to mine. "I don't think that would be a good idea." He nods at Daddy. "Nice meeting you, Mr. Anderson."

"Likewise," Daddy says.

"Um, bye," Jack says, and I watch him go out the front door! And I don't move a single inch!

"Your mama's waiting," Daddy says.

I set my jaw, clench my fist, turn, and march down the

hall into my kitchen. Mama sits at the table, her hands folded in front of her, her lips tight.

I don't sit. "Mama, what just happened?"

"You might want to sit down," she says.

"I'll stand because I've been sitting too *long* today," I say, with attitude.

She looks up. "Suit yourself." She blinks. "Your daddy and I will be leaving tomorrow."

Huh? "What?"

She smiles that self-assured smile of hers. "My work here is done."

I fall into a seat across from her. "What do you mean?"

"Just that . . . my work here is done. I've met Jack, and"—she shrugs—"I can go home now."

"What do you mean, you can go home now?"

"Dee-Dee, oh, I'm sorry, I know you prefer to be called Diane now. Diane, I am speaking English, am I not?"

There she goes calling me Diane again! "Yes, Mama, you are, but you're not making sense."

She furrows her eyebrows. "To anyone but you, I am. Let me spell it out for you. I've met Jack. Are you with me?"

"Yes, but—"

"So I've met him, and now I can go home. What's so hard to understand about that?"

I'm so confused I can't even blink!

"Mama, what did you two talk about all that time?"

She smiles. "A little bit of everything, but it doesn't concern you anymore."

I don't like the sound of that! "What do you mean it doesn't concern me?"

"Bill!" Mama calls, and Daddy steps into the room. "Get us a flight back home for tomorrow."

Daddy looks at me. "Tomorrow?"

"Yes," Mama says.

"What's going on?" Daddy mouths to me.

I can only shake my head.

"Go on, now," Mama says. "And try to get us window seats this time."

Daddy leaves.

"You're . . . seriously leaving tomorrow."

Mama nods. "We are."

"But . . . but you just got here." I can't believe I'm saying this. "Four days tops" has turned into two days in a matter of minutes. "You couldn't have had time to . . . to . . ."

She smiles. "To what?"

I jump up. "To . . . to properly assess Jack."

"Assess? I thought I was only meeting him."

I slap my right hand on the table. I will never slap my left hand on any table. I may even stop using my left hand completely. "You know what I mean, Mama."

She pushes back her chair and crosses her legs. "No, I'm afraid I don't."

I hold up both hands. "Enough of these games."

"What games?"

I sigh so hard I think her hair moves. "Do you accept Jack or not?"

"Accept? What do you mean by 'accept'?"

I want to curse her so bad! "Mama, I am engaged to be married to him in August. Now, do you accept—"

"You're not getting married to him in August, Diane."

I suck in a breath. "What?"

She looks around. "The acoustics in here must be terrible. Have you had your hearing checked lately?"

"I heard you, Mama." I clench my fists. "What do you mean I'm not marrying him?"

"In August," she adds.

"Whatever. What do you mean?"

She smiles. "Diane, you're hearing me, but you're not *feeling* what I'm saying."

"What's there to feel? You haven't said anything!"

Or has she? Wait a minute. She's leaving tomorrow, even though she brought six suitcases. Who brings six suitcases only to stay for two days? I'm not marrying Jack. . . .

"Mama, could you . . ." *In August.* I'm not marrying Jack in August. She emphasized that. "Mama, is it okay?"

"Is what okay?"

Jack looked so miserable, though! And he left without even giving me a peck on the cheek. "Mama, what do you think of Jack?"

"I like him."

I'm not going to say, "What?" again. "You like him."

"Yes."

My fingers tingle. "But if you like him, why can't I marry him in August?"

She looks at the ceiling and shakes her head. "You *could* marry him in August, Diane, but I don't think you two can wait that long. *He* definitely can't, but if you want to wait . . ."

"What?" escapes before I can catch it.

She slides her chair back to the table, reaches out, and takes my hands. "My work here is done. There will be no August wedding. I like Jack. You two have to get married as soon as possible."

Blink blink.

"Can I make it any clearer than that, Diane?"

"No, Mama." I can't believe this is happening. I mean, I've been hoping that this very thing would happen, and now that it has, I don't believe it!

She squeezes my hands. "So, why don't you go on this tour and find time to, you know, get married?"

I pull back my hands. "You mean, elope?"

She shrugs. "Your daddy and I did it, and we've done okay."

No way. "You and Daddy . . . eloped?"

She nods.

Why wasn't I told this? "Can I ask why?"

"Sure."

Mama doesn't answer.

"*Why* did you and Daddy elope?" I ask.

"I couldn't wait," she says, with a giggle. "I wanted your daddy that badly. I prayed and prayed for God to take away that want—and, Diane, it was a serious want—but it just wouldn't go away. And since I didn't want to do anything I would be ashamed of before I was married, I talked your daddy into taking me down to Kentucky, where we found us a justice of the peace at three in the morning, and," she sighs, "we didn't even have any rings."

This is so incredible. This is so . . . wonderful!

I see a tear slip from her eye, and my throat gets tight.

"I came down here to stop you, Diane, partially because I thought I could, but mostly because I, um, because someone told me that I look at life too much on the surface of things. She said I was 'skin-deep.' I'm sorry about that."

I reach out and take her hands. "It's okay."

"But when I saw you and Jack and the way you two have been looking at each other all day, I saw your daddy and me all over again, and it brought back so many wonderful memories." She shakes her head. "You don't need a church wedding to be blessed by God, Diane. God has already blessed Jack with you."

"And God has blessed me with Jack."

"Yes, I think He has." She adjusts my ring. "It's a lovely ring."

"Thank you."

She nods. "Jack has good taste."

"He does."

She stands, taking my hands in hers, so I have to stand with her. "And right now, Jack is packing two suitcases."

What? "How do you know that?"

She puts her arm around me, moving me down the hall. "Oh, technically he's only packing one. The other one is empty."

I stop. "How do you know this, Mama?"

"It was my idea."

"It was your—"

She pushes me gently into the living room. "Bill, when does our flight leave?"

Daddy waves the phone in the air. "I'm still on hold."

"Well, hurry up." She turns to me. "Diane has to call Jack."

I can't think! "But he left here so—"

"That was my idea, too. He was *acting,* Diane."

That sneaky man. And the whole time he knew— "So, the other suitcase is for me?"

Mama shakes her head. "Are you kidding? That's for what he'll be bringing back."

Bringing back? "From where?"

She smiles. "From your honeymoon."

"From my . . ."

Honeymoon.

"Daddy, give me the phone!"

"But, baby, I've been waiting for half an hour," he says.

The cell phone. I have a cell phone. Now, where did I put it?

"It's in your car," Mama says.

"What?"

"Your cell phone. It's in your car." She smiles. "I hope it has enough juice left."

58
Jack

"Look, Nina, she's not going, and there's nothing I can do about it." *Don't forget to pack extra boxers.*

I won't.

They tear so easily, and Diane has some seriously long nails.

"Jackie, you're not considering the big picture here," Nina says.

And that cologne she likes.

I'll get it.

"If she doesn't go, there will be no tour."

This might be pushing it, but . . . a can of whipped cream?

They scan the luggage. They may think it's a bomb.

Well, something will explode.

Ha-ha.

"Look, Nina," I say, "you know I didn't want to go on a tour in the first place, so I don't care if they cancel it or not."

What about . . . some chocolate syrup?

I could put some in a freezer bag.

Make sure it's a Ziploc.

Yeah.

"Your career may be hanging in the balance here, Jackie."

What is she talking about?

I have no idea. Now where's the sunscreen?

You're not actually going to wear that stuff, are you?

What do you suggest?

Baby oil! And it has other uses as well. . . .

Baby oil is good.

"What am I going to do with you, Jackie? This is the opportunity of a lifetime. Can't you make Diane see that?"

I already have.

He already has.

"Her mind is made up, and so is mine," I say. "I don't want my fiancée to be used as window dressing to sell more books."

I would have said "eye candy."

Yes, you would have.

She is *going to be tasty.*

Hmm. Where's my lip balm? I can't be tasting her with chapped lips.

"It's only for a week, for Christ's sake!" Nina yells.

"No," I say. "You're wrong. It's for a lifetime, Nina, and I prefer to say 'for Jesus' sake.' Good-bye."

I hang up.

How about throwing in a deck of cards?

What for?

So you two can play strip poker.

I don't intend to be clothed.

So, play for favors, you know, like—

I don't think I'll have to win any favors.

True.

The phone rings. I check the Caller ID. It's Diane . . . on her cell phone.

"Hello, beautiful."

"Jack, I am going on your tour," she says.

She never beats around the bush, does she?

I like that about her.

"Are you sure?" I ask.

"Positive."

"It may get rough, you know."

Ooh, kinky.

I'm thinking about us having to change planes so quickly.

Oh.

"I don't care, Jack. I am going with you. When are you picking me up?"

"Oh, in about . . . two hours."

Silence.

"Diane?"

"Two hours? I thought your plane left tomorrow!"

There has been a change in plans.

Shh. That's my line.

"There's been a change in plans, Diane."

"Oh."

I close my suitcase. "Can you be ready in an hour?"

All at once, this life, this life.

I'm beginning to like the all-at-once-ness of this life.

All-at-once-ness?

Can you think of a better word?

Uh, no.

"I'll, uh, try to be ready," she says. "Will I need an extra suitcase?"

Hmm. She may be on to us. "Yes."

"Should it be empty?"

She might be on to us. "Yes."

"I'm so excited!"

So are we.

"See you in an hour."

"I'll be ready."

Click.

Should I have told her to pack a swimsuit?

You devil, you! You forgot on purpose!

Maybe I did.

Do you think she has any idea of what's about to happen?

You know, I don't think she does.

59

Diane

"**S**low down!" Mama shouts.

"He'll be here in an hour!" I shout back, throwing more clothes into a suitcase while she packs up most of my dressing table in a carry-on bag.

"You're so unorganized, Diane!"

"No, I'm not."

She reaches into the suitcase I've been filling and starts counting. "Five, six, seven . . . *twelve* pairs of underwear for a week? And only one bra?"

For some reason, that sounds about right for a honeymoon!

"Slow down," she says again. "You have time to do this right."

I grab my iron, wrapping the cord around it quickly. "Put the spray starch in that bag, too."

She puts the can of Niagra in the bag. "They have irons at hotels, Diane. And ironing boards, too."

I put the iron back on the floor. "I'm not a world traveler like you, Mama."

I throw open my closet door. What am I going to wear? It's April, so it might be cold in New York, Boston, and Philadelphia at night. I take down several long-sleeved outfits and toss them near my hanging bag. I'm not even sure they fit anymore! I wish I had more time to choose!

"I suppose I should be telling you what a mother is supposed to be telling her daughter before her wedding night," Mama says.

I stare her down.

"But I won't."

Shoes! Man, I can't take an empty suitcase if I'm bringing all the shoes that match these outfits! I'll need another carry-on.

"Mama, let me borrow one of your smaller suitcases to carry on the plane."

She leaves the room and comes back with a small soft-sided suitcase. "Don't you think you're overdoing it?"

"Mama, I am going to be in public in front of lots of people. There will likely be photographers. . . ." I cram six pairs of shoes into the small suitcase. "And you wouldn't want anyone to talk bad about me, would you?"

She sits on the bed. "No one will talk bad about you, Diane."

"Did you pack all my make-up?"

"Yes."

I pull out my top drawer, looking for the sexy, satiny Victoria's Secret outfit that Jack's gift certificate "bought" me for Valentine's Day, find it, ball it up, and stuff it in a zippered pocket of my hanging bag.

"What was that?" Mama asks.

Shoot. "Um, some pajamas."

"Uh-huh." She unzips the pocket and takes out the top, a satin black tank top. She checks the label. "Size six?"

I know I'm blushing. "It fits, okay?" And it makes my girls seem *so* much bigger.

She pulls out the matching shorts, stretching them as wide as she can. "You'd need baby oil and a shoehorn to get into these."

I snatch them from her and stuff them back in the pocket. "They fit, okay?"

She smiles. "Can you move in them?"

I ignore her and look for— Ah, the burgundy see-through teddy I've been saving. But how do I get it from the drawer to the bag without Mama seeing it?

"Mama, I think there's some clean laundry in the dryer. Could you get it for me?"

She stands. "Sure." She moves to the door. "And burgundy looks good on you, Diane."

"Mama!" I pull out the teddy. "You went through my drawers!"

She winks. "Now *that one* will fit. Those others . . ."

I shoo her away with the teddy.

I check the clock. I have less than thirty minutes! I pull open every drawer and just start grabbing, stuffing, and hoping until Mama comes back with a single sock.

She waves it at me like a sock puppet. "Are you going to need this?"

I snatch it off her hand. "I might."

Okay, okay, what else might I need? Money? No, it's all supposed to be paid for. ID? Yes. What else? My camera! I'll need film—

"Diane?"

I turn to Mama, who is sitting on the bed, pulling clothes from the other suitcase and folding them neatly. "What are you doing?"

"Helping."

I check the clock again. "He'll be here in twenty minutes!"

"You want this suitcase to close, don't you?"

"Yes, but—"

"And I have yet to see you packing any deodorant, perfume, toothpaste, toothbrush—"

I rush to the bathroom, and scoop everything on the counter into a pile. "Mama, bring me that bag with the shoes!"

She brings it to me, and I push the pile into the bag.

"That's going to be one big mess by the time—"

"I don't have time, Mama!" I interrupt, carrying the bag to my bedroom. "Now . . . let's close up everything and get it outside!"

"I'll get your father," she says, then leaves me alone with a small carry-on bag, a small suitcase I intend to carry on, a large suitcase, and a hanging bag, all of them stuffed to bursting.

I have become my mama in less than forty-five minutes!

Daddy comes in and whistles. "Good thing you're only going for a week." He smiles and hoists the big suitcase. "I thought you were supposed to take an empty one."

"I can't," I say.

He shakes his head as he loads up. "You're going to break poor Jack's back."

When Jack arrives early—and for the second time today!—I tell Mama, "You can just leave my car at the airport and lock my house key inside. I have a spare."

"We're taking a cab tomorrow," Daddy says, taking the suitcases and bags outside.

"Oh. Well . . . lock up before you go."

Mama pushes me toward the door. "We will."

"And, uh, and leave the outside lights on."

She sighs. "Diane, we know how to leave a house, so unless you want to get left, get a move on."

I stop. "What about my mail?" Not that I get that much.

"Your mailbox is big enough," Mama says. "Now go on."

I kiss her cheek. "Bye, Mama."

She hugs me. "Bye. Send us postcards."

I look into her eyes. "I love you, Mama."

She pushes a lock of hair out of my eyes. "I'm proud of you, Diane. I've always been proud of you."

I hug her closely. "Thank you, Mama."

She turns me to the door, where Daddy stands, holding it open. "Mr. Browning awaits your presence," he says.

I hug Daddy, kiss his cheek, and run down the sidewalk into Jack's arms.

He checks his watch. "We're going to be late."

"Listen to you," I say, hugging him tightly. "And anyway, aren't we really going to be early?"

He nods. "Good point."

60
Jack

You're driving too fast!
The streets are practically empty.
Slow down!
Just trying to keep up with my heart!

"Sorry I brought so much," Diane says, gripping the door handle and steadying herself with a hand on the dashboard.

"It's okay," I say, turning in to long-term parking and getting a ticket from the machine.

"Did, um, did Noël travel as heavy?"

"Heavier," I say.

Two pairs of shoes for every day of the week.

I park, pop the trunk, somehow manage to carry all six bags—

Watch your step!

And we run to the terminal.

You're not exactly running.

Shh.

"How late are we?" Diane asks.

I check my watch again. "I'm sure they're boarding already." I dump the luggage at the counter, telling the woman behind the counter, "Tickets for Browning."

"Oh, yes," she says, finding a little folder and placing it in my hand. "You'll have to hurry, but I think you'll make it. Gate three."

I take the two carry-on bags, and we race to the escalator.

You're in pretty good shape for an old man. Save some of your energy for later.

I'm sure I'll be able to muster up something.

After a few minutes waiting for security to give us evil looks, we get to the gate, both of us out of breath, and I hand the folder to the attendant. "Just made it," he says, and he waves us through.

"Um, Jack," Diane says, "this flight is going to Charlotte."

I smile. "Another change in plans."

"We have to fly south to go north?" she asks as we stow the carry-on bags.

We squeeze into two tiny seats. "Crazy, isn't it?"

And after that, I can't think of a single thing to say but "We're here."

"We're here," Diane echoes. She takes my hand. "Whoo. I didn't think we'd make it."

You might have a little trouble making that next flight. You'd better tell her to get some rest.

But that would spoil the surprise.

Trust me. Tell her to get some rest.

"Um, you'd better rest while you can," I say.

She squeezes my hand. "Don't you worry about me, Jack. I am primed and ready."

But she's thinking about—

Aren't you?

I smile.

"What are you smiling about?" Diane asks as the plane pulls away from the terminal.

I lean close to her ear. "The night and the morning to come."

"Mmm," she says.

We like the sound of that.

Yes, we do.

The flight to Charlotte is uneventful and actually arrives a few minutes early. When we head through the tube into the terminal, Diane slows almost to a stop. "It feels so good to stretch my legs."

I try to picture the map of the airport in my head. The international terminal is . . . "We'll just, um, go this way."

You have less than twenty minutes, Jack. Tell her!

I take her hand. "Um, I know a shortcut."

"To where?" she asks.

I would have asked the same thing. Tell her!

"Diane, do you have your license with you?"

"Yes. What, are we renting a car?"

I shake my head. "No."

Tell her!

"What's going on, Jack?"

I drop the carry-on bags and take both of her hands.

So she doesn't try to run away.

Shh.

"Diane, there's been another change in plans. There is no tour."

"What?"

"Well, actually there *is* a tour, only it doesn't involve books."

Except for The Kama Sutra.

Oh yeah. Except for that.

Diane shakes her head and blinks repeatedly. "What are you telling me, Jack?"

"The only tour we're going on is the grand tour called marriage, and if we don't hurry, we'll miss our flight to Jamaica."

Her mouth drops open.

I turn her gently. "We need to run that way as fast as we can, okay?"

She nods.

"Ready?"

She nods again, and then we . . . run—

Haul ass, book, bolt, jet—

To the international terminal, where we hear "Last call . . ." as we near the counter. I slap our boarding passes on the counter, the attendant checks our IDs, and we run through the tube into the plane. Diane turns right in to the coach section, but I pull her back.

"Um, I got us first-class seats," I say.

Her mouth drops open a lot more than I remember, Jack.

She's so fun to surprise!

After we sit in the most comfortable seats and gulp two glasses of some really fine champagne, she finally finds her voice.

"Are there going to be any more surprises?"

I nod.

She looks at her empty glass. "I'm going to need another one of these."

Don't let her get drunk.

This statement, from *you?*

You want her completely sober for—

I know, I know.

I ask for another glass of champagne once the plane levels off, and Diane sips this one, smiling and . . . giggling?

She's drunk.

She's happy.

Okay, she's a happy drunk.

"I can't believe we're doing this," she says. "Where are we going anyway?"

"Jamaica," I say.

Diane growls. "*Where* in Jamaica?"

"Some place . . . Jamaican?"

She squeezes my leg. "Tell me."

We like her squeezing our leg. Don't tell her.
I don't intend to.
"It's a surprise," I say.
She giggles again! "All this has been a surprise."
And there are more surprises to come. . . .
Yup.

61

Diane

I'm buzzing. First class. Sweet champagne. A smooth flight. Jack's hand *under* my hand so the world can see my ring. A soft pillow. *No* idea where we're going only that we're going to Jamaica. . . .

To get seriously busy.

Oh, and get married, too.

And no amount of squeezing Jack's leg or whispering in Jack's ear will get him to reveal all his secrets. But that's okay.

But then I realize . . . "Jack, what if our bags don't catch up to us?"

"We, um, won't need any clothes for a few days, right?"

And that sets me buzzing again, until I remember . . . "Jack, I only have shoes, toiletries, and my make-up and hair stuff in the carry-ons. You don't have a single thing."

"I know."

And *that* sets me buzzing until we land, because once I take his clothes off—and hide them somewhere, of course—

he won't be able to leave the room, not that I could either. I could . . . Hmm. At least my hair and make-up would look good as I walk around in my high heels. . . .

"Jack," I whisper as we leave the plane, "is this one of those clothing-optional places?"

He kisses me softly on the lips. "It *can* be."

I may *never* stop buzzing!

Inside the terminal, I see a short black man in a dark uniform holding a sign that says, "Mr. and Mrs. Browning."

"Is that for us?" I ask. I mean, who else would it be for?

Jack nods and approaches the man. "I'm Jack Browning, and this is the future Mrs. Browning."

"We've been expecting you," the man says in beautiful, cultured *English* English. "I am Paul. Do you have many bags?"

Jack shakes his head, showing him my two carry-on bags. "Just these."

"Follow me," Paul says, and we trail behind him to . . . a taxi? I was expecting a limo. But once we're moving through the tropical night, I know why we're not in a limo—the roads are barely wide enough for this taxi.

Not that Jack lets me look out the window much. We make out and touch and squeeze all the way to . . . Firefly Beach. It's too dark to see much, but I do see a skinny *pink* Victorian house and lots of palm trees teeming with coconuts.

Paul opens my door, and I step out. "Thank you, Paul." I smell a mixture of hibiscus, oleander, and the sea, delightful bougainvillea hedges brightening the night.

"A pleasure," he says, and he backs away to Jack, who pays him . . . a *lot* of money. How long were we in the taxi? I was too busy to notice the passing of time.

Jack holds his hand out to me. "Come on," he says.

I take Jack's hand. "Where are we going, Mr. Browning?"

"To the beach," he says.

Now? "What for?" I mean, shouldn't we be checking in or going to our room and ripping each other's clothes off?

Jack squeezes my hand. "You haven't figured it out?"

"Our room isn't ready or something?"

He laughs. "It's ready, and it isn't a room. It's a cozy cottage just a few yards from the water. We're just not ready for our cottage."

And that makes no sense whatsoever until we stop at the edge of the beach, kicking off our shoes. The sand is so soft and silvery. "It's still warm," I say, digging in my toes.

He leads me where waves sigh gently on the sand, and we look at the stars lighting up the sky, a little sliver of the moon glowing in the darkest patch. "I wish we could have gotten a later flight so we could do this at sunrise."

Here? We're going to do *it* here? This wasn't in that sex scene. Did I print out all of it?

He steps into the foamy edge of the waves, pulling me close. Somewhere reggae plays in perfect rhythm to the surf. Well, I suppose I could do it here in this paradise, but . . .

"Diane, um . . ." He sighs. "I wanted to do this legally, but . . ." He smiles. "The requirements are a bit much."

He has completely lost me.

"In order to get married here, we would have had to send our birth certificates one month in advance."

I swallow. Am I about to—

"And I would have had to bring Noël's death certificate, too, and we would have had to be in the country for twenty-four hours before we could—"

"Jack?"

"Yes, Diane?"

"You mean, we can't . . ." I close my eyes. "But I thought—"

He puts his finger to my lips. "We're in paradise, Diane, a real Garden of Eden. We have too many clothes on to be Adam and Eve, but . . . this is how they got married." He looks up. "In the sight of God." His eyes, those soft blue eyes of his, rest on mine. "They didn't need any certificates. They didn't need any witnesses. They only needed each other." He squeezes my hands tightly. "Diane Anderson, I will love and cherish you forever from this moment forth, and I will do my best to be a good husband and father to our children."

Goose bumps are leaving my body and traveling into space!

He blinks at me several times. Oh. Those were his vows! And now it's my turn!

"Uh, Jack Browning, I will love, honor, and . . ." I look down. "Obey you forever." I look up. "As long as what you ask of me is reasonable."

He nods.

"And I will be your wife, your best friend, and the mother of your children."

And I'm not crying, though I have goose bumps even on the tip of my nose!

"I, uh, don't have a wedding band for you," Jack says, "but your mother said—"

"I know what she said," I interrupt. Lord, I'm getting to be more and more like Mama. I know I wasn't adopted now.

He pulls my ring gently toward the tip of my finger.

"Don't," I whisper. "Don't take it off."

He stops pulling. "With this ring, I thee wed."

I put my fingers on the ring. "With this ring," I repeat, "I thee wed."

We slide the ring back to its rightful place.

And we kiss, while waves of the warmest water kiss our feet. "Hello, Mrs. Browning," he whispers.

"Hello, Mr. Browning."

He turns us slightly toward shore. "We can watch the sunrise from our cottage if you like."

"I'd like that."

Then, leisurely slipping through soft sand, we walk into

cottage #19, pausing on the veranda to look back at the water. "What time is it?" I whisper as Jack slides off my pants from behind me. The air feels good on my skin, and I barely feel him remove my underwear.

"Maybe . . . three."

I turn and take off his shirt, looking past him to two double beds. "There are two beds, Mr. Browning."

He smiles. "How nice of them."

He removes my top and bra in mere seconds, and seconds later I've reduced him to Adam. We embrace, and though for a fleeting second I worry about someone seeing us, I don't let go, I can't let go, and right there with my caboose sitting on the rail of a veranda in cottage #19 at Firefly Beach in Jamaica, I thank God I have this man whom I let completely inside me for the first time in my life—

"Oh, Jack," I say.

"Are you all right?" he whispers.

"Yes." I pull him deeper into me. "Can we stay like this until the sunrise?" I don't want this moment to end!

"Not if we stay out here," he pants, little beads of sweat forming on his forehead. "You feel so good, Diane."

Oh, God, if he only knew how good I feel in my *soul* at this moment. I waited twenty-five years for this man and this moment, and it was definitely worth the wait. And I wrap my legs around his back to prove it. "Take me to the bed, Jack."

He lifts me up. "Which one?"

"It doesn't matter," I say.

He carries me past the bed closest to the veranda and sits us gently *between* the two beds on a smooth wood floor. "Jack, what are you doing?"

"I'd rather be doing this on the beach, but . . ."

We're high enough that we can see over the first bed past the veranda to the water and the stars.

"So," he says, "we'll just sit here, moving to the rhythm of the waves while we watch the sun rise."

"We'll look like prairie dogs," I giggle.

"I love your laugh," he says, kissing my neck. "And I love you."

I hold him close, saying, "I love you, Jack," riding him in rhythm to the waves as the sky turns red . . . then orange . . . then gold.

62
Jack

When are we going to get into a bed?
If I move, I'll, you know, again.
We're going to get splinters.
I don't care.
I'll bet we're making a baby right now.
I hope so. God, I hope so.
"Diane?"
"Hmm?"
She has incredible stamina!
I know!
"Um, Diane, honey, my butt's asleep."
She opens her eyes. "Do you want to take me to bed, Mr. Browning?"
I nod.
"Not until I . . ." And then she grinds against me just right, and I can't hold back anymore.
At this rate, you'll have triplets for sure!
She eases off me and climbs into the bed closest to the

sunrise, and I slide in behind her, wrapping my arm around her stomach.

"It's so beautiful," she whispers.

"You're beautiful," I whisper.

She grabs my arms and holds on to them tightly. "Thank you."

"I'll bet you never expected this," I say, snuggling closer.

"Not in a million years," she says. "Not in a million-trillion years."

63

Diane

No. I didn't just say— I mean, five months ago, I *hated* that line. And now look at me. Look at us! I may have to make up a whole different definition of romance now.

"Jack?"

"Yes, Diane."

"*Wishful Thinking* now gets two stars from Nisi."

He drops his hand to my booty and begins to rub it oh so nicely. Here come the goose bumps. "What rating would Diane Anderson Browning give it?"

I feel him growing again behind me. *Lord, thank You for a virile man.* "Five stars, and if I could give it six, I would."

"Yeah?" He pulls me closer to him. "Five? Hmm. Well, I'd better get back to work."

"What do you mean, work? This isn't work, is it?"

"It is for me," he says. "I mean, if you want to have five kids, I have lots of work to do."

"I said five *stars*, Jack."

"And they will be," he says.

And in my heart, I know he's right.

Former boxing champion Dante "Blood and Guts" Lattanza is being featured in *Personality* magazine's "Sexiest Men Alive" issue, and reporter Christiana Artis has the scoop. There's just one hitch: she'll have to fly to her elusive subject's home in Canada. But once she lays eyes on Dante's chiseled physique and sultry Italian looks, she decides it was worth every mile. Too bad his icy demeanor doesn't match his hot body.

Since he lost his last fight ten years ago, Dante has led a reclusive life—and he *never* gives interviews. But he's making a comeback, ready to prove to the world—and his ex-wife—that he can still win a championship. He gives Christiana an ultimatum: if she can perform five tasks, she can ask him five questions. And then she can be on her way. Yet Dante's always had a weakness for beautiful black women, and seeing Christiana every day is enough to melt his defenses. Soon Christiana is an intimate part of the very story she came to write. But when the line between personal and professional gets blurred, it can be difficult to see when you've found the real thing . . .

**Please turn the page for an exciting sneak peek at
J. J. Murray's
THE REAL THING
coming next month!**

"**D**o you know where Dante Lattanza lives?"

The towheaded child on the wooden dock jutting off Turkey Island whizzes a long silver lure past the prow of my rented aluminum boat. "You talk funny, eh?"

It's because I'm from Red Hook in Brooklyn. At least I don't say, "Eh?" after every sentence. "I'm from New York City," I say not wanting to confuse him. "So, do you know where he lives?"

"Yeah."

This Canadian kid is obviously more interested in catching a fish than answering questions from a black woman in jeans, waterproof Timberlands, and a red and black flannel shirt.

"Your outfit will help you blend in," Shelley, my editor at *Personality* magazine told me.

"I'll still be black in the Great White North," I had complained, "no matter what I wear."

Shelley only rolled her eyes. She does that a lot whenever

I'm around. I think she has a wandering eye. She never seems to focus on me when I talk to her.

"Um," I say, turning off the ten-horsepower motor and drifting toward the shore, "where exactly is Dante Lattanza's house?"

The kid's eyes stay glued to the lure sluicing through the water. "He lives in a cottage."

Cottage, house, what difference does it make? "Which *cottage* does he live in?"

The lure flies up from the water and zips immediately toward me, missing the stern of the boat by inches, er, centimeters, or whatever archaic units these Canadians use. "What time is it?"

I ask which cottage, and he asks me for the time. "Almost four-thirty, but I really need to know . . ."

The kid reels in the lure rapidly, throws down his pole, and takes off up some stairs to a house, er, cottage. It looks like a *house* with a huge screen porch and some decking in front of another house-like section. "Where are you going?"

The kid doesn't turn or even acknowledge me. What? Is it time for his meds? Maybe he'll come back with some intelligence and some respect for his elders.

This is such a waste of time. I had gotten an anonymous letter last month telling me where to find the reclusive, elusive Dante "Blood and Guts" Lattanza, former middleweight champion and boxing wunderkind of the mid-1990's until he lost two bloody brawls to better, faster, and stronger fighters. "He's training at Aylen Lake, Ontario, from the end of August through November," the letter said. Retired for ten years, Lattanza was making a comeback just as *Personality* had named him one of the sexiest men alive based on a bit part he had in a recent *Rocky*-rip-off called *Heavy Leather*. Normally, *Personality* magazine only chooses from the Hollywood ranks, but someone in editorial must have a crush on Lattanza.

It has been a slow year for sexy men. "The older ones

keep dying off," Shelley had told me, "and the younger ones just don't seem to know anything about cultivating sex appeal." Except for Denzel Washington in 1996, all the winners since 1985 have been white, with Richard Gere, Brad Pitt, and George Clooney winning twice. There has yet to be a single Italian winner, and I, for one, think Italians are very sexy.

Something about their eyes just moves me.

Shelley wants me to get a few good close-ups of Lattanza's face before Tank "The Lion" Washington, the current undisputed middleweight champion and the man who originally took Dante's title, splits it open and generally rearranges it during their rematch this December. "We can't put bloody-faced Italian men in *Personality*," Shelley had explained. "Oh, I suppose we can if it's a shot from a *Sopranos* episode or one of whosawwhatsit's model boy-toys."

I had to fly from LaGuardia to Ottawa and rent a car to drive 225 kilometers (about 135 miles) through the towns of Kanata, Carp, Golden Lake, Killaloe Station, and Barry's Bay to this little strangely shaped lake. It was kind of like escaping Red Hook, where I live in a renovated warehouse at Reed and Brunt Streets with a lovely view of the East River, which my insane Realtor called "Buttermilk Channel." It actually looks like buttermilk some days, but . . . it's the freaking East River! Calling it something else does *not* make it any cleaner.

Now, I'm floating on Aylen Lake in front of Turkey Island, feeling like a flannelled turkey and waiting for a blonde-headed, freckled kid with selective hearing to—

Oh, there he is, and he's carrying a . . . stopwatch? Is he going to time the gaps in his synapses?

"Dante will be by here in a few minutes," the boy says.

"By here, as in *here*. He'll be by *this* island?" I take a weather-beaten paddle and dip it in the water, pushing the boat away from the shore.

"Yeah. He comes right by here, eh?"

I look around. I see no boats, canoes, or sailboats on the lake, not a single person other than Towhead out on a dock, not even any of the moose, bear, or loons I've read about cavorting on the shoreline. "Really?"

The kid points to a rocky outcropping bathed in sunlight and jutting off the northeast shore maybe a quarter mile away. "He's about to begin."

I look at the outcropping and don't see anyone. "Begin what?"

"The last part of his workout," the kid says. "He broke his record by twelve seconds yesterday."

I get my camera ready anyway, screwing on a telephoto lens. "You don't say? What exactly am I going to . . . see?"

Then I see a man diving off the rocks at least thirty feet above the water. He wears what looks like a parachute or a backpack on his back. *That's* Dante Lattanza? He's also a cliff diver?

The kid starts the stopwatch. "He'll swim across the channel to the point of our island, run across to the other point, swim the other channel to that cottage over there, run up the hill, ring a bell, run down the hill, and swim back."

I zoom in on a man's arms furiously cutting through the waves, his head bobbing up every ten strokes. "What's on his back?"

"Twenty kilos in a backpack," Tow Head says. "He has weights on his wrists and ankles to. It adds a total of thirty kilos."

This means absolutely nothing to me.

I snap a few shots of Lattanza's flailing arms, the sunny outcropping in the background. He is an extremely strong swimmer, cutting through the water like . . . well, like a man carrying an extra thirty kilos, practically disappearing underwater occasionally. These shots won't do. I couldn't sell these to even the most desperate tabloids. Lattanza isn't, however, exactly tabloid material. He's practically unknown.

And then . . .

Lattanza reaches the northeast point of Turkey Island, rising out of the blue-green water like a cut sculpture, tanned and toned and looking like Carrara marble. He sprints down the somewhat sandy shore in bare feet. I click away on auto as he glides closer.

"Ciao, David," Lattanza says with a smile as he passes the dock.

"Ciao, Dante," David says.

I keep my finger on the trigger, so to speak, taking Lattanza in, keeping him framed until he dives off the other point into the water. I sit and review the pictures I've taken and see a man defying nature. Lattanza is forty-two but hasn't an ounce of fat on him. His entire body is cut like one of Michelangelo's models. He has such dark eyes, dark eyebrows, dark stubble, and thick, wavy black hair. His signature high cheekbones make his smile even more effective because of his squint. I can't believe Shelley and the rest of the editorial staff only have him at number thirteen.

I'd, um, I'd put him in the top . . . seven. But then again, I've been single a long time. When was the last time? Who was I with? Who was president? Ooh, look at his—

"Hey," David says.

"Yes?" I look up briefly. Lattanza has a seriously interesting butt, as if he has two huge fists back there. Our readers will rejoice. I my damn self may rejoice a little bit later. He has a nice, muscular booty.

"Listen for the bell," David says.

"What bell?"

"Shh. You'll hear it, eh?"

I look at the southeast shore about another quarter mile away and see Lattanza rise from the water onto a dock, run up some steps, and disappear into the woods . . .

A bell rings.

Then I hear shouts, "Yoo-hoos," and car and boat horns honking. What's all this about?

"He's ahead of his record," David says.

"What was all that noise?"

David grins. "I'm not the only one timing him, eh?"

So at least the residents, vacationers, and cottagers on Aylen Lake know they have a celebrity among them. This must be the highlight of their day. Whoopee.

I see Lattanza bouncing down the steps to another dock and zooming off. Thirty kilos extra and he's flying like that. Tank Washington may be in for more of a fight than he has imagined. Lattanza will still lose, but maybe the fight won't be the bloodbath Las Vegas is predicting and HBO Pay-Per-View is counting on. They're already touting the rematch as "The Lion vs. the Legend—*Twice* in a Lifetime." The first fight was *Ring* magazine's "Fight of the Year" ten years ago. The two had combined for over eighteen hundred punches, eight hundred of which connected—five *hundred* or so to Lattanza's face and body. Most folks, though, don't expect a repeat performance, especially from Lattanza. The experts think he'll run out of gas after the third round.

I see Lattanza using his legs now, hairy things, strong kicks, no letup as he comes back, silhouetted against the sun, powerful, virile, truly not number thirteen. I let the camera fire away. With that background, that face, and that body, he should be at least in the top five. I'll have to talk to Shelley about his placement. Unlike many on this year's list, every bit of Dante Lattanza is real and as God made him. He has no blonde highlights in his hair, no calf implants, no caps for his teeth, and no sex appeal based on whom he's sleeping with, adopting children with, or dating. In addition, he doesn't need a personal trainer because he's his *own* personal trainer.

I am witnessing an atypical typical boxer's workout. My graddaddy fought in the amateurs, getting pretty far in the New York Gold Gloves, and he maintained a boxing workout throughout the rest of his life at Gleason's Gym, so I know boxing. Granddaddy ran in the morning, went to work, then picked me up after school to spend a few hours in the gym shadowboxing, pounding the heavy bag, popping the focus mitts, peppering the speed and double-end bags, jumping rope, and sparring whenever he could. Yet here's Dante swimming a total of a mile or so and playing a hunchbacked lifeguard on *Baywatch*.

Lattanza is on the island again, and he's not slowing down. He only nods at David, shoots—is that a grin?—at me, and again he's crunching down the beach to the point and flying into the water again.

I check to see if I snapped the grin, and I did. It's a nice grin. I'm not sure if all those teeth are originally his, but . . . Nice. The squint makes his eyes twinkle. On the other hand, maybe they just twinkle and the squint . . .

Listen to me. Daydreaming about a photograph.

Hmm.

Okay, top three.

David runs out onto the dock. "This is my favorite part."

I zoom in on the rocks, expecting Lattanza to stop to catch his breath. He doesn't. He literally leaps from rock to rock, handhold to handhold, almost hopping up that rock formation to the top where he rings another bell.

David clicks the stopwatch. "He beat yesterday by fifteen seconds!"

More noise, yelling—what is this "Yoo-hoo!" business?—horns blaring.

"He's going to get that title back for sure," David says.

Not.

Lattanza turns, addresses the noise, and bows, sunlight drenching him in amber.

Damn. I forgot to keep shooting. I click one of him taking off the backpack and raising his arms into the air. It reminds me of a scene from *Rocky*. That scene gave me goosebumps.

I look at my arms. They are long brown goosebumps that end with nails that desperately need a manicure.

Well.

Hmm.

Lattanza's bow would have been a cheesy shot, but I wish I had taken it.

Hmm.

I may have to, um, make the interview last longer than my usual thirty minutes. You know, stretch it a bit. I need to make sure I probe this man and get to his essence. Except for *Heavy Leather,* Lattanza has been out of the spotlight for ten years. This is an important interview. Readers will want to know why he's been hiding for so long.

I also, um, have to check out his abs up close.

My last short-lived boyfriend, whose name still escapes me (Chuck? Howard?) had love handles, which turned simply to fat, and I quickly returned to a single life.

Dante Lattanza has love ripples.

I wonder what those feel like.